HIGHER THAN THE ANGELS

ALSO BY CHARLES WILLIAMS

In Close Proximity
-an action/thriller-

Nor Tolerate Among Us
-a novel of the Air Force Academy-

ACKNOWLEDGEMENTS

Were I to write of all the fighter pilots and fighter gators I knew and flew with, this novel would have no chance of being completed. Nor would it be a novel. Likewise, if I acknowledged every one that influenced me in one way or another, the name-filled pages would invariably be absent those lost in the years of my memory.

I can and will acknowledge those past friends who most significantly touched my life and those who have more recently offered and/or given assistance and advice in recalling memories or critiquing those of which I have written.

Chris Campbell, who, as we sat decades ago contemplating life at the edge of a western cliff on the island of Zakynthos, gave me the idea for the title of the novel I could not know then I would write.

George Lint who for decades kept the post-Vietnam 613th TFS Squid family together with updated addresses, emails, social media, and reunions at his house. Thank you, Flounder. I wish you and Maria were still here. We all do.

David Wells, who has offered detailed memories, some we shared, some I had forgotten, some I never knew. Thank you for your patience, Dave.

Gary Kaskela, the only WSO I ever let land my F-4 from the backseat, and who reanimated faded memories of an earlier time.

Jim "Babymac" McCormick who years ago encouraged me to publish despite the obstacles along the way.

Rich "Richie" Cole who nurtured me, taking me under his wing so long ago. You are certainly your father's son.

Jerre "Bull" Kittle who has always made me smile while reminding me of what is important.

I greatly appreciate those friends who have read, critiqued and offered correction to my work. Thank you, Sabrina Afflixio, Sidney "Fuzzy" Thurston, Gary Mitchell, Sherry Varner, Gary Kaskela, Laura Lee Scott, and Lynda Kalantzakis.

I consider myself extremely fortunate that my parents, Kenneth and Charlene, were always so supportive of me and of each other from the very beginning to now and beyond. My loving mother read everything I wrote, every novel I drafted or published or planned to publish. Thank you, mom. You married a good man. I miss you both.

My loving brothers:

Jeff Alan, who reads my work even when he does not have time to between working at NASA and playing with his martins or his plants, and

Paul Wayne, a fellow F-16 fighter pilot now American Captain, who read, critiqued, and edited my first 800 page draft many years ago and insisted I continue. And cut a bit.

Forrest Taylor Kirk Williams, who created my first website for me. Thank you, son. You are a good and talented man.

And finally, my beautiful wife - and personal Master Gardener - my angel of unconditional love, my most trusted advisor, my closest friend who always has my six. Karen, you are the love of my life.

THOUGHTS AND DEDICATIONS

This novel took me the better part of three decades to get right or, rather, right enough. Many times, I put it away, even as it tossed in the turbulence that swirls in the back of my mind. It is not meant to reflect the current times, neither of fighter planes nor the men and women who fly them. It is a story of a more chauvinistic, less politically correct era in the evolution of the fighter pilot.

Among the most challenging tasks in making this novel complete was portraying as accurately as possible the mixed and many emotions people feel when they lose someone close, someone they have admired and loved. That is as much true now as it was then. I found the very nature of it to be spiritually exhausting.

No less challenging was the construction of my dedications in memory and honor of those whose last time aloft in a fighter became the first leg on that final flight west into the sun.

Flying fighters is exhilarating and challenging and dangerous. It is also fun. Still, the danger that threatens to end the fun is like a shadow that hides a lingering reality. I have lost good friends to that reality, friends who were overcome by the shadow at a time when they were most alive.

It is appropriate to dedicate this novel in remembrance of all those who have made that supreme sacrifice. And in honor and memory of all fighter pilots and those that love and have loved them.

One final thought ...

Military service is not for everyone, nor should it be. It is an arduous path for those who choose to follow it; it may be difficult to reconcile for those who do not. Yet even the kindest and gentlest can see the wisdom of holding a fist in reserve for despots who would deny the rights of mind and soul.

Sadly, there will always be those who prefer to debase rather than respect that choice, let alone honor it. They will never grasp what it means to place love of country above love of self or wealth or the pursuit of power. Nor will they ever understand the depth of character that makes one willing to die for those who would never return the favor.

A TOAST IN MEMORIAM FOR FRIENDS WHO WERE DONE TOO SOON

George "Buddy" Mason	Aircraft Commander and Mentor
Bradley "Brad" Scott	Aircraft Commander and Friend
Richard "Rich" Cali	Weapon Systems Officer and Poker Buddy
Mark Melancon	Golf Buddy and Teacher - Thunderbird T-38 Diamond Formation Slot Pilot whose final flight was with:
Norman "Norm" Lowry	Thunderbird T-38 Diamond Formation Lead
William "Willie" Mayes	Thunderbird T-38 Diamond Formation Left Wing
Joseph "Pete" Peterson	Thunderbird T-38 Diamond Formation Right Wing

and

Julie Campbell	Beloved Wife of Christopher Campbell: Flying Buddy, Golfing Buddy, Drinking Buddy, Best Friend and one of the finest Men I have ever known

"...who for a little while was made lower than the angels, crowned with glory and honor because of the suffering of death ..."

"For it was not to angels that God subjected the world to come ..."

The Holy Bible

By the angels, who tear forth the souls of men with violence, and by those who draw forth the souls of others with gentleness, by those who glide swimmingly through the air with the commands of Allah, by those who proceed and usher the righteous into Paradise, and by those who subordinately govern the affairs of the world ...

The Holy Qur'an

PROLOGUE

To fly. To really fly.

To ascend above the common ground we walk each day and become one of those few who understand movement in three dimensions - into a world where imagination was Man's only experience one hundred years ago. I feel the initial sensation ... I am no longer a part of the land. I am free ... and yet totally dependent upon the wings Man's intellect has given me. Men far more intelligent than I.

Now, to climb higher - to be farther away, to be closer - to see it all. I draw in my breath and wait to be overwhelmed by the reality. But I am rarely overwhelmed anymore. It is too natural. Flying is not simply flying now. It is living. It is my way of life.

I fly. With the help of my machine, I do it well. Now, until I am ready to return, the Earth is at once my friend and my nemesis. I joust with Her - behind Her mountains, down Her valleys, using Her to hide from the Hunter that would harm me, knowing all the while that She could harm me most effectively - most permanently.

Then, I return to Her, proving my mortality. I return to talk of my flying with others who will understand until the next time I really fly. And as I talk, and they talk, I reflect on how it was. I have time to think of the flying instead of the mission, and I realize its true wonder. I feel the sensation which accompanies the remembrance of something beautiful.

Then I feel the impatience, the restlessness to be back in the cockpit, to feel the stick in my hand again. I have just returned, yet because I am not touching my aircraft now, it seems an eternity since I last flew. I need to be back in the air again - to be me, I need to have the aircraft strapped to my body, and man and machine take to the sky again as one.

To fly. To really fly.

To be.

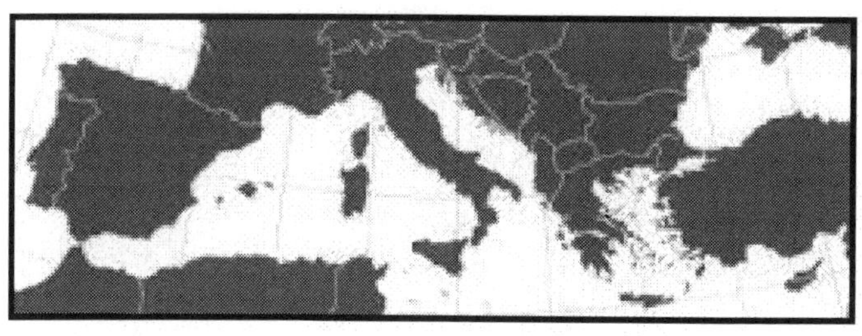

PART ONE

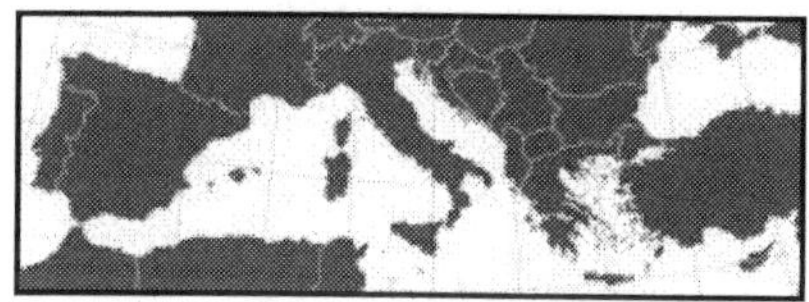

FIRST FALL
CHAPTER ONE

The flight from New York to Madrid was unpleasant. Neither hope nor anticipation could change that. A journey that should have heralded fresh possibilities was instead fraught with misgivings. He felt stifled. Despite securing an aisle seat before leaving JFK, the lack of space for his long legs left little room for expression of movement, which accentuated his uneasiness.

The airplane, a stretch DC-8, was configured with more seats than its commercial counterpart, and even those people short of Alan Wayne's six-foot two stature were becoming all too familiar with their knees. In Alan's mind, the lumbering craft did not rightly belong in the jet category. It was a "cattle car," commissioned by the government to move as many people as possible as inhospitably as possible from west to east.

The flight attendants working the chartered flight did so with an air of impersonal distraction, as if they, too, found themselves rendered indifferent by the emotionless complexion of a military operation. When speaking among themselves, they did not refer to the people as passengers, deferring instead to the dehumanizing, non-word "pax." They formed no attachments, offered few smiles, keeping themselves and their sentiments at arm's length as they served.

Not once in the small cockpit of an Air Force fighter had Alan felt as confined as he did on this dark, turbulent night, thirty-seven thousand feet above the Atlantic Ocean. Yet, it was not the skin of the aircraft Alan felt closing in on him.

He stole glances at the unfamiliar faces around him, his eyes hidden by the shadows of the cabin's dim reading lights. The majority of his fellow passengers were single military men, along with a few uniformed women. There were also families - wives and some children traveling with their warriors. He imagined the idea of living in Europe was luxurious for some, frightening for others, but the Spartan fashion in which they traveled left no doubt of their true status. They were all cargo.

The unrelenting turbulence of the past three hours had been difficult to endure and offered little promise of a smoother ride. The young woman seated in front of Alan complained again of nausea to her uniformed husband.

Alan listened in quiet sympathy. As the soldier turned to her, Alan spotted the small round adhesive bandage that clung below and behind the soldier's left ear. Scopolamine. Alan smirked at the idea and, searching the necks of sailors he could see, tried to guess which of those without patches might nonetheless have popped a little Dramamine to avoid getting sick on this flight across the ocean. Looking to his left he found, in fitful sleep, the pale adolescent face of a sailor he recognized.

He had witnessed the young man, his bearing tall and straight, hug and kiss his mother ritualistically back at JFK. The sailor had been gentle with her, even tolerant, allowing the woman to cling shamelessly to him as she openly vented her emotions through her tears.

The sailor's father, a large man in his fifties, had displayed an exaggerated smile of pride, patting the young sailor on the back that others might know this fine example of an American male was his son. When the flight was called to board, the big man walked away from mother and child to look through the large window at the air machine that would transport his son far from home, perhaps never to return. No longer able to restrain himself, the man's eyes reddened as his proud face turned sour. Pretending to scratch his eyebrows, the man suddenly seemed very old as he fought to regain his composure, wiping away his tears before turning from the window for one last inaudible gesture of good-bye. Despite this gallantry, Alan sensed the old man's vision was yet blurred, the complexities of the present time making little sense to him.

A painful twinge of guilt hit Alan's stomach, like the unexpected blow from a boxer, momentarily making it hard for him to breath. He had not given his own father a proper good-bye. In fact, he had harshly denied his father's pleas for reconciliation. Wallowing in a tepid bath of self-righteousness, it had seemed the manly way to handle it. Too late, he regretted his ill-founded defiance.

His father had always been a wonderful, caring man, but Alan understood his mother's decision to leave him. She had given at least the appearance of trying to make things work, but in the end, brief though it had been, she could no longer live with the idea of her husband's descent into debauchery.

Two nights before Alan was to leave for Spain, his mother confided to him that she still loved his father. Through her tears, she explained that his father's infidelity would perhaps have been a painful but tolerable episode had it been one drunken night of passionate indiscretion. But the fact that the man had entered into it soberly and deliberately had been too much. There had been only the one time, followed by two years without so much as a passing flirtatious glance at another woman, yet the only thing his father could do to influence his wife's final decision was the one thing he refused.

"I will not lie," he had said. "I will not demean her, myself or you by saying it meant nothing."

"I don't care how much of it there was!" Alan's mother cried. "You took too much from it. And it took too much from us." To the very end, she refused to accept her complicity in allowing their life together to self-destruct. She had blinded Alan to it as well.

The last time Alan had seen his father, at his own wedding, he seemed a beaten man. Admission of guilt followed by years of penance and proven integrity lost in the end to irreconcilable emotions. Alan's father conceded his life's greatest battle to the inharmonious concepts of honesty, honor, and that indefinable sense of feeling completely alive.

The sleeping sailor's head jerked involuntarily against an invisible demon haunting his dreams. Alan looked away as the soldier's wife voiced an exaggerated gasp when the plane rudely bounced them in a heavy pocket of turbulent air.

The situation was a mockery of the significance of life. And Alan needed to feel that his life, that all life, was significant. Ernie was still fresh in his mind. Ernie was significant. Ernie haunted him, a fact he refused to admit to anyone else. His face tugged at the edge of Alan's consciousness, reminding him that if he had been more aware, Ernie would be on this airplane to Spain, and he, instead, would be in Korea.

And Bill Fisch would have meant nothing more to him than a fighter pilot he cared little for and would probably never see again.

Tonight, on this bumpy ride, with the renewed realization that his friend was gone came the same fresh tinge of disbelief that made Alan twitch as if he was seeing it happen again for the first time. Unless Heaven was a barren landscape where souls wandered aimlessly in a fog of forgetfulness, nothing it offered could placate the horror of Ernie's last memory of life. And the chaplain's well-meaning memorial assurances had done little to placate Alan's anger against a God who did nothing to hinder Ernie's horrible, untimely, and unnecessary death. Nor had his words erased the guilt Alan felt for being alive.

Why had this young officer been called upon for the supreme sacrifice when, just seven days earlier, Ernie had embraced them all as he announced his engagement? Now there was nothing to hold but the flag that covered his near-empty coffin.

This being too much to bear, Ernie's mother had fallen prostrate over his honored remains and sobbed uncontrollably. The roar of the fighter planes passing overhead in the Missing Man formation did not touch her shell of despair, and the significance was lost on them all.

Alan leaned back on the uncomfortable airliner seat that seemed to shake out of sequence with the rest of the airplane. If they went down tonight, there would be something very painful to the soul about dying in the middle of the Atlantic Ocean among people he would never know.

At least Ernie had died in a fighter, and death had been swift. There had been little time for fear and no time for regrets.

Consumed in rage, Alan fought to turn his thoughts away from his friend and his antagonist. But his anger consumed him like a fire that refused to be extinguished. Damn you, Bill Fisch! Damn you for being right!

The woman in the row ahead complained to the soldier about the late time of night they were traveling, then redirected her attack by admonishing him for drinking too much at the airport bar. Alan's earlier sympathy for her dissipated behind a mask of indifference.

Alan glanced quickly to his right at Sloan, his own bride of but a few weeks. Having met by chance while he was in attending Undergraduate

Pilot Training in Arizona, they decided within the first week that they were in love. Later, she made regular trips to Florida when Alan was assigned to MacDill Air Force Base for F-4 training. But he was not ready to get married, and she seemed willing enough to await his return from a one year tour of duty in Korea to decide if they had a future together.

When, after the accident, he was reassigned to Torrejon Air Base, Alan broke the news to Sloan that he would be in Spain for at least two years. Once she recovered from the initial shock, she suggested, with no uncertain finality, they either get married or call the whole thing off. He realized now that Sloan was here because Ernie was not. And because she was, they would spend the first three years of their married life away from family and friends and the stability that comes from being home.

Watching her quietly whisper Spanish phrases as she read them in a Berlitz book, Alan felt glad she was with him. She seemed much more excited about living in Spain than he was. Her excitement underscored his need for something fresh in life, something good. Perhaps that something would be Sloan.

He kissed her on the cheek. "How do you say, 'Where's the restroom, I need to know now!'"

Sloan's blue eyes did not leave the page as she grimaced in mock frustration. "I think it would be easier if you crossed your legs and screwed up your face." She closed the book and flashed a crooked smile at him. "They'd get the idea a lot quicker, and you just might have a chance of making it!"

Alan forced a laugh. "I guess that's the universal language." He turned away from her, lay back and closed his eyes.

When the transport touched down in Spain, he was still searching for sleep, but his conscience would not allow it.

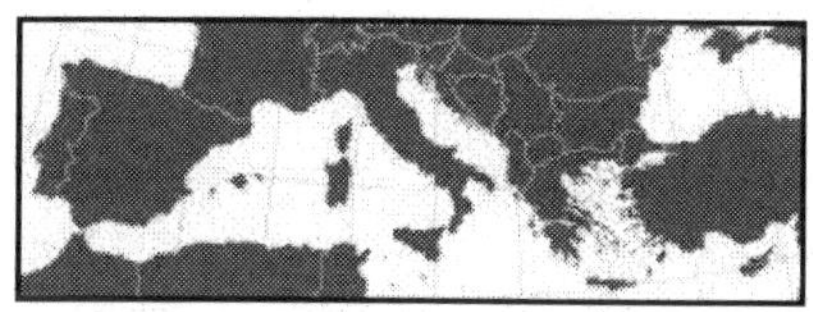

CHAPTER TWO

Mid-morning, Alan awoke with a violent shudder, limp with exhaustion, wet from perspiration precipitated by a dream he found himself unable to replay in consciousness. He knew it had been The Dream, or one of its haunting variations, but all that remained was an ephemeral memory of an obscure face twisted in fear.

The bright August sun shining through the window caught his eyes, momentarily enhancing the feeling of disorientation the dream had cast over him. He closed his eyes, searching for a calm, semiconscious state that would allow the dream to continue. The inward search faded as he remembered that, for the first time in his life, he was in a foreign country.

Snuggled next to him, oblivious to his agitation, Sloan snored softly, her lively blue eyes hidden beneath the delicate patches of skin as wrinkle-free as the rest of her young body. Alan studied her. She was beautiful, better than he deserved. He wished again, as he had so often before, that he was madly in love with her. But he was not, and maybe that was good. He did love her, there was little doubt about that, but he felt no desperate lust, no primitive animalistic urges that he imagined should accompany truly passionate love. Perhaps that was why he tended to exaggerate his desire for her.

Not wishing to disturb her, Alan rose quietly and went to the window for his first, private glimpse of Spain. The only other sound on this quiet morning was the steady dripping from the leaking faucet in the minuscule bathroom. No lively conversations beyond the walls. No "sound of freedom" from fighter jets in the pattern.

The curtains were partially open, allowing the unfiltered warmth of the sun to flood a portion of the room. Sloan's side of the bed remained in the shadows.

What a difference between darkness and light, he mused, making me come to life while in her innocence she sleeps soundly, unaware of so much.

The view through the window was of a thinly grassed quadrangle encompassed on three sides by the BOQ building that housed their small room. These temporary quarters would be the extent of their living space until they found a place to call home somewhere out beyond the boundaries of Torrejon Air Base.

'So, this is Spain,' he thought to himself. What was he feeling? Foreign? Out of place? A long way from home? Drugged.

He looked again at his young wife still immersed in sweet repose. How did she do it?

There was a knock on the door, which Alan found and opened.

A black man of fair complexion, average height and perhaps three years Alan's senior looked up at him from the hallway. The fellow had a sly, secretive grin on his face that seemed to say he understood the situation immediately. It had been but a few hours since Alan first met that grin.

"Lieutenant Wayne!" the grin said. "You look terrible!"

"I can't figure why," Alan answered, "just because I've been awakened in the middle of the night by a loud banging on a strange door."

"It's ten o'clock in the morning."

Alan glanced at his watch. "Here, maybe, but in the real world, it's three A.M., and the entire state of Texas is in REM sleep."

"You consider Texas the real world?"

"Parts of it."

"Well, you're in Spain now. Set your watch back twenty years."

Alan allowed himself to laugh. Ron Butler had been at the terminal to meet them as they deplaned, and Alan took an instant liking to him. Although black fighter pilots were, regrettably, somewhat rare, Alan was not surprised. Sloan had openly expressed her relief upon seeing an obviously American face.

"I was already awake," Alan admitted. "I don't sleep too soundly in strange surroundings."

Ron eyed Alan closer as the grin faded. "Is Sloan up?" he asked, peering in from the hall.

"Not yet," Alan answered, looking over his shoulder at his sleeping bride. What an angelic face, he thought. Even in sleep, her countenance was perfect. He looked back at Ron. "The sleep of the innocent."

"Innocent or not, it's time to get moving. For the sake of your lady, the sooner you find a place to call home, the better she'll feel about being here."

"Sloan will be okay."

Ron glanced at his watch. "We'll start with lunch at my place. Jennifer is making sandwiches."

"Lunch ... Jennifer ... your wife ...?"

Ron seemed amused. He nodded. "At those apartments I wrote you about - Parque de Cataluña. This evening, we're going to a squadron 'Hail and Farewell' party. Some folks are being bid farewell. You might be hailed."

Alan nodded sleepily. "When's siesta time?"

The scheming grin returned to Ron Butler's face. "Forget that. It's not what you think over here, anyway." He paused to smile. "The best way to adjust to the time change is to stay up all day and sleep well tonight."

"We'll be dragging butt! That won't help the impression we make on our new squadron."

Ron waved his hand beside his face. "It's a fighter pilot party. If you pass out, you won't be alone." He turned to leave. "I'll be back in an hour."

"We won't be here," Alan said. "We're moving to an unlisted room."

"One hour," Ron called over his shoulder, disappearing down the stairs.

Alan closed the door and went to the bed. Sloan had not stirred.

He lay down gently beside her and brushed a lock of brunette hair from her eyes. He kissed her smooth forehead. Slowly, as if coming out of a coma, she subdued a yawn and looked up at her husband with deep blue eyes.

She raised herself on her elbows. "What time is it?"

Alan cupped one of her small breasts in his big hand. "It's time for you to get ready."

"Ready for what?" She struggled only slightly for a look at the clock.

"Ready to learn the pleasures of Spain, a country where romance is legend."

Sloan frowned cutely. "I thought that was more like Italy ... maybe France."

"We'll get to those soon enough," Alan said.

Sloan glanced around the small room, noting the window frames scarred with rust, the walls in dire need of paint, the dripping bathroom faucet. She screwed up her eyes and looked playfully at Alan. "And just what exactly are these Spanish pleasures?"

"You have awakened in a BOQ room on an Air Force base in the middle of Spain, sharing a bathroom with God knows who, lying on a squeaky bed that threatens to give way at any moment." He stroked her slender neck. "I say we find that moment."

Her lips formed a thin smile. "You've certainly set the mood."

He kissed her flushed cheek. "Did I mention the paper-thin walls? This place absolutely reeks of atmosphere."

He reached to her knee and stroked her soft inner thigh. She raised her tanned lean arms, allowing him to pull her nightgown over her head. He let it fall to the floor beside the bed.

He rubbed her smooth stomach, caressing her belly button.

"Is this the new Spanish foreplay?" she asked. "You should at least get a towel. You know I like to watch you get the towel."

"No time for a towel!" Alan grimaced in mock urgency. "Ron will be back in an hour.

"But ..."

"I'm sure they change the sheets once a month whether they need to or not."

She closed her eyes, aroused by the urgency of his touch. "Ron was here?" she breathed.

"He better not have been," Alan said, tickling her ear with his breath as he caressed her.

Sloan giggled. "We'll have to be very quiet," she whispered as he smothered her lips with his. He thought her words funny. She rarely made a sound in her passion. Hers was a quiet love.

But the bed betrayed them.

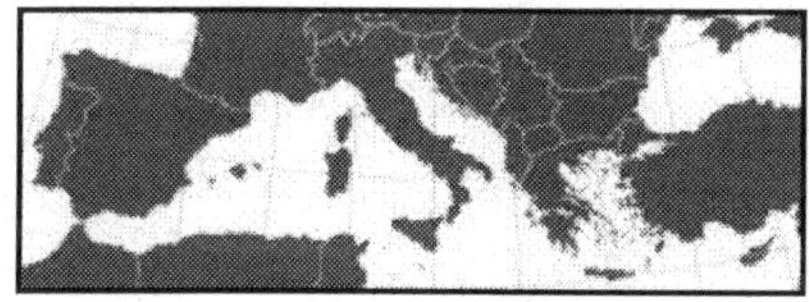

CHAPTER THREE

Spain is a beautiful, dry country that feels foreign until it becomes home. The flat, dry plateau that stretches southeast from Madrid forms a majestic border south of the lower land where the autopista connects Madrid to Alcala and Alcala to Guadalajara. In the spring, this lower land is enlivened briefly with the natural colors of green wheat fields and the red poppies that grow wild in the uncultivated open lands.

Traveling west on the autopista toward Madrid, the higher plateau forms a delightful backdrop in the distance. Closer in, the view is less romantic, the parched land there being interspersed with concrete business buildings, high-rise apartments and other developments. The town of Torrejon de Ardoz is south of the highway and east of Madrid. Not what one would call a typically styled Spanish village, Torrejon takes on the appearance of an awkward, ill-conceived suburb, reaching in its stumbling development toward a grouping of small, more typically Spanish hills on the western horizon.

Except for about two months in the spring, all these lands are brown and barren. The rain that falls in the winter is immediately absorbed by the thirsty, dry earth, and the sun bakes the land unmercifully in the summer, sapping the life from anything not hardy enough to withstand the heat.

As Ron finessed the little green Spanish Seat down the ill-kept road that led into the country-side away from Madrid, Alan felt a tinge of confusion brought on by the strange time of day. The sun seemed much too high in the sky for this late hour, and it lingered as if avoiding the inevitable setting that history required of it.

In the absence of air conditioning, the windows of the car were down, allowing the hot breeze to mingle the road dust with the four sweating bodies packed tightly in its confines.

The road was paved but broken and must have been important at one time. Ron weaved from side to side, avoiding the large holes spawned by age and apathy. What could only be called craters, some as large as the car, gave stuttering testimony to the years of neglect.

"Notice anything about Spain?" Ron asked Alan.

Romance, Alan thought, turning to wink over his shoulder at Sloan seated in the back with Jennifer Butler.

When he did not answer, Ron said, "No trees."

Alan gazed through the small dusty windshield. "Very few."

"They cut them all down to build the Spanish Armada."

Alan glanced at Ron. He saw neither truth nor deception.

They hit a large hole.

"How much further to this Spanish fink house?" Sloan asked.

"Finca," Ron answered, "and do you want that in minutes or miles?"

"Minutes," Alan answered for her. "When we left your apartment, you said it was less than ten miles away. That's lost something in the translation."

Ron exhaled heavily. "We're in the farm area now, and the house is in a small valley called Finca Avalon, just over that hill to our right."

"Any places for rent out there?" Alan asked.

Ron shrugged his shoulders. "I don't know of any." He turned the car onto a dirt road that went up and over a hill beyond old, unplayable tennis courts from which point they could see the houses in the valley.

"Civilization," Sloan said.

"Hold that thought," Jennifer said, smiling. She was a slight girl, just over five feet tall with a small mouth, pale brown skin, and brown eyes. She wore a pair of large-rimmed glasses that slid regularly down her small nose, making it appear even smaller. "You may not always feel that way."

"After our tour in Spain?" Sloan asked guardedly.

"In about an hour," Jennifer answered, glancing at Sloan. "These parties can get rowdy. It depends on the mood of the night." Jennifer playfully tapped the back of Ron's head. "We have to keep these boys under control."

"Standard," Alan said, ignoring Sloan's frown.

They turned onto a side road. A mixture of Spanish and American cars parked at awkward angles lined both sides of the street, giving the appearance of a junk yard where cars go to die.

The white stucco houses, several of them accented with red geraniums in their windows, were spaced at comfortable intervals along the dirt road, and more closely approximated Alan's image of Spanish dwellings than the unromantic high-rise apartments where Ron and Jennifer lived.

Ron stopped the car in front of a house. Small groups of people, drinking and talking, were scattered in the front yard inside a short stucco wall. They greeted Jennifer and Ron casually as they walked up the sidewalk and nodded with interest at the newcomers.

Sloan attached her hand under Alan's arm as the four of them entered the open front door without knocking. Several of the squadron pilots and wives were gathered around a table covered with picked-over plates of finger food. They turned to tacitly assess the new arrivals.

Jennifer introduced them without hesitation. "This is Alan and Sloan Wayne, the newcomers who arrived on the redeye rocket."

"Recovered from the jet lag yet?" a fellow about Alan's age asked. "When we first got over here, our sponsors kept us up all night to adjust to the time change."

"Our tyrants have the same game plan," Alan replied, surprised how quickly someone struck up a conversation. "They got us out of bed at an ungodly hour and haven't let up on us since. I feel pretty good now ... I should, anyway. Back home, the afternoon is just beginning."

"Going east is harder than going west," the fellow said. "It's harder to adjust. But east is how you get here. And east is where you go to nuke the Commies." He smiled, and Alan imagined the pleasantness of his face came from a deeper source than the glass of Scotch he held in his hand. He was around five feet eight inches tall and of average weight and build. His shortly cropped blond hair was very straight and refused to lie flat on his head. He had a rugged, handsome face, high cheekbones and green eyes that teemed with life. "The way I see it," the young man continued, "there's everything bad about going east and everything good about going west." He shifted his glass to his left hand and offered Alan his right. "I'm Sam Christopher. We'll probably fly together. I'm a back seater, a WSO," he said, pronouncing it 'wizzo'.

Alan shook his hand, noting the strong grip. "Alan Wayne. This is Sloan, my bride."

"I have one of those around here somewhere," Sam said. He stirred the ice in his drink with his finger and looked at Sloan.

Ron cut the conversation short, pulling Alan toward a group of five men in the center of the adjacent room.

"If you meet a good-looking gal named Michelle," Sam called after him, "that's my better half."

In the corner of the next room, Alan noticed an attractive woman in perhaps her mid-twenties talking to two men. The older of the two men was lavishing just enough attention on the woman for Alan to think he might be more than casually interested. The other man appeared to be bored and more than a little uncomfortable. He got up and walked into the kitchen, leaving the older man and the woman alone. The woman touched the man's hand softly as he whispered something into her ear.

'I hope that doesn't turn out to be Michelle,' Alan thought.

The men in the middle of the room were deeply immersed in discussion. A tall, lanky fellow was centered in the group. He held an empty whisky tumbler in his big right hand and listened without emotion to the arguments of a younger man with a red mustache who spilled a little gin from his glass as he gestured. Standing among the group, his legs spread wide in masculine stance with a highball glass in his hand, was Bill Fisch.

"But, damn it, Whiskey!" the redheaded gent with the gin was saying. "We have to train as low as we can go! Otherwise, we won't be able to do it when the time comes and our lives depend on it. We aren't ready to go in and get the hostages. What good is all our training if we don't train the way we are going to fight?"

The skinny fellow waved his disproportionately large hand as if to clear the air of what was just said. "Now keep your zipper locked, Buck."

"You learned to fly low at Weapon's School back in the States," Fisch interrupted loudly. "Why can't we train that way over here, closer to the war where it really counts?"

"We don't have a war, yet," Whiskey Wilson said. "Yeah, we should train the way we're gonna fight. But it don't make a hare's ass bit of sense to lose half of you hard-knots to the rocks before we ever get started for real."

"Then let's weed out the one's that can't hack it," Bill Fisch said arrogantly. "They'll be gone the first day of the war anyway." He was obviously already drunk.

Alan clenched his fists as he listened. While he had anticipated running into Bill Fisch sooner or later, he had never imagined the two of them would be in the same squadron.

"A dead man can't cover your six, Billy," Wilson answered. "Even a new bean like you knows that."

Fisch flinched when the lanky man referred to him as "new" and took a quick gulp of his bourbon and Coke.

"You're an experienced Weapon Systems Officer, Buck," Whiskey Wilson said, turning to the redheaded man. "Interesting phrase Billy used there - 'weed out'. It fits. Weeds grow out of rocks and rocks kill airplanes that fly too low. Are you willin' to take the risk of being weeded out by some green-tailed front-seater?"

Buck eyed Fisch before saying, "I wouldn't let him. I'd be watching him."

"If you're watching him, and he's watching the rocks, who's gonna check six?"

"If we're that low, it isn't as important," Fisch chimed in.

Whiskey eyed him with interest. "And your WSO's out of a job."

As Alan listened, he felt flushed. Fisch had to know how foolish his words were.

Buck was quiet for a moment. He glanced at Fisch, then took a sip of gin. Watching him drink, Alan thought again of the day Ernie died. Was that all it meant to Fisch, that Ernie had merely been "weeded out"?

"Have you ever lost a close friend to the rocks?" Alan directed the question at Buck, but the reaction he was really hoping for came from Bill Fisch.

Fisch jerked his head in recognition of the voice. The smirk of a smile crept across his wide, circular face, but he said nothing.

Buck Buchannan gazed over the top of his glass with a quizzical eye. He was a squarish, bulky man of obvious physical strength. Thick red hair covered his arms and the backs of his hands and flowed from his chest at the top of his polo shirt. The sandals he wore exposed large, wide feet and stubby toes. "Friends of friends," he said. "Who are you?"

"I lost a friend, a good pilot," Alan said, ignoring Buck's call for introduction. "He was weeded out by somebody's poor judgment." He waited as his words pierced the air.

Buck's eyes widened knowingly. He cast a glance around the group and then back at Alan. "That latest accident ... at MacDill?"

"I was there," Alan said pointedly. He cast his eyes briefly to the floor for affect. "Ernest Goddard." He focused his gaze on Fisch. "He was my best friend."

Buck sobered somewhat as he silently studied Alan's rigid face, recalling the details from the accident report. He considered for a moment what it must be like to lose a friend in a way that brought Death to your front door step, as if maybe it reached out and caressed you briefly before deciding to take someone else. "I didn't mean it that way ..." he said finally. "We heard that guy was supposed to be in our squadron ..."

"Instead of me," Alan finished for him.

Buck nodded in sudden understanding.

"But he couldn't hack it," Fisch interjected before taking another large drink from his glass.

Alan narrowed his eyes as he turned to look squarely at Fisch, angered by the harshness of his statement. His words formed slowly. "Bullshit ... Carp."

Fisch winced when he heard the nickname an instructor had christened him with at MacDill. He glanced around, hoping none of the fighter pilots had picked up on Alan Wayne's subtle interjection.

Whiskey rubbed his narrow chin as he listened, finding it interesting to watch the WSO and the New Guys go at it. He understood Buck well enough to know he could not mean that only the best deserved to survive. He was less sure about Bill Fisch, whose careless choice of words had suddenly put him in a precarious position with little room for retreat. Yet, it appeared Fisch would stand his ground, even if it was the quicksand of arrogant ignorance.

"Death ain't discriminate," Whiskey said suddenly, glancing at Alan. He spoke with the confidence that experience and stature afforded him. "She takes the good and the mediocre. Look at the guys we just lost six months ago up in Germany. They were both experienced. And the F-5 driver that hit 'em had nearly two thousand fighter hours. He was not only experienced, he was one of the Weapon School's finest. Was he weak?"

He paused. No one spoke.

"Who can know for sure why that happened?" he continued, as if to himself. "Each of us can probably remember a close call, when circumstances alone made the difference. We say we cheated Death by our superior flying skills. We may even be so cocky as to say that a lesser pilot would not have survived. I don't believe all that crap that says a pilot died because he didn't have what it takes. He was just unlucky." After a moment he looked around the group and added, "For whatever reason, we've lost another fly-buddy who might otherwise have saved our own undeservin' ass."

Bill Fisch looked at Alan who held his gaze for a moment before letting it drift away to another part of the room. The attractive woman and the older man were still sitting in the corner, whispering and laughing softly.

Buck drained his glass. "I need a refill," he said and walked away.

Fisch returned Alan's stare in search of words. "If you're going to fight your battles from your bleeding heart," he said, contemptuously curling his upper lip, "you might as well stay on the ground." He spun away and followed Buck toward the kitchen.

Alan glanced at Ron, his eyes intense, his mouth drawn tight. "How do you like me so far?"

Whiskey looked at him with interest. "Buck was just tossin' out an idea he found in the bottom of a gin glass."

"I like you well enough," Ron said. "How your Flight Commander feels about you remains to be seen."

Alan whirled around to see Buck gesturing with a fresh glass of gin in another group. Bill Fisch had his back to him. "My Flight Commander?"

"Alan Wayne meet Buck Buchannan," Ron said with a sly grin.

Alan groaned. "I've been here less than twenty hours and already my career is on a banana peel!" He made the joke lightly, knowing that he did not yet have his emotions under control.

"I was going to introduce you," Ron said. "But you did a fair job of breaking the ice on your own."

Whiskey Wilson looked at his empty his glass, nodded and said, "Gotta drain it," as he strolled away.

Sloan and Jennifer appeared with an attractive young woman of Sloan's height and age.

"You guys can't wait to get into the bar talk," Sloan teased.

Alan winced. "I'm not making friends, but I am influencing people."

Ron grinned. "You haven't been doing so bad. You only pissed off a couple of guys."

"And who was that?" Jennifer asked, winking at Alan in anticipation of one of Ron's exaggerations.

"Buck ..." Ron began.

"My flight commander," Alan added for clarity.

"What does he do?" Sloan asked cautiously.

Alan shook his head. "For starters, he writes my efficiency report. I just crossed swords with my immediate supervisor."

Sloan gasped involuntarily. "Alan, don't do that!" she said, but recognizing the look of distraction on his face, she softened her voice. "You'll make enough enemies when you start taking their money on the bombing range." She winked at him.

"Knock it off, Sloan," Alan said, shaking his head.

The pretty woman with short blond hair spoke for the first time. "You talk like you already know a lot about this stuff," she said to Sloan.

"Alan was the top gun in his graduating RTU class," Sloan said with obvious pride.

'If you don't count Ernie,' Alan thought. "Come on, Sloan, cut it out." He felt his face redden.

But Sloan liked bragging about him. She wanted her man to excel. The better he was, the better was she. "Well, it's true," she continued, though she changed to her cute voice. "You drop good pickleth!" she said, purposely lisping the "s."

"Pickleth?" Jennifer questioned. She tilted her head to look up at Alan. Her glasses sat on the end of her nose. She pushed them back into place.

"You know," Alan gestured with a pushing down movement of his thumb. "Pickling off bombs ... at the range. Her word, not mine." He felt embarrassed. "I'm Alan Wayne," he said, offering his hand to the new lady. "You must be Michelle. I met Sam a little while ago."

She smiled pleasantly but eyed Alan with quiet, questioning eyes. "No," she drawled slowly. "I'm Denise. Denise Fisch." She furrowed her brow for a second in momentary confusion. "But thanks for the compliment." She took Alan's hand.

Alan squeezed her hand gently, noting that it was soft but firm. "Compliment?" He looked steadily into her pale blue eyes. They each had a dark blue, almost black ring around the edge of the iris. With her pupils dilated as they were now, they looked like targets, like open bullseyes awaiting the unpredictable darts of life. Alan was momentarily ashamed by the open honesty they seemed to portray. He recalled that Ernie had once spoken of a girl named Denise, even describing her eyes.

Denise returned his gaze. "You obviously don't know her."

"Know who?" Alan said.

Denise held her smile. "Michelle Christopher."

"No," Alan said.

Sloan reached for Alan's free hand and held it in both of hers. "They're renting a house in a place called ..." She looked at Denise. "How do you say it?"

"Eurovillas," she answered.

"That's it!" Sloan acknowledged.

Suddenly aware Alan's hand was still in hers, Denise released it and reached up to put a loose lock of her pale-yellow hair behind her ear. "We haven't been there long," Denise said almost apologetically. "But maybe we can get together some time soon."

"We'll have to come see you," Alan said.

At Jennifer's urging, Ron took pity on the newcomers, and they left the party early. As they settled in for the ride back to the base, Sloan rested her head on Alan's broad shoulder and said sleepily, "I like Ron and Jennifer's apartment."

Alan was surprised. "You two ladies have obviously been talking about this."

"Those apartments may not be what you would think of as classic Spain," Jennifer leaned around her seat to say, "but they're convenient to the base." She looked small, even in this little Spanish automobile. "There's one for rent two floors above us on the eighth."

"There are several options for houses," Ron said.

Jennifer glared at him from behind her seat.

"But," he added while trying to appear unintimidated, "it's hard to find one close to the base. Even Royal Oaks, the base housing, is forty-five minutes away."

"How far is Eurovillas?" Alan heard himself ask.

"At least a thirty-five-minute drive on bad roads. Built to be summer homes for rich Spaniards. Most of the houses don't have radiators."

"I want a place like theirs," Sloan said. Her soft begging eyes rested on Alan's.

He whispered in her ear, "Those apartments are nice enough, but they're ugly. They are not Spain. The houses like we saw tonight ... that's Spain. I want it to be Spain."

She whispered, "And I want us to be happy."

Alan was inwardly relieved. He had transplanted her across an ocean, thousands of miles from her family and friends. He owed her. Not because he felt lucky to have her, although he was. It was not that. He had felt uncomfortable tonight with Sloan and Denise standing side by side. While he would have preferred a small Spanish house garnished with red geraniums, the last thing he wanted was for them to become suburbanite neighbors with Bill Fisch.

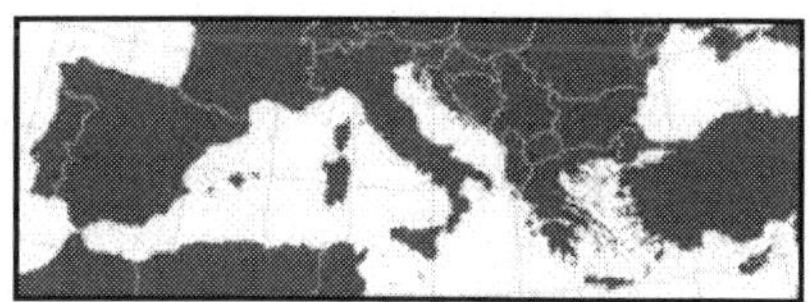

CHAPTER FOUR

The dream startled Alan into consciousness, and he opened his eyes, staring at the ceiling in the darkness. He focused on the digital numbers of the alarm clock glowing an eerie luminescent green. 2:57A.

He sat on the edge of the bed and stared out the window into the night. Across the quadrangle in another high-rise apartment building, a light was on in a room on the sixth floor. Maybe another pilot getting dressed to go fly. It could not be a Julio, Alan decided ... much too early, and some of them were probably just going to bed. He laughed to himself at how quickly he had adopted the word some of the Americans used when referring to the Spaniards. Allowing himself to awaken a bit more, he contemplated possible origins.

Yesterday's September heat was just beginning to dissipate. The cool of the morning had not yet begun. Sloan moaned softly and rolled over toward him. He turned away from the window to look at her. The bed sheets covered only part of her shapely calves.

He stretched out gently beside her.

She did not open her eyes. "What time is it?"

"Early." Alan pulled her shoulders to his bare chest and caressed her back through the negligee, smelling the fresh fragrance of her hair. Her eyes remained closed as he kissed her cheek. She did not respond to his touch. He left the bed and turned on the hot water for the shower.

Sloan was sleeping soundly when he closed the apartment door behind him.

He strode out of the building and into the darkness of this warm September morning. A Spanish man, dressed poorly but clean shaven, pushed an old wheelbarrow, top-heavy with cardboard, down the street. He carried himself well, his head high as he strained against the weight of his load, driven with purpose to provide for his family. The man stopped at the garbage cans in front of the building, ignoring Alan, while with noble dignity he inspected the refuse, looking, not for something to eat, but for something to sell.

Ron waited in the small car. Alan got in on the passenger's side. A small clock Velcro-ed to the dashboard glowed 4:01.

"Good morning," Alan offered.

"Mornin'!" said Ron. Looking amazingly well rested and alert, he grinned knowingly at his companion. "How'd you sleep?"

"Fine," Alan lied.

Ron gunned the air-cooled four-cylinder engine and pulled away from the apartments of Parque de Cataluña. "How's the new casa?"

"Sloan likes it. We got the transformer installed so the fans are working. But it's still hot at bedtime. I have trouble sleeping before these 0-dark thirty briefs anyway."

"You'll get used to it," Ron said. "Once you've spent a year here, your body will adjust."

There was no moon, and the darkness lingered as they entered the squadron building fifteen minutes later. Alan followed Ron down the hallway and into a room which served as a lounge during working hours and morphed into the squadron bar once the last flight of the day was airborne. The lights of the building were bright everywhere except in the lounge which was softly lit to ease the transition from peaceful slumber to the aggressive, often abrasive world of fighter pilots.

Whiskey Wilson, having just finished pouring his first mug of coffee, was weighing himself on the scales in the corner of the room. He stood statuesque, his coffee mug upheld and level in his right hand as he tapped the counterweight with his left. One more small movement of the weight and the scale balanced with the gangly man and his coffee. Grunting his satisfaction, Whiskey strolled out of the lounge on his way upstairs.

"Tell me again the name of that guy weighing his coffee," Alan said quietly. "I remember him from the party, but we never really met."

Ron poured coffee into a mug that bore the 613th TFS Squid patch on one side and his name on the other. "That's our resident 'fwick.' He got in on the tail-end of Vietnam."

Alan hesitated. "Fwick," he repeated.

"F W I C." Ron added a spoonful of sweetener to his mug. "A graduate of that exclusive school of fighter learning in Nevada, The Fighter Weapon's School," he offered in explanation, although he seemed unimpressed. "Frederick 'Whiskey' Wilson. He wasn't weighing his coffee."

Ron picked out a random cup, filled it with coffee, and handed it to Alan. Alan added powdered creamer, and they sat to drink in the quiet of the dark morning. Five minutes later, Whiskey Wilson returned, now with an empty coffee mug. He stepped on the scales, holding the mug aloft, and maneuvered the weight again. Again, the scales balanced to his satisfaction, Whiskey stepped down and walked to the coffee maker for his second cup. "How much?" Ron asked.

"Pound and a quarter," Whiskey answered as he poured. Black. No cream. No sugar. He looked at Alan and offered his hand. "Sorry we weren't introduced before. Name's Wilson."

"Alan Wayne."

They shook hands briefly.

"Yeah. First flight in Spain today?"

"First flight to the range," Alan answered coolly.

"Wake up the Julios," Whiskey Wilson said. "Have you gotten much Julio gut-stuffing yet? I ate at a place called 'Kiko's' last night. In Torrejon de Ardoz. Great yard-perch asado. Give it a try. Butler knows where it is."

He walked out of the lounge again.

Alan turned to Ron with a confused look on his early morning face. "Yard-perch?"

"Chicken," Ron said without further explanation.

"Oh." Alan sipped his coffee. "Well, what was he weighing? A pound of what?"

"Whiskey's morning ritual." Ron's face portrayed indifference as he explained. "Every morning he weighs himself with his coffee. He then proceeds upstairs to the head for his morning constitutional. He weighs himself again to determine how much it weighed."

"How much what weighed?"

Whiskey Wilson's voice broke in loudly over the squadron interphone, disrupting the early morning tranquility. "Looks like a pound and a quarter this morning," his voice boomed throughout the building. "Resembles my Uncle Sidney on my mother's side. Yard-perch at Kiko's."

Ron eyed Alan without smiling.

Alan looked at his watch. Thirty minutes before brief time. "Time to check the weather," he said.

"See you in the briefing."

Alan nodded, poured another mug of coffee, put his quarter in the "Feed Me" can, and went to the front desk to sign out and prepare his line-up card. Grabbing a copy of the weather sheet, he bounded up the stairs.

Sam Christopher found Alan deeply engrossed in a low-level map in the Navigation Planning Room.

"Alan Wayne!" Sam called to him.

Alan's head snapped up from his work to look at Sam, his countenance changing from one of deep concentration to that of concern. Instinctively, he looked at his watch - he still had twenty minutes.

"What's up?" Alan asked stiffly.

Standing to one side, Sam perused Alan's half-finished map with the amused eye of experience. "What could hold your attention so completely? It's just a standard range mission, not a nuke run on Budapest."

"Budapest?"

"They're all a pest," Sam grinned. "I say nuke 'em all and let God sort it out." Experience gave Sam the luxury of levity Alan could not yet express.

Serious lines formed on Alan's forehead. "I need to learn the area. This is good practice." He used a ruler to draw a line between points labeled "C" and "D", then penned timing marks on the line.

Watching Alan's long fingers move across the map, Sam quietly considered this new AC, as the pilots were called, this serious fighter jock on the border of becoming too serious. All new Aircraft Commanders desired to fit the "image." If initial indicators held true, only the lack of war would keep them all from becoming heroes. But it did not work that way. There were disappointments.

Sam picked up a pre-made low-level book. Having flown this "canned" route to Bardenas Reales bombing range many times, he knew every turn point and timing mark by heart. "Who's in your pit today?" He knew the answer.

Alan looked up. "Buck," he said. "Buck's in my pit."

Sam thumbed through the low-level book, but his eyes did not focus on the pages. "This is your first flight with him?"

"Yeah. I get the impression he doesn't think much of me."

"You won't last very long being thin-skinned. It comes with the territory. And Buck's a thick-skinned fighter 'gator. He knows his shit."

"And how to jump into mine," Alan interrupted

Sam smiled. "It was the other way around, wasn't it?"

"Hard to remember, now ..."

"Buck may not be the best at expressing himself, but he's a genius at threat warning and counter measures. He beeps and squeaks when he walks."

Alan allowed himself to laugh at the WSO infatuation with electrons. "He seems more aggressive than the ones at MacDill."

Sam tossed the book on the table and stared hard into Alan's eyes. "He's a frustrated fighter pilot. Like most wizzos. Forced by the shortcomings of eyesight or just dumb luck to spend their Air Force flying career in the rear cockpit, looking over the shoulders of luckier and, in some cases, less talented men."

Sam sat down in a swivel chair at an empty desk, leaned back and crossed his arms. "And it gets worse with experience. You sit there in the pit and watch front seaters make mistakes that in a war could cost us our lives, or at least our freedom." He stared out the window into the darkness. "The AC will press on, going against what his experienced WSO is telling him, even if it's the wrong thing to do. Some guys would rather die than look bad."

"I'll learn whatever I can from whoever I can, "Alan said awkwardly. "Dying is not part of my game plan."

Sam stared silently across the room at the large map of Spain.

Alan was thoughtful for a moment, then threw Sam a line. "I know it's your experience that might keep a young pup like me alive long enough to learn."

"That's a good attitude," Sam returned, aware of its origin. "If you believe it." He grinned. "Just remember to keep your wizzo alive, too!" He stood and walked to the door. "I'll get the weather."

"Done already," Alan called after him.

"Well, finish coloring your maps. I'll see you at the briefing."

"Sam."

Sam looked back. "Yeah?"

"I do believe it."

With less than five minutes remaining before brief time, the number three Aircraft Commander was not in the room.

As the flight lead, Ron was all business. "Go get Lieutenant Colonel Hargrove," he directed Alan.

Alan descended the stairs and walked the long hallway past the squadron lounge to the far end of the building where the administration room joined the Squadron Commander's office. The door was open. Lt. Colonel Hargrove sat behind a large cherry-wood desk, talking into a phone pressed tightly against his ear. Hearing Alan's knock on the open door, the Squadron Commander pivoted his chair to face him and, returning his salute, motioned for him to enter and take a seat on the brown vinyl couch. The rhythm of his early morning phone banter never faltered.

Alan sat on the edge of the couch with his hands on his knees, a posture he hoped would communicate a sense of urgency. He eyed Hargrove intently, realizing this was the first time since his arrival in Spain that he had seen him wearing something other than the more formal Air Force blues.

Daryl Hargrove was a short, slight man, weighing barely 140 pounds. He looked out of place in the olive drab Nomex flight suit. Spray starched by his equally slight wife, Marcy, the utility uniform hung loosely on his bony shoulders and rarely seemed to come in contact with his skinny legs and arms.

The features of his face were rather soft, belying his reputation as a hard-ball player. His nose was too large for his thin face, bulbous on the end and placed between two large brown "puppy dog" eyes that could, with little warning, become black and lifeless, like forbidding caves.

He was a very intense man, with a clear, analytical mind. When he spoke, as he did into the phone now, his words were punctuated, the ends of the words crisp, creating the image of computer-like precision, which was precisely what he wanted.

He considered the foundation for his career to be the Pentagon, where his unquestionable intelligence and a capacity for enduring long hours of tedious tasks while creating and destroying multiple paperwork empires had won him the friendship and favor of a small but powerful handful of high ranking generals. This propensity for hard work along with his untiring, strategic use of a telephone were legend. It had made his career. However, but for her total devotion, it had more than once nearly cost him his Marcy.

And Marcy had not held on to Daryl so much out of love as she had out of character. It was character that, after much soul-searching, convinced her the job of an Air Force wife was to be devoted and to sacrifice and to become totally encompassed in her husband's life and work.

That was not easily done. The essence of "the boy colonel," as Hargrove liked to refer to himself, was carefully constructed in a binary plane of "yes" and "no." All gray areas were quickly resolved into black or white.

Ironically, in the years to come, his hair, once pitch black, would become prematurely gray before at last turning snow white. The transition, however, and the years it would take to happen would go almost completely unnoticed in his mind. His ambition threatened to carry him to a point where he would simply awaken one morning to discover that his hair was all but completely gone, his life all but completely over.

For now, he was the commander of a fighter squadron, and that was different from the Pentagon. He yearned to display his leadership abilities through methods he thought already perfected, but he possessed a background much weaker than he realized. He did not see himself as the way he was, but rather as the way he wished to be.

Alan grew anxious thinking of the seven crew members waiting impatiently upstairs in the briefing room. After many pointed attempts, Alan caught Hargrove's eye and quickly tapped his watch. The boy colonel nodded and spoke into the phone, giving no indication that the conversation was over. Suddenly, Lt. Colonel Hargrove got what he wanted, or decided he no longer wanted it, and returned the receiver firmly to its cradle.

"Let's go fly!" Daryl said.

With Alan in close trail, the Squadron Commander strode purposefully down the hallway, his flight suit rippling crisply over his black, spit-shined boots. He grabbed a line-up card at the duty desk and bounded energetically up the stairs. Alan closed the door to the briefing room as they entered.

When the briefing was over, Alan opened the door.

"Standard bet," Ron called out as the fighter pilots and gators filed out of the room.

"What's the standard bet?" Alan asked Sam covertly as they descended downstairs.

"A quarter a blue bomb, fifty cents for nukes," Sam answered.

"And we're carrying eight blue and four orange?" Alan groaned. "Good-bye lunch money. Guess I'm not as hungry as I thought ..."

"Then get hungry!"

"Maybe I can find some dog biscuits to gnaw on."

"Or puppy chow," Sam said.

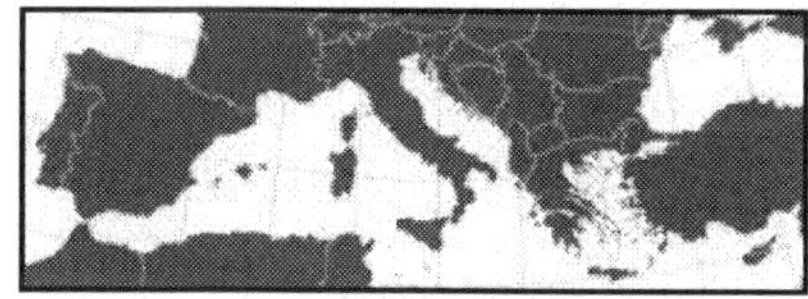

CHAPTER FIVE

In the Life Support section of the squadron, Alan put on his parachute harness, tested his flight helmet and put it into his helmet bag, as per the standard ritual. He threw his G-suit over his arm.

Buck Buchannan stared at him, his red eyebrows raised in mock perplexity. "Are you going to wear that go-fast suit, or dry dishes with it?"

Alan stammered, "Uh, it's probably getting hot outside. I thought I'd wait until the airplane ..." It sounded ridiculous as soon as he said it.

Buck flinched, but his thick lips curled slightly upward. "A real fighter pilot never waits to put on his G-suit."

Alan quickly donned the G-suit, zipping it on each leg from crotch to ankle. Bedecked in this flying and fighting regalia, a cross between gladiator and armored knight errant, he followed his WSO out the doors to the ramp as the first glimmerings of daybreak unraveled in the east.

Fifty-four F-4Ds rose from the concrete of the large ramp parking area, precisely aligned in six rows - statuesque fighting machines standing still and somber, ready for the call to combat. The soft glow of the new morning molded the hard-lined silhouettes of these dinosaurs of the fighter fleet, giving eerie meaning to the designation "Phantom." As the light of dawn bled over them, the jets' patterns of brown and green camouflage were unsheathed from the darkness, giving them the appearance of aerodynamically designed mounds of earth suspended atop the heavy-duty tricycle gear originally designed to sustain the high impact forces of carrier landings.

The ramp was very quiet now, with only the intermittent sounds of trucks and men at its perimeter, muffled from time to time by wispy gusts of the warm early morning breeze. Soon, the machines and the jet-powered air carts that helped start the machines would come to life, one by one, erupting in a crescendo of ear-splitting, earth rumbling noise. The Sound of Freedom.

As the fighter pilots approached their Phantom, the crew chief cranked the Dash-60 power cart to provide electrical power to the jet prior to engine start.

Alan checked the maintenance log while Buck made a quick inspection of the practice bombs. Buck put his foot on the cockpit ladder and said flatly, "The crew coordination briefing is standard. Any questions?"

"Only one," Alan answered. "Doesn't the aircraft commander give the briefing?"

Buck stepped down, put his helmet bag on the ground beside the nose gear, clamped his hands on his hips, and looked at Alan in bored anticipation.

When Alan had finished, Buck nodded, picked up his helmet bag, and, without looking back, said, "Standard" as he ascended the ladder. Lowering himself into the rear cockpit ejection seat, he yelled to be heard above the Dash-60, "Kick the tires and let's light the fires!"

After a thorough preflight check, confident that all was as well as it could be with this fifteen-year-old jet, Alan climbed his ladder with the crew chief in close trail. Resting his helmet on the canopy rail, he stepped into the cockpit, stood on the seat bottom cushion while he adjusted his parachute harness, then slid down into the snug ejection seat. The crew chief helped him strap-in, then scrambled down the ladder and removed it from the aircraft.

Alan made a glancing check of his instruments and switches as he fitted on the leg restraints designed to pull his legs in tightly against the seat so they would not flail and break against the tight cockpit should the need to eject arise.

He put on his helmet, adjusted the strap and hooked up his oxygen mask and interphone. Each additional step that served to connect him to his machine decreased his freedom of movement a bit more. Through the intercom system, he could hear Buck breathing in the back. "How do you read?" he said.

"Loud and clear," Buck answered. Their helmets muffled the blare from the M-60, allowing them to speak in normal, conversational voice. "You feel good on your emergency procedures?"

"I think so," Alan answered, quickly adding, "No problem."

"How will you recognize an engine fire during start?"

"I ... uh ..."

Buck cut him off. "The crew chief running rapidly away from the aircraft may be construed as a reliable indication of a fire." Buck recited the well-worn joke as if reading from a cue card. "One more thing ... you do what you are supposed to do. I won't do any instructing today unless it becomes painfully obvious you need it. There are two types of pilots ... fighter pilots and pilots who fly fighters. Today we'll find out which one you are."

After engine start, Ron's voice came over the radio, "Duddy four one, check!"

"Two!" Bill Fisch acknowledged.

"Three!" From Hargrove.

"Four!" Alan called.

"Torrejon ground, Duddy four one flight taxi four Phantoms." Ron's voice sounded deeper on the radio. Alan recalled back in pilot training that his favorite instructor, Wheels Delong, taught him to "put some balls in your voice" when talking on the radio. It was universal.

"Duddy four one, taxi to runway 2-3. Wind 2-2-0 at 8 knots, altimeter 3-0-0-3." The ground controller had no balls in her voice.

Alan theatrically signaled the crew chief with his fists closed, thumbs out, and the crew chief relayed the signal to unknown faces beneath the aircraft who removed the chocks. With the run-up signal from the crew chief, Alan pushed the throttles forward ten percent above idle RPM, and the 24-ton fighter reluctantly rolled forward, coaxed from its resting place by the brute power of the twin General Electric J-79 engines. As the fighter accelerated to taxi speed, Alan brought the throttles back to idle, turned the corner at the taxi way, and fell in line 150 feet behind the jet Lt. Colonel Hargrove and Sam were in. Like elephants, they lumbered slowly in staggered trail to the end of the runway.

They took off as single ships. Releasing his brakes and slamming his engines into afterburner ten seconds behind Hargrove, Alan felt the subdued flush of excitement as the powerful jet accelerated rapidly down the runway. At 155 knots, he eased back on the stick, and the nose-wheel strut extended as the pitch attitude of the F-4 increased above the horizon. Alan held the attitude at ten degrees nose high, and the main gear struts extended as the weight of the fighter was transferred from the wheels to the wings.

The jet continued to accelerate and climb. Alan raised first the landing gear and then the flaps while making the immediate left turn required to avoid over-flying Barajas, Madrid's International Airport. He rolled out heading southeast, 6000 feet behind Hargrove's jet, and kept the afterburners cooking a few seconds more to gain closure speed. The sun, low on his left, was bright and clear on the green and brown camouflage paint scheme of his leader's jet as Alan moved his great metal bird silently into fingertip formation, allowing only three feet of wing tip clearance.

Flying so close to another fighter at over 400 miles per hour, Alan found he was still awed when he realized what he was actually doing. Looking across his right shoulder, he lined up his lead's afterburner cans only twenty feet away. The canopy of his jet and the padding of his helmet cushioned external noises to a whisper. He heard neither the rushing wind nor the ear-splitting roar he knew was bellowing from the bowels of the two powerful engines. There was no sensation of speed. Except for the sound of his own breathing and the occasional voices on the radio, the morning was quiet.

Hargrove rolled out heading east behind Ron's element. He looked over his left shoulder and turned to look forward again. He "kicked" Alan out with a brief fishtail of the rudder, checking again over his shoulder to see that his command was being executed. Alan moved out, 500 feet down his leader's wing-line to the route formation.

Buck was silent. No encouragement. No rebukes.

Alan decided to initiate a conversation. "Climb check," he called over the intercom. Buck coughed and recited the checklist items from memory. Alan responded, and with the checklist complete, they were silent again until Buck said, "Twin Buttes," to point out the distant landmark to their left.

The land showed signs of millions of years of erosion. Wind, water and time had worn away the earth to form a relatively thin, sheer mesa, which, a third of the way from the top, had been worn through the middle leaving two elongated, flat-topped peaks separated by a narrow gap. The buttes looked to have risen as two huge horns from the bowels of the earth, only to be subsequently lopped cleanly flat by a superhuman something from above.

"That's a good landmark for finding the entrance to the VFR corridor underneath the Madrid Terminal Control Area," Buck said.

Alan squinted. "Looks like an F-4 might just fit between them."

"Might just."

As the four aircraft leveled at 31,000 feet, Alan called for the cruise check, and they sang the second verse of their routine. In the silence that followed, Alan turned his attention to his first real look at Spain.

There are many ways to see a country and many ways a country can be seen. A country can be seen as a tourist attraction, something to have done. It can be experienced, which would imply a desire to learn. Or it can be lived, as by one who wants to understand. There can be no better way to see, experience, or look to understand a country and its people than to live inside of it - within its borders, its laws and its culture.

To be able to use the wings of an airplane to fly above it adds a rare dimension that is panoramic, inspiring and personal. Then, the only limits are one's own desire. And it is the magnitude of this desire that will finally dictate how close a person will come to understanding.

The flight of four fighters turned south, above the arid land of La Mancha, and a fraction of the mystery that is Spain unfolded before Alan. As he took his first glimpse of the Mediterranean Sea over the nose of the Phantom, Buck came to life.

"We're coming up on Granada," he said. "The mountains to the left are the Sierra Nevada, the highest in Spain ... The Pyrenees up north are better for skiing - more slopes and better snow."

"Do you ski?" Alan asked.

Buck did not answer. Alan waited. "What's at Granada?"

"I've never been there," Buck said.

Ron switched them to the tanker frequency when they were "feet wet" over the Med.

On his repeater radar scope, Alan could see Buck was moving the acquisition cursors and changing ranges on the radar.

"Call the first contact," Ron radioed.

"Roger." Buck keyed the mike before Alan could acknowledge. "Four's got a contact 10 left, 32 miles."

"Roger," Ron responded.

They accomplished the rendezvous with the KC-135 tanker south of Malaga. As they closed in, Buck said, "That's Gibraltar over there to your right."

"I can't see much, but it looks like a pretty big rock."

"Uh, huh."

Having flown on the wing of a Phantom for the past forty minutes, the tanker loomed large and close, and Alan had to adjust his perspective to keep an eye on all four fighters while flying his briefed position on the tanker's wing. He glanced away at Gibraltar from time to time, trying to see more than just a rock.

"Four's cleared precontact," the boom operator radioed as Fisch's aircraft moved from beneath the tanker and back up to Ron's outside wing.

Alan opened his jet's refueling door and slid down to the ready position where the boom hung aft and down from the rear of the modified Boeing 707 like a stinger with two black wings. "Four's ready!"

The boom operator said, "Four's cleared contact."

"Real fine, nose gunner," Buck said. "That's a good position. You'd almost think you know what you're doing."

After four extremely long minutes, the boom operator said, "Four, I show a no-flow."

Alan looked quickly at the green lights on his canopy bow. "Roger, Four's full. Disconnect now!" He heard the clunk as the boom operator and he simultaneously initiated the disconnect. Holding his position for a moment as the boom swung clear, he then slowly backed away from the tanker and flew up once again on Lt. Colonel Hargrove's wing.

Looking beyond Hargrove's jet, he could see the sand dunes of Morocco. The country looked dry and empty and starkly uninviting. The wind lifted the sand off the dunes, making it difficult to distinguish the land from the sea and the sky.

Ron led the flight of fighters away from Morocco as they descended below the tanker. Heading due north, the fighters approached the southern coast of Spain, the Costa del Sol. The rugged land seemed to rise up to greet them.

The formation turned eastbound four miles from the land, paralleling the coast. Sheer rock cliffs held back the Mediterranean Sea, forming a stark demarcation between land and water. The sea approached this barrier in continuous columns of energy that turned to white foam, hammering relentlessly against the land, brushing over the smoother rock already partially or nearly completely eroded away.

Magnificent! Alan thought. Strong and beautiful. He felt awe and wonder and a deep desire to stand on those cliffs and look out to sea, perhaps to look up at them as they passed by in their fighters. "Pretty, isn't it?" he said to Buck in a voice deepened to cloak his trite statement in detached dignity.

"Yeah," said Buck.

As they continued northeast, the rocky coast gave way to beaches.

"That's the Costa Blanca," Buck said. "The area ahead to our left is Benidorm. There's a nude beach there. Valencia's ahead to the right." He used the Castilian pronunciation, 'Balanthea'. "That's where they make Lladrós."

"Make what?" Alan asked.

"Lladrós. Porcelain figurines," Buck answered dryly. "If Sloan hasn't asked for them already, she will soon. Nothing you've seen in The States can match the conspicuous consumption your wife will indulge in during your tour here in Europe."

"Duddy four one, go tactical!" Ron directed over the radio. Bill Fisch pulled away to a point 7000 feet from Ron's aircraft to a line abreast position. Alan did the same, flying abeam Hargrove as the Boy Colonel dropped back to put his element two miles in trail.

The formation descended to 2000 feet AGL (above ground level). The sensation of speed was somewhat exciting here, but nothing like what it would be at 200 feet where death was but a few heartbeats away.

The first leg of the low-level route took the F-4s west of Sierra del Moncayo, the tall peak the pilots called "Bust Your Butt," and into the foothills of the Sierra de la Demanda.

The demanding mountains, Alan thought, but not much demand made on us this high above the rocks.

Fighter pilots tend to lump the mountains and the trees and all else attached to Mother Earth into a single category: The Rocks. The Rocks pose the biggest threat, in war and peace, and jets that hit them share a finality unparalleled by missile or cannon hits or even the side effects of a nuclear blast. The Probability of Kill (PK) of The Rocks is said to be 99.9 percent, being kept from a perfect score only by the miraculous survival of a handful of lucky souls.

In war, depending upon the theater, not flying close to the ground can be very dangerous as it makes it easier for the enemy's radar to find you and gives its missiles and guns a clearer shot at bringing you down. In peace-time, Mother Earth is by far the biggest killer, and flying very close to Her is the most dangerous thing a pilot can do.

In this environment, the fighter plane bears the ultimate wings. It is the ultimate vehicle, and the ultimate toy. Out of its versatility created in complex technology demanded by war is born its simple beauty. The fighter pilot, while honing his skills to perfect the lethality that may one day be required of him, can use those skills in the equally courageous task of understanding a land that is at peace. Within the laws of the land, he can fly his fighter to forty thousand feet above the ground and take in the whole of it, its mountains and its plains, its lakes and its forests. From this lofty height, he may choose a town and descend upon it, watching the dot that is the place grow to the significance of buildings and parks and neighborhoods that are the homes and livelihood of its people.

He may climb again at a rate exceeding 6000 feet per minute to find a river in a canyon, then once again fling the aircraft down very near the earth to follow the canyon, flying in excess of 700 miles an hour, now truly feeling the sensation of speed. Nearing treetop level, the pilot can navigate the river to find where it leads. Or, tiring of the chase, he may pull his jet suddenly and quickly up many thousands of feet to gain an all-encompassing view and thereby solve the mystery.

That is the beauty of the fighter plane. In peacetime, it is fantasy reflecting reality without touching it. In war, it is reality amid the fantastic.

At 2000 feet, Alan could easily stay in position while watching The Rocks. He glanced at the commander's jet from time to time but made no positional changes without Buck's direction to which he responded with stick and throttle.

"We're converging ... check right," Buck said.

Alan made an aggressive five degree turn and immediately rolled wings level.

"Push it up, we're falling back," Buck said.

Alan pushed the throttles forward and looked over his right shoulder at Lt. Colonel Hargrove's airplane, casually noting that Buck was correct.

Seeing Alan's head movement, Buck growled, "Watch the rocks!"

Snapping his head forward, Alan expected to see a mountain suddenly appearing in front of them out of nowhere, and he braced himself for an immediate climbing turn. There was nothing. They were still safely above the terrain.

Alan cleared his throat and answered, "Roger!"

Over the Spanish town of Logroño, Alan knew it was time to turn to the east, having seen the lead element do so two miles in front of them. He checked Hargrove's jet, expecting to see the initiation of a turn.

"We're turning. Check thirty right," Buck instructed. "Watch the rocks, goddammit!"

Looking forward again, Alan felt his frustration level rising. "Shit ... sorry."

"Don't be sorry. Fly the fucking jet."

"I think I should check him from time to time." Alan rolled out of the turn. "Single-seat pilots do it." As soon as he spoke, he wished he had not.

"We'll talk about it on the ground," Buck said flatly. "Come right."

Alan put a four "g" turn on the jet.

"Roll out," Buck grunted at the completion of the turn.

Alan rolled the wings of the Phantom level. They were in a valley now with the mountains rising above them on the left. He looked to the horizon. Their flight path was clear.

The thought occurred to him that even at two thousand feet, they were not safe. Inattention at the wrong time could kill them. That was the point. Whether at 200 feet or 2000 feet, the biggest threat to his existence as a fighter pilot would always be Mother Earth, and for his life to end by that threat, he would have to hit Her.

"It would be my fault," he said aloud.

"What's that?" Buck stared at the green camouflaged back of Alan's helmet.

"Duddy four one, button 8, green 'em up!" Ron's voice broke over the radio as they neared the Bardenas Reales Bombing Range.

"2!" Fisch acknowledged.

"3!" said the Boy Colonel.

"4!" Alan responded.

Buck changed the radio frequency to the preset channel.

"Duddy four one, check!"

"2!"

"3!"

"4!"

Thirty-five miles north of Zaragoza, just northwest of the town of Tudela, in a mostly unpopulated stretch of the Ebro river valley, the Spaniards and Americans maintained the Bardenas-Reales practice bombing range. The town of Guernica, Hitler's one-time "practice bombing range" and the subject of Picasso's resultant rage lies eighty-five miles to the northwest.

On a call from Ron, the flight maneuvered for spacing to line up in trail with two to three miles between each aircraft, insuring fifteen seconds between deliveries on the simulated target. Buck initiated the nuclear checklist to which Alan responded as he positioned the switches while checking The Rocks.

At five miles from the target, Alan accelerated to 480 knots ground speed. He set his iron bombing sight at 198 mils and descended until the radar altimeter read 200 feet AGL. The first two passes would be visual laydowns (VLDs), simulating a high-speed low altitude nuclear bomb run. The bright orange practice bomb, weighing only six pounds, was designed to simulate a 750 pound high-yield nuclear weapon that would deploy a parachute to decelerate.

Alan's first bomb dropped 150 feet short.

"You were climbing when you pickled," Buck said as they turned downwind of the pylon.

"Roger."

On the second pass, Alan concentrated on fighting the subconscious desire to diverge from The Rocks. Everything looked good.

The range controller in the tower was Mervin Vandersnoot, a Squid everyone called "Shooter."

"Bull, four!" Shooter called after Alan's second pass.

"Four!" Alan acknowledged.

"Nice pass," Buck said. "Do you have number three in sight?"

"11 o'clock, slightly high," Alan answered.

"Tally."

The conventional bombing pattern was very tight, requiring the full concentration of all the fighter pilots and gators. It could be exciting, although a fighter pilot would never admit to it. It could also be deadly. If the pilot just coming off the target did not see the jet on downwind and turned too early, the result would be a conflict at the part of the pattern called the "Coffin Corner," the worst possibility being a mid-air collision.

Ron was pulling off the target from his first ten-degree dive pass just as Alan leveled his wings on downwind. This is not the only place for a coffin corner, Alan thought. They were everywhere.

Ron's bomb hit at the ten o'clock position, 40 feet from the target.

"40 at ten, 1," Shooter called from the range tower.

"1," Ron responded.

Fisch's bomb was short by eighty feet. Hargrove's bomb was long, 50 at twelve.

"4 is in," Alan radioed.

"Cleared four," Shooter returned.

Alan rolled into a ten-degree dive, allowing the jet to accelerate.

"Dive angle's good," Buck called from the back seat.

At 450 knots, Alan pulled the throttles back to hold that airspeed. He watched the pipper track along the ground toward the target, barely noticing the rush of the ground coming toward him.

At 1100 feet above the target altitude, Buck began a countdown. "5 ... 4 ... 3 ... 2 ... ready ... pickle!"

The pipper was just short of the pylon. Alan pushed the bomb release button on the stick. The bomb hit fifteen feet short.

"Bull, 4," Shooter called the score.

"He gave it to you," Buck said.

"It looked close enough," Alan said somewhat defensively.

Ron's second pass was a "bull." Fisch and Hargrove both dropped their bombs long.

Alan's second pass hit 50 feet from the pylon at four o'clock.

"Fly your ass over the target!" Buck instructed.

"Roger."

The flight of F-4s climbed to 6500 feet in the same pattern to drop from twenty degrees of dive.

"One's in for twenty degree on the pylon!" Ron called.

"Cleared, One."

"2's base," Fisch called.

"45 at five, One," Shooter called.

"0ne."

"2's in."

"Cleared, 2."

"3's base," Hargrove radioed as he turned the base leg just ahead of Alan's jet.

Then Hargrove announced, "3's in."

"Cleared, three," Shooter said. "30 at six, 2."

"2," Fisch responded.

"4's base." Alan adjusted his piper to the sight depression required for twenty-degree dive bomb.

"4's in!" Alan rolled into an over-bank of 110 degrees, pulling four g's in the turn to the final attack heading and holding it until he had twenty degrees of dive.

"Cleared, 4. 60 at one, three."

"This pass is still wide open!" Buck said. "No bulls yet ... you can take the money."

"1's base."

Ron was already right there behind him. The pressure never let up. Blocking out all else, Alan concentrated on the target and what he was doing with his jet.

Buck called, "5 ... 4 ... 3 ... 2 ... ready ... pickle!"

The pipper was there. Alan pickled and pulled on the stick, putting five g's on them as he climbed and turned.

"Shack, 4!" Shooter radioed.

"4, roger," Alan called as coolly as he could.

"Shit hot!" Buck laughed.

Bill Fisch radioed, "Two requests a replot of number 4's bomb."

"What?" Alan said to Buck. "Why does he want a replot of my bomb?"

"He's pissed off!" Buck sneered. "You're taking their money!"

"Replot stands as a Bull," Shooter announced almost immediately. "Who's your number four man today?"

"Wayne." Ron answered.

"Alan Wayne?" Shooter exclaimed in disbelief. "The new bean?"

"Roger."

Shooter was incredulous. "Good bombs!"

"Roger. 1's in on the Tab Vee."

"Cleared, 1."

Ron watched his pipper track to the target thinking to himself, 'I'm going to take this one from you, Alan Wayne.' The pipper was at the bottom of the Tab Vee doors. Ron pickled when Sam in his rear cockpit called "... ready ..."

"Bull, 1," Shooter called as the white smoke rose from the doors.

Fisch dropped his bomb 50 feet at 6 o'clock. The Squadron Commander's bomb went wide.

"75 at ten, 3."

"3."

"Watch your parameters!" Buck barked at his aggressive young AC. "You're three hundred feet low on base, here, and you're way wide!"

Alan was slightly annoyed. "I'm flying a curvilinear pattern! I don't want them to say I took the money because I was flying the beginner's box."

"You haven't taken their money, yet. And I've seen prettier curves on my grandmother's ass!" Buck watched his altimeter as they rolled in, noting they had only fifteen degrees of dive. "You're shallow."

"I'll press a little."

From the corner of his eye, Buck watched the dive angle as he counted down the altitude, "... 5 ... 4 ... 3 ... 2 ... ready ... pickle ... Pull!"

Alan continued the dive, his pipper still one hundred feet short of the Tab Vee.

"Pull!" Buck yelled, putting his hand on the rear cockpit stick.

Releasing the bomb, Alan instantly put 6.5 g's on the jet and their bodies. They grunted as their G-suits inflated. With the nose of the aircraft above the horizon and in a climb, Alan whipped into a hard left turn to spot his bomb.

The smoke was a hundred and fifty feet short of the target.

"Foul, four!" Shooter's voice was gruff.

"Foul! Shit!" Alan said to Buck as he rolled out, still climbing.

"No shit!" Buck was truly angry. "You pressed too far! You'd have fragged us! With live bombs, there'd be shrapnel all over this jet! Not to mention getting too damn close to the ground!"

"Shit!"

"Acknowledge the foul, four." Shooter again.

"4 copies!" Buck answered for him.

"Shit!"

"Shit, yeah," Buck said, regaining his normal tone of voice. "That was too fucking close. Don't do that shit. In the air to mud business, there's no real future in building yourself a square corner like that." Buck paused. "It only takes one 'Ah shit!' to erase a hundred Attaboys!" He glanced at his g-meter. "You almost over-'g'-ed the jet, too."

Alan looked at his meter. It was an over-g. He knew what that meant. Buck was letting him get away with it. What he had done, he knew, was stupid. Buck was covering for him. He reset the meter as he was sure Buck was doing in the back. He understood now that, through all of this, perhaps Buck was on his side.

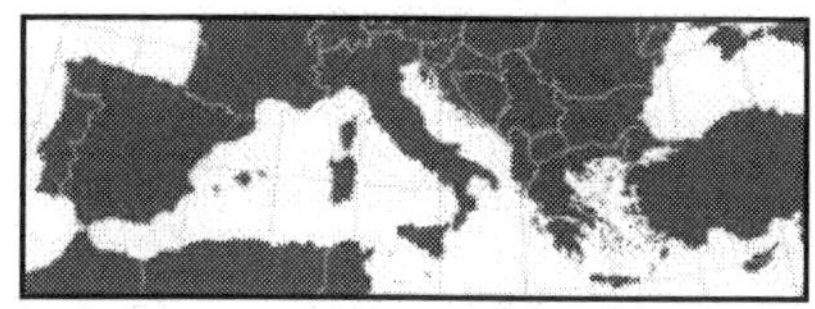

CHAPTER SIX

"I want Lladrós!" Sloan said after she quickly kissed Alan at the door.

Alan closed the door behind him. "Is this any way to treat a warrior returning from his first operational flight in the land of the Julios?"

"Did everything go well? Did you have a good flight? Did you drop good pickles?"

"Yes and no. I did drop pretty good bombs and a couple not so good."

"Good. I'm proud of you," Sloan said. "I want Lladrós."

Alan exhaled noisily. "Well, I know where they are. But it's a long way by foot. You'll have to wait a while ... at least until our car gets here."

"Valencia," she said slowly, pronouncing it as Buck had while ignoring Alan's diversionary tactic. "But we don't have to go to the Lladró factory. You can get 'em right here on the base!"

"Oh, great," Alan said in feigned distraction.

"I know we can't afford too many of them right now, but they sure would make good Christmas presents ..."

"Especially for you."

Sloan pouted playfully.

"How expensive?"

"Not near as much as they would be in the States. They are fine porcelain and very Spanish! You said you wanted things Spanish, to live Spain. Lladrós represent Spanish art and culture."

"We'll talk about it later." Alan appeared drawn out.

"I want some ..."

There was a knock on the apartment door. Alan turned his body away from Sloan just enough to allow his long arm the reach required to turn the door knob and open it. His movement gave Sloan the impression he was expecting whoever was at the door. She tilted her head to look around him at the figure in the landing, at once recognizing the clean-cut mustache above the grin.

"Well?" Ron spoke from beyond the door. He wore his flight cap with a tuck in the back in the cocky manner of the fighter pilot.

"Hi, Ron," Sloan greeted him, moving around Alan to the doorway.

"It hasn't come up, yet," Alan said.

"What's that?" she asked, looking back at Alan. "What are you guys scheming?"

"It's Friday afternoon ..." Alan began by way of explanation.

"So?"

"So, we're going to the bar," Ron finished Alan's reluctant statement.

"The bar?" Sloan took a step back. "You just got home. I've got supper defrosting in the sink. Probably the homeliest chicken you've ever seen." Her eyes narrowed as she peered at Alan. "And you want to leave me to get drunk with your new-found cronies at some smelly bar?"

Ron held the elevator door open with his combat-booted right foot to keep what was happening fluid, hoping Sloan would feel swept up in the notion to leave it all behind. And the thought had not escaped him that, should the situation get out of hand, it would also facilitate a clean get-away.

"No, we want you to go with us," Alan said looking convincingly hurt. "Jennifer's going, too. I would never desert you like that ... not without asking anyway."

Sloan's expression softened.

Alan's face became devilish. "Besides, why would I get drunk with a bunch of smelly fighter pilots when I can get drunk with you?"

"No!" Sloan barked at him. "You cannot get drunk! We'll have a few drinks and then come back home for dinner and that's it." She moved closer and said quietly, "I have other plans for you tonight."

Alan winked at Ron.

"And I'm not saying I'm going," she added with no finality, pulling away from Alan. "I don't like bars."

"It's a good way to meet other people on the base," Ron offered, seeing Alan was having trouble on his own. "Everybody goes to the bar on Friday. We won't stay long. Just a couple of social drinks and then head to Madrid for dinner."

Alan looked questioningly at Ron who was obviously improvising.

"Now you're talking!" Sloan said excitedly, her dubious committal turned suddenly enthusiastic. "Where are we going? I need to change clothes. Is a sun dress okay?" Sloan's genuine excitement about the prospect of an evening in Madrid chased the scrawny, half-thawed chicken in the sink completely from her mind.

"That'll be fine," Ron said, curling his lips over his teeth to control his grin. "We're going to Botin's."

"I've heard of it!" She turned away. "Put the chicken in the fridge," she called back to Alan as she disappeared beyond the living room.

"Botin's?" Alan questioned Ron after Sloan closed the bedroom door.

Ron shrugged his shoulders. "If they're losing interest, you up the ante." He was still holding the elevator door open.

An American, obviously military but in civilian clothes came puffing up the stairs. He looked at Ron and the open elevator door. "Have you been standing there with door open all this time?" he asked Ron pointedly.

Ron said, "Yeah," his eyes widening in anticipated confrontation. He knew he was in the wrong, but he did not see that as the issue now. He not only expected a confrontation, he welcomed one. They stared at each other. With each second that passed in silence, the chances of extracting an apology from Ron dwindled. The man shook his head from side to side and, looking down at the floor said, "Shit!" He continued up the stairs, puffing excessively.

Ron watched him without comment.

"Do you know him?" Alan asked.

"No," Ron said as he stepped into the elevator. "We'll meet you downstairs in fifteen minutes. Don't forget your civvies." He closed the elevator door to ride the two floors down to his apartment.

Waiting inside near the glass doors of the lobby, Alan and Sloan watched the portero, the apartment handyman, water the grassy knoll between the street and the building using a large diameter hose. The hose snaked from a faucet on the side of the building, along the concrete sidewalk and between the legs of the portero who held the oversize hose in his right hand, his left hand resting on his hip.

"He's holding that thing like it's his own," Sloan whispered to Alan.

Alan nudged her playfully. "He thinks he's a fighter pilot."

Ron and Jennifer joined them, and together they walked out of the building and down the steps to the car. "He's disgusting!" Sloan said, looking back at the portero who stared back at them as if he understood. "He always looks at us as if we're the ones that are weird."

Staring shamelessly, the portero furrowed his tawny brow at the two nicely dressed, aromatic ladies accompanied by the two men in wrinkled, odorous, olive drab flight suits.

The Officer's Club parking lot was full, making it necessary for them to park along the side of the street behind several other cars. Once inside, Jennifer said, "Let's go freshen up," and guided Sloan to the restroom. Alan followed Ron.

The bar was inside a large open rectangular room. At the near end stood a long counter with a mirrored back wall. Three bartenders, two American and one Spanish, hustled to fill orders. It was still early, but the room was filling up with pilots wearing green "bags" and other officers in Air Force blues or fatigues. A number of ladies formed three or four circles separate from the flight suits and other uniforms. Some were single, but the majority were married to officers either in the bar or who normally would be but were absent this night due to late office duties or perhaps on temporary duty somewhere else in Europe.

The floor around the counter where the majority of the people stood was of Spanish tile. The middle section of the room was dimly lit, and tables and chairs, most of them unoccupied this early in the evening, rested on a carpeted portion of the floor. At the very far end, a dormant fireplace formed the larger part of the wall near a tile dance floor. A juke box in the corner could be faintly heard when it was played.

Someone was ringing a bell that hung beside the counter. Alan glanced around the room at this interesting group and realized they all seemed interested in him. Ron was looking at his head and smiling.

"What is it?" Alan asked. A shiver of awareness crept up his neck, flushed his face crimson, and tickled the hairs of his still covered head. He snatched at his flight cap.

"Too slow!" Bill Fisch snorted, walking toward Alan. "I'll have a bourbon and Coke."

Alan clinched his teeth as he tucked the cap in the calf-pocket of his flight suit. "Dammit," he said under his breath.

Ron smirked slyly. "Remember to watch your lead."

"The New Guy's gonna buy the round!" Fisch said loudly.

Someone yelled, "Let's say hello to the New Guy!"

The fighter pilots yelled in unison, "Hello, asshole!"

Fisch said, "Let's say hello to the asshole!"

"Hello, New Guy!"

Alan strolled to the counter as casually as he could and asked the Spanish bartender his name.

"Everyone knows my name, Señor," he said. "I am Pepe."

"Start a tab for me, will you, Pepe ... I'm buying the house!" Alan said loudly. He leaned over the counter, getting closer to Pepe, and whispered, "Try to keep it at one to a customer, okay?"

"Si, Señor, what would you like?"

"I'll take a beer."

"San Miguel?"

"Miller."

Whiskey Wilson sidled up to the bar holding a bottle of San Miguel by the neck in his left hand, a cigarette in his right. Lifting his long skinny leg enough to rest his size thirteen boot on the bar rail, he drawled to Alan, "Got caught with your skull jacket on, eh? Nothing escapes these hardtails in here."

"Yeah, I wasn't watching my lead."

Whiskey nodded. "I hear you done good today, but I don't consider you're ready to proceed autonomous, yet." He shifted his weight. "How's the bag-drag going ... you all settled in cozy?"

"Just about," Alan answered as Pepe placed another San Miguel in front of Whiskey. "Still waiting for our car to get here."

"What kind of wheels?"

"Camaro."

"Good. Yankee made. Most of it. Where'd you decide to pitch your tent?"

"Parque de Cataluña."

"Can o' tuna, eh? Little America." Whiskey took a long drag on his cigarette, carefully rubbed the butt out on his large boot, opened the left sleeve pocket of his flight suit and pulled another cigarette out of the pack that was stored inside. The little sleeve pocket was perfectly sized and served better in that capacity than any other role the Air Force might have originally had in mind. He lit a match with his thumbnail, put it to the cigarette while the sulfur was still burning, took a deep draw on the smoke and blew out the match. Returning the matchbook to the pocket, he zipped it up again.

"You got American electricity yet?" Whiskey asked.

Alan nodded. "The transformer was installed last weekend."

"Good ol' one ten," Whiskey Wilson said approvingly.

"Whiskey!" Sam Christopher called from the end of the bar. "Haven't seen you for a while." He took a fresh beer from Pepe and walked to them.

Whiskey inhaled deeply. "Well, I figured while I was here on the Iberian Pinensula I might as well get a little cultural enlightenment, so I packed my woolybears and went over to Benidorm for a few days in search of the elusive European Bearded Clam. And I'll tell you that little devil is much more plentiful on the beach than in these more hostile urban environs. Also, much more willing to be dug for." As he spoke, the smoke escaped from his mouth, giving body to his words.

"Was it a successful dig?" Sam asked, watching his eyes with amusement.

Whiskey took a long drink. "A man needs to polish his rocket in Virgin territory from time to time to keep it shiny and smooth," he began. "I met a young thing on the beach, most beautiful life-support system for the bearded clam I've ever seen. In my most practiced Spanish, I explained to her how big feet on a man are a true-to-life reflection of his God given endowment. See what I'm sayin'?" Whiskey took another long swig of beer before continuing. "Actually, I kinda had trouble with the Spanish for all that, so I just pointed and said 'Grande.' She seemed to get the picture because we spent the rest of the afternoon testin' the theory." He paused for their reaction.

"I took her back to my imitation hotel room that I was payin' a million pesetas an hour for. I laid her down gently in the old fart sack ... she was a young thing and had been virginal quite a while. After I strapped on ol' Elmer's protection, I put earplugs in my ears, and cotton balls in my nose."

"What the hell?" Fisch put in from behind him.

"Parenthetically, those were her words," Whiskey said, briefly looking over his shoulder at Fisch. "So, I explained to her that there are two things I absolutely cannot stand ... the smell of burnin' rubber and the sound of a woman screamin'."

The laughter intensified as several more flight suits joined the audience listening to Whiskey's tale.

"Sounds like something that happened to me a couple of times," Fisch said with a self-satisfying smile.

Someone said, "I don't think you can get the same results with only three inches, Fisch."

Above the laughter, Fisch answered, "Mine may be only three inches, but some women like it that wide."

"That's not what your wife told me!"

Someone else said, "Yeah, right, Fisch. If a woman tells you to give her nine inches and make it hurt, you think she means for you to do it three times and hit her in the face."

Fisch went silent. He was an average looking fellow of average height. He wore his hair combed straight back in a modified Air Force pompadour. The fact that he appeared genuinely hurt by these goodhearted insults seemed out of character for a man so modest of chin.

Whiskey looked at him critically for a moment. "There are many ways to measure a man," he said with the furrowed-brow look of a sage. He turned away from Fisch. "But the only true measure is how many crows can stand on his pecker at one time." The laughter began again. "Thirteen crows can stand on mine." He raised his right leg. "But the last one's on one foot."

Under the cover of the laughter that followed, Alan watched Bill Fisch who seemed unsure whether to laugh or scowl.

Jennifer and Sloan heard the uproar as they rounded the corner into the bar. Michelle Christopher was with them, and the three wives walked sheepishly to their men.

"Oops!" Sam joked. "The missesses!"

Sloan punched Alan lightly in the ribs. "What have you guys been up to?" She put her arm in Alan's.

"Losing the rent money." Alan looked at her apologetically. He turned around to Pepe who was shaking a vodka martini for a colonel in blues. "What's the damage now, Pepe?"

"About thirty dollars, Señor."

"That sounds about enough," Whiskey said.

Sam gave the order, "Close it out, Pepe!"

Pepe looked up at Alan from under his heavy eyebrows and wrinkled forehead.

Alan nodded. "Close it out."

Sloan pulled her arm away from Alan. "You bought the bar?!"

"I broke a rule," he answered defensively, "... and I got caught."

"You fuss about buying me a Lladró," Sloan said quietly, "and then you turn around and buy your buddies' drinks."

He leaned close to her. "I'm sorry, Babe. I'll make it up to you. You know I couldn't back down."

She squeezed his arm and pulled herself close. "Well, see that you do make it up to me."

Jennifer bumped Ron on the arm. "How much did you lose?" She threatened him, making cute, feminine fists, curled up tightly with her long-nailed thumbs sticking out. She looked to be winding up something as she whirled them in front of her chest.

"We're safe from poverty," Ron said.

Michelle Christopher stood shoulder to shoulder with Sam, looking at him with soft brown eyes in a pose Alan could only describe as adoring. She was a very pretty girl of twenty-three years, with long straight brown hair that caressed her shoulders, soft brown eyes and a turned-up nose. Endearing shallow dimples appeared in her cheeks when she politely laughed. Not necessarily sensuous, she nonetheless possessed a simple attractiveness that made it understandable why the men in the bar kept stealing glances at her. She seemed oblivious to everyone except Sam, keeping her arm tightly in his, holding it in place with her free hand.

"I'm dry," Whiskey Wilson said to Alan, "and you've got the hammer."

Alan nodded. "What can I do?"

"What can you do?" Whiskey seemed taken aback and almost showed emotion. "So you don't dick it up again ... excuse me, ladies ... I'll help you this time. Young pups like you need help." Whiskey went behind the bar counter and began a furtive search as the bartenders scurried out of his way. "I'm sure what we need is back here." He disappeared under the counter.

"Puppy! That's a good call sign!" Fisch said with obvious delight.

Alan flushed red. "Thanks, Carp."

Bill Fisch's face flashed his anger. He had tried to ditch the moniker given to him at MacDill, hoping instead to be called "Marlin." He turned and walked away to another part of the bar and leaned against it. Nick Dawson patted him on the back. "You seem depressed, Carp. Let your main most woozo buy you a drink."

"Buzz off, Nick!" Fisch said. The name was going to stick.

Whiskey returned from his mission holding a dead roach by one leg. The girls jumped backed in unison voicing words of disgust.

"This," Whiskey said, pointing to the roach with the same hand that held his cigarette, "is your basic deceased insect." Motioning for Alan to follow, he walked toward the middle of the room and placed the roach ceremoniously on the tile floor. "I hope you can figure what to do from here," he said and walked alone back to the group.

Alan peered at the insect on its back, its feet up in the air, and knelt down as if inspecting it. Nodding his head in satisfaction, he stood, faced the patrons at the bar, pointed at the insect and yelled, "Dead bug!"

In what looked like a rough-cut rehearsal of The June Taylor Dancers, all the officers in the bar, including those in blue, dropped to the floor on their backs and threw their arms and legs into the air. Only the bartenders remained standing, along with the ladies who, with drinks in hand, watched the spectacle feeling awkwardly out of place.

The men looked around at each other from their positions, then returned to their feet and seats as if nothing had happened. The noise in the bar returned to its previous hum.

"Much better job of watching your lead," Ron said to Alan.

"Who's it gonna be?" Fisch asked Alan.

"Who's going to be what?"

"Who was last down? Who's going to buy the bar? There has to be a buyer." Fisch snickered.

"I don't know," Alan said.

"You don't know much about being a fighter pilot, do you?" Fisch said, his words drenched in the drink of sarcasm. "There's always a loser. Combat rules!"

"It isn't important." Alan was beginning to get heated.

"Then you'll be buying the round again. I'll have another bourbon and Coke."

"It's okay, Carp," Sam said, stepping in. "I was a bit slow gettin' my cheeks to the floor." He turned to Alan. "It's on me." He nodded to Pepe.

Fisch looked at Alan with genuine hatred in his blue eyes. Neither spoke, but obvious heat passed between them. Staring back at Fisch, Alan thought of backing down. There was something at stake here. His conscience told him to give in. But lower down, in his more primitive areas, he could not.

The fighter pilots around them gave Pepe their drink orders. Others, unaware of the exchange and knowing only that a loser had at last been determined, were more than willing to help him along to speedy restitution, whoever he might be.

Fisch ordered a bourbon and coke and joined another group of pilots wearing yellow Squid patches who were 'shooting their watches,' using their hands to depict two aircraft engaged in one-versus-one aerial combat.

"Don't worry about Carp," Whiskey said to Alan so that only he could hear. "He's sort of suffering from a recto-cranial inversion."

Alan looked at Whiskey. "A what?"

Whiskey barely smiled. "He's got his head up his ass." He looked at Alan. "Socially. See what I'm sayin.' But he'll make a good fighter pilot."

Alan glanced at Fisch from time to time, wondering if he had done any permanent damage to his own reputation. He spotted Denise at a table with several ladies he guessed were fighter pilots' wives. She caught his glance and smiled at him. He found himself curious what she saw in a man like Bill Fisch. Too bad, he thought.

"Gotta drain it," Whiskey said. He put his empty San Miguel bottle on the counter and walked out of the bar.

Jennifer and Sloan went to find a table. Alan saw that Ron was following the ladies and so pushed away from the counter to join them.

Ron seemed tense. When Alan sat beside Sloan, Ron remained standing. After a moment, he walked away toward the bar.

Jennifer's eyes shown wide through the glasses that always made them seem bigger than life. She reached to place her half-empty drink on the table. "How were your pickles today?" she asked Alan. Leaning back, her small body was almost swallowed up in the chair.

Alan hesitated to answer. "I did okay." He looked away to the bar. Larry Bryant was talking to Whiskey Wilson who, having returned from the latrine, was pulling a cigarette from the packet in his flight suit pocket. At the other end of the bar, JG Nutter was with Larry's wife, Ramona. They seemed to be whispering a continuation of the conversation Alan had witnessed at the Finca party.

Ron returned with two San Miguels. He sat down and silently shoved one towards Alan. After a long, thoughtful drink, Ron said, "Have you ever heard the expression 'Never try to teach a pig to sing?'"

Alan nodded. "It wastes your time and annoys the pig."

Ron tapped the table. "The next time the squadron commander says you pushed it too far, the better part of valor would be to agree with him. Think about it."

Embarrassed, Alan glanced at Sloan. She was watching Ron intently, evaluating every word. Alan nodded without comment as he recalled the defensiveness he had felt in the flight debrief. After a moment, he said, "I guess it's hard for me to take instruction because I thought I left it all behind at MacDill. I thought I was one of the big boys now."

"At MacDill, you only learned how to learn," Ron said.

"That's true," Sloan commented. She looked at Alan and nodded.

Alan looked away. Nutter's lips nearly touched Ramona's ear as he shared some secret with her.

Following Alan's eyes, Ron said, "He'd better hurry."

Alan took a long drink from his beer.

Ron looked at Alan. "Larry says he's leaving the Air Force because he's tired of the bullshit. But the only bullshit he's tired of is Nutter hitting on his wife. You can see she's a looker. He stayed over here too long. He has to do something to get her away from Nutter, even if it means getting out completely."

"What will he do?"

"Probably join some Guard unit in the States. But he'll have to do more than leave Europe. You can't just keep running from all the JG Nutters in the world."

Alan nodded in silent agreement. He looked at Ramona with an inner feeling of disgust. In his mind, it was all up to her. He was glad Nutter was not a Squid. His poison was deadly enough as it was.

A low din of moaning voices began to rise in pitch and volume to become recognizable, to some degree, as singing. The fighter pilots sang to the tune of "The Bells of Saint Mary," but the words projected different objects of reverence.

> The Balls of O'Leary are wrinkled and weary
> They're shapely and stately, like the Dome of
> Saint Paul
> The women all muster to view that great cluster
> And they stand, and they stare at the bloody red pair
> Of O'Leary's balls!

The end of the song approached with a dramatic rise in volume and feeling as the true tenors reached the high notes while the majority bellowed and strained in a gut-wrenching alternative.

"What a song!" Sloan exclaimed looking into Alan's brown eyes in a way that revealed she was both embarrassed and amused. "Bloody balls? What a disgusting idea!"

"It's just from battle fatigue," Alan answered.

Sloan looked confused, but her droll mouth was twisted as she fought against a smile. "What kind of battle are we talking here?"

Alan leaned close to whisper his reply for her tender ears alone. "From slapping those hummers ..."

"Oh! Alan!" She pushed away before he could finish. She tried her best to look disgustedly annoyed, but an aroused grin formed on her tulip lips. The picture she had in her mind was of Alan and not some bloody fellow named O'Leary.

"Here's to the real fighter pilots!" Someone very close to them offered his beer bottle in a toast. "There ain't many of us left!"

"And the fighter gators!" Another added.

"Here here!"

They drank.

After another drink, Ron said, "Time to go. We need to get to Botin's before the Spaniards do." He left for the men's room to change.

Jennifer rose to tell Michelle it was time to leave.

"What was all that talk with Ron about?" Sloan asked when they were alone at the table. The look on her face turned intense.

Alan grimaced. "Larry's about to lose his wife."

"What? No, I mean about listening to the Squadron Commander."

Alan shrugged his shoulders. "I got a foul on the range today."

Sloan's look was one of concern. "What's that mean?"

"I broke the rules. I went too low. Buck had a few words for me ... so did the Squadron Commander."

"Colonel Hargrove?" She was astonished.

"Lieutenant Colonel Hargrove ... and it's no big deal."

"Ron seems to think it was."

"It was my fault. They were just trying to help me."

"They?" Sloan imagined a group of fighter pilots yelling at her beloved Alan. A lump formed in her throat. "Were they right?"

"Yes and no ... more yes than no. I got a little too close to the ground."

"Alan!"

"It was no big deal." He looked away.

Sloan lowered her voice. "Well, listen to them. And listen to Ron." Sloan hated to say it that way. She wanted Alan to be the best. He had to be. She did not like the idea of other people criticizing her man, but she concluded, as a mother would, that it must be for his own good.

"You're going to tell me how to fly, too?" Alan rose from the table and turned away from her. "I'm going to change."

Feeling awkward, Sloan got up with him. "No, I won't ever try to tell you how to fly. I just want you to do your best."

"I'm doing my best. I need you to stay on my side. It's hard enough as it is."

"I am on your side!" Noticing they were attracting attention, Sloan lowered her voice. "I just don't want you to get in trouble." She put an arm around his waist and looked up at him with her "cute" face. "I just want you to drop the best pickleth." She hugged him tightly. "And I need you to stay with me, to stay alive. I've got plans for us."

Alan looked around the barroom at the gathering of warriors. "I'm going to be the best damn fighter pilot this base has ever seen." He pulled away from her.

When he reemerged from the men's room in his civvies, his flight suit and combat boots tucked under his arm, Sloan was talking to Ramona Bryant who returned to the bar as Alan approached.

"What did she want?" Alan asked with obvious distaste in his voice.

Sloan looked after her. "She just wanted to give me some phone numbers of the people lucky enough to have phones. Not many do. Very expensive to have one installed."

"That's all?"

"Yes. What else would she have to say?"

"I just wouldn't want you taking any advice from her," Alan answered, ignoring Sloan's frown.

Sam gestured to them, and the three couples walked out of the club together. The Spanish fall was coming on. The evenings would begin to get cooler soon.

"Thanks for stepping in there for me," Alan said to Sam as they walked through the parking lot. "With Fisch ..."

Sam shrugged. "He's not a bad person, really. He and Denise haven't been here much longer than you, but I guess he wants you to be the New Guy ... or maybe he sees you as competition." Sam winked knowingly. "You did beat up on him some today. On the range and off. If you want to be the best, you can't expect everyone to like you."

"I guess not," Alan answered. He glanced away toward the flight line where he knew the fighters waited in silent vigil. He imagined he could smell the JP-4.

"I'll pay you back," Alan said.

Sam shook his head. "What for?"

CHAPTER SEVEN

Ron skillfully maneuvered the Seat down the Avenida de America and onto Calle de Maria de Molina. The traffic was characteristically heavy this Friday evening, and the gray exhaust of the cars that traversed this artery billowed skyward as if to compliment the gray buildings that lined the boulevard.

"The Julios are back from their August vacations," Ron said as he stopped at a red light.

Alan and Sloan watched intently from the cramped rear seat while Sam and Michelle followed in their baby blue Ford Fiesta, doing whatever it took to stay with the green Seat. Ron decelerated suddenly and turned left onto the Paseo de Castellana, the main street running north and south through the center of Madrid. They continued through the Plaza de Colon, so named to commemorate Christopher Columbus, where the street became Paseo de Recoletos. Ron stopped at another red light.

"They don't pay much attention to the white lines," Alan observed.

"No," Ron said keeping his eye on the light. "And it would be dangerous if I did." He glanced in the rearview mirror, beyond Alan and Sloan, and saw Sam was still with him. "Sam's a good wingman," he said.

When the light turned green, two high-pitched horns honked plaintively. "Do you know the definition of a nanosecond?" Ron asked as he gunned the four-cylinder engine.

"Well I ..." Alan began.

"It's the measure of time between when the light turns green and the Spaniard behind you honks," Ron answered for him. He veered to the right of a majestic fountain, a statue of a woman in flowing robes riding a chariot pulled by beautifully sculpted horses.

"Wow! What's that?" Sloan asked.

"Cibeles," Jennifer answered, pronouncing the name in the Castilian 'The -bay-laze.' "We call her Dotty on the Potty."

Sloan laughed.

"This is Plaza de la Cibeles," Ron said. Converging Spanish cars made the turn onto the side street a tight squeeze, but Ron persevered, pulling ahead of two of them. "Nose position is everything," he said to Alan, citing the well-known fighter pilot adage.

"And speed is life," Alan added.

"Yeah."

"What was that place back there?" Sloan asked excitedly, moving her head around to get a better view. "It looked like a castle."

"It does look like a castle ..." Jennifer began.

"That's the post office," Ron put in, depriving Jennifer of the chance to showcase her knowledge to the newcomers. She glared at Ron from behind her glasses.

"This is Puerta del Sol," Ron said as they emerged into a more open area packed with cars and pedestrians.

He slowed nearly to a stop as Spaniards crossed the road in front of the Seat, some even brushing against the slow-moving cars.

"You have to be careful," Ron said, hitting the brakes to avoid two male teenagers. "The men pretend they are matadors, seeing how close they can come to the moving cars."

An old man dressed in gray and black and wearing a black beret caught Alan's eye. The man walked slowly along a sidewalk, his head lowered, his hands behind his back as if in deep thought. He seemed oblivious to the bustling activity of the teenagers on the walkway around him. Undisturbed by the vitality of their youth, he was engrossed in the business of being old.

"You see that old man?" Ron pointed. "You see that hat he's wearing with the little knob on the top? They all wear those hats, the old men. If the little knob is still standing, it means he still has his stuff, he's still virile. If it has flopped down, he's lost it. Macho is very important in Spain."

Alan and Sloan looked at each other, then back at the old man. Neither said anything. They were new to this country. Who were they to dispute the word of experience? Perhaps it was true.

After negotiating a couple of narrow side streets, they turned onto a smaller road and into the parking area marked with a "P" under the Plaza Mayor.

Ron and Jennifer led the way up a flight of old stairs and into the large square plaza surrounded completely by buildings. Alan got the impression they were in a huge brick box, the four sides formed by windowed apartments meeting at the corners, enclosing the plaza. The first level was recessed under the buildings, creating a covered walkway.

A raised statue adorned the middle of the open quadrangle.

"That's the 'man on a horse'," Ron said, pointing to the statue. "I don't know what it's really called."

"It's a statue of Phillip the 3rd," Jennifer said in triumph.

"Yeah, anyway, it's a good landmark for finding your way around this place. Botin's is in the corner of the plaza off the horses right rear cheek." He pointed to the far corner of the Plaza Mayor. "Over there."

For the first time, Alan felt he was truly in a European city. The old brick, the stone steps, the gypsies on the sidewalks begging for money all made this adventure come to life.

They found Botin's with little trouble, although the unassuming entrance made Sloan curious how it ever became so famous. Alan looked at the menu on the outside window but saw nothing he recognized. They waited ten minutes before being led to a table near the window. Alan pulled Sloan's chair for her, then made sure everyone was seated before taking his own.

Sloan opened the menu. "Looks kind of expensive. And I don't even know what everything is."

"We'll help," Michelle said.

Alan eyed the price list. "What's the current exchange?"

"Sixty-seven pesetas to the dollar," Sloan answered quickly. She glanced at Alan. "I got pesetas today."

"You should try the peseta lady," Jennifer said. "She'll get 'em to you for seventy."

"How does she do that?" Alan asked.

Jennifer winked at him. "Black market."

He rubbed his chin. "Three pesetas doesn't seem worth it."

"It is when it comes time to pay the rent," Jennifer said smiling.

Alan nodded. "So, a thousand pesetas for this," he said, pointing to an item on the menu. "That's what? Fifteen bucks?"

"There about," Sam confirmed.

The appetizers arrived with the wine, which, as the waiter showed them, was a fine red from the Rioja region. In movements that implied confidence, preoccupation and a bit of European snobbery, and with his elbows wide apart, the waiter peeled the top cover off and maneuvered the corkscrew deep into the cork. He braced the bottle between his hands, pulled out the cork and placed it beside Alan.

His nose tipped ever so slightly into the air, the waiter poured a small portion of wine into Alan's glass and waited for him to taste it and nod his approval. Alan did not do so, the gesture being lost on him. He examined the cork. Realizing this American was not going to sample the wine, the waiter filled six small glasses precisely two-thirds full, placed the near-empty wine bottle on the table and bowed slightly.

Ron said, "Gracias," in Castilian. The waiter returned with a subdued "De nada," thinking to himself 'Typical ignorant Americans.'

Jennifer offered a toast. "To our friends and their first real taste of Europe."

"Hear! Hear!" Alan answered loudly.

"Hear, hear, but not all here tonight," Sloan said as she eyed Alan.

"Why not all night every night?" Alan asked looking around the table. He caught Michelle's gaze and, feeling himself to be more animated than usual, said, "You only go around once. You never know when things are going to end."

"In moderation," Jennifer said, putting down her wine. "All things in moderation." She pushed her glasses up on her nose.

"Moderation is not what being a fighter pilot is about," Alan countered. Aided by the wine, the words came easily.

"No," said Ron. With intense curiosity, he watched Alan, an enthusiastic but inexperienced young jock in search of an image. "But tact is."

"You're right!" Alan said rather loudly, as if seeing some very important and heretofore hidden truth. "Tact is everything!"

"Alan! Lower your voice," Sloan admonished him. She stole a glance around the little room. "Remember we are guests in a foreign country."

Sam sought to change the subject. "Where did you guys meet?"

Sloan touched Alan's leg under the table. "It's an interesting story," she began.

Alan interrupted. "I was white water rafting on a treacherous stretch of the Colorado River. I saw her sunbathing nude on a rock and stopped by to ask directions."

Michelle's laugh caught Alan's attention. Hers was a simple, sincere laugh, neither too loud nor too giggly. She was, he decided, the most attractive woman he had ever seen married to a fighter jock. When she laughed, her face seemed to glow with life.

Sam looked covertly at Sloan, envisioning the scene in his mind.

"That's not what happened at all!" Sloan exclaimed, recoiling from Alan. She slapped his leg and looked at him from this position before turning to face the others as she explained. "You were tubing down the Salt River and popped your inner-tube on some rocks and lost your shorts in the process." She glanced at Jennifer and continued. "I happened along with a spare inner-tube that he asked if he could borrow."

Alan rolled his eyes in exaggerated boredom as she retold the story he had heard many times before.

"We floated the rest of the way down the Salt with Alan wearing only his water-soaked drawers! He tried to hide his predicament by burying his butt so deep in the inner-tube that he dragged it on every shallow spot we passed saying 'Who-boy! Who-boy!'"

"Tried to hide your what?" Michelle giggled.

Alan flushed red.

Michelle imagined he looked now exactly as he must have then.

"So you're from Arizona?" Sam asked.

"Sloan is. I'm not." Alan struggled to regain his composure. The story was funny, he had to admit that. But it made him look a bit of the fool. "I'm from Texas."

"You look like a long tall Texan," Jennifer said.

"I am not a cowboy."

"Oh, I didn't mean that! You just look like a big Texan."

"Well, you know what they say about men with big feet," Alan said, alluding to Whiskey's boast.

Michelle cleared her throat and said, "But you don't have an accent."

"No, I lost it somewhere in the mountains of Colorado."

"Puppy! You're an Academy grad!" Sam said knowingly. "A career man?"

"Yes and no," Alan answered, thinking now was the time for tact. "I am a Zoomie but I'm not thinking career right now. I'm thinking fighter pilot."

"Just fighter pilot?" Sam prodded him.

Sloan looked at Jennifer and said, "How long have you been in Spain?"

In grateful relief, Jennifer answered quickly, "Two and a half years."

"So you'll be leaving soon?"

"We extended to stay in Spain another year," Ron interjected. He glanced at Jennifer. "There's rumors the wing might transition to the F-16."

"Will you try for something else if you don't get it?" Alan asked.

"Such as?"

Alan shrugged. "The Thunderbirds, maybe ..."

"Why?" Ron's one-word question was pointed.

Alan looked briefly at Sloan. "I think it would be interesting ..." he began.

Ron interrupted. "I mean why would you want to do that?"

Alan frowned. "What do you mean?"

"Do you want to get out of the mission of flying fighters just when you've gotten into it?"

Alan put down his wine glass and looked at the others around the table in confused amusement. "But those are fighters. The average guy doesn't get the chance to do that. That makes it more desirable. Doesn't it?"

Ron stared at Alan noncommittally. "The Thunderbirds don't fly air-to-air. They don't train every day to drop nukes on Ivan and his Communist Pinko buddies. It's like going to the circus. It's just a show."

Alan felt himself taking the defensive. "A fantastic air show ... They fly all over the country."

"You'll never see them over here."

"They are very good at what they do."

"It's not the flying for a fighter pilot. It's not the life of a fighter pilot. You don't want to do that stuff."

Alan quieted, hoping to let it drop. Sloan knew his future dreams as he as well as he did, but they were young and new, and the future was just that.

Jennifer cleared her throat. "You guys save that talk for the bar," she said, looking at Sloan and Michelle.

Sam studied Alan with curious eyes. Ron was silent. Something stuck in the back of Alan's mind. What was it Buck had said? Something about the difference between fighter pilots and pilots who fly fighters?

Alan said, "Back in pilot training, I briefly considered flying cargo because I thought of flying for the airlines. But I preferred the idea of fighters because I liked aerobatics. I had little understanding of the real difference between flying an F-4 and flying an RF-4." He paused. "The reconnaissance version," he explained for the ladies. "I didn't know recces were armed only with camera film."

"Kill 'em with fil-lem," Sam interjected.

"Right! One day during pilot training, a fighter pilot came to talk to us and told us if we wanted to be like him, we had better be interested in gun bores and bullet calibers and bomb fragmentation damage assessment. I thought he was just trying to intimidate us. But I was sure I wanted to be a fighter jock. I wavered only once."

"How do you mean?" Jennifer asked, sipping her wine.

"During fighter lead-in at Holloman, over the White Sands of New Mexico, I was on a solo defensive BFM mission in a T-38 with an Instructor Pilot in another T-38 at my deep six o'clock."

"Also trying to rip into your shorts." Sam smiled at Sloan.

"Right!"

Resting her chin on her open palm, Michelle watched her husband casually as Alan told his story. He was watching Alan intently, smiling often now. Sam is a good man, she thought. He got along well with people, and they liked him. She glanced at Alan who was adding flair to his animated tale. He seemed more devil-may-care, perhaps even bordering on what she had heard people refer to as a "loose cannon." She felt a sudden flush of exhilaration when his gaze caught her eyes.

“I was working hard,” Alan continued, “sweating and hurting, trying to fly my airplane and keep my maneuvering speed up and look back over my shoulder at the same time while pulling six g’s. I thought to myself in the middle of all this ‘Why didn’t I fly cargo?!’ But I got over that quick.”

“How’d you get over it?” Michelle asked with a cute smile that showcased her dimples. “All that sweating and grunting.”

Alan looked into her eyes for effect, noting how pretty they were. “I rolled my jet to put the IP at the top of my canopy and pulled as hard as I could straight into him. He overshot, I reversed and gunned his brains out ... on gun camera film only, of course.” He looked at Sam who nodded. “I got some good pictures of my pipper on his head and then called ‘Knock it off!’ I had over-stressed my jet.”

“Over g-ed,” Sam said flatly.

“Yeah. A momentary loss of awareness as to the physical capabilities of my aircraft. I caught a lot of flak for that, but it cured my little attitude problem. I decided I never wanted to be on the defensive again.”

The waiter returned, balancing a large metal tray on his right shoulder which he deftly swung in one motion onto a small serving table, allowing the Americans their first look at the feast. Sam had ordered squid cooked in its own ink. The cruelest way to go, Sloan thought, as, with obvious distaste, she watched the waiter place the bowl of blue-black liquid in front of Sam. White squid bodies surfaced in the bowl like whales in a lagoon. “They’re not still alive, are they?” she asked.

The waiter grimaced.

Ah, thought Alan, so he does understand English.

The waiter served Sloan and Michelle biftec and Jennifer her pollo asado. He returned to the little table and uncovered Alan’s roast suckling pig. With European flair, he transferred the hind quarter of the pig with a large fork and spoon from the tin dish to a plate, then used the spoon to scoop the juices from the tin dish over the meat. With practiced precision, he placed a few small potatoes delicately around the periphery of the plate, finally placing the small work of art ceremoniously in front of Alan.

“I was expecting the whole thing,” Alan said. “With maybe an apple in its mouth.”

"Just the ass end," Sam said. "They could shove an olive up there if you like."

Sloan vocalized her feelings. "Yuck!" The wine tempered her powers of articulation.

"The skin is great!" Sam said. "It's usually very crunchy, with a touch of garlic."

Ron spoke in Spanish to the waiter who nodded and left them.

"What did you say to him?" Sloan asked.

"Yes, your Spanish is impressive," Alan added.

Ron grinned. "I think I said, 'Us to have some wine more please would like'."

As the second bottle arrived, a group of young men dressed as troubadours in tight-fitting purple doublets over white shirts and black tights came into the room playing mandolins and guitars, singing as they made their entrance.

"Ah! The Tunas!" Jennifer said.

In fine harmony, these university students sang lively songs of Madrid and Spain.

The music made conversation difficult. The Americans quieted, settling into the business of eating.

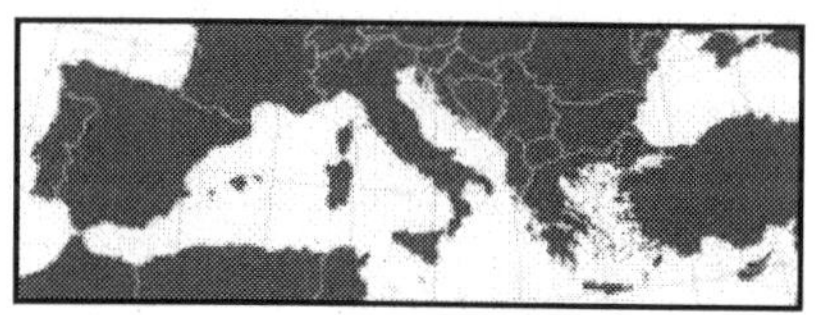

WINTER
CHAPTER EIGHT

"No one is going to spend Christmas TDY," Lt. Colonel Hargrove said in "The Announcement" two days before Thanksgiving.

As turkey was hard to come by, Ron and Jennifer Butler shared their dinner with Alan and Sloan. The American holiday about sharing and giving thanks reminded the ladies how thankful they were to be sharing it with their men who were not away, especially not away at war.

But Thanksgiving in Spain was over, and their contentment was curtailed by "The Updated Announcement."

Now, the Squids began making hurried preparations to deploy for a month of temporary duty at Incirlik Air Base in Turkey where they would most likely remain beyond Christmas. Could the Boy Colonel not have known? More likely, he had known all along but considered this the best way, to hold off the bad news until the last minute, thereby keeping the troops and their wives happy in their ignorance.

There was anticipation and unspoken anxiety. The 613th would be away from their families at Christmas ... to do what?

That was Sloan's question. That was Sloan's worry.

"Why do you have to be TDY over Christmas?" she asked him with a hint of tears in her brave eyes. "Will it take that long to do what you have to do? What do you have to do? Is this a test?"

"We don't know why they are suddenly telling us to go. They say it has nothing to do with Iran."

"Iran!" The thought made her worse fears fly to the surface of her feelings.

Alan searched for something to make her laugh. "Two days ago, turkeys were rare. Now, suddenly, they're all over the place."

Sloan did not look up from the chair.

"This turkey Hargrove is packing us up to go TDY," Alan said. "And we're going because of the way some turkeys in the White House or the Congress are reacting to the situation these Iranian turkeys have caused by holding Americans hostage." He waited for a reaction from Sloan.

She only shook her head.

"And to what square on the playing board are we being moved for our role in this game? Turkey. Incirlik Air Base, Turkey!" He laughed without feeling.

Sloan saw no humor in his story.

The possibility that Alan might go into combat was something Sloan could not let herself believe. She looked intently at her husband, fighting back the tears. After staring at him for some time, she straightened her hair and said, "It's probably nothing big. I'm sure it's nothing big. It's probably just as they said, the beginning of regular deployments to Turkey just like they did before, just like we heard about at MacDill. This Iran thing is just an excuse to start going there again."

"I hope so," Alan said.

He disliked the idea of leaving Sloan for what would be their first Christmas together, but he could not complain any more than the more senior members of the squadron. It was depressing enough being in a foreign country this time of year. Yet, having accepted the deployment as an irreversible fact, the attitude of these fighter pilots became one of pointed determination to make the most of it. This was the military, and they were military men and there was nothing more to be said about that.

Meanwhile, Alan was left to find the balance between tempered remorse with Sloan and enthusiastic involvement in the squadron preparations. He was, after all, a fighter pilot, ready, willing and able when called upon to deploy to any forward operating location. He was also a young man in his first year of marriage, and he certainly did not want his bride to think he preferred to be anywhere other than by her side.

Still, he was inwardly excited at the prospect that something might indeed happen, that they might become part of a rescue effort.

The call to battle is deeply embedded in all true fighter pilots. All fighter pilots harbor the desire to prove themselves, to prove they can survive, that the way they have trained is right, even if it means leaving family and friends behind. Alan was becoming a fighter pilot, and this was simply part of it.

As Hargrove was not yet a fully qualified flight lead - a bit unusual for a squadron commander - he delegated the role of leading the first flight of six F-4s from Spain to Incirlik to his second in command, the new Operations Officer Major Doug Sherman.

On Sherman's head signal, Alan, with Sam in his pit, released brakes and quickly selected the afterburners to stay tight on the Ops Officer's wing. As they accelerated rapidly down the runway, Alan smoothly matched his lead's rotation, keeping it in tight, and the F-4s lifted off together. Head signal - gear up. Head signal - out of afterburner. Rudder kick - Alan moved out to route formation, 200 feet from Major Sherman. As the other four aircraft joined up with them, they continued to climb to 27,000 feet heading northeast toward Barcelona.

It was a beautiful, clear morning. East of Barcelona, they rendezvoused over the Mediterranean with the KC-135 tanker that would take them as far as the east coast of Sicily before leaving them to continue to Turkey on their own.

"The Med's bigger than I realized," Alan said to Sam. It was an observation that could either begin a conversation to pass the time or be taken with a grunt of agreement from the other crew member followed again by silence from both. It tested the waters.

"Yeah. It's hard to imagine that at one time it wasn't there," Sam mused.

Alan hesitated, remembering Ron's tale about the old men and their berets. He had been "bamboozled" quite often lately, to use Whiskey Wilson's word. "So," he said finally, "did the dinosaurs drink that sucker dry?"

"Yeah, right." Sam had found another non-believer. "Actually, the entire Mediterranean Basin was dry land. All these islands were just tall mountainous areas. Gibraltar was closed off, and the place dried up."

"You're serious," Alan grunted. "How do you know that? How do they know that?"

Sam was not affronted. "Deposits. Found on the bottom. And river beds that wouldn't be there if the Med had always been full." Sam spoke matter-of-factly, just one of the guys passing the time in the airplane.

When Sam offered nothing more, Alan said, "Well, what happened?"

Sam breathed in deeply. "You have to think in terms of geological time, where a thousand years is nothing. If the strait was closed, the Med would evaporate in about a thousand years, give or take a rainy season. That's probably what happened. Then, a little later, say five and a half million years ago, the glaciers melted, and the oceans began to rise, and the tectonic plate that Gibraltar is on shifted, and in came the water. It wasn't just a trickle, either. They say it came rushing in at about 1000 times the volume of Niagara Falls. Imagine that. All that water being held back, and then to be suddenly released."

Alan imagined himself standing on the dry floor of the Mediterranean Sea, looking up at the Rock of Gibraltar as the strait gave way and the Atlantic Ocean gushed past a barrier that had been keeping it out for eons. He thought it might be a relief, to be washed clean by those incoming waters. "Is that the Noah's Ark theory?"

"Not likely," Sam said quietly.

When their time came to take gas from the tanker, Alan was on and off, taking the release of gas the tanker offered quickly and uneventfully.

Again they were silent, each to his own meditations. As the Med drifted beneath them, Alan's thoughts turned to Ernie. Perhaps if he had been more aware, or a bit less bold, Ernie would be seated in this F-4 with Sam en route to Turkey.

Thinking of Ernie took him back to the genesis of their friendship. Fate had put them together at the Air Force Water Survival Training course in the warm southern water of Florida's Biscayne Bay where future fighter pilots were instructed in the proper procedures to be followed in the event of a forced bailout over the open ocean. Attendance at water survival training was mandatory. Knowing how to swim was not.

Non-swimmers were issued red football helmets to facilitate easy recognition by the Water Survival Instructors - who were required to know how to swim. The other helmets were generally white. Aside from being used as an indicator of aquatic traits, the ill-fitting head gear, smelling of age and abuse, roughly simulated the real helmets each fighter pilot would be wearing until he was safely in the one-man raft. Alan singled out Ernie when he noticed his helmet was painted a pale green.

"Lt. Goddard," Alan had said, "do you know why your helmet is green?"

Ernie Goddard stared at Alan, allowing a thin smile to form on his slightly blistered lips. He sensed a joke in the making and sought to gain the advantage. "Recognition of superiority," Ernie answered. "I say that in all humility, of course."

"Of course," Alan had returned, nodding his head before shaking it. "Sadly, that's not the case." Creasing his brow in studied sympathy, Alan said, "They look at all the trainees and find the one that is the size and shape most likely to attract sharks. He gets the green helmet. So, in a way, you're right. They recognize you as superior, Grade A shark bait."

In the heat of the midday sun, the smile on Ernie's face melted as a mustache of perspiration beaded above his upper lip. The green of his helmet blurred briefly as he turned his head and looked out across the large expanse of the bay. Sharks were a part of the Great Unknown, and Ernie's Illinois upbringing had not mentally prepared him for the reality of floating around in potentially shark-infested ocean waters in a well-worn, Air Force issue "one each type" life raft kept in service only by a multiplicity of generously applied patches.

"That's so much shark feces!" Ernie spewed finally even as his eyes widened in potential belief.

Alan pressed the attack. "And it's not even for your protection. If anyone yells 'Shark!' they know where it must be. They tell everyone else to get away from him, away from the sacrificial lamb wearing the green helmet."

After a noticeable hesitation, Ernie answered, "Bull ..." in a low, guttural voice, but he was trapped between what he believed was reality and what he feared could be real.

Alan said grimly, "You are devoured that we may survive to fight another day."

Ernie's eyes widened as he scanned the suddenly hostile waters of Biscayne Bay. "Bullshit!" he replied flatly.

Sensing he had hit a nerve he had not known was there, Alan said, "Then why the green?"

Ernie blinked and looked back at Alan. "I prefer my original idea."

Smiling, Alan had said, "Then perhaps his Excellency would do me the honor of joining me for dinner at the Ocean Beach Club tonight. We'll begin with an appetizing bowl of shark-fin soup and thereby reclaim our dominance of the sea."

"Hell no!" Ernie answered. "The sharks would be circling tomorrow, bent on retaliation!" Feeling now what he had wanted to all along, he played into the joke.

Alan nodded. "What would you prefer?"

Ernie smiled. "I'm thinking chicken."

Thus, with a joke and a chicken dinner began a friendship that seemed to have started long before it did. It was during that first dinner when, much to Ernie's amusement, Alan confessed he should have been wearing a red helmet.

Five hours is a long time to sit in a fighter. The time can feel even longer if a pilot or WSO develops a bladder problem while having failed to bring along a piddle-pack for relief. Even one who has a piddle-pack and develops the necessity to use it can find himself in progressively deeper trouble if he does not have a plan of execution. Add to this the typical tendency to hold off the moment for as long as possible, and the buildup of back pressure that results can render the situation almost uncontrollable. The last and, for the WSO, most devastating factor in this ever-expanding equation is the possibility of discovering too late that the pilot flying the fighter is unsympathetic to the waterlogged WSO's plight. He could be the kind that sports an eight-hour bladder or one who was not so foolish, as he might acerbically point out, to have downed five mugs of the squadron's chest-hair-burning coffee just prior to departure.

The use of a piddle-pack, perhaps in contrast with its user, is no small thing. If one decides to proceed with the inevitable, the logistics of such an endeavor can become quite involved. Once the parachute, seat belt and seat kit are unhooked, the flight suit unzipped, and the proper position of half-sit-half-stand is achieved, the moment of truth begins. From this point, what is going to happen is irreversible. Where it is going to happen remains to be seen. Should a slip occur now, a sudden loss of control, if the situation gets somehow out of hand - which is quite possible, considering the confines of the cockpit - one can imagine the likeness to a fire hose being turned on full force and then flailing with fervent indiscretion on the cockpit instruments.

One can also imagine the accompanying embarrassment, the hapless soul's confession being preambled by such statements as, "I don't think the radios are going to work from back here anymore ..."

The motivation to hold out until the end of the flight might be enough to avoid this scene. The pain and uncertainty, however, could make each turn with even the slightest onset of g-forces a short but substantial nightmare. A full bladder suddenly weighing twice as much due to a simple 60° bank turn can result in agony of the most unpleasant sort.

Such was the misery of Sam Christopher as the flight of six F-4 fighters turned north near Cyprus. It had begun earlier, when they received their last fuel top-off from the tanker. Initially, it was merely uneasiness that caused him to reposition himself in his seat a little more often than usual. Uneasiness turned to discomfort when it was once more their turn on the boom, and it seemed to Sam that Alan was taking longer than was necessary and was not nearly as smooth as before.

Sam tried to concentrate on holding back as the boomer plugged their airplane and the tanker began to release its gas. The boomer called for a disconnect when their tanks were obviously full as the excess gas vented from the tips of both the fighter's wings. Alan disconnected, and the boom pulled away, leaking a little more JP-4 when it was retracted to its stored position on the tanker. Alan then flew to the observation position on the starboard side of the tanker where he noted that the co-pilot was drinking a large cup of coffee.

Two more hours would pass before they landed at Incirlik.

And now, west of Cyprus, Sam's situation was inflated.

"You sure you don't want me to pass you my spare piddle-pack?" Alan asked.

"No," Sam groaned. "I think I can make it. Don't talk about it. Talk about something else."

"Okay." Alan looked east toward the island. "Very interesting. I had no idea Cyprus looked like that, with that long thin mountain range running along the northern coast. A lot of water around it." He paused. "Some pretty hefty erosion must have taken place when the Med waters came rushing over Gibraltar. Like the Atlantic Ocean just could not hold back anymore. A thousand times Niagara, you said."

"Oh!" Sam voiced a subdued groan.

Holding the clear plastic bag with two gloved fingers, Alan dangled it over his left shoulder where Sam could see it.

"Keep it." Sam looked away to the dry landscape of Turkey. "It's too late now, anyway. We'll be doing too much maneuvering. Just put the first pass on the runway ... no go-arounds, or I'll be forced to kill you."

"I'll do my best," Alan answered, stuffing the precious piddle-pack into his helmet bag. "I don't want to drown."

Most of what they saw of Turkey was brown and barren and rugged. Like Spain, Alan thought. They flew over a mountain range that was stark and bold. At Tarsus, they left the mountains behind them and could see the large town of Adana in the coastal flat lands.

"That must be Incirlik," Alan said. "That runway east of the city. The other runway over there must be the Adana civil air patch."

"Great," Sam said without enthusiasm. "Land this pig. Anywhere is good."

In response to the wing rock given them by Major Sherman, the six-ship joined in tight fingertip formation. Approaching the air base, they formed an echelon on the left side of the Operations Officer's wing who said over the radio, "Make it look good, boys." Alan pitched aggressively five seconds after the Major.

"Take it easy!" Sam complained.

Alan tried not to laugh. "You heard the major." He put the gear down and began the final turn. His spacing behind Major Sherman looked good.

"I don't know," Alan said to Sam. "It looks pretty bad, and this is my first time here. I may have to take it around."

"Bullshit!" Sam said. "You want me to land it for you?"

"Okay." Alan shook the stick. "You've got the airplane!"

"Land this sonovabitch now!"

"I wonder where the re-entry point is ..."

"On the ground, you bastard!"

The wheels of the F-4D squeaked down, and the nose of the fighter dropped until the nose gear supported its weight. Alan deployed the drag chute and gingerly applied the brakes.

"You weren't much help on final approach," Alan said jokingly. "Your demeanor was terrible, and the more you talked, da meaner you got."

"Eat me."

"There you go."

Alan released the drag chute and taxied in behind Major Sherman.

Torrejon maintenance personnel, having arrived earlier by C-141, joined Incirlik's staff officers in waiting for the six aircraft as they pulled into the designated parking area. Alan shut down the right engine and followed the visual signals of the crew chief.

He shut down the remaining engine and saw Sam was already crawling stiffly out of the rear cockpit. Sam would be the first on Turkish soil, and his immediate plan was to quickly get somewhere semi-secluded and piddle on it. He moved awkwardly as he scrambled down to the ramp, reaching the bottom of the ladder at the same time as the Incirlik Wing Commander approached to greet him.

Colonel Ramos slapped Sam heartily on the back. "Welcome to Incirlik!" the Colonel beamed. "Have a beer!" He opened a can of Budweiser and thrust it at Sam. "To Turkey!"

Sam saluted while trying to take the beer and dropped his helmet on the concrete ramp. He groaned and took a sip of beer, a gesture of congeniality, then, trying to put the beer back into the Colonel's hand, dropped it on the tarmac beside his helmet. Beer and foamed gushed from the can as it rolled against Sam's boot.

Mumbling something about plans to move liquid in a different direction, Sam stumbled away toward what he assumed was the maintenance hangar in a cross-legged walk that developed into a stutter-stepping trot. Colonel Ramos and his staff looked after him, wondering what the hell had arrived at Incirlik Air Base.

CHAPTER NINE

The airman from the Incirlik weather shop began his segment of the inbrief saying, "The weather around here is usually good. But we don't have the best equipment for forecasting, so we do the best with what we have to work with. Sometimes, state of the art for us means calling the Control Tower for a weather update." He paused for the muffled laughter he had stirred. "They help us out with things like 'it's raining,' 'it's dark,' 'it's windy.' Things like that."

It was 1730 on Friday afternoon, and the bar had been open for some time. The inbrief, as all inbriefs go, was agonizingly long, particularly for the several crew members who were into their third beer when the briefing began. Their misery, subtle at first, rose with a torturous crescendo as each new speaker was introduced.

When the weatherman was finished, the sergeant from the Control Tower began his briefing with obvious disdain, using slides to enhance the effectiveness of his presentation. He concluded by flashing an out-of-focus slide of the Incirlik Detachment 10 emblem on the wall with an inscription that read "Our eyes are your life."

At last, the Incirlik Weapons Liaison Officer, Captain "Pep" Peplinski, took the podium and briefed them as quickly and painlessly as possible on the local flying procedures. Once again, due to time constraints, the most important subject held a back seat to the mundane.

"Faster, funnier!" Reggie Swartz said loudly from the back of the room when Pep paused to consider his notes.

Terrance Reginald Swartz was a somewhat overweight WSO with a unique approach to life and the military. "They both suck," he said, "but at least you don't have to die to get out of the military." Reggie was too easy going, and, by some accounts, too privileged, to be very serious about either one. He did not take himself seriously, and, in his own way, was intolerant of people who did. He possessed a knack for pointing out the ridiculous in any situation, or any person for that matter, mocking his targets by word or by deed.

Rumor had it that Reggie was the rarest of breeds, an independently wealthy officer who preferred the risks of flying in the backseat of an F-4 to the comforts of the gilded life. He had never fessed up to the accusation of being rich, and seldom was it pressed upon him, as many of his comrades believed he possessed any number of shortcomings warranting greater attention.

"Before I conclude," Pep said, clearing his throat, "in accordance with the procedures established by the Air Force Department of Redundancy Department, I am required to cover everything that everyone else has already covered at least twice ..."

"No! No! No!" He was shouted down.

He backed away as if insulted. "Okay," he laughed. "One more thing ... the step vans ... don't abuse them. They're the only one's we've got or can expect to get for some time. They are not for driving down to the strip for copper shopping. And use the 'bottle to throttle' rule ... don't drive them within twelve hours of drinking booze."

From the back, Reggie yelled, "Then how are we supposed to get to our briefings?"

"That's all I've got," Pep said. "Any questions?"

Butts squirmed. There was but one obvious question.

For a time, the two urinals in the restroom located on the opposite side of the hanger were very busy. "The auto-flush-mode," Sam called it. As the action slowed, the crew members piled into the government trucks and step vans to descend on the Incirlik Officer's Club en masse where Mike, the Turkish bartender, anticipated their arrival in trepidation.

When the squadron of fighter pilots arrived at the bar, several locals were well settled into their Friday after-hours routine of quaffing a few quiet brews and mixed drinks. In five minutes, the bar noise transformed from an almost inaudible murmur to a pulsating roar fueled by thirty-plus thirsty fighter pilots placing their orders and discussing the day in review. The local officers, dressed in Air Force blues, some with neatly starched shirts and ties, quieted and watched with furrowed brows, unsure of what was about to unfold before them. They returned to their conversations, shifting their eyes warily to the sea of green Nomex flight suits that ebbed and flowed around the bar. One of the flight suits put a quarter in the juke box and all hope of a quiet evening's drinking was shattered.

Alan leaned on the bar, sipping on his first bottle of Efes beer and listening to Shooter and Ron exchange opinions about how the low-level training in Turkey should be accomplished and how best to convince Lt. Col. Hargrove to allow them to train down to 250 feet.

Shooter's flight suit zipper was down at "TDY bar talk" level in his image of the fighter pilot, exposing a good bit of his pale, hairless chest. A leather cup with five dice in it was shoved his way. Instinctively, Shooter clamped his cigarette in his mouth, squinted his eyes as the smoke swirled past them into his hair, grabbed the cup, and, shaking it with both hands asked, "What's the point?"

Gary "Bull" Boulder, the big, gray-haired Lt. Colonel WSO and Assistant Ops Officer, said, "Seven."

"I can beat seven," Shooter said. He rolled the dice. After rolling four times, he said, "Five," and pushed the cup of dice at Alan who stared blankly at it.

Realizing the new pup was unfamiliar with the game, Whiskey Wilson pushed past Alan and took the cup. "Take another gander," he said.

"How did you get five?" Alan asked Shooter as Whiskey rolled. "Was that good or bad?"

Hooter gasped in mock astonishment. "You've never played Korean Zap before?" He addressed the group. "We've got a virgin zapper here!"

He turned to Alan. "You'd better learn in a hurry, or you'll be buying everyone's whiskey for the rest of this deployment. First of all, 5 was good. Okay? It beat seven. Seven was the point, okay?" Sometimes when he said "okay," his voice went up like a question, and sometimes his voice stayed level, like a statement.

"You want to get under the point, okay." He gestured with his cigarette at Whiskey's roll. "He's got eight already, and he's still rolling. Whatever he ends up with will be the new point. It's like golf. The one with the biggest score ... with the highest points, wins, okay?"

"Wins?"

"Well, loses."

"How do you know points?"

Hooter slapped him on the back. "We'll tell you, Puppy." He winked. "You're up."

"Not with those rules!"

"Okay, then listen up." Shooter explained the rules of Zap. "On each roll, you must turn over one die. The number on that die is added to your total points. For example, if all five dice on your first roll were sixes, you would turn over one and you would have one point so far, okay? Then you roll the remaining four dice, okay? Now, threes are worth zero and are free. If on your first roll you had five 3s, you would have to flip one which would become a four and you would be done rolling because the rest were 3s which are worth nothing and are free, okay. Your point would be four. So you always roll to get the lowest number."

"Point's 9." Whiskey pushed the cup to Alan. "You're welcome."

Alan eyed the cup like it was a loaded gun pointed at his nose.

"Come on, roll 'em!" Bull said, watching him with a curious eye. "You can't lose in a big game!"

"I can beat 9," Alan said, aware of the sly grin appearing on Ron's face. But luck was not with him. When he was finally finished suffering, he was looking at twelve points.

"Damn! I can't afford to lose," he said, passing the dice.

Carp Fisch took the cup. "You whimpering again, Puppy?" He laughed and began to roll, not returning Alan's heavy stare.

"You got your TDY advance pay," Whiskey said. "Contrary to what your wife may have told you, gamblin' and bar games is what it's really for, especially at The Lik. But if you like to eat or tend to get your skivvies soiled, you'd better learn the game."

"But it's just a game of chance," Alan complained.

"Any game that tests skill," Whiskey countered philosophically, "is a game of chance."

Carp finished with 10. Alan bought the round.

Colonel Ramos strolled into the bar with his wife on his arm. The Deputy Commander for Operations and the Base Commander, Colonel Fuqua, walked in behind them with their wives in trail. All three Colonels carried walkie-talkies, their "bricks," as they were referred to. They were there as a presence, to be with the TDY Squids. And to keep an eye on them.

Ramos cornered Bull Boulder and bought him a beer. With little preamble, Ramos began a practiced dissertation on the scant pros and many and varied cons of allowing the Squids to train down to 250 feet while at his air base. He was a big handsome man, well-groomed and obviously on his way up in the ranks. Being a fighter pilot himself and now a Wing Commander, he understood low level flying to be a necessary evil. He also knew he could not keep fighter pilots from flying too low. That bothered him.

Experience informed him that when fighter pilots were told to fly at a minimum of 2000 feet, they would sneak down to 500 feet. If he told them to fly no lower than 500 feet, there were sure to be some excursions down below 300 feet. And if the limit was 250 feet ...

There had to be a margin. If a crew was lost to The Rocks, or anything else, for that matter, someone would pay with his career.

For the next hour, all was fairly calm, and the whiskey flowed freely. The fighter jocks continued to drink and talk and shoot their watches. Shooter lost at Zap and bought a round of drinks. A group of five female nurses from the base hospital walked in shortly after 1900 hours. As a group, the eyes of the fighter pilots began to wander, although it took them longer to focus.

Alan looked from time to time at the nurses, and Shooter caught his glances.

"It's better to go ugly early," he said.

"It is?" Alan looked back at him as he finished another beer.

"Go ugly early and avoid the rush," Shooter said. "And remember, on a scale of one to ten, a normal '3' is a TDY '7'." He downed a shot of bourbon. "With enough whiskey, you can turn that '7' into a '9', okay."

"I'm married," Alan said, sounding a bit too self-righteous.

"Yeah, yeah," Shooter grunted. "How long?"

"Less than a year."

Shooter eyed the nurses. "Then you're forgiven, okay. But never think you aren't corruptible. Because what happens TDY, stays TDY, okay. And, some day, that may be too much temptation to resist. Remember that."

Shooter walked over to the nurses and told them who he was, although his manner and exposed chest spoke louder than his words.

Alan did not follow. Three more beers did. Then the songs began.

I don't want to join the Air Corps
I don't want to go to war
I'd just rather sit around
Piccadilly underground
Living off the earnings of a high-born lady
I don't want a bullet up me arsehole
I don't want me buttox shot away
I just want to stay in England
In jolly, jolly England
And fornicate me bloomin' life away!

Shooter left the nurses to sing with the boys. It was part of the image, and it was too early for anything else.

The D.O. was a good friend of Bull's, dating back to Vietnam. He had a new motorcycle, a Kawasaki 600, that he wanted to show off and so brought it into the bar. It was a nice bike, but the Squids howled their disapproval when the D.O. declined to allow Bull to ride it just to the juke box and back. He took it outside again without so much as an engine run.

A beeper went off on the Wing Commander's brick. He talked into it for a moment, looked at Sherman in a strange way, and then both he and the Base Commander left the bar.

With the "heavies" gone, and the booze flowing continuously, a mischievous attitude filled the hearts and minds of the fighter pilots and gators. It was something that came over them as it came over most fighter jocks at one time or another. A way of venting the stress that came with the job.

"This night could be a quality drunk," Sam said to Alan. "The 'Desire to Disgust' is alive and well."

"The what?" Alan asked.

Sam stirred the ice in his Scotch with his finger before taking a sip. "Desire to Disgust. A phrase coined by Michelle. She says fighter pilots practically plan their off time around it, looking for reactions from the rest of the world. In the air, we want to make a bridge implode or a MiG explode. In the bar, we desire to disgust those that are not us ... and sometimes even those that are."

Shooter and Carp went down on their knees. Someone shouted out the warning, "Land shark!" as several of the green flight suits voiced their best rendition of the theme song from "Jaws!"

Carp and Shooter sneaked around the far corner of the bar where Col. Ramos's wife was talking to the wife of Col. Fuqua. The background "music" grew louder, picking up tempo. Suddenly, both ladies jumped, and Mrs. Ramos screeched, "My God!" They looked over their shoulders as they lunged into each other. The assassins beat a hasty retreat amid the ensuing confusion, absorbed once again in an ecstatically turbulent green sea of Nomex.

Dorothy Fuqua stared menacingly at the group of flight suits whose faces were partially camouflaged by the shadows cast from the dim lights above the bar. Some of the faces grinned with pleasure, but the preoccupied air with which they continued to converse among themselves implied they admitted neither awareness nor memory of whatever may or may not have just occurred. Dorothy stormed out of the bar, staring coldly at the fighter pilots she passed on her way. Reluctantly, the Wing Commander's wife trailed behind her.

Bull Boulder whispered into the ear of the D.O.'s wife, and her laughter could be heard above the din of conversation.

Major Sherman showed more concern.

Bull said loudly, "Gentlemen, I do not think the pleasure of our company will be appreciated here much longer." He smiled to himself, realizing the potential gravity of the situation. Having decided that being in big trouble was not much different from being in really big trouble, he yelled, "Socks check!" Several of the Squids who had served a tour in South Korea quickly unzipped their flight suits and pulled them down to their ankles, revealing nearly all were wearing white socks with stripes. As quickly as they had partially disrobed, the fighter pilots pulled up their flight suits and zipped them securely.

Bull confronted Shooter. "For failure to partake, you owe a round of cheer!"

Shooter turned to Mike, the bartender, to make the order, then said, "I had no choice."

"No choice?"

"No skivvies."

As Mike worked to fill the drink orders, Colonel Ramos burst through the swinging bar doors like an avenging Old West gun slinger. Colonel Fuqua was in close trail. He glared at the suddenly silent crowd for a moment before spewing, "Who bit my wife on the ... on her ... who assaulted my wife?!"

The bar was very quiet as the Base Commander stared at the fighter pilots. He was a short, rather obese man, with glasses that nestled on a pug nose. He appeared out of shape and out of sorts. He wore no wings on his uniform.

Fuqua stepped toward the crowd of fighter pilots, holding his brick in his hand like a weapon. He seemed undecided whether to throw it, swing it, or parry and thrust. Many of the local officers anticipated that finally something favorable was going to happen to quell this infestation from Spain.

The Base Commander hesitated, trying to use the silence for effect. "I tell you all, I will find out. And when I do, it will not be pleasant!" He glared at Major Sherman. "It's time you got control of your squadron, Major." He glared some more. "Mike!" He turned to the bar tender who cowered in response. "Mike, the bar is closed to these ... Squids, these ... gentlemen from Torrejon. You men can come back when you are ready to behave as such. And when I find out who is responsible for tonight's ... debacle ... well ... I promise you ... this is not over!"

The D.O.'s wife snickered and tugged at Bull's leg from under the counter. Fuqua shot her a harsh look, then turned his stare once more on the Squids.

"Get out!" He wheeled and pushed through the swinging doors.

Colonel Ramos eyed the fighter pilots, more frustrated than angry. "Beat it, you guys." He glanced briefly at Bull Boulder before leaving.

"Shit!" Major Sherman cursed under his breath. He lowered his eyes to the floor. "You guys go to the Q," he said as he envisioned his career flying out those swinging doors.

The fighter pilots filed out as Mike brought up the lights. The nurses, drinks in hand, some clenching straws in their teeth, looked after the men sullenly. The bar was quiet and now seemed very empty.

Alan and Sam walked with Shooter and Reggie Swartz as the Squids ambled in small groups along the dark street that would take them to the BOQ. Passing the base pool, Shooter suddenly stopped and walked back toward the pool as if possessed by a power beyond his control. He stopped at the fence and peered through. "There's only one thing to do at a time like this, okay."

"Yeah," Reggie Swartz said. "Start our own bar."

Shooter turned to him, forgetting the pool for a moment. "Swartz, that's pure genius. And we'll begin work on that illustrious project tomorrow, okay? But right now, an unavoidable mission looms before us." He winked. "Are ye with me, me hearties?!"

"I don't like that look in your one good eye," Alan said, turning to assess the pool. "What mission?"

"Our destiny!" he drawled for emphasis. "TASMO!"

"TASMO!" Sam repeated.

"TASMO?" Alan questioned.

"Tactical Air Support of Maritime Operations," Sam said watching Reggie and Shooter shimmy up the fence which gave precariously under their combined weight. "You're a Tactical Fighter Pilot, aren't you?"

"Yeah."

"Beyond this obviously inadequate barrier," Sam continued, "lies a maritime opportunity upon which to operate. We must support our comrades in arms."

"Seems like suicide ..." Alan began.

"TASMO is a suicide mission. Ours is not to reason why ..."

Like an unwitting spectator suddenly along for the ride, Alan followed Sam over the fence, a nervous excitement building in his stomach. This was the climax a night entrenched in the "Desire to Disgust" demanded. Alan thought it just might be something fun enough to cost him his career, assuming he did not drown first. He followed the others up the ladder to the high diving board as, one by one, they jumped into the icy water below. Alan let out a yell as his numbed face broke the surface. His combat boots and winter flight jacket weighed him down.

A surge of panic ebbed and flowed as he treaded water, making his way toward the ladder.

"Can it, the cops!" Sam warned in a terse whisper.

The men moved quickly to the edge of the pool, keeping their heads as low as they could stand in the frigid water. The headlights of a Security Police patrol car brushed above them as it turned onto the street that paralleled the swimming pool.

"Damn it! They're stopping!" Sam whispered.

"Quiet!" Shooter shot back. "They probably saw our ripples. Prepare to suck air and dive!"

"I can't hold my breath!" Sam whispered hoarsely. "My damn nuts have crawled up inside my stomach!"

Reggie snickered quietly. "This water's so cold, if they don't see our ripples, they'll still see our nipples."

"Can it, okay!" Shooter hissed.

The car began to move again.

"Let's go," Sam suggested.

"Hold it a minute," Shooter instructed him.

"Shit! I'm dyin''!"

When the car was gone, Sam clawed his way out over Shooter. "Dammit! It's colder here in the wind. Let's go!"

They rushed to the fence and clumsily scaled it. As the chill of sobriety crept upon them, Shooter and Reggie laughed out loud.

Approaching the safety of the BOQ, they were hit by a stream of water. Bull Boulder held a fire hose on them from the second floor. He stopped laughing when he noticed that he was merely adding to previously acquired damage. "Hey, you guys are wet already. Where the hell have you been?"

"TASMO," Reggie said wearily, walking toward the room he shared with Bill Fisch. "Consider your ox gored at a later date, Colonel."

Sam and Alan each took a hot shower before crawling into bed. As Alan turned out the light, Sam smiled to himself.

"See what I meant, Puppy? I knew it."

Alan wondered what Sloan would think of this first night of TDY antics and smiled to himself. With the morning might come consequences, but for now they would savor what had definitely been a quality drunk.

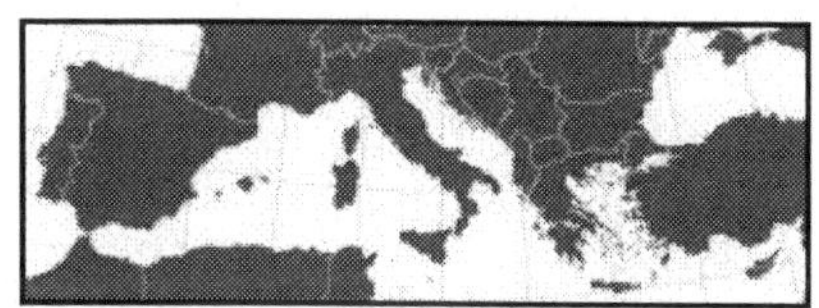

CHAPTER TEN

The wrinkled old Turkish man sat on a chipped wooden stool, methodically shining the American pilot's boots. His hands moved deftly and quickly, applying the polish to the toes and heels of each.

Alan sat in a folding chair, balancing his combat footwear on the horn of the Turk's wooden shoeshine box and reading an article entitled *The Image* in the quarterly *Fighter Weapons Review.* The Turk worked to return a deep black shine to Alan's dank boots. It was taking extra time. The base was thin.

The old man was there every day in the front room of the squadron Ops hanger, calling "Need shine, Albaý?" to the squadron members as they wandered in and out. The fighter pilots began calling him "Albay," thinking he was using the Turkish word for "friend."

Alan looked up when Carp sauntered in.

"We've got jets," Carp said blandly. He looked over Alan's shoulder as the old man worked in the black polish. "What are you reading there, Puppy ... 'The Image'!" His voice slid lower in sarcasm. "If you can't do it in the airplane, you can at least pretend to yourself in the bar, eh?" He walked out of the room with a quizzical smirk on his large round face.

"Gimme nudder one, Albaý!" the old man said loudly as he finished the first boot.

"Sorry, Albay," Alan answered. "Gotta go fly now. We'll finish when I get back."

"Okay, Albaý!"

"How much do I owe so far?"

"Whatever you want, Albaý!"

Alan handed him two quarters. Albay pouted.

"I'll be back with the rest, Albay," Alan assured him. "Soon."

"Okay, Albaý!" The old man opened a small drawer of the well-worn wooden box and flipped the coins inside.

Alan placed the magazine where he could find it later and walked out of the room to pretend to blow Carp Fisch out of the sky over the waters of the Gulf of Iskenderun.

Shooter and Carp took off in formation. Alan, flying this mission with Bull Boulder in his pit, released brakes ten seconds behind them. En route to the over-water area, he performed a quick weapons system check before taking the lead to allow Shooter and Carp to work on their ranging and bogie calls.

When they reached the beach, Shooter called, "Okay, Puppy, you are cleared to your point."

"Roger," Alan acknowledged and turned the Phantom to the southeast corner of the area. "This will be good," he said to Bull. "We'll come from high, out of the sun."

"And supersonic," Bull added.

"You bet."

Shooter's voice came over the radio, "Puppy, you're cleared down track, heading 3-0-0."

"Look for them low," Alan said to Bull as he rolled left to the heading and lit the burners. He flew to the high-altitude block.

"Right." Bull worked the controls, setting the tilt of the radar antenna to sweep the airspace below their altitude. "I've got one contact 20 degrees right, about 18 miles ... Now I've got two of them, going to about thirty right."

"Okay," Alan said. He did not look at his repeater scope, but searched below the distant horizon, hoping to see a wing flash or burner plume that would show him where they were. "30 right ... are they, uh ..."

"30 right, slightly low, a couple of degrees."

They were supersonic. "We're Mach 1.2," Alan said.

"Want me to lock up?"

Alan guessed correctly that neither Buck in Carp's pit nor Reggie Swartz in Shooter's had found them yet. He had the advantage. Locking on to them now would make their radar warning receivers light up, giving Shooter information that might help him determine where they were.

"Don't lock, but keep talking to me," Alan said to Bull.

"Twelve miles, now."

Alan did not see the bandits. "Roger, no tally yet." He banked the jet to the left for the turning room he would soon need.

Shooter's excited voice came over the radio, "Shooter's got one wing flash, right one o'clock high!"

The element of surprise was gone. "Okay, lock him on," Alan said.

Shooter called to Carp, "Check thirty right." The two ship made the check turn, putting Alan on Shooter's nose. Shooter did not yet see him, but now he knew where he was.

"Checking my switches," Alan said to Bull. "Three up, one down."

"Locked on and counting," Bull said.

"We're 1.4 now," Alan said. "I'm coming out of burner."

"No!" Bull said too late.

Fisch made his first radio call. "Carp's got a burner plume!"

"Shit!" Alan cursed his stupidity. "Now they both see us, and I still don't have a tally!"

Shooter said, "I've got the bandit five high, now ... let's take it up!"

The two-ship nosed up toward Alan as his RWR gear lit up.

"Thirty-five right, eight miles. Do you see 'em?" Bull's voice showed only the slightest bit of agitation. They were approaching the merge without a tally, a tenuous situation if they were fighting real bad guys with real bullets.

"Carp's tally-ho!"

"Damn!" Alan squinted. "Oh! Tally one ... tally both!" He started a hard turn into the two ship that was now five miles away.

"You're locked on," Bull reminded him.

Alan squeezed the trigger on the stick and keyed the mike. "Fox one on the left hand man."

"Fox one!" Shooter countered with a return shot.

"They're both on our right side," Alan said to Bull.

"Roger, looking." Bull did not see them, having had his head in the radar scope until now.

Carp said, “I lost my tally.”

“I still have my tally! Keep it coming, keep it coming!” Shooter said, coaxing his wingman to continue turning toward a bandit he did not see.

“I think Carp’s out to lunch,” Alan said. “If I can figure out which one his is, I’ll try to kill him first ... okay, we’ve got two F-4s, both nose up, going behind us.”

He made a hard, level right hand turn as the two F-4s turned back toward him from above. They had passed quickly and were now three miles away again.

“He’s at you three o’clock!” Shooter called to Carp, trying to talk his eyes onto Alan’s jet.

“Carp’s tally-ho!”

“I wish I knew which one is Carp,” Alan said to Bull.

“Okay, he’s going north!” Shooter called, the excitement in his normally subdued voice now obvious.

“Tally-ho both!” Bull said to Alan. “Got ‘em at two o’clock and one o’clock.”

Alan continued the hard right turn. The fighter went subsonic and dug in at 7.5 g’s.

“Watch the g!” Bull groaned.

“Roger!”

The fight was tightening now. As all three fighters went subsonic and began hard maneuvering, the airspeeds bled off, making the turns tighter and the fight smaller.

“I’ve got one high, one low!” Bull said to Alan.

“Roger!” Alan answered. “The high man must be Carp! I’ll go for him, you watch the low man!”

Alan lit the burners and Immelmann-ed. At the completion of the half-loop, he was inverted, seven thousand feet behind Carp and two thousand feet above him. He quickly rolled upright, pointing at the bogie. Watching the fight from below, Shooter maneuvered for the turning room he needed to gain an offensive advantage behind the ever tightening “furball.”

Alan aggressively pulled the nose of his fighter in lead pursuit, cutting across the circle that was Carp’s projected flight path as he went into a hard left turn.

"The bandit's at my right two o'clock high!" Shooter said, as yet unaware that Carp was in trouble and needed more than a helpful hint from his flight lead.

Carp re-acquired Alan's aircraft behind him. "Tally, visual!" he cried. He increased his turn to seven g's, lowering the nose of his jet to maintain the airspeed he needed to maneuver. Alan followed him, closing rapidly now.

Alan called, "Snap shot!" while squeezing the trigger as the gun sight passed momentarily through Carp's helmet.

"Watch the range!" Carp grunted in anger at being on the defensive.

Shooter was now four thousand feet above the fight. Straining his stomach muscles to keep the blood flowing to his brain, he re-acquired Alan's jet over his right shoulder as he continued the six-g turn. A bead of sweat from his forehead ran down into his right eye.

"Let's run!" Bull said to Alan.

"No! They're still split up," Alan countered. He turned left and began to climb with the burners cooking. "We can kill them both."

"Okay," Boulder said, thinking to himself, I've said my peace, let's see what you can do. "Check gas!"

Looking quickly inside, then back out again, Alan answered, "Gas is good!"

Feeling the blood of anger clouding the vision in his eyes, Alan repositioned to press his attack. "I'm going for guns," he said to Bull as he checked the Master Arm switch. "Watch the guy on the right!"

"Tally! He's still turning." Working against the g's, Bull maneuvered in his seat to watch Shooter. His body and line of sight were oriented counter to the movement of the jet as he strained to maintain his tally. It was hard work that experience and time had made second nature to his mind and body. "The other guy will be on us soon," he warned.

Alan repositioned high above Carp.

Carp unloaded his aircraft to gain fighting speed.

Shooter descended below Alan to get turning room.

Alan pointed the nose of his fighter at the glow of Carp's two burner cans.

"Going heat!" he informed Bull and changed his switches for the new shot opportunity. The dummy Sidewinder missile head under his left wing detected the heat source from the afterburner cans and gave the characteristic growl in Alan's headset that told him the missile had acquired the heat source.

Alan squeezed the trigger and keyed the radio. "Fox 2! Fox 2!"

"Carp, go hard left!" Shooter called. "HARD!"

Carp pulled the joy stick into his lap, putting seven g's on his jet in a left hand turn. Alan selected the gun again and closed to within 2500 feet of Carp.

As Alan and Carp turned away from him, Shooter got the turning room he needed to press the attack on Alan.

"I've lost the other guy!" Bull warned Alan. "You've got boresight and ten. Get an auto-lock!"

Alan hit the throttle switch, and the radar locked on. The range bar showed Alan to be 1800 feet from Carp's jet and closing rapidly. At fifteen hundred feet, Alan pulled on the stick until the pipper in the center of the sight was just in front of the F-4's vertical stabilizer. After the initial transient instability, the pipper settled on the target's canopy. The ranging on the sight showed 1200 feet, but he was not watching that now.

"Check our six!" he commanded.

Bull grunted, "I am checking six, dammit! ... I don't see him!"

"I'm going to guns track Carp," Alan said flatly.

"We're staying too long!" Bull yelled. "This turning and burning will get us killed!"

"This won't take long."

Aware of the threat of a gunshot, Carp began to maneuver his jet erratically through the sky in a series of turns and reversals commonly known as "doing the chicken." His airspeed bled rapidly away.

Alan was in range, his radar was locked on to Carp's airplane, and his gunsight was on Carp's head. He concentrated on holding the pipper on the aircraft as he squeezed the trigger.

"Fox 2!" Shooter called. Alan's RWR lit up and the warning tone was loud in his head set.

"Shit!" Bull growled.

Alan keyed the mic. "Tracking guns kill!" The excitement in his voice was not from the shot.

He pulled the airplane away at nearly 8 g's, momentarily blinded as the blood drained from his eyes. He felt himself graying out as he continued the pull.

He could hear a voice. Who was it? Ernie?

"Knock it off!" Shooter called. "I've got a Fox 2, kill, on the bandit."

"Knock it off, Alan," Bull grunted, sounding somewhat angry. "We're dead."

"3, knock it off," Alan acknowledged.

"Looked like a good shot on Carp, anyway," Bull said. "Was it?"

"Yeah." Alan's voice shook. "Stitched him from nose to tail ..." he heard himself say. "Could have made a blanket out of him ..."

His heart was beating wildly. A sudden rush of adrenaline flooded his senses, making his hands and face tingle. He felt flushed. The thrill of flying the fighter, the excitement of the gun shot, and the sensation of being near Death ran together in a swelling sea of agitation that made him feel at once terrified and exhilarated.

It had been a close call, and Bull seemed unaware of it.

Bull broke the ensuing silence, his voice disavowing the heat of battle that had seared the cockpit just moments before. "We stayed too long," he said.

"Yeah, we stayed too long, but what the hell," Alan answered, regaining his breath. "It was good training for them."

Bull grunted. "It wasn't good training for us, unless you're trying to learn how to die ... and we died today ... wholesale."

CHAPTER ELEVEN

The Squid bar was a money maker, serving beer and mixed drinks for fifty cents, soft drinks for a quarter. It was dubbed unoriginally "The Pagoda Hell Saloon" which Bull had embossed on a brass sign ordered from Ali's Copper Shop just outside the base. They headquartered the bar in an empty room of the BOQ building, and the fighter pilots and fighter gators took turns bartending like any other squadron additional duty.

On this night, behind the bar, Reggie Swartz reasoned that since it was Friday, the boys deserved a little something extra. He spent a full week's TDY money in the BX, shopping in the women's lingerie section under the speechless scrutiny of the floor manager.

After serious consideration, Reggie decided to go with virginal white, finding it more conspicuous and less flattering on him than the black sheer. He did not, after all, want to look too good. The brassiere was a 38E, the hose was also white, and the girdle fit snugly over his ample waist. At five feet nine inches tall in the stilettos, sporting a thin mustache and bristly short hair, Reginald Swartz, in his typical dead-pan fashion, presented himself to the bar's evening clientele in this dubiously provocative attire.

In truth, whore-ishly dressed as he was now, if his goal was to be as lasciviously undesirable as possible, he attained it dramatically.

"Swartz, you're gross!" Shooter said, throwing him a dollar. "You've got to be the ugliest woman I've never wanted." He looked Reggie up one side and down the other. "Give me two beers, sweet cheeks, and don't breathe on 'em."

Stone-faced, as if totally indifferent to the manner of his dress, Reggie took Shooter's money and wordlessly handed him two Budweisers. No winks, no blinks, he did not play the role. He simply served drinks as they were ordered in his heels and hose and girdle and bra.

Lt. Colonel Hargrove walked into the bar with his brick in his hand, his hat on his small head, and Major Sherman at his heels. Reggie rang the bronze bell he had purchased from Ali. A cheer rang out from the patrons of the bar. Realizing his error too late, Hargrove left his hat in place.

"Well, this is a bar, isn't it?" He looked around the room. "I'd like to stay tonight and drink with you fellas, but I have some meetings to attend, which brings me to an announcement of good news."

"I doubt it," Sam said to Alan under his breath.

"... the good news is that I have convinced Colonel South back home that, since we will be away at Christmas, we deserve a free phone call to our families at Torrejon."

He looked around in anticipation. For some reason he could not fathom, his troops were skeptically silent.

"A week before Christmas, we are going to have a Happy Talk by way of a priority Autovon line. Everyone will be allowed five minutes. The ladies will hear about it at home, but it wouldn't hurt for you to write them as well. We have trouble sometimes getting the word out to everyone."

Alan touched the pocket of his flight jacket, feeling for the unopened letter from Sloan. Did she already know? Since their arrival in Spain, she seemed to hear all the gossip before he did.

Hargrove did not pause to see how this news affected his troops. "I strongly urge each of you to participate in this Happy Talk. Now, I owe you some drinks." He turned to the make-shift bar constructed from a bed frame turned on its side with a piece of plywood thrown across the top. "Put it on my tab ..." He gawked. "Swartz, you're gross! Who's got your hand receipt tonight?" He turned and left the room.

"Great," Shooter said to Major Sherman. "A mandatory phone call to the misses. That gives me the beak." He put his hand against his face to simulate a bird's beak. "Next he'll be making us write weekly letters to our parents! What does he think this is, goddamn summer camp?"

Sherman looked sheepishly around the room, then at Shooter. "Lt. Colonel Hargrove wanted me to remind you guys to write your folks ..."

"Shit hot!" Shooter said.

"What if I ain't got no one to talk happy with?" Reggie asked from behind the plywood counter.

"You can talk to my wife, sweet cheeks," Shooter said. "She'll have plenty to say and all you have to do is listen. She won't know the difference, and neither will you."

Alan found an empty barstool away from the fighter pilots huddled around Whiskey and sat down to read Sloan's letter. Checking to ensure no one was looking, he sniffed the envelope. There was no scent other than that of the blue ink.

After he had finished, he reread the letter, looking for signs of malcontent from his lonely young wife. Awareness of another presence rescued him from his thoughts. He raised his head to see Whiskey Wilson staring down at him.

"Form letter from the misses, eh?" He took a swig of Efes. "How are things back at the ol' Báse Aréa de Torrejon?"

"Fine. The misses misses me."

Whiskey grunted. "A good sign."

"She wants to find a job."

Whiskey raised his eyebrows slightly. "Civilians have trouble getting jobs on base," he said, drawing deeply on the butt of a cigarette. "With us TDY all the time, the ladies could use a little moral diversion, to keep 'em busy ... to keep 'em from finding other things to do while we're away." He paused for another drink of Efes. "I say we ... I'm not married ... not anymore, anyway. Used to be."

For the first time, Alan thought he saw a glimmer of emotion in Frederick Wilson's eyes. There for but a moment, it was drowned with his next swallow of beer.

"Yeah, I was married once," Whiskey continued as if Alan had asked, "but TDYs kind of killed it. I reconciled it in my mind, though. I look at it this way: It's better to have loved and lost than to have to spend the rest of my life with that bitch." He looked at Alan as if to say, 'Don't let it happen to you.' He took another cigarette from the pouch in his pocket, lit it, and took a long draw. "How'd your little air-to-air sort-tee go today? Was it a John Wayne? Or a Jane Fonda."

Alan sensed he already knew. He rubbed his chin. "It was an Alan Wayne."

"Bit of both then."

"Yeah."

"Yeah." Whiskey looked away. "Gotta drain it," he said. He nodded to Alan and strolled out the door into the night.

Shooter tapped Alan on the shoulder. "Buy you a drink," he said to Alan without looking at him.

"Thanks." Together they walked to the bar.

Bull Boulder, Buck, and Fisch leaned gingerly on the plywood counter, beers in hand and deep in discussion.

"You can never be sure how many MiGs are out there," Fisch was saying. "You have to fight as if you are one-vee-many all the time." He spoke authoritatively, as if these were original ideas.

"That's always been true," Bull said, "but our job is to kill, and when you see an opportunity to kill two MiGs, you take it."

Bull looked over Fisch's shoulder. Nodding to Alan and Shooter as they approached, he continued listening to Fisch.

"I didn't want you to leave thinking you didn't do good today," Shooter said to Alan after ordering the beer.

Fisch glared at Alan, then turned suddenly away from Bull and began a conversation with Sam who reacted uncomfortably to Fisch's manner.

"You did good," Bull confirmed. "But we still died."

"You split us up," Shooter acknowledged. "Played havoc on our formation for a while. But you stayed too long. You probably learned something from that, okay."

"I learned not to stay too long," Alan said, taking the bottle of Efes Shooter thrust at him. He glanced at Fisch who was doing his best to pointedly ignore them all.

Shooter watched Alan as his tipped his beer. "Never stay too long. That's a good axiom for a fighter pilot," he said knowingly. "Never stay too long. Anywhere."

Bull whispered something to Shooter who nodded in agreement.

Alan turned to Sam. "What's Michelle up to while you're gone?" he asked, interrupting Fisch's conversation.

Sam laughed to himself. "She has her job at the BX. When she's not doing that, she's busy spending my TDY money."

"You want to play some tennis tomorrow?" Alan knew Fisch did not play. He did not have to look at Fisch to know he was stewing. "When we're sober."

"Sounds like a good way to work the evil out," Sam answered.

Fisch stood silent, his jaws locked, glaring at Alan. There was no kindness in his eyes.

"Do you play by the rules, Puppy?" Carp looked hard at him before taking another drink. "You cheat the wrong person, and you'll get your ass kicked for real."

Alan felt his face redden in a fire of anger he could not always control. What was it with this guy? "It would surprise me if you knew them."

Carp put his drink on the counter. "Knew what?"

"Tennis ROE."

Carp stared at him in disgust and worked his jaw.

Alan did not flinch. "You're still urinated off about today's fight. You should be. You got your ass kicked."

Sam winced as Carp moved closer to Alan and said, "You died. We lived. By the ROE."

Alan made a noise through his nose. "If you can live with a brain riddled with 20-millimeter bullets and an Aim-9 up your anus! You can't be resurrected by the ROE. It won't save your butt in combat."

Carp glared at him, an appropriate retort evading his angry mind.

Their eyes burned fire. Neither one flinched.

Bull Boulder tapped Alan on the shoulder. "We're getting up a card game. You interested?"

Alan turned to face Bull, putting his back to Carp. "Yeah, sure. Where?"

"Shooter's room. Ten minutes."

"I'll be there." Alan was pleased to be invited into this inner circle of card players, even if it was, as he realized, only to avert an immediate showdown with Carp. It made for a good exit. He looked at Sam. "Tennis tomorrow," he said to him, finished his beer and left for his room under the hateful glare of Carp's narrow eyes.

Waiting at home, living a life not completely her own, Sloan beat a daily nurturing path between their Spanish apartment and the Air Base.

Having little else to do, she found comfort in driving the Camaro to the base for the reassuring feeling she derived from being near Alan's life. A few AC's and WSO's who would not go to Turkey or would go for only part of the deployment manned the otherwise deserted squadron building. At her bravest, Sloan tried not to pout, even to herself, because Alan was not among them. She drove past the building, and sometimes to it, looking for signs of life among the skeletal remains, the favored few that stayed behind.

The days would get so long, and she wished she could be working. Anything would be better than the nothing she was employed in now. Every day that she could, she bought a little insignificant something at one of the shops on base in hopes of bringing home a spot of cheer to fill the void of their scantily furnished apartment on the eighth floor.

Despite these regular treks, she could not disguise the fact that she was young and alone in a foreign land with no family within a thousand miles. In the evening, she would write a letter to Alan for solace, to touch him, to see him smile and laugh in her mind's eye. She tried to be funny when she wrote, to make herself happy, but found that she could not always do so.

She started books she did not finish, unable to concentrate. When she received a letter from Alan, she escaped on a cloud of detachment the rest of the day. Every day without a letter from Alan brought bitterness and tears. What was happening? What was he doing? It was driving her crazy! She needed to talk to Alan, to hear his reassuring voice.

The nights were black and faceless. She tried to fill them with activity, either physical or mental, but found neither to be particularly rewarding. She was hollow, her life on standby until her man came back to her.

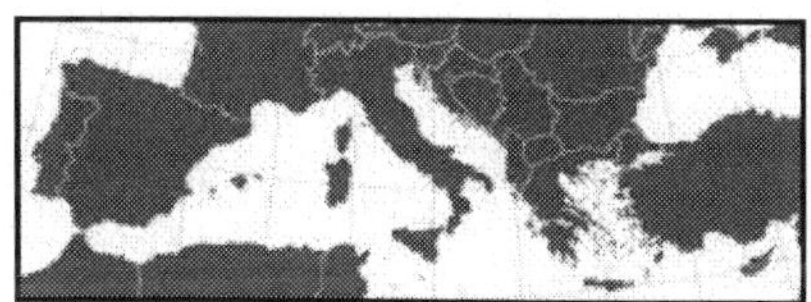

CHAPTER TWELVE

The Turkish days were occupied with flying and waiting. The flying was good. All other activities, regardless of value, merely time killers.

Beyond the mountains to the northwest, the land was barren, harsh and dry. But from inside a fighter, it was paradise with limited restrictions. Within a fifty-mile radius of The Lik they flew where they wanted, did what they needed, explored whatever attracted them.

They passed the nights with drinking at the Pagoda Hell or poker games in Shooter's room. On weekends, they recovered and played - tennis, "combat golf," more poker. Shooter continued to play his favorite game, Push, Pass or Puke, and continued to lose money in his uncongenial manner. Shooter Vandersnoot was a lot of things to a lot of people, mostly to himself, but he was not a poker player.

The men and women of the U.S. Air Force were required each year to prove their physical fitness by way of an aerobics test which, for most of them, involved running a mile and a half somewhere under eleven minutes. Quite often, in a fighter squadron this square was filled by the Administration Officer asking a pilot how fast he thought he could run a mile and a half. He would then dutifully record the officer's answer, thus fulfilling the requirement for another year.

Lt Colonel Hargrove possessed a more literal take on the annual test. He devised the idea that the most moral-mending way to perform this necessary diversion was to wrap it up and sell it as an all-out squadron gathering with loftier goals.

He devised a "Great Race" and a "Not-so-great Race" to be run on a glorious Saturday morning the weekend before the long awaited, longer dreaded military exercise. The Great Race, for those that wished to punish and prove themselves, would be six miles, and the Not-so-great Race of three miles was for those less capable but no less ambitious. Almost as an afterthought, he offered a run of a mile and a half to fill the minimal aerobics square with no prize other than to be done with it for another year.

On the morning of the run, Reggie Swartz awoke the hung-over members of the 613th by cranking up his new portable tape player which he dubbed his "BOQ Blaster." He claimed to have purchased the player with his massive, though unsubstantiated, poker winnings.

Few believed him. Bull Boulder knew absolutely otherwise.

Still heavily laden with whiskey and beer, the Squids fumbled into their running attire to partake in the festivities.

Whiskey Wilson wore ragged shorts and a sweatshirt with "Fuck, Fight or go for your Guns!" stenciled on it. He was incensed. "I can't believe we got to participate in this damn mandatory leg wobble," he said as he stretched his skinny legs.

"Whiskey," Reggie said, "it's a Happy Run."

"My hairy white buttocks! Who knows what's going on with the hostages! And here we are, having a 'Happy Run'!"

Putting his hand pointedly to his face, Shooter said, "Beak! Mosambeak!"

"Roger!"

Warming up by running in place, Sam asked, "What are you going to run, Shooter? The Great Race or the Not-so-great Race?"

Shooter looked at him as if looking at an idiot. "Neither. It's doubtful I'll even make it through the hardly mentionable push, pass or puke."

"I'll be pushing you," Reggie said. "In fact, I'll be pushing everyone, because I'll be in dead last."

Sam paused his warmup. "You plan to come in last?"

"Never be good at anything you don't want to have to do all the time."

Shooter eyed Reggie, half smiling. "Ok, Sweet Cheeks. Care to lay a little wager on who can come in last and still be under the time limit?"

"How much?"

"What'd you do with your brassiere?"

Without cracking a smile, Reggie answered, "Returned it. It made me itch. Besides, it wasn't your color."

"How 'bout that damn buttox blaster?"

"My radio?"

"Yeah."

"No way."

Shooter contemplated other options. "Alright," he said finally. "Whoever loses has to get the keys to the step van, okay."

"What for?" Reggie asked warily.

"To drive us to Mersin."

"Mersin? Where's that?"

"About fifty miles that way." Shooter pointed to the west.

"Why do we want to go there?" Reggie asked.

"To get shrimp, Sweet Cheeks." Shooter looked around. "You in, Whiskey?"

Whiskey Wilson nodded. "Possibly."

Shooter eyed Sam and Alan. "How about you guys?"

Alan and Sam exchanged glances.

"Can we really do that?" Sam asked.

"Yeah," Shooter said. "Bull already said he'd drive."

"Legit enough for me," Whiskey said.

Alan looked at Sam before saying, "I'll see how I'm doing after this."

Sam nodded and began running in place again. "This is a good way to run the evil out."

"What evil?" Reggie snorted.

Sam stretched. "The booze, the gambling, the straying thoughts of scantily clad, fluffy white sheep." He laughed. "The fact that we might be about to get ourselves into serious trouble."

"What are you going to run?" Alan asked Sam.

"The 'Not-so'."

"I'll push you along," Alan said. "Until you pass me, or I puke."

Despite the difference in their heights, Sam ran the race with Alan step for step until the last half-mile, at which point, slowly, almost apologetically Sam pulled ahead.

Ironic, Alan thought as they walked back to the BOQ after the race. Fifty-two Americans were being held hostage in the next country to the east while the members of the 613th Tactical Fighter Squadron spent their Saturday morning filling their Air Force "squares." Life went on, but 52 people remained in captivity. And it appeared the Squids would not be called upon to get them out.

In the late afternoon, the military van carrying eight fighter pilots and three large newly-purchased ice chests packed with ice and shrimp returned to Incirlik Air Base from Mersin. Alan approached the van as it stopped in the BOQ parking area. Sam stepped out.

"You should have gone with us, Puppy!" Sam said as he retrieved one of the ice chests and lowered it to the ground. "It was a quality time."

Alan nodded, sorry now he had opted out of going with them. Especially as it seemed they had all survived the experience seemingly unscathed. "How much shrimp did you get?" He opened the ice chest.

"A shitload," Shooter answered as he removed another chest from the van.

"So, what happens now?" Alan asked.

"We boil 'em up and feast! You can join us. For the right price."

"What's the right price?"

Shooter jerked his thumb. "Sweet Cheeks can tell you. He handles the money." He opened the chest and inspected the shrimp. "It'll be more than if you had gone with us, okay."

Reggie nodded. "Timidity has its price. None but the brave deserve the cheap shrimp."

Alan opened his mouth to protest but said nothing.

"Mersin was fascinating," Sam said.

"Yeah. I especially liked the skinned sheep's heads on the spikes," Reggie put in.

Alan smiled wryly. "Relatives of yours, Sweet Cheeks?"

"Eat shit and bark at the moon, Puppy."

"You could have had one for lunch," Sam said. "Raki can make anything test good," he added, referring to Turkey's popular anise-flavored drink.

"You ate there?" Alan asked.

"Yeah. We found a small kind of restaurant that was willing to boil up some of the shrimp for us."

Shooter emptied a large bag of charcoal on the brick bar-b-que pit and doused it with a bottle of boot-legged JP-4. Reggie went to his room and returned with a water fire extinguisher.

"It was funny," Sam continued. "It was taking a long time for the restaurant to boil the shrimp, so Bull sent me to check on their progress. I caught several of the Turks sitting around in the back watching some of our shrimp cook on a kebab skewer over an open fire. They knew they were busted, but they just kind of shrugged it off. The price of doing business, I guess. Our boiled shrimp was cooling on a big platter on some ice. I guess they think Americans prefer their shrimp cold."

Shooter stood back and threw a lighted match into the pit. The fire erupted immediately, flaring from the jet fuel.

"I'll go next time," Alan said, jumping away from the flames.

"If there is one," Shooter said. "You new guys need to go with us so you can teach the next New Beans how to do it."

Sam nodded as he took the fire extinguisher from Reggie. "You won't see much of the world sitting around the base the whole time. You have to get out among the natives."

Early Monday morning, Alan awoke to a pounding on the door. "Recall! Squadron recall!" Operations Sergeant, Jose' Montoya yelled from the other side of the door. Not waiting for an answer, Montoya went to the next door, pounding and repeating his message declaring the beginning of the exercise.

A dream circulated dully in Alan's throbbing head. He sat up in his bed and remembered.

A howling, cold, foul wind blew the shingles off the simple wooden houses, imploding the lattice work that hid the stilts the houses were built upon. The wind blew the screens from the windows and doors as it circulated dust and stench around their porches. The wind was strong, cracking the wooden four by fours that held the roof above the porch.

Next came the beating sound of hooves, then the dust, and then the Pig People were upon them, spurring their ugly horses to chase the town's people who scattered and ran from them. Laughing in a voice half-human, half-squeal, the riders roped the people around their waists and faces, pulling the ropes around them several times, tightening them until their red eyes bulged, ready to burst from their faces.

At nightfall, the fires burned against the darkness as the Pig People raped and pillaged, silhouetted against the red and yellow flames. The shadows of their evil danced across the fallen town. Suddenly, at midnight, they were gone.

In the morning, the town's people awoke early and began to rebuild their town, finally finishing in time for dinner.

Then the evening, and the sun setting, and the foul wind rose again from the east. And the hollow sound. The dust.

In his dream, Alan realized in horror that the Pig People were coming again. Every morning the town was rebuilt. Every evening, the foul wind blew. Every night the Pig People came, riding their ugly horses.

CHAPTER THIRTEEN

The exercise began in a benign vein that belied the chaos and groping that would fill the next three days.

The lack of coordination between operations, maintenance, and Incirlik headquarters personnel resulted in more finger pointing than mission planning. They were at each other's throats, the true enemy remembered only as a necessary afterthought.

Thinking there would be no air raids and therefore no chemical warfare drills, many of the base personnel had stuffed their gas mask bags with toilet paper for appearance sake. When the first simulated air-raid did come, they were caught short with no gas masks and so became simulated kills. And for those who looked to hide for a few moments from the chaos, a trip to the latrine proved traumatic when, only too late, the toilet paper deficit was discovered.

Sergeant Montoya, who had been doing most of the driving, discovered that the brakes on the step van were wearing thin. Suspecting the illicit trip to Mersin had something to do with their degraded condition, he repeatedly informed Lt. Colonel Hargrove of his concern, only to be repeatedly informed it would be taken care of when this damn exercise was over.

Now, the step van sat idle near the front of the squadron building, partially wrapped around the power pole that had finally brought it to a stop when Montoya's repeated pumping of the brakes could not. There it would remain, a mechanical monument to the dissonance that pervaded the exercise.

Sam's anticipation of another trip to Mersin and the "Castle by the Sea" dissipated amid the wreckage.

Walking into the operations room with Sam, Alan felt an uneasy tension. It was not the picture of chaos he had expected, but some of the faces registered growing concern. Hargrove was not there. Major Sherman leaned over the duty desk, trying to bring some semblance of order to the aircraft generation schedule.

And Albay was gone, having left in a huff when Major Sherman explained to him that he could not be in the squadron building during an exercise. Albay had not understood why an old man could not make his daily bread just because the Americans wanted to play their war games.

Shooter was slouched in a chair in the corner of the front room with a look on his face that expressed both amusement and contempt. A white plastic spoon was sticking out of a slit on his sleeve pocket that would normally hold a pencil or pen.

"Where's the Colonel?" Alan asked.

Sam walked to the opened door to Hargrove's office and peered in. Hundreds of little white, doughnut-like paper reinforcers were scattered on top of the mounds of paperwork that covered the desk. He turned to Shooter. "What's with the paper assholes?"

Shooter grinned knowingly. "It seems someone wanted to make a statement about our paper-pushing squadron commander."

Sam nodded in understanding.

"Where is the Colonel?" Alan repeated.

Shooter snickered. "He's on the carpet in Colonel Ramos's office."

"Already?"

"The whole exercise is FUBAR, okay."

"Fucked up beyond all recognition," Sam said.

"Yeah," Shooter affirmed. "Completely. Maintenance is putting the wrong bombs on the wrong airplanes, so now none of them are loaded for air defense." Shooter zipped open his sleeve pocket and removed a cigarette and matches. He lit the cigarette and returned the matches to the pocket. "But Maintenance is blaming Ops. When it comes right down to it, Maintenance is never responsible for anything that goes wrong, okay." He clasped the cigarette between his lips as he spoke.

"Why the plastic spoon?" Sam asked.

Shooter looked sideways at it. "Because we've been more like a MAC squadron than a fighter squadron, okay? They run this base like a bunch of MAC pukes. And Hargrove ..." He went silent, letting his words hang in the stiff air that permeated the room.

Bull Boulder walked in. "Whiskey's ready," he said to Major Sherman.

"Okay," Sherman said. He turned to the group of fighter jocks milling around the room. "For everyone who is available and interested - and that's every one of you in this room - I've asked Captain Wilson to give us a talk on BFM, as a diversion."

"A different kind of Happy Talk," Reggie said as he and Alan followed the others into the squadron meeting room.

Wearing his chemical warfare gear, his steel helmet shoved to the back of his narrow head, Whiskey Wilson hovered comfortably around the lectern at the front of the room. When everyone was seated, he said, "Major Sherman asked me to tell you what little I know about flying air-to-air in the old F-4 Double-Ugly, so I'm gonna talk about defensive BFM. Maybe it'll give you something to think about at night while you're spankin' your monkey."

The men laughed.

"What do you do when you're surprised, caught from behind?" Whiskey began. "Well, usually some of you grunt and groan and thrash about and go into your imitation of a headless chicken. So, one of the things I want to talk about is thinking while somebody's gnawin' at your ass.

"It's just like real life. If some hood shows up behind you with a gun in a dark alley, your first thought will probably be 'How the hell did he get there?'

"Well, you shouldn't dwell too much on that because it don't matter. He's there. And he's got the jump on you. Your immediate thought should be 'How can I survive this nasty turn of events?' Hopefully, you haven't waited until that moment to begin your finest creative thinking. To the guy who's holding me up I might say that I've got the three worst kinds of herpes known to man and then blow chow on him.

"To the guy who's trying to kill me in an airplane, I want to say, with my actions, that I'm not going to be easy, and that he's gonna have to stay with me a long time to even get a chance to kill me, that I'm gonna be as unpredictable as I can be, and that it ain't gonna be fun for him because I plan to make him very uncomfortable."

As Whiskey talked, he put his thumbs in his web belt and stood with his legs spread apart. With his steel pot tilted back, he looked like the modern-day reincarnation of a gunslinger from Tombstone.

"I'm looking to give him a corner he can't make, a turn that will overshoot him if he makes a mistake. If he sees the corner too late, he can't make it, he overshoots, I gun his Commie brains out.

"Unless it's me ..." He grinned. "Just so you young studs'll know, I ain't never found a corner I can't make. You try to overshoot me, I'll clean your clock." He grinned amiably, but he meant it.

Alan considered how curious it was that Whiskey always related flying fighters to real life. To him, they were one and the same. There were essentially two types of fighter pilots. There were those who, like Whiskey, wore the life of the fighter pilot every day. For those guys that liked to take it off when they got home, these long TDYs must have made it difficult to reconcile the extremes.

Alan felt a tap on his shoulder and turned to see Lt. Colonel Boulder.

"Alan, we need you to go to the RSU," Bull said. "I'll drive you out."

Alan left with Bull as Whiskey went on with his dissertation.

As Bull steered the six-pack truck along the perimeter road to the Runway Supervisory Unit, Alan said, "I hope I don't sit out the real war in the RSU."

"You won't. But in this war, the RSU is not a bad place to hide," Bull said with the touch of a smile on his broad face. "There are worse places to be. Hell, I volunteered to be the Supervisor of Flying today. I'd much rather be monitoring the flying as SOF from out here than floundering with gas mask drills back at the squadron."

Alan could not tell if Bull really meant all he was saying or if he was just trying to make him feel better. "I'd rather be flying," Alan said.

"You will."

At the approach end of the runway, Boulder stopped the truck in front of a small building about ten feet high with several antennae attached to the top of its square roof. The upper half of the hut-sized structure was made entirely of tinted glass, allowing observers on the inside an unobstructed 360-degree view.

"Don't get impatient," Bull said after they set up the RSU radios, then sat down to await the first F4s that would takeoff. "You'll fly plenty."

A single F-4 taxied into the quick-check area.

"That would be Fisch and Fuzzy," Bull said. "Special tasking," he added, indicating the simulated selective release of a nuclear weapon.

Alan was silent as he watched Fisch's head move from one side of the cockpit to the other, checking the jet one last time before acknowledging the take-off clearance from the tower. Alan longed to be in his place.

Bull looked covertly at Alan, noting the furrowed brow and seriously squared chin of this young fighter buck. He recalled that same look of quiet defiance at the squadron finca party.

"You have a lot of potential, Lt. Wayne. You have the choice to be either a good fighter pilot and officer, or just another angry young man." Through a pair of binoculars, he watched as Carp ran the engines of the F-4 up to 85 percent. "I know you lost a friend very early in your career. It doesn't mean you have more to prove than any other young jock. I was in Nam. I lost a lot of friends. It didn't make me any better or any worse. It just made me different."

The F-4 began to roll. Carp lit the afterburners, and the jet accelerated quickly. The roar from the engines shook the little building with a deafening thunder. The blue flames from the engines' Mach cones were as two huge Bunsen burners. The sound the flames made was a continuous snap, like that of an enormous bonfire.

"That's part of our profession," Bull Boulder continued. "People lose friends, wingmen, husbands and wives. But when everyone else seems to be going in different directions, fighter pilots keep it together."

Alan watched silently as Fisch's F-4 turned to the right and disappeared to the north, a trailing line of black smoke the sole indicator of where it had been.

After four days of confusion, ENDEX was declared. The Squids gathered in the Officer's Club bar waiting for Colonel Ramos to make his End of Exercise remarks. Ignoring the protocol of having such a briefing in a more secure location, Ramos' transparent gesture left little doubt that he intended for the Squids to buy drinks before and after the debrief. After that, he hoped the fighter pilots would stay to finish out the evening drinking at the bar, which would return at least some of the revenue lost since the Squids first abandoned it. Ramos hoped to retreat quietly without admitting defeat, and all would return to the status quo.

Colonel Ramos failed to understand the extent to which he had alienated the 613th Tactical Fighter Squadron with his flawed finger-pointing leadership technique. The exercise, and his conduct of it, had reopened old wounds and sliced new deeper ones.

Intentionally arriving ten minutes late, Ramos was surprised to see none of the fighter pilots with drink in hand. As the room was called to attention, he held up his hands as if to say, 'Oh please, not for me.' He said, "Sorry I'm late. We'll give you guys a chance to buy another beer before we begin."

Whiskey was the first to the bar. "I'll take a coke," he said to Mike.

"One coke coming up!" Mike said as he went to work. He was obviously glad to see the Squids return. "Fifty cents."

Whiskey paid the fifty cents and added a dollar tip.

"Make mine a coke, too," Shooter said.

"You want bourbon with that?" Mike held up the bottle.

"Just a coke," Shooter repeated. He put a dollar and a quarter on the bar and went to find a chair in the corner.

"Seven-Up," Sam said when it was his turn.

"Seven and seven?" Mike asked hopefully.

"Nope. Just the one seven."

Sam took his drink and turned to Reggie Swartz. "You're up, Sweet Cheeks."

"Got any ice water?" Reggie asked.

Mike looked tormented. "Water?"

"Yeah," Reggie answered. "I'm on a diet."

Mike poured the water and handed it to Reggie. There was no charge. Sweet Cheeks put down a five dollar bill and said, "Mike, why don't you come work for us?"

Mike shrugged and placed the bill in his tip jar.

The orders continued with no requests for alcohol. Mike could not decide whether to be disappointed or grateful. Their intention was obvious, but he could not complain about the tips.

When they were once again seated, Ramos noticed there was not a single beer among them. He decided they must all be having mixed drinks.

Forty-five minutes elapsed before the Colonel had heard himself speak enough. He looked at Hargrove. "Do you have anything to add before we cut these men loose, Daryl?"

Lt. Colonel Hargrove stood in front of his fighter squadron. He was obviously exhausted. Deep circles darkened the perimeter of his large brown eyes. The look he passed to Ramos left no doubt that much love had been lost between the two leaders.

"No, sir," he began. "Except to say that I am proud of your efforts during difficult times, men. And it is time to declare 'begin weekend'."

"Yeah!" Shooter yelled from the corner. "Merry Fuckin' Christmas!"

Ramos glanced around at the fighter pilots' stoic faces. "Gentlemen, you are dismissed to the bar!"

Quietly, deliberately, devoid of the fanfare Ramos anticipated, the Squids of the 613th Tactical Fighter Squadron stood. In a kind of Squid pro quo, they wordlessly added more tips to Mike's jar before filing out of the room through the swinging doors and into the street.

"You're welcome to join us for a drink sir," the Boy Colonel said to the Wing Commander.

"I'm thinking of closing that ... damn thing of yours down!" Ramos answered. He looked at Hargrove long and hard for a moment, but the Boy Colonel did not flinch. Finally, Ramos spoke again, biting his words as they left his lips. "Not tonight, Daryl."

Daryl Hargrove nodded silently and, as he strode out of the bar through the swinging doors, the Boy Colonel began to look like a man.

On Sunday, everyone who wanted to participate got five minutes alone in Hargrove's office, the "Happy Room" as Reggie christened it, to talk to their wives. Alan's turn came after Sam.

"Hello," he said, taking the phone.

"Hi, Alan!" Sloan's voice did not sound right.

"Sloan?"

"This is Michelle Christopher."

Alan flinched. "Is everything okay?"

"Fine. Forgive me for using a few of your precious 300 seconds ... bring him home safe."

"What?"

"Bring Sam home to me."

Alan detected the quiver in her soft voice. "If he beats me at tennis one more time, I'll kill him myself."

"He beat you?" She laughed.

"I'll get him to you in one piece."

"One live piece."

"Right."

Michelle hesitated, and Alan could feel something behind her silence. "He likes you Alan."

Unsure if it was the right thing to say, Alan said, "I like him, too."

Suddenly Michelle laughed, changing her voice. "I look forward to getting together with you guys when you get home."

"We'll have to do it," Alan answered.

"It's a deal. Here's Sloan."

"Alan." Sloan's voice was coarse. "What was that about?"

He felt the lump in his throat. "Hi, Babe." He paused. "Michelle misses Sam."

"What about you?" Sloan breathed.

"I'm missing you."

"I miss you tons!"

Alan could hear her swallow. "What's going on there? What are you hearing? Michelle seems upset."

"We're not hearing anything. We can only guess."

"Well, nothing is going on here. Is Michelle still there?"

"No. I'm alone. The door is closed."

He looked around quickly. The door to the room was open, but he heard no one outside.

"I need you here," Sloan said softly.

Alan could hear the lump in her throat. "I needed to hear that," he said.

"I do! I love you!" Her voice was guttural.

"I love you, Babe."

There was a pause.

"How's Turkey?" Sloan asked.

"When you get wheels in the well, it's great."

"When you what?"

"Get airborne. It's the most fun you can have with your clothes on."

He heard her exhale through her nose into the phone. "You'd better wait until you get home to take them off!"

"They'll smell sort of gamy by then ..."

"I won't notice."

"I wish I could hold you."

"I hold you every night ... are you getting my letters?"

"Yes. They help." He sighed.

"I hope so." She paused. "I want to buy another car."

"What?"

"The Gilliard's are selling their Citroën before they leave. It's a really good deal."

"Can it wait until I get home?"

She hesitated before saying, "I don't think so."

"Seems rather extravagant. Our budget's really tight."

"I'll need it for work."

"You got a job?"

He sounded excited. She thought he might actually be. "Yes!"

"I'm happy for you, Babe."

"When will you be home?"

"The day after Christmas."

"Why does it have to be the day after?"

"I don't know."

"Will you fly or get flown?"

"The Lump."

"Oh."

"But at least I can get all your boodle on it."

"Goodies?"

"Trinkets. Copper. Spoils of war."

"I don't want to talk about war."

"Oh."

"But I'll take the spoils! Are all the TDY's going to be like this?"

He laughed. "You mean bringing home the spoils?"

She was silent long enough for it to bother him. "Sloan?"

Her voice was softer. "I mean ... are they all going to be this long and mysterious?" She paused. "And so many of them?"

"I think it'll get easier, Babe." He was not sure if that was a lie or not. He hoped the time away would get easier once they were used to it ... if that could ever happen.

Ron walked into the room and gave the cut-throat sign.

"I've got to go, Babe."

"No!"

"I love you."

"Come home to me."

"Five days."

"Merry Christmas."

"Not till I get home."

Ron's eyes widened. Alan turned away from him in the swivel chair and whispered, "Hold my place for me."

"You come home and do it yourself."

"I will."

"Alan ... I need you here with me."

"I want that, too." He gave the phone to Ron.

"Where's my wife?" Ron said into the receiver.

"With another man," Sloan teased.

"So, let's talk dirty."

"I'll get Jennifer."

It was Christmas Eve, but Alan lacked the fervor he usually felt. He sipped on the beer Ron bought for him, eyeing his fellow fighter pilots and the squadron enlisted personnel who on this evening, talked with only a subdued regard for rank. "We don't have much of a Christmas spirit, do we?" he remarked to Ron.

"We will when we get home," Ron answered, looking away. "Without the buildup or the hype."

"I feel robbed," Alan answered, curious what Ron meant by "hype."

Ron looked at him and raised his eyebrows. "You were robbed."

"This will be the year that I missed it."

Ron smirked. "If you feel the need for spiritual enlightenment, discuss it with our resident Christian." He made no mention of a name.

Alan had entertained the notion of talking to Camron Ransom about it, perhaps to get a sort of pep talk. But he knew where it would lead, and he did not feel like starting any arguments this night. He just wanted the magic he felt as a little boy when he would sneak into the living room in the early morning hours to see the Christmas tree and all the gifts beneath it. He would quietly turn on the tree lights and then curl up on the sofa to bath in the rhythmic glow of blinking lights and youthful anticipation.

"I don't know how they do it, anyway," Ron was saying.

"Do what?" Alan asked, returning from his brief reverie.

Ron looked at Camron Ransom, who was drinking a soft drink. "How can a real Christian fly fighters? Live our life?"

Alan did not answer but looked away at Camron who was talking to Sherman.

He felt very strange, very foreign, as if everything he believed in, everything that mattered, was being pushed aside by his chosen way of life. Living it is one thing, he thought to himself. Justifying it is another.

"Up for some poker, Puppy?" It was Shooter.

Alan contemplated for a moment.

Smiling to himself, Shooter said, "It ain't a live or die question."

"I don't think so ... tonight," Alan answered and walked off by himself.

He found Sam in their room. "Ever been to Midnight Mass?" Alan asked him.

"I'm not Catholic," Sam said, putting on a light jacket and a festive plaid scarf.

"Neither am I."

Together, they walked silently to the chapel.

The eerie chords of the organ could be heard from outside. There was the solemn shuffling of feet as they entered with several other attendees and took their seats. It was a somber celebration. The people were a long way from home, and their seasonal spirit was subdued. The colors and carols of the Mass made Alan feel something, but not enough. It was not going to happen for him, not on this night.

They walked back to the BOQ in a silence Sam found most interesting. He would have liked to know where Alan was. Returning to their room, Sam went to bed.

Alan walked outside, down the way to the open door to Shooter's room. With cards in hand, an open bottle of Raki by his stash of chips, an unlit cigar clinched between his teeth, Bull Boulder said, "Puppy, pull up a chair!"

"Yeah, Bull," Alan said as his mind drifted into the room following his body. "Deal me a no-brainer."

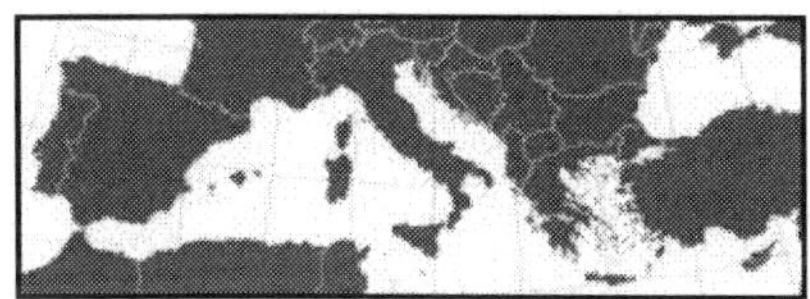

CHAPTER FOURTEEN

Sloan opened the door to their Spanish apartment while Alan waited in the landing holding the two olive drab canvass bags of his dirty laundry and Turkish treasures of copper, whirling dervish figurines and pistachios. The light from the landing flowed into the little foyer of the dark apartment. Alan followed her inside, awkwardly shifting the bulky bags to get them through the doorway, one in front of him and one behind. He placed them gently on the foyer floor and went for the light switch.

Sloan reached for his hand. "No lights," she said, sounding very mysterious and sexy. She pulled his hand to her side and closed the door behind them. They shuffled only a few feet together before she said, "Wait here," and walked away. He could hear her groping for something in the darkness.

"What are you doing?" Alan laughed finally.

"Nothing. Just wait a minute."

As his eyes adjusted to the darkness, Alan could see her kneeling in the far corner.

Sloan found the extension cord with the European adapter and plugged it into the wall socket. The brilliance of transformed electricity brought a modest Christmas tree to life. Standing alone at the far end of the sparsely furnished front room, a warm, multi-colored glow from a hundred little lights reflected off the large glass windows, casting shadows of Scotch pine needles on the walls. The apartment smelled of Spain, but this glowing tree, its soft colors outlining the silhouettes, transformed him, and he felt it once again.

And there was Sloan, her eyes glowing in anticipation. He came to her, held her tightly against him and smothered her soft lips with his. Her kiss was long and deep.

"That is the most beautiful tree I have ever seen," he said. "And you are the most beautiful woman I have ever known."

"I love you, Alan! I missed you so much!" A tear began to form in her eye, and she lay her head against his chest. "Welcome home. Merry Christmas!"

"You have made this a home."

"This is home. Our home," she said, looking up at him with blue eyes full of love. She put her head back against his chest. "But it's not much of one when you aren't here."

"I'm here now."

"Yes, and safely!" She squeezed him tighter.

"Other Americans aren't so lucky," he said. "We spent Christmas at that place and then did absolutely nothing."

"Nothing?" Sloan asked pulling away only slightly. "You did the most important thing. You came back."

Alan decided not to talk of it. He kissed her again, and his mouth began to water as if he was about to eat a delectable meal. He lowered his hands from her back to her thighs. "Let's make love under this beautiful tree."

She pulled away again and gave him a funny look. "Trees are for putting goodies from Turkey under. Beds are for making love, and a big bed waits for us. A very big bed! I noticed that while you were gone."

"Let's go make it smaller."

"Don't you want to shower or anything first?" she asked with a sly grin.

Alan sniffed under his left arm. I don't need a bath, he thought. I need to be disinfected. To Sloan he said wryly, "No, I'm all right."

"No, you're not, either!" she groaned, turning him toward the bathroom.

"It's too cold to shower!" he pleaded.

"I'll turn on the electric blanket. You'll have a warm bed and a hot wife waiting for you."

"We have an electric blanket?"

"I bought it with my first pay check. That and a flannel nightgown that's longer than I am."

Alan pouted. "No flannel tonight, please." He gave her his best hurt look.

"Only until you get out of the shower."

When Alan reemerged from the bathroom, the Christmas tree glowed beyond the hallway, softly framing the door to their bedroom. Sloan was under the electric blanket. A red flannel nightgown lay neatly folded at the foot of the bed.

PART TWO

FIRST SPRING
CHAPTER FIFTEEN

Spring brought with it enough rain to turn the dry land between Madrid and Alcala and Torrejon Air Base a refreshing green. The large brown dirt fields were transformed, however temporarily, into large rectangles of life as wheat planted by local farmers began its short cycle of life. Other colorless uncultivated fields and vacant lots, bland landscapes that normally passed the eye unnoticed, briefly became the focal point of travelers along the autopista between Madrid and Alcala as large patches of wild poppies sprung up among them.

Sometimes the rain came in great storms that could almost make the inexperienced visitor feel perhaps the whole climate of central Spain was going through some meteorological metamorphosis. For the more experienced soul, the rain offered some hope that the green would remain longer this year. But the thirsty, dry earth absorbed the rain, and even the cheerful red poppies seemed to cling to life one day at a time.

This time of year also brought Death. The Feria de San Isidro officially ushered in the warming days of spring with two weeks of daily bullfights. Each day for two weeks, six brave bulls would run onto the sand of the large arena and chase whatever they found inside and fight and die by a sword pierced through the heart in their last act of life. Then, with their tongues hanging out, their lifeless bodies would plow up the bloody stage as they were dragged away behind two old geldings.

Alan and Sloan were not sure they wanted to see a bullfight, but Ron and Jennifer insisted they needed to experience this central lifeblood of Spanish culture. They invited Sam and Michelle Christopher to come along.

On the middle Sunday of the Festival, they drove in two cars to the Plaza Toros de Madrid. The Plaza was hot and crowded, but the parking lot was large, and they found two places together with little trouble.

Approaching the ticket counters, Ron said, "Do we want 'sol y sombre'?"

"Yes," Jennifer answered.

"What's that?" Sloan asked, studying a group of old Spanish men wearing black berets talking and pointing to the names on the bullfight poster.

"Sun and shade," Jennifer said. "Sol is the cheapest seats because it's always in the sun. Sombre is more expensive because it's always in the shade. Sol y sombre is the in-between. Sun part of the time and shade part of the time. That's what we want."

The smell of stale urine was prevalent along the outside walls. Alan involuntarily curled his lip. "Do they have restrooms?" he asked Jennifer as they waited for Ron to purchase their seats.

"Yes, inside."

Ron returned with the tickets and, after winning the standard argument of who was going to pay for them, acted as director and guide, retaining possession of the tickets so that he alone would know where they were sitting. The others followed him through the gate to the ramp that led to the seats of "sol y sombre." The ramp was crowded with Spaniards pushing their way into the arena. A gray-haired woman pushed against the crowd in front of her. The Spaniards she pushed paid no attention to her as they pushed on those in front of them.

"That's the way they are," Ron said. He spoke loud enough for them all to hear, knowing the Spaniards would probably be unaware of what he was saying. And he knew if there were those that did understand him, to acknowledge this small insult would be an admittance that would make eavesdropping on the Americans more difficult later. "It's cultural for them to push and shove, to be impatient."

"It is?" Michelle said.

"It must be."

Alan watched the old woman elbow her way along. She was not trying to get in ahead of anyone else. She was simply maintaining her position in the sea of people.

The crowd thinned at the other end of the ramp as the people parted, going in different directions. Ron led his group to six wooden seats.

"We're right in the sun!" Sloan said. "Where's the sombre?"

Jennifer laughed. "We'll get into it about halfway through." She looked up at the sky. "But these seats look like they might have more sol than sombre." She glanced at Ron. "These the best you could do?"

Ron said nothing, and they took their seats: Ron, Jennifer, Sloan, Alan, Michelle, Sam.

The procession began with the ceremonial walk through the two large doors of the gate that led into the arena. Four men dressed as matadors on four beautiful horses lead the way. Ron pointed at them. "Those are the picadors," he said. "They are the ones that cut the neck muscle on the bull so that it cannot lift its head. The horse's vocal chords have been cut so that you can't hear them scream when the bull hooks them."

Sloan's face formed a wretched look. "That's terrible! Why don't they have some sort of padding?"

"They usually do," Ron said. "They'll probably put it on after this. The horses are the comical part of a bullfight."

Sam whispered something in Michelle's ear that made her respond with a slight nod and a grin.

Alan looked around the ring at the processional. "It takes that many men to kill a bull? Where are the matadors?"

"They are the guys with the pink and orange capes," Ron answered just as Sam was about to offer an explanation.

Sam leaned across Michelle. "A guy at the squadron told me this would be a Portuguese style fight," he said to Alan.

"What does that mean?"

"It will be fought on horseback. The matadors, called 'rejoneadors' in this case, will ride horses instead of standing on the ground with the bulls."

"That doesn't sound very brave," Alan said. "What are those Portuguese ... cowards?"

"No," Sam said, looking back to the ring. "There aren't any picadors. In a regular bullfight, they let the bull run around in the ring by itself for a while, then the guys with the pink capes come out and the bull chases them for a time. They start wearing the bull down that way. Then the picador comes out on a horse with padding on. He uses a big sharp lance to cut the bull's neck muscles while the bull tries to gore his horse."

Alan felt a tinge of disgust. "What's the purpose of that?"

"To keep the bull's head down," Michelle said. "It makes it harder for the bull to hurt the matador."

"The whole idea is to wear the bull down before the matador fights it," Sam said.

"And then there's the banderilleros," Michelle added.

"What do they do?"

"They put the colorful barbed sticks in the bull's shoulder. You have probably noticed them on bullfight posters."

Alan did not admit he had not.

Sam continued, "After all that is done, the matador fights the bull with the cape called a muleta."

"Well, what will this be like today?"

Sam pointed at the riders on the pretty horses. "I think those are the rejoneadors. Everything will be done on horseback."

Alan considered this for a minute. "That doesn't seem fair for the bull."

"It's more fair than wearing him down and slicing him up first," Michelle said. Her pretty eyes flashed with a touch of pain.

"Who ever said bullfighting was fair?" Sam said.

Impressed with their collective knowledge, Alan felt a tinge of embarrassment that he did not know more. "I don't know, who did?"

"I think Hemmingway believed it was," Michelle said, looking at him and revealing her source.

Alan found the little Spanish woman among the spectators. She was seated on the first row of seats behind the barrera, the wall that separated the fight from the observers. It was a good place to see and hear the gore and the glory.

The members of the paseo bowed to the president's box, centered in the middle of the sombre section, then exited through the wooden gate. After a moment, the doors opened again, and the first bull of the afternoon ran into the ring. As the aggressive and headstrong beast raced around the enclosed battleground in search of a target at which to vent its fury, a short red streamer flew from where it had been inserted on the animal's shoulder. Three fighters with pink capes emerged from behind three different barriers around the ring. The bull spotted the movement and ran at full gallop toward the closest man.

The man hid immediately behind the barrier. The bull looked for him a moment, then, seeing the next one across the ring, turned and made for him with no less enthusiasm. The second man hid behind his barrier. The bull hesitated, waiting like a cat to see if his prey would reappear.

The sound of the big doors opening caught the bull's attention, and it quickly turned its powerful body to face the horse and rider. The bull began a gentle trot toward the new intruder. The trot turned into a dead run when the rejoneador, Jorge de Oliveira, spurred his horse into motion as the bull gave chase.

After one full circle around the perimeter of the ring, the bull stopped as if waiting to see if the horse would continue and come back around to him. The rejoneador reigned his horse and turned it around to face the stationary bull. Realizing the bull was not ready to charge, he spurred his brave and trusting steed ahead until the bull countered the assault. At seemingly the last possible moment, he turned his horse and the chase began anew with the bull right on the horse's tail, its dangerous horns but inches from the horse which appeared to tuck in its rump to avoid them. The horse outlasted the bull, widening the gap to several meters until the bull slowed to a halt.

At the end of two more such rounds of cat and mouse, the bull stopped in the middle of the arena, eyeing horse and rider circling at a distance. There was still plenty of fight in the bull, but it was beginning to breathe heavily in the heat.

Sloan leaned to Alan. "I'm thirsty," she said. "Do you think they serve drinks here?"

The horseman rode to the barrier nearest them where a peon gave him a banderilla. Turning to the bull, he raised the banderilla above his head in his right hand and, holding the reins in his left, charged the bull, enticing it to counter with a charge of its own. As the combatants closed on each other, Jorge steered the horse to feint right, which the bull followed, then pulled the horse hard back to the left. With too little time to react, the bull was slow to follow the maneuver, and horse and bull passed each other like two knights in a joust. At the pass, the bull threw its head in the direction of the blur that it saw but met only empty air.

The man plunged the barbed razor-sharp end of the colorful baton deeply and firmly into the fleshy shoulder of the beast. The bull whirled to face its adversary with a look in its black eyes that bespoke confusion and contempt.

The eyes of a bull are like that of the great white shark, being black, cold and lifeless. It is by its breath and its pawing of the earth and the movement of its head that its meaning is clearly understood.

A matador, if confronted about his feelings, is likely to say he loves the bull. No one could ever confuse that emotion with what the bull must feel for the matador.

Jorge rode to the barrier where a peon gave him two banderillas. He then rode to the center of the ring, stopping short of a distance from the bull that he supposed would incite a charge. Placing the reins between his teeth, he made another charge at the bull with a weapon in each hand. The bull charged. With a twist of his head, Jorge steered his horse in a feint to the right. When the bull took the feint, he reversed the turn of the horse with another jerk of his head and again passed close to the bull, driving both banderillas home while the bull made a harmless swipe at the horse.

The fluid movement of man and horse captivated Alan's thoughts like a beautiful, provocative poem. The horses were not comic, but well trained, intelligent and beautiful. The bullfight unfolded before him like a ballet, causing him to ponder the destiny of horses. Who or what determined their station in life, hero or comic victim?

Jorge made one more double banderilla pass. The bull's exhaustion was evidenced by its labored breathing.

Alan turned to Michelle. "About now the bull must be thinking 'What in hell brought this on?!'" She smiled at him, and, for a moment, he was caught in her eyes.

Jorge encouraged the tiring bull to chase the horse twice again, but the runs were short. It was time for the kill while there was still fight in the beast.

Jorge armed himself with his weapon of Death, a long javelin with a sharp blade at the end of it, the "rejon." He would fool the animal one last time. He charged the bull. The horse faked right. The bull followed. The horse swung back left, and the man thrust the blade through the animal's shoulder at the base of its neck. The force gained from the power and speed of the horse drove the blade deep into the animal's large heart. Mortally wounded, the black blood-soaked bull fell to its forelimbs. A few heartbeats more and it fell on its side. It was a well-fought fight, a brilliant kill. There was no need for the atronar, the coup de grace.

Alan turned to Sloan. "Are you still thirsty?"

She answered with a silent grimace.

With the bull in the sand, the spectators rose to their feet and cheered. From his horse, Jorge watched his kill die. The crowd demanded both ears be given to the rejoneador. The judges in the booth decided to allow him one. Jorge rode his talented horse around the perimeter of the ring and was showered with hats and flowers, a few seat cushions and a fine leather coat as he held high his ear of victory. It had been a good fight. He had drawn a very brave bull, and the crowd loved him. Rarely did the Madrileños see this style of fighting. They were taken in totally by the finesse and coordination required between man and horse.

Three more bulls met and died at the hands of the other three matadors. All but one were clean kills. Rauol Zoilo had trouble with his bull.

The bull had been reluctant to fight. It would not charge unless Rauol took his horse dangerously close. When the bull did finally charge, Rauol had very little time to react and give the bull the feint required to plant the banderillas in its shoulder.

The bull was either a coward or very smart. Rauol got in only two banderillas.

Sam again leaned over Michelle's lap. "This is a bad bull, I think," he said to Alan.

"How's that?" Alan answered watching the bull. "He seems smart."

"But not brave," Michelle said. Her eyes flashed something at Alan he could not completely understand.

"He's unpredictable," Sam said. "That makes him dangerous."

"That seems to me the best way to be if he wants to stay alive," Alan answered.

"But he won't," Michelle turned to him to say.

Alan looked at her curiously.

When the time came for the kill, Rauol again had to get close to make the bull charge. He jabbed a glancing blow with the rejon that missed the heart and met mostly flesh. The bull shook with rage and threw the rejon free. Rauol made another pass with another rejon that took enough energy from the bull to make it waiver from the loss of blood. It fell to its fore-knees but with enough remaining strength to keep that stance, refusing to fall.

While Rauol held the beast's attention, a peon crept up behind it and applied the atronar, scrambling its spinal cord at the base of the brain.

The bull fell. Neither Rauol nor the bull was honored with the cutting of an ear.

For the final fight of the day, a beautiful large black specimen of a bull entered the ring as the wooden doors swung shut behind it. The red tag appeared insignificant to its size. The bull did not run but turned to see its only means of escape removed. A pink cape at the far end beckoned. Still the bull did not charge, but only watched the cape intently. Another cape appeared from behind a barrier closer to the bull. The man taunted the beast with movement and words it did not understand.

A third peon appeared. The bull started into a trot, making the rounds of the ring as each of the men successively disappeared behind a barrier. When the first reappeared, the bull loped toward him for a closer look. The man was very close to the safety of the barrier and so remained a bit longer to display his bravado. When it became apparent the bull showed more interest in the man than his cape, he jumped to safety as the bull tossed its head, hitting the wood soundly with a horn.

Rauol and Jorge rode side by side into the ring. The bull did not charge. Instead, it appeared to assess the situation as if mulling over a plan of action in its small mind. Jorge rode to the left and Rauol to the right. The bull began an experimental trot toward Rauol's horse, possibly anticipating that the horse and rider would themselves disappear behind some invisible barrier. Rauol spurred his horse into a gallop, and the bull gave chase. Halfway around the ring, the animal switched its attack to Jorge, who rode away from Rauol with the bull hot on his heels.

Alan watched the exchange with great interest. "A two vee one," he turned to Sam to say.

"What's that?" Michelle asked.

"Yeah," Sam answered. "Two against one. Like an air-to-air engagement. The bull is the bogie and the matadors are making coordinated sequential attacks on it."

Sloan overheard the exchange. "You guys compare everything to flying," she said in exasperation.

"It fits," Alan said.

The crowd was alive, emotionally bonded to the fight. Alan watched his little Spanish lady react with the enthusiasm of the other spectators. She waved a white scarf and cheered when the bull charged.

The two rejoneadors acted with caution. The bull was unpredictable.

Jorge took a banderilla for his first pass. It was a clean pass, and he controlled his horse brilliantly, and still the bull came dangerously close to the horse. The crowd cheered the matador's apparent courage.

Rauol made two attempts to match his skill with that of his companion, but each time the bull was slow to take the fake and quick to react to the horse's change of direction. Two ill-handled banderillas lay trampled in the sand.

The crowd became concerned. Rauol appeared afraid of the bull. To dispel any doubts of his bravado, Rauol took two banderillas and fitted the reins in his teeth. It was a dangerous thing to think more of the crowd than of the bull.

Jorge urged his horse to creep closer to the bull to confuse the animal and perhaps give Rauol a better chance.

The bull pawed the ground in determined anger. Rauol began his charge. With the first feint, the reins fell from his mouth. Bull and horse rapidly closed the gap that separated them. In fear, the horse lurched from the charging bull. Rauol spurred the horse left, using his legs to guide the horse away. The resultant turn brought the fight close to Jorge, who suddenly realized he had no means of escape. He was cornered against the wooden wall.

Veering away from Rauol, the bull caught Jorge's horse squarely with its massive head, its horns piercing deeply into Jorge's upper thigh. The force of the charge threw Jorge against the top of the barrier. His body bent oddly backward over the wall and then dropped limply on the far side of the barrera.

The horse screamed as the bull gored it again. Rauol brought his horse to the bull and stabbed at it with a banderilla. The bull turned, chasing him to the other end of the ring.

A crowd rushed to the matador who was not moving.

"What's happened?!" Sloan heard herself scream.

The men over the matador began to yell and motion for help.

The Americans looked on with curiosity and horror as the excitement in the Plaza Toros de Madrid grew to a frenzy.

CHAPTER SIXTEEN

The drive down Calle Alcalá from the Plaza Toros to the Plaza Major was quiet. Through separate windows, Alan and Sloan watched Madrid pass by without comment. Jennifer stared through her large, drooping glasses into unfocused space. Ron drove as if preoccupied with something that had nothing to do with the day, gazing from time to time in the rearview mirror to insure Sam and Michelle still followed.

As they traversed the half-circle around the Plaza Independencia, Alan's lips parted as he thought to remark on this 200 year old monument of enduring Spanish history. He exhaled without comment, his words corralled by the sullen mood that pervaded the small confines of the car.

Plaza Major was crowded, but the patrons were curiously reserved. Few at the Plaza could know of the afternoon's events at the bull ring, but for whatever reason, a subdued mist engulfed this normally enlivened meeting place.

Although Sam and Michelle seemed to know where they were going, Ron lead the way as they walked past the "Man on the Horse" to the far corner of the Plaza and down the same steps Alan remembered had taken them to Botin's. At the street level, they turned right and followed Ron along the Avenida de Cuchilleros and into the Meson de Champignon, a tosca built into the outside wall of the Plaza Major.

The front room of the dimly lit tosca was crowded, and the smell of smoke, garlic and stale dampness that clung to the walls obscured the atmosphere from the hot outside city air.

The smell of garlic was strong. The specialty of the house, mushrooms with pieces of serrano ham stuffed into each, smoldered on a grill behind the bar counter. Ron placed an order. The man behind the bar brought them three plates of the cooked mushrooms, with flat toothpicks in them for easier eating, then placed six small glasses of red wine in front of the Americans.

"This is good stuff," Jennifer said. "You'll love it."

"It looks good," Alan said. The bullfight had made him thirsty. He took a drink of the wine. He was unable to hide the fact that the raw taste caught him by surprise.

Ron watched with amused eyes. "What do you think?" he smiled.

In the spirit of making a valid judgment, Alan took another sip. It was as bad as the first. "I've never claimed to be a connoisseur of fine wines, but on a scale of one to ten, I'd rate this as horse tee tee."

"Gross!" Sloan said, looking at her untouched glass with a developing distaste for Spain that had grown throughout the day.

"It's really not that bad," Alan decided after another drink. "Sort of grows on you."

"It's tinto," Ron said. "It's part of Spain."

"Ah, another part of Spain," Sloan groaned.

Sipping on their tinto, Michelle and Sam listened quietly. Alan noticed that, unlike Sloan, they, especially Michelle, seemed to want to touch everything, to feel everything. Even if they should find the need to complain, they would do so as Spaniards. They each ate another of the stuffed mushrooms.

"It's the blood of the bull," Ron said watching them.

Alan emptied his glass. "What is?"

"After the bullfights, Spaniards go to the toscas and drink tinto, to symbolize the blood of the bull, like we're doing."

"It's not what I'm doing," Sloan argued.

"Oh, he's making it up as he goes," Jennifer said. She elbowed her husband in the ribs.

Ron looked at Sloan who winced at the idea of drinking real blood. The mischievous grin formed on his brown face. "That's what they do."

"We drank blood in survival training," Alan said for effect.

"Don't believe them," Jennifer reassured Sloan. "They're both full of it."

"We did," Alan insisted.

"What about the blood of the matador?" Sloan complained. "Or doesn't that matter?"

Sam became suddenly enlivened by Sloan's concern. "It's just like flying fighters," he said. "Each depending on the other to cover his six. But one of them did not. The incompetence of one caused the death ... possible death, of the other."

"That was terrible!" Sloan winced. "I wish that had not happened. Let's not talk about it. I think that was my last, bullfight."

Alan looked at her crossly, embarrassed by her words. "It wasn't that bad." He spoke to her as if to a child.

"Wasn't that bad!" Sloan returned his look with one of uncertain defiance. "A man was probably killed today! In my book, that's bad."

"What I mean is, it can't get any worse."

"I don't plan to find out."

"Sloan ..." he began.

"No! What I saw today just proves what I thought all along. It's just a mindless slaughter. There's nothing sporting about it."

Alan tried a different approach. "You have to admit, it wasn't as one-sided as we had heard. The bull won today."

"The bull did not win," Michelle said.

Alan looked at her. Her brown eyes seemed especially soft in the dim light of the tosca. "What do you mean? The bull got the matador. This time, the bull won. He walked out of the ring the same way he came in. Maybe they should have cut off the matador's ear and given it to the bull."

She looked at him and tilted her head slightly. "Well, you know, they have to kill the bull after the fight no matter what happens." She did not speak aggressively. She did not have to. The truth blazed in her eyes.

"Even if it wins?"

She nodded. "They can't let the bull fight again. He knows too much." Her eyes crinkled as she laughed at her joke. "He would probably kill the next matador he meets."

"I think he killed this one ..." Sam interjected.

"They don't just put him out to pasture?" Sloan asked.

"Why not out to stud?" Alan put in.

"It would make more sense," Michelle answered with a light touch in her voice.

Alan looked into her eyes. "A bull that wins should be rewarded."

"And what better reward than to be a bull gigolo?" Sam laughed his full, healthy laugh. "But, would you want to be put out to pasture, retired at your finest hour? The boring life of growing old being so much longer than the one, brief, glorious fight?"

"I wouldn't want to be killed for it," Alan answered. "I think I understand the concept of bull fighting, that it is supposed to be an art form and all, but to me that is all bull shit. They are murdering the bull at tremendous odds against it. He has only one option. If you've kicked some butt and come out on top, you should at least get the womens!" He laughed to soften his words.

Jennifer spoke from under her glasses, "If they want to see some real butt-kicking, they should let them fight female bulls."

"Yeah!" Sloan laughed in agreement.

"Female bulls?" Ron said.

"You can't put prissy little cows in there and expect them to fight with their udders flopping all over the place," Alan said with a comical grin. He was glad to see Sloan smile, and he tried to make her do it more.

"Why not?" Sloan retorted. "They put those male bulls in there with their things flopping everywhere."

"Oh, so you were watching that," Alan said lightly.

"Yep," she nudged him. "I was checkin' 'em out."

"Not comparatively, I hope."

She laughed and put her arm inside his, looking up at him lovingly. "You never know what it takes to get the womens."

"Cojones," Ron said simply.

"What?" Alan said.

"That's what they're called."

Sloan looked at him. "What are?"

"What were we talking about?"

"Oh."

They had another glass of tinto.

"Let's go find another tosca," Sam suggested.

"What's wrong with this one?" Alan asked.

"Nothing," Jennifer said. "But there are bars all over this place. You're supposed to go from one tosca to the next. It's called 'tosca hopping.' Haven't you noticed there's no real place to sit, except maybe in the back? Even the owners don't expect for you to hang around. You come in, they serve you their specialty, whether it's mushrooms or ham or pulpo or whatever, and give you some tinto or beer to wash it down, and then you leave and go somewhere else to make room for other hoppers."

"Pulpo?" Sloan said.

"Octopus. It's pretty good."

"What if you meet someone and want to start talking to that person?" Alan asked. He stole a glance at Michelle and caught her eye. She looked away.

"Hopping from bar to bar," Ron interjected, "keeps the conversation from getting too heavy." He placed his glass on the counter. "Come on, let's go get some tortillas."

Sloan tried to look confused. "Tortillas? In Spain?"

"Spanish tortillas," Jennifer explained. "Made with potatoes."

They left the bar and walked slowly up the Avenida de Cuchilleros, giving their eyes a chance to adjust to the late afternoon light. People milled around the sidewalk and outside the bars in small groups.

In the tosca, they had Spanish tortillas, served hot from the oven. The waiter shot Ron a funny look when he ordered a second round of tinto.

The bullfight was still on Sam's mind. "Those matadors, the ones that fight the bulls on foot must have big cojones."

Alan nodded in agreement. "So does the bull." He tapped his wife and took another bite of tortilla. "He walks into that ring, not knowing he's in the last hour of his life. Suddenly, he finds himself fighting for every minute."

"That's life," Ron said simply.

"Maybe the true intelligence of animals is that they all live each minute as if it might be the last," Sam put in.

Alan looked into Sam's eyes for a moment, noting the depth of character that seemed to shine from behind them. "That could be," he acknowledged. "But when they run the bull into the ring, they make it his life's last great challenge. And the whole idea seems to be to determine if he has something he will never be able to use again."

"And what is that?" Michelle asked.

"The balls ... the cojones to die bravely," Alan answered. He shook his head. "But when he does, they drag his carcass out of the arena with the least amount of dignity I can think of. I hope, if I ever get the chance to die bravely, I'm treated with more dignity than the bull."

Michelle said, "That's not the point."

"What is the point?"

"The point," Michelle said, "is that it is tragic. How the bull faces death is important. But how the matador administers that death is more important. It's the measure of everything else."

"The matador plays God."

"No, God is still in charge."

"Then the bull ought to have a chance. At least in this fight today they didn't cut his neck. He had a fighting chance."

"If the bull had any more of a chance, it wouldn't be a sport. Just a gruesome spectacle."

"Like war," Jennifer said.

"I think it's horrid as it is," Sloan said.

"It's a hell of a way to die," Alan said, sipping his tinto, "alone in the dust against all odds."

CHAPTER SEVENTEEN

In ways both subtle and dramatic, the fighter-jock persona was developing in Alan, a kind of metamorphosis that, to a greater or lesser extent, all fighter pilots and fighter gators experience. Existing personalities of previous years are molded and then adjusted to fit in a niche each claims in the unique world that belongs to those who fly and fight. It is like an expandable puzzle - given the right initial edges, each unique peace can be trimmed to fit.

The essence of the being of the fighter pilot lies in the fact that he is usually a person of ordinary background and upbringing who has been thrust into an environment completely foreign to the majority of the world and, in most cases, his past. He is potentially a slightly above average man (or woman) of moderate means and mental faculties, possessing a certain degree of athletic ability and competitiveness. Were he never to become a part of the fighter world, his entire being would project priorities reflecting a totally separate reality.

He is tested and trained, and then delivered into the environment and given the most important command as a primal directive: Survive.

Understandably, a common misconception is to think that the fighter pilot is a special breed of human being, destined from birth to be a defender of the skies. There is even the romantic fantasy that, in earlier times, he might have been a gladiator or a knight. This is not true. There is really nothing in the past that hints of anything like the fighter pilot. Before the age of fighter planes, he did not exist. He is, in fact, a person of brain power and coordination moderately above average who has been indoctrinated into the world of legalized killing made possible through Man's technology and the declaration of war.

What sets him apart is desire. It is this desire which enables him to hurdle the physical and mental obstacles that would otherwise keep him from ever knowing the very life he comes to love. He is never off-duty. He is always a fighter pilot. Because of this, he entertains unique diversions devised to release stored up energy and relieve pent up stress.

It takes a mature, disciplined person to effectively fly a fighter plane in preparation for combat. The majority of fighter pilots fit this mold. The pressure resulting from practicing maneuvers that test one's skill, and from abiding by the whims of commanders that tests one's patience, could become overwhelming and drive the fighter pilot to the edge. Yet the training he receives somehow incorporates the innate ability to scoff at this pressure and even deny its existence, not only in himself, but in his environment.

To admit the reality of this pressure and thereby react to it might indicate one was affected by it. The result could be to transform a commander's feelings of trust into those of concern. Since the greatest fighter pilot in the world would not let this happen, and since all fighter pilots are the greatest, the pressure would have to be so great that all cry out in unison. The lonely cry of one is but a whimper.

This does not mean that fighter pilots do not belly-ache. In fact, some of them are among the most eloquent, gifted grumblers in the world. But these complaints do not concern that which is required in the job of flying and fighting. They do not complain that they must face the enemy in a life and death struggle. They are fighter pilots.

The clamor arises when they are expected to perform this mission with limited ordnance on weapons systems that are not combat ready and with antiquated tactics in scenarios untouched by reality. They complain of commanders that handcuff them with murderous, obscene regulations and "fire only when fired upon" rules of engagement. They complain when a high-level decision makes the survival aspect of flying and fighting just a little harder to achieve.

Fighter pilots can be defined as either Old Heads or New Guys. There is really very little in between. Old Heads look upon New Guys as fumbling, awkward infants in the serious world of fighter pilots. Squadron leaders rush to get these young pups combat ready, even as they are frustrated by the tail-dragging pace the inexperience of the New Guys often demands. The Old Heads tolerate them with the restrained patience of an old dog who suffers the young pups that bite and tug on his ears, sometimes ignoring them, sometimes enticing them to the game, sometimes snapping at them and wandering off when patience runs dry.

Nonetheless, New Guys are refreshing. Old Head ACs and WSOs like the new blood because it gives them something to train and mold, and influence, like the propagation of an elite fraternity.

Aldous Huxley wrote, "To his dog, every man is Napoleon; hence the constant popularity of dogs." So it is with New Guys.

But additional duties run the squadron. More importantly, additional duties make careers. Though seemingly inconceivable, "excessive paperwork" has at times been an accepted excuse for arriving at a flight briefing late or unprepared, and the higher up the hierarchy a pilot is, the easier the rational becomes. When their "additional duties" require too much of their time, the training for war, the flying and fighting takes a back seat to the perpetual paperwork. Studying tactics, enemy defenses and threats, and ordnance knowledge requires the luxury of time few possess.

The New Guys then, having few other responsibilities, are generally more up to date on the latest developments and technological advances. They are free to read and learn. The Old Heads have the experience, the New Guys have the books.

In reality, it is a question of priorities, of realizing what is at the forefront. That is survival. During war, survival depends absolutely on skill and cunning and knowledge. In peacetime, promotability, job retention, and salary are survival, making paperwork a priority. That sort of survival becomes worthless if you get yourself killed in some "meaningless" training mission.

From the "butter bars" to the four-star generals, there are good leaders, and there are bad leaders, just as there are good fighter pilots and not-so-good fighter pilots. And a fighter jock will follow a good leader into battle anytime, anywhere. It is the pompous, self-centered leader who says, "I will be proud to lead you guys ..." It is the true leader who hears, "We would proudly follow you ..."

And what makes him the man to follow? Priorities. What comes first: the pilots? Or his career. Is being the commander of a fighter squadron the goal or just a stepping stone? If it is the goal, then all are polished and protected.

If it is a mere stepping stone, then all in it come under his boot, and they, as a squadron, are a detriment to the defense of the country until he is either transformed or gone.

And what of the fighter pilot? If his concerns are for his wingman or flight lead, he will strive to keep them alive. They will bond in a fashion that echoes their common need for survival.

However, if his priorities reflect a different, more personal agenda, or he allows himself to waiver from reality and forget that which is most important, he is potentially a thief of life, or of love, and more dangerous than any other enemy, imagined or real. Such a man cannot long be tolerated among the ranks of those who have chosen the honorable, more difficult road necessary for the common good.

FIRST SUMMER
CHAPTER EIGHTEEN

The days grew longer and hotter as the summer progressed. And there was no more rain.

As the Fourth of July approached, awareness that the Spanish populace took no notice of this celebration punctuated the preparations of the Americans. Beyond the gates, there were no fireworks stands popping up along the road, no advertisements for Fourth of July sales at El Corte Ingles in Madrid. Encapsulated amid the surrounding vacuum, the enthusiasm of the Americans assigned to Torrejon Air Base intensified to a climactic nationalism far beyond that which they may have displayed back home.

The structured celebration on the base promised to be oriented toward the military family, with the wing's high rollers taking full advantage of this exaggerated patriotism. The planning behind the planning insured a celebration arranged in true military fashion with a rigid timetable, and an event by event layout of festivities that accounted for the day from start to finish. "Bring the kids for softball, hot-dogs, American beer and lemonade."

Alan agreed with Sam that this would be a good time to celebrate the three-day weekend somewhere, anywhere, other than on the base. Sam opined that a camping trip was the ideal solution. Alan liked the idea and, with some difficulty, sold Sloan on it. Buck and his wife, Kathleen, agreed to go with them, to flee to the country for a few nights of roughing it under the hot, cloudless Spanish sky.

They drove to the lake they incorrectly referred to as Sacedon in three cars full of people and the necessities required for the three-day excursion with nothing but the lake in which to bathe. Following the road, they topped the rolling hills that led east toward the town of Sacedon and the lake beyond. Although the vegetation along the road seemed full enough, they were surprised to discover that the green trees the fighter pilots had seen from the air - and therefore promised to their wives in talking them into this venture - were nothing more than small olive trees capable of providing little shade and far-removed from the receding waterline. The drought of this and preceding years had resulted in a steady shrinking of the lake, leaving an ever-widening shore of hot sand with no trees of any kind near the water. It would be like camping on the beach of a Caribbean island without the benefit of either palm trees or ocean breezes.

It was after noon when they finished setting up their camp at the water's edge, and the hot sun chased them under the shade of the hastily erected tarpaulin to rest and eat cold sandwiches. They ate and drank and watched Buck and Kathleen's young toddler, Jason, run naked along the shore before taking the first plunge themselves into the cold, inviting lake water.

Sloan looked good in her two-piece as she always did. The smallness of her breasts detracted only slightly from her figure in a swim suit. Her fair skin, round hips and muscular but soft and shapely legs always made Alan proud of her, for her shapeliness said that she was an athlete. She was a positive reflection on him.

Out of the corner of his eye, Alan caught Sam's covert gaze. He obviously liked the way she looked as well.

When Michelle came out from the other tent, Alan found it equally hard to keep from staring at her. The one-piece suit she wore, meant to be conservative, accentuated the comely curvature of her lean body. To anyone who would be infatuated with it, her beauty was striking. For Alan, her exterior only complimented the person he was beginning to like, perhaps too much. He finally turned his body completely away from her in an exaggerated display of indifference.

He turned again to see her running lightly toward the water's edge. He was entranced and felt self-conscious. He closed his mouth. She ran straight on into the lake until its depth arrested her movement where, with a laugh, she fell face first into the water.

This is ridiculous, he silently admonished himself. I have no feelings for her and would have no one think otherwise.

Buck wore a simple swimsuit, befitting the image of a father and flight commander. The red hair on his chest sparkled in the bright afternoon sun. His large wide feet left significant footprints in the sand as he strolled into the lake. Kathleen, becoming heavy with their second child, did not dress to go into the water, but remained seated under the tarpaulin, watching Jason.

Sam's body was muscular, though not bulky in his cut-offs, and a deep tan gave him a healthy glow that contrasted sharply to Alan's pale skin.

"Puppy! You're blinding me!" Sam said, shielding his eyes with his hand.

Alan felt himself redden with embarrassment as he walked into the lake. Michelle stood in waist-deep water, swirling it around her hips with her hands, her long wet hair clinging to her neck, shoulders and chest. Catching Alan's gaze, she smiled coyly at him, then laughed as Sam jumped at her with a body tackle that sent them both under the water. She reemerged first, her entire body shooting out of the water as Sam appeared beneath her, hurling her further out into the lake.

Alan waded near Sloan then lowered his body until only his head and neck were above the surface.

The water was a cool and refreshing escape from the summer sun. After a short while, Sloan and Michelle left the water, brought the men some beer at Sam's request, then sat under the shade of the tarpaulin to keep Kathleen company.

When they were no longer within ear shot, Alan said, "Michelle is taller than I realized." Meaning no offence, he asked Sam, "Are you two the same height?"

Sam took a quick drink of beer. "Nearly," he said and drank again. "But there is a definite advantage to being married to a tall woman."

They looked at Michelle. "What's the advantage?" Alan asked.

"I can think of several," Buck said. "None with your wife, of course!" He smiled an awkward smile. "I mean none that I would want to do with your wife ..." he coughed and grabbed his throat. "I mean, not that I wouldn't want to do them to your wife ... I mean I would do them with your wife ... with a woman like your wife ... if I didn't have a wife ... but I wouldn't want to ..." Sam tried to dunk Buck's head in the water to save him the further misery he was sure to bring upon himself. Buck's thick body resisted, and a short wrestling match ensued. They released each other only when they realized they were spilling an unacceptable amount of beer.

"What's the advantage of being married to a tall woman?" Alan asked again.

A serious look came across Sam's face. "Well, for one thing, when you're toes to toes, your nose is in it, and when you're nose to nose, your toes is in it."

They burst into laughter, and Sam's punctuated laugh could be heard above the others.

"What's gotten into them?" Sloan asked, sitting under the tarp. "They'd better not be talking about us!"

Kathleen looked at the men from above her glasses. "They are either talking about us or they are talking about flying."

"They'd better be talking about flying."

"Either way," Michelle said, "it's hormonal."

The other two looked at her and she started to giggle which brought s brief smile to Kathleen's freckled face.

Fanning herself, Sloan said, "Thank God for sombre!" She looked at Alan and thought to herself how much she liked his looks, so tall and well proportioned, though she had to admit, compared to Buck and Sam, he appeared to be on the skinny side. Still, he looked good to her. She hoped she always looked good to him. She stole a quick glance at Michelle, looked down at her own chest, then away toward the men.

In cooling silence, the ladies watched Jason play in the sand and sipped on their wine.

Kathleen kept her head down as she worked the needles. "Do you want children?"

Sloan and Michelle looked quickly at each other, unsure who Kathleen was addressing. "I do," Sloan said. "Eventually. I have to do something to justify my existence." She laughed weakly and looked out across the water at Alan.

Michelle nodded, but said nothing.

Kathleen looked up from her needlepoint, scrutinizing the younger women as she adjusted her glasses. "Well, you should do whatever is best for your husband's career, I suppose."

Again, Sloan and Michelle traded questioning glances.

"That's probably true," Michelle said finally.

Sloan said. "There's plenty of time for children."

"Yes," Michelle agreed. "And there are things I want to do before I start having kids. There's a lot out there I want to experience."

"Don't you get bored when Sam goes TDY?" Kathleen asked.

Michelle smiled. "I miss him. I am glad I have my little BX job."

"So am I," Sloan put in.

"I'm not just sitting around waiting for Sam to come back," Michelle said.

Kathleen adjusted herself in the lawn chair.

"I know that's not what you're doing," Michelle added, smiling. "I know I'll be plenty busy when the kids start coming."

"Yes, you will," Kathleen said. She lowered her head to her work.

After several minutes of silence, Sloan said, "I wish we knew what is going to happen to this base."

"What do you mean?" Kathleen asked. "Have you heard something?"

Sloan shifted in her chair. "We've heard that they might transition to F-16s here ... is that true?"

Kathleen sighed heavily. "Don't talk about that in front of Buck."

"Why not?"

"Because the back-seaters aren't too happy about it. The F-16 is a single seat fighter, and that doesn't leave much room for wizzos. Buck doesn't think one head is better than two. And, having met some of the ACs that somehow made it through RTU, I agree with him. He could probably fly as good as some of them, but that doesn't make any difference."

"Some of them aren't so good," Sloan said. "I've heard Ron say that." She put on her sunglasses.

"Sam says the F-16 is a good jet," Michelle said, trying to sound non-committal. "He just thinks it would be better with two crewmembers."

"A lot of aircraft commanders get that macho feeling of wanting to fly alone," Kathleen continued. "I'm sure if a war broke out, they would really miss the guy in back."

"I know Alan would miss Sam," Sloan said, looking out across the lake. "And Buck. He likes flying with them."

Michelle crossed her legs and sipped wine from her glass. "Does Alan want to fly the F-16?"

"I think he does," Sloan answered. She knew he did. It was foremost in his mind.

"Are you willing to stay in Spain that long?" Kathleen asked her.

Sloan flinched, as if she was hearing something for the first time.

Kathleen grimaced. "Hasn't he told you? You'd have to extend."

"How long?"

"Well, I don't know." Kathleen furrowed her brow. "I guess it would depend on when they actually begin the transition. I would guess a year before and a year after ... you could end up staying here four or five years."

"Five years!" Sloan blurted. She briefly considered what that could mean. "Well, if that's what he wants, and it's good for his career, I'm all for it." She did not sound convincing.

"You think you'll feel that way another two years down the road? You don't think that will be too long?"

"I'll always feel that way," Sloan answered defensively.

"I'll always feel that way about Sam's career, too," Michelle said. She sipped her wine, curious to know but not willing to ask if Sloan meant what she said.

The men returned from the lake and shook water on the ladies.

"Cut it out!" Sloan yelled.

"Knock it off! Knock it off!" Sam called.

Alan said, "More beer!" He opened the cooler and pulled out a can of Budweiser, popped the top and took a long swig.

A cooling breeze caressed them under the tarpaulin. The men drank beer and the women drank a German Auslese, relaxing in lawn chairs or sitting on the sand watching little Jason run gleefully in and out of the water. He plopped himself down in three inches of water and splashed in it for a while with his little plastic shovel and grinned a joyous grin. Then, after two attempts, he stood up and returned to the beach to plop himself there, oblivious of the adults watching him. After a time in the sand, and having dug a small hole between his legs, he made for the water again with the fine sand sticking to his butt and legs and little crotch.

"Why do parents like to let their boys run around naked?" Alan asked as Buck handed him another beer.

Buck sat in the sand beside him. "Well, it's better than cleaning all the clothes he would soil if he had them on."

"Yeah, but you see pictures of it all the time, little boys running around naked."

Sloan and Michelle laughed as Jason ran in small circles in the sand. His private parts flopped when he jumped.

"It's because he's so cute!" Sloan laughed. "He's a little angel."

Alan was not completely sure why he felt argumentative. "But you never see little girls running around naked. I think this running around naked thing is prejudicial toward little boys."

"Would you like to see little girls running around naked?" Kathleen asked him.

Alan looked at her. She was not what he would call enticing, although she was certainly not unattractive. As she sat cross-legged in the lawn chair, her stomach under her blouse showing the presence of their second child, he decided she was pleasant enough, although somewhat homely. Her red hair was short, and the white baseball cap she wore to protect her tender face from the sun made her head look almost like that of a man's. She wore wide lens prescription sunglasses balanced on an ample nose that, despite the protection of the tarpaulin, she had coated with a white greasy sun screen.

"Depends on the girl," Sam finished for him.

Alan looked squarely at Kathleen. "I think you see little boys running around naked because woman, their mothers and their friends, think it is so cute to see their little tallywackers flopping in the breeze and their dads like it because it shows off to the world that their little boy has one and proud of it. But for little girls to run around naked in front of men is not as culturally acceptable ... men with their dirty minds and all."

"No," Michelle said, "Some wait until they get older and can do it for a living."

With some effort, Kathleen pushed herself out of the lawn chair and stood up. "Well, I'm not putting my child on display. I'm just saving time." She turned to her son. "Come on, my little exhibitionist ... it's time for you to get dressed for your nap."

Kathleen disappeared into the tent she and Buck would share with Sam and Michelle. Jason did not follow her but wandered around for a minute as if in search of something important, then walked into the other tent.

"I think he's cute," Michelle said, "and he's free."

"He's free, but he's also confused," Sloan said, and rose to retrieve him.

He came out of the tent just as she reached the opening.

"Whatcha been doin'?" she asked him.

"My ting!" he said and walked off to find his mother. Sloan looked inside.

"Oh boy!" she said loud enough for all to hear.

Alan got up and strode to the tent. "What is it?"

"I think he disagrees with you and wants to let you know the only way a little boy knows how."

"Well feces," Alan said as he glanced inside the tent.

"That's right!" Sam laughed looking from behind him.

"Double feces!" Alan said.

"Don't say that!" Sloan laughed. "He might!"

"I'll get something to take care of this," Buck said.

"No problem," Alan said. "Leave it ... we'll just change tents."

"Wait a minute," Michelle interjected. "I had nothing to do with this. I'm staying in the clean tent with you guys. An innocent bystander shouldn't have to pay for this."

"You don't want to sleep in the same tent with a dirty old man, do you?" Alan looked at her soft brown eyes.

"Between a dirty old man and that ..." She pointed. "... I'll take my chances with the dirty old man."

CHAPTER NINETEEN

The heat of the afternoon intensified, keeping them under the tarpaulin or in the tents. After several more beers, Alan closed his eyes, drifting into semi-conscious awareness. He heard Jason telling his mother he did not need a nap. He could hear the incoherent buzz of conversation coming from the tent where Sam and Michelle had taken refuge from the cloudless summer sky. The drone of Sam's voice made Alan think of Ernie, an indulgence he had not allowed himself for many months.

He recalled the Sunday afternoon when, curious where and how his friend was spending the valuable commodity of free time, he had covertly followed Ernie's pale-yellow Volkswagen into an older section of Tampa near the Air Force base.

From a vantage point a block away, he had stopped and watched Ernie enter a small house in much need of repair and yard work. After several minutes when he did not see Ernie reappear, Alan got out of his car, adjusted his sunglasses, and walked toward the house, all the while watching to see if anyone was aware of, or cared about, his presence.

Behind the cover of an ancient oak tree in an empty lot across the street, Alan peered covertly as Ernie emerged from the house with a young woman, who, at one time in her life, had probably been more interested in being attractive than being a mother. Two energetic children scampered for the Volkswagen ahead of them as if they had played this scene many times before.

Alan moved to hide himself quickly behind the large trunk when one of the children, a skinny dark-haired girl, glanced his way. When he dared to peek around the tree again, her soft brown eyes met his, and she stared wordlessly from the edge of the street as if having asked him a question he could not understand.

Ernie, the woman and the little boy, seemingly unaware of Alan's presence, climbed into the small vehicle and coaxed the young girl in with them. With one last glimpse at the shadows under the tree, the girl ran silently to the car, crawling over Ernie's lap into the rear seat. They drove away in the direction where Alan's Camaro was parked.

The following Monday, Ernie was uncharacteristically quiet. Over a beer at the Officer's Club, Alan asked if he felt okay.

"Fine," Ernie said, watching Alan as if trying to find a way to negotiate a business contract. "How was your weekend?"

Alan was caught, and he knew it. There was no need to act the innocent. "You know how it was."

Ernie coughed and looked quickly around the room. "I know about part of it."

"Is this something I'm not supposed to know? Something the Air Force should not know?"

Ernie shook his head. "No. It's just something."

"Something ..."

Ernie was silent.

"What are they to you?" Alan did not mean to be harsh, but he could think of no other way to ask.

"Just people."

"Just?"

"Alan," he said heavily. "It's personal."

"But it's not, uh, they're not ..."

"No." Ernie looked quickly around the dimly lit bar room.

Surprised, Alan felt put upon that his friend was being so non-committal. He worked a different angle. "How did you meet them?"

Ernie shrugged uncomfortably. "I was riding my bike near the bay, in that park west of the base. They were there, although I didn't know it at the time. All I saw was the little boy floundering in the water."

"Drowning?" Alan said. He felt a slight, involuntary shudder.

"Yes."

Alan was stunned. "And you saved him?"

Ernie nodded. "There was no one else there who could."

"What about sharks?" Alan teased half seriously.

Ernie grimaced. "It didn't matter at the time."

Alan contemplated the implications. If he had been the one on the bike instead of Ernie, the kid would probably be dead now. Or they both would be. After a moment, he said, "You never told me anything ... I never saw anything in the paper."

"There was no reason ..."

"You saved a kid's life. You're a hero!"

"No," Ernie said simply. "My life was never in danger."

Alan frowned and nodded. "So you got attached to the kid."

"I liked them both. They don't have much. Their father is some local toad who left them ... he never married her."

"And you feel obligated?"

"No. I feel good."

"You take them places?"

"And they do the same for me."

Alan had not completely understood. "Is what you're doing part of the base good will thing?"

"No. I don't like to get wrapped up with things on the base. Things like that always seem like self-serving, political PR."

"There must be some other reason why you do this for them."

Ernie seemed embarrassed that Alan knew so much and was trying to find out so much more. "They're just kids. And already life has dumped on them. They're not nearly so unlucky as others, but these I can help. I can reach them. The question is, what will they grow up thinking? Hate? Or hope. It may help them to know someone outside their world cares."

"Oh."

After another beer, Ernie said, "Why don't you go with me next Sunday?"

Feeling at once uncomfortable and out of place, Alan had gone with his friend, but his concern was born of curiosity rather than compassion, and therefore not genuine. When they left to return to the base, looking to express some emotion, Alan said, "I feel so sorry for them."

Ernie stopped abruptly at a traffic light. "They don't need pity, Alan! Pity is too easy. Pity is our problem. It's too easy to say 'it's such a shame' and let it go at that." He had then looked out the window of the car and said, "These little cherubs matter too much to be pawns in an empathy game."

Alan put his hand to his forehead to block the sun as he opened his eyes. The sun glinted off the calm water near the barren shore, but on the far side, the lake mirrored the scant puffy clouds in reflected images amid the deep blue sky above. There was no noise. Jason was sleeping now.

The water. Ernie had saved a little child from the same water that had abruptly ended his life. Alan had felt something for the kids, but pity was not enough to make a difference.

It was very late when darkness began to cover this part of the earth. The late setting of the sun and the heat of the Spanish summer removed any need for a campfire, assuming they would have been able to round up enough dry wood.

The sky was clear, the moon three days past new. Sloan declined Alan's invitation to sleep outside with him.

"Stay in the tent," she said. "With me." She flashed her long lashes at him.

"I came camping to sleep under the stars. A tent is for when it's cold or it rains. Not much chance for either here."

They had the tent to themselves, but he knew nothing would happen if he stayed inside with her. She would never do anything the least bit provocative while there were people so close, even in her quiet love. She just wanted him with her, to do what she was doing.

This night, he preferred the romance of the stars.

After the others retired inside the tents, Alan reclined on the sleeping bag, watching the heavens, waiting and hoping to see a shooting star. Looking south, he spotted Sloan's Zodiac sign, Scorpius, and thought he saw a satellite drift across it.

He was awake an hour later, unable to sleep, not wanting to lose the serenity of the night. He sat up and looked at the tents some twenty feet away. They was no movement, no noise. Standing and stretching, his eyes followed the curve of the water's edge to the north. He glanced once more at the tents, then walked away from them along the shore line, stopping when their camp was but a shadow in the distance.

He looked at the dark water, contemplating his next move. Years earlier, his father had paraphrased Mark Twain, telling Alan that courage was simply the mastery of fear. Alan had decided he wanted more than to simply master his fear. He wanted to be devoid of it. That desire made him reckless at times, but his greatest fear was being accused of cowardice.

He stripped, hiding his underwear in a leg of his jeans just in case, and walked cautiously into the water that seemed much cooler than it had at midday. He felt exhilarated in his nakedness, but lowered his chest gently, disturbing the waters only slightly, watching the small ripples rush away from his body. When the water was deeper, he stopped and looked to the shore, making sure he was not too far away.

A figure was standing at the water's edge. He lowered himself until only his head was above water and looked to the south toward the tents. He was a long way from them, perhaps even too far to yell if he had to.

Looking again at the figure, he could tell by the stance it was female. He felt less threatened. Perhaps it was Sloan. Working his hands and feet below the surface, he glided toward the shore.

The woman did not appear aware of his presence. Her hands were in the pockets of her loosely fitting shorts, and she was staring at the distant shore. Closer now, he recognized her.

"Michelle?"

She jumped with a start as her hands went to her throat, then looked in the direction of his voice. "Alan?"

He stood in the chest-deep water. His heart was pounding, but he could not be sure it was from the fear he had felt moments earlier.

She put her hands back into her pants pockets and walked down the shoreline toward him. "You scared me. You weren't in your sleeping bag. I figured you had gone off in the woods for something."

"What are you doing out here?"

"I came out to do the same thing I thought you were doing."

"Oh."

"Are you?"

"Michelle!"

She giggled.

Pushing against the sandy bottom of the lake, he waded toward her until the water was at his stomach.

She kicked his clothes before knowing they were there. "I'm sorry." She looked at them. "My night vision isn't so good."

"I hope that's true."

She knelt to straighten his clothes.

"Don't do that. Really. It's okay."

She shook the sand from his underwear before tucking them back in his jeans. She stood, her hands once again in her pockets, and glanced back in the direction of the cars and tents. "It's a beautiful night. A good night for a swim."

"You should join me." His heart leapt in his throat as he said the words, making them come out raspy and guttural.

She turned to look at him and twisted slightly on her bare feet in the sand. She was silent for a moment, just long enough to give Alan the impression she might seriously consider doing so, then laughed her pretty laugh. "I don't think that would be a good idea."

He could see she was smiling. "Why not? It's nice."

"But hard to explain," she said. "If someone came out."

"You mean, if we were caught."

"Yeah. Well, no. Not caught. We wouldn't be being caught."

"No." He felt a flush of relief.

She looked at him then back toward the tents. "I think I'm going to bed. Enjoy your swim."

"Did you do what you came out here to do?" He moved closer to shore, lowering himself to a sitting position to keep his hips below the water.

She looked above his head at the stars and the clear night sky. "No. But if you'll stay down here, I'll be able to, closer to them." She nodded with her head as she lowered her gaze. "Nearer the tents."

She turned and walked away from him.

"I'll stay." He said.

Michelle laughed over her shoulder. "You'd better. And don't try to peek, either!"

"Trust me."

"I have no choice."

As she approached the tents, she turned to look back along the edge of the lake. She could dimly see him standing on the shore, his body silhouetted against the sand and water. She thought it was his back.

CHAPTER TWENTY

It was Friday night, and the bar came alive. Around 4:00 P.M., the early birds began to arrive. They ordered their drinks, and Pepe served them quietly. His perpetually serious countenance portrayed the single-mindedness of his work while, deep inside, his thoughts turned to the place where he really wanted to be.

It was a pretty chalet in the mountains near Segovia where he had grown up. His aging parents still lived there, but he found little time to visit them these days. His mother grew red geraniums in long, thin planters in the windows of the white house, and his father kept a horse in the small barn in the back. The air was crisp and clean, and there was not much noise except for the bees and the horse and the sound of the wind.

At 1700 hours, the pace quickened as more people entered the Officer's Club bar in larger numbers, and, by 1730, the noise level began to rise with the smoke from the cigarettes and a few cigars. The wives of fighter pilots, having either driven in together or met in the lobby, arrived in groups of two or three. From time to time, a lone wife entered and quickly joined an established group. Single female officers, although sometimes alone, were usually with a group of male officers from the same office, and almost always in the uniform of the day.

Fighter pilots from the 613th Squids gathered and intermingled with those of the 612th "Eagles" and the 614th "Lucky Devils."

Several female nurses were together in civilian clothes, mostly dresses. More of them would arrive after working the late shift. A few young Spanish women also attended the bar regularly on Friday nights before hitting the discos in Madrid. Although they had no military connections, no one ever stopped them from going into the bar, and no one ever asked any of them to leave except to go with them.

Non-flying officers wearing Air Force blues or fatigues gathered in small groups at the edge of the bar or at tables. Those that were or had at one time been fighter pilots would talk with the men in the green Nomex flight suits, have a beer or two with them, then, in consideration of priorities, return to the group of officers they now worked with to talk a different kind of shop.

Sloan and Jennifer arrived to discover their husbands were not yet there. Each ordered a white wine as they continued the same idle conversation they had enjoyed during the drive to the base. While they talked and sipped wine and waited, Buck walked in with Denise.

"Where's Kathleen? Waiting for the sitter? Should I call her?" Jennifer said in one breath.

"No. She's at home, at the Oaks." Buck squeezed his thick neck with his left hand. He turned to Denise. "Let me buy you a drink."

"Thanks," Denise answered, looking at Sloan and Jennifer. "White wine."

As Buck waited for Pepe to pour the drinks, Michelle entered the bar alone. Her small purse hung from her right shoulder by a long strap, her hands were shoved casually into the side pockets of a sleeveless sun dress that modestly accentuated her features. She stood near the entrance for a moment with a preoccupied look on her face and expectantly searched the room, her brown eyes darting from group to group, catching the attention of the men as her eyes left them. Seeing Sloan, Denise, and Jennifer, she smiled and walked to them, seemingly unaware of the many male eyes that followed her path.

Buck returned with Denise's white wine, and gin for himself. "Hey there!" Buck said to Michelle. He put his arm around her thin waist and pulled her shoulder into his hefty chest.

Michelle's hands remained in her pockets. Leaning away from him, she smiled and said, "How's it goin'?"

"Where's Sam?" he asked, not releasing his grip.

"I don't know!" She laughed. "That guy was supposed to meet me here, you know?"

"You can never count on that guy."

"Yeah," she smiled. "I don't know. He's a pretty good kid. He'll be around soon."

Buck put his arm back to his side. "I think he was about on his way out when I left the squadron." Surrounded by attractive young women, Buck became overly animated. As secure as he was in a fighter, so was he clumsy when away from one. Impressing women had never been his strong suit. When Bill Fisch and Sam appeared, Michelle went immediately to Sam's side, and Buck's flirtation ceased along with his self-imagined prestige.

Practically ignoring his own wife, Fisch feigned an amorous attack on Michelle, grabbing her waist and kissing her neck. "Hola, you beautiful hunk of woman!" he said loudly. "You free tonight?"

Denise put her drink to her lips, caustically watching her husband's antics but saying nothing.

Bill backed away to stand between Denise and Sloan, aloof and uncaring of the immature appearance of his act. "Gotta drain it," he announced, imitating Whiskey Wilson. He departed as quickly as he had arrived.

Michelle's thick black hair swirled gracefully as she turned her head toward Sam. Buck watched her every move. She looked back in his direction. Seeing her eyes brighten, Buck's chest heaved slightly. But she was looking beyond him. He swiveled to see Alan and Ron walking toward the group.

"At last, the dead have arisen!" Jennifer said. She flashed Ron a secretive smile and waited for him to come to her.

"They are risen indeed," Alan said, giving Sloan a shoulder hug.

Sloan looked at him quizzically. "Did your flight go well?" she asked.

He focused on her. "Well enough. We killed them."

She flinched. "Oh. Are you okay?"

"Fine." He whispered to her and kissed her cheek.

Alan followed Sam to the bar.

When they returned, Michelle took the wine Sam handed her and smiled. Her countenance beamed as she watched Sam's eyes and asked, "How was your day?"

Alan had noticed the way she always looked at Sam when he returned from a flight. It was a look that combined love with relief and gratitude, as if she was happy he had gotten to fly but happier still to have him once again safely at her side.

An image of her on a clear summer night at the water's edge of Lake Sacedon flashed in his mind. He involuntarily shook his head.

"I didn't do much," Sam answered Michelle apologetically. He looked at the ground and shuffled his feet. "We briefed a four-ship flight, but Carp and I were the only jet that actually got airborne. Everybody else aborted."

"No IFE?" Buck asked with laugh.

Sam looked at Carp. "No, we were lucky."

"The old 'Brief four, step three, taxi two, take-off one and return it IFE' was almost a player today, eh?" Buck said with a smile.

Sam nodded. "Almost."

"What does that mean?" Sloan asked. "What's 'I ... F ... E ...'?"

Sam looked at his wife. "Michelle knows what an IFE is, don't you, 'Chelle?"

The smile disappeared from her face for a moment, then returned less convincingly. "These guys are good pilots," Michelle said nudging Alan with her hip. "They can handle any inflight emergency, right?" She looked at Sam with her endearing smile and soft eyes in a way that for some reason seemed to embarrass him.

Looking around the barroom as he drank, Alan spotted Hargrove talking to the Torrejon Assistant Deputy of Operations, Lt. Colonel Lemon, who leaned on the counter in his Air Force blues. Alan lifted his glass in a brief salute to which Hargrove nodded acknowledgment. Alan looked back at Michelle. "So, have you given Sam a list of what to bring back from Aviano? Better make it a good one. This may be our last TDY to Italy for a while."

"Oh, yeah," Michelle squeezed Sam's arm. "I've got lots of plans for Italian goodies ... inlaid wood, Maniago knives, an onyx phone ..."

"Quite a shopping list," Alan said giving Sam a sympathetic frown.

"Don't be so smug," Sloan said. "You've got the same list."

Alan grinned. "Looks like you've got it all figured out."

"Yep," Sloan said, smiling cutely. "I've been snoopin' around, and I've got a wish litht ready to go." She lisped to be cute. "And it's at least as long as Sam's."

"As long as Sam's what?" Fisch said, returning with another glass of chardonnay for Denise and bourbon and coke for himself. He smirked and let out a quick laugh, but his was the only response.

Michelle grinned knowingly. "It's not his list. I'm going, too."

Buck flinched, then looked questioningly at Sam. "Wives on a TDY?"

Sam shrugged, but before he could offer an explanation, Michelle said, "It's not his choice." She smiled an easy smile, but Alan could tell she meant it.

Sloan felt a surge of painful envy. Wives were discouraged from following their husbands on TDY. Michelle did not seem concerned with any such unwritten law. Sloan glanced at Alan who said nothing.

"Are you going alone?" Sloan asked.

"Nope," Michelle answered. "We've got a car full."

Denise's lips parted, but she did not speak.

Alan looked at Ron and saw amusement on his face. "Don't you have a list?"

"I would if I were going."

Another bite of jealousy nipped at Sloan. "You're not even going?"

Ron held the moment, anticipating the reaction his announcement would bring, especially from Alan. He baited them further. "I'll be in Nevada."

Sloan's jaw dropped. "The States?"

"The land of the big BX."

"What for?" Sloan glanced at Jennifer's nodding head for confirmation.

Looking at Alan, Ron said, "I'm going to fly in the trial for the Thunderbirds." He waited for the news to soak in. He had caught them off-guard. He was pleased.

Alan said evenly, "You're going to be a Thunderbird."

"I'm going to try out for the Thunderbirds."

"Wasn't it you who told me that flying for the Thunderbirds was the last thing a real fighter pilot would want to do? What happened to those words?"

Ron grinned his stealthy grin. As Jennifer knew all too well, he liked keeping people in suspense. "I've developed new career goals."

"You mean you've changed them."

"No," Ron said. "Things never change. Your life doesn't change ... it develops."

"It'll be good for his career," Jennifer said, hoping she sounded sincere.

Alan looked from Jennifer back to Ron. "You're doing this to enhance your career?"

Ron held up his hand. "It probably wouldn't hurt, but that's not my reason."

"With all the arguments you gave me for not doing it, it's the only reason that fits," Alan countered.

Ron was silent. His smile said, I'll do it because it is what I choose to do now.

Alan gave Ron a sardonic grin. "You sly dog ... you have any other advice for me ... things I shouldn't do that you'll turn around and do the first chance you get?"

Ron covered his teeth with his lips in an act of suppression. "I'll let you know."

"You should be buying drinks," Denise said.

"I haven't made it yet," Ron protested in unconvincing humility.

"A round of cheer!" Carp demanded.

Ron recoiled defensively. "Okay, okay." He started toward the bar.

Alan followed him to an open spot at the end of the bar next to Lt. Colonels Lemon and Hargrove.

"Friends and foes!" Hargrove greeted them and offered his hand. "Good fight today, Captain Butler," he said.

Ron nodded wordlessly.

In turn, Alan took his hand, saying, "Seems we only traded blows."

"And experience," Hargrove answered.

Alan nodded, not understanding completely. He looked at Lemon. The ADO kept his hands on his glass.

"You fought a good fight today," Hargrove repeated, then turning to Lemon said, "This is Lieutenant Wayne, the fighter pilot who kicked my butt in a two-vee-two today."

"Ah," said Lemon, deliberately swirling the ice in his glass. "Lieutenant Colonel Hargrove was just telling me he thinks you're the best young F-4 pilot he's seen in a while."

Alan swallowed hard, not sure how to take the compliment obviously intended to bring the ADO's attention to him. "He nearly blew my butt out of the sky," Alan said finally.

"But you did shoot mine off," Hargrove added quickly. "And, more importantly, you were there when your leader needed you." He looked at Ron who remained silent.

"That's important," Lemon said, draining his drink and chewing on the ice. "You have to trust your lead, so he can trust you to help him when he needs it for mutual support. If a four-ship lead runs into the side of a mountain, there should be three other smoking holes around his." He chewed on more ice.

Hargrove looked away from the ADO. "Well, you did good. Keep it up." He paused. "So did you, Ron. Seems we all traded blows, as Lieutenant Wayne put it."

"Right," Ron said.

The Lt. Colonels returned to themselves, making the junior officers aware the discussion with them was ended.

Ron ordered the drinks, but his mind was elsewhere. "That was bullshit."

"The act?" Alan said. "A bit of crap, I suppose ..."

"No," Ron said. "I mean that bullshit Lemon said about leaders. This is a thinking man's Air Force, now. The days of four smoking holes are gone. That stuff about following your lead into the side of a mountain is all old Vietnam bullshit. You don't follow a bad leader into the ground to show your loyalty. You owe a lot more to yourself and your country than you do to a fool who should never have been a leader in the first place."

They returned to the group. Alan was reflective and looked away often, stealing glances at the two Lt. Colonels across the room. That was the way of the bar, Alan decided. Light conversation hiding heavy meaning. Ron was going away. The Air Force changed, despite the inertia that tried to keep it the same. Or maybe it was as Ron said ... it only developed as time required because nothing ever changed the fact that you could die in this business.

PART THREE

SECOND FALL
CHAPTER TWENTY-ONE

In late August, the dry intense heat of the Spanish summer, while building toward a crescendo, lacked the required moisture to create the refreshing thunderstorms that so often develop in other parts of the world under similar circumstances. As a result, it only got hotter, driving the Spaniards to seek relief from the heat in large scale evacuations out of the cities toward the beaches or mountains. The streets were, for the most part, deserted, shops closed, and the bars and restaurants that remained open were minimally staffed as even the small town of Torrejon de Ardoz appeared lifeless by comparison.

Bombarded by the sweltering afternoon heat, Alan labored awkwardly down the steps of Parque de Cataluña. He sweated freely under his green Nomex flight suit, the unwieldy canvas A-3 bag bouncing heavily against his leg with every step. Sorry to be leaving Sloan again, he was nonetheless ready for the cooler air that awaited him at the foot of the Italian Alps. He heaved the bulky bag into the backseat of the Citroën.

Across the street, the restaurant and bar, El Rincon del Jamon, was open for business, though quite nearly devoid of patrons. The letters of various colors that spelled out the name of the bar, although appearing lively and gay at night, looked somewhat ridiculous and out of place in the bright, hot afternoon sun. Driving slowly past the bar in idle curiosity, Alan noticed two men walking toward the edge of the street. Beyond a parked car, he caught sight of a small brown short-haired dog lying at the edge of the road, panting heavily.

At first, he thought the dog was either a pet or perhaps a stray the men were going to chase it away. The dog barked threateningly. As the men stepped back, Alan noticed the dog's insides were flowing from its body through a large gash in its stomach, its warm, wet viscera lying on the hot and dirty street. A short, bloody trail was drying out quickly, marking the place where a passing car had slashed the dog open to where it now lay dying. Able to go no further, the dog had plopped its desecrated body here to recover what strength it could while awaiting whatever would happen next.

When the men retreated, the dog closed its eyes again, panting heavily, fighting the pain and heat in the only way it knew how.

Alan accelerated away from the scene, but the picture of the dying dog burned in his mind.

Pulling up to the squadron building, he still carried the image of the disemboweled dog, its eyes shut, its tongue hanging heavily from its dry mouth, its breath quick and shallow, vainly trying to comfort itself. Should human thoughts be attributed to the dog, he imagined it would be, 'This has not been my day. What did I do to deserve this?'

But, more likely, if the dog could reason at all, it would only be to think, 'So, in the short journey that is my life, this is what happens next.'

Aviano cannot be found on many maps of Italy, being one of the smaller, less significant towns that apparently many World Atlas makers find unworthy of the time required to accurately plot what would be the town's unique dot. Like so many small European towns claiming little if any cultural or historical significance, Aviano induces no inquisitive passion from the undiscerning traveler who might see the town's name on a detailed road map or highway sign, other than for him or her to momentarily consider, absent mindedly, if there might be anything noteworthy to be experienced there. Should this traveler, by way of a wrong turn, find his automobile wandering through the streets of the little town, his only concern might be to find his way out again, carrying with him only the experience of confusion which would be forgotten in thirty minutes time.

But to the eye of the true lover, the northeastern corner of Italy is a beautifully serene garden, as yet untouched by the most damaging aspects of man's progress. A little over one hundred miles south of Salzburg,

Austria, in the southern foothills of the Alps, Aviano is nestled in breath taking countryside that matches if not exceeds the tranquility of the Austrian city.

Although tourists might often miss the beauty that is northern Italy, spending their time on the dirty canals of Venice or the even dirtier streets of more southern Italian cities, Soviet Intelligence was intimately familiar with it. They knew of Aviano's location precisely, with the most possible accuracy known to man, "right down to the gnat's ass," as a fighter pilot would say. The Soviets planned to obliterate this base in a pre-emptive strike, thereby negating the devastating effect that nuclear loaded American fighters, if successfully launched, would have had on any Warsaw Pact offensive through Hungary and what was then Yugoslavia.

This small base served as the Forward Operating Location of the 401st Tactical Fighter Wing. The open green land surrounding it, a pleasantly quiet corner of the earth that would be scorched by war, was their playground.

Stepping off the C-141 cargo plane at Aviano Air Base, Alan raised his head from the weight of the A-3 bag and took in his first eyeful of Italy. There were the usual, drab and, for some reason on this day, depressing concrete hangars and the assorted equipment required for military aviation. Looking back toward the runway, he saw a cornfield beyond the fence that marked the base boundary.

Deplaning behind him, Whiskey Wilson watched with amused interest as Alan's head swiveled about, his intense awareness glowing on his sunburned face. Whiskey glanced reflectively beyond the hangars. "They've taken the mountains down again," he said so Alan would hear.

Alan looked at him, briefly diverting his attention from the awkward bag. "What's that?" he said heavily, trying to show interest. The canvas bag encumbered his steps as he walked with Whiskey. He stopped to change hands. "Where are they supposed to be?"

"Well," Whiskey drawled, "when they're up, you usually see them over there." He pointed to the north, beyond the hangars.

Alan saw only haze. He tried to think of something to say that was somewhere between casual interest and overwhelmed amazement. "I guess that haze would be pretty dangerous to the wrong people."

"It can be if you don't think about it. You might be cruising along on a low level and suddenly find yourself in a face-off with cumulo-granite in a corner you can't get out of."

"Humph," Alan answered, climbing on a blue Air Force bus parked near an open hangar. He threw his bag on a seat behind him and sat down. The others tossed their bags where they could find a place and took the remaining vacant seats.

The blue bus followed a small road that wound around the perimeter of the base. Hangars and administration buildings were to the left, open fields beyond the high fence to the right. Some of the fields were planted in corn, others were bare but green. The bus paralleled the runway driving northeast before coming to a grouping of concrete Tab Vees, hardened shelters that resembled huge concrete culverts buried halfway in the ground. A circular taxiway ran among them with stems of the taxiway branching off to each of the Tab Vees where several 613th F-4s were already parked.

The bus turned left into an open gate and stopped in front of an old, moderately sized green building with a flat roof. Stepping off the bus, an unusual sight caught Alan's eye. Next to the sidewalk that led to the building was a three-foot square concrete platform. Rising out of the platform was a heavy-duty spring of some six to eight inches in diameter showing signs of rust and age. On top of the spring sat a small, fat, faded merry-go-round horse that looked like it could accommodate an eight-year old child. Grass had overgrown part of the building, the shell driveway and the horse's platform.

In the haze, below the overcast skies, the building looked like a dismally aged apparition from past wars.

"Welcome to your new home!" Major Sherman greeted the newly arriving warriors.

Alan looked with disbelief at the green edifice. "Bullshit!" he said under his breath. "That wouldn't even survive a conventional attack. And a nuke would only laugh at it!"

Whiskey said, "Not a chance, but who wants to survive a nuke attack anyway? It's just a place to hang our go-fast suits until we take to the air to stop the dirty rotten Commie pinkie bastards. When the bomb hits here, most of us will be fighting the airborne war."

Being an Air Force fighter pilot stationed in Europe made a war seem closer. Now, looking around at the fighters parked in front of Tab Vees in the northeast corner of Italy, it seemed imminent.

"Most of us?" the concern in Alan's voice was obvious.

"If you haven't noticed," Whiskey said, "there ain't enough jets to go around."

"They're working on a hardened Ops building in the Zulu area," Major Sherman said in consolation, "and new improved Tab Vees. That's where we would fight the war."

"As long as it doesn't come in the next two or three years," Whiskey added. "Seems there's a minor problem with the doors." He smirked at the unspoken question on Alan's face before saying, "They won't close."

Alan blurted, "You're kidding!" He felt suddenly vulnerable, as he realized any attempts to survive a nuclear war would be futile. "What good's a hardened shelter if you can't close the damn doors?" Something about Aviano, perhaps the dreary haze of the day, made a war, any war, seem almost unavoidable. "The doors won't close," he repeated.

"Nope."

"Will they ever?"

Major Sherman grinned mischievously and glanced sideways at Whiskey. With that grin on his round face that anchored his large head atop his five-foot six frame, Sherman looked every bit like an elf in a flight suit. "The contractor skipped town."

Whiskey stopped to look at him. "Are you slippin' us the high hard one?"

"They finished just enough, then took the money and ran."

"Those communist bastards!"

Clarence Bailey, a newly arrived WSO followed behind them, listening. Eager to join in on this fighter jock conversation, he said, "Typical 'screw the US ploy' again, eh?"

"Something like that," Sherman said, glancing at Clarence over his shoulder as they entered the squadron building.

Inside, there was a large room to the right with folding chairs arranged in rows in the middle and several rather battered looking green vinyl chairs with matching sofas. An old refrigerator stood rusting in one corner next to a nasty looking sink. Some of the squadron members were gathered in the room, sitting in the folding chairs and on the sofas or standing with coffee mugs in hand near the coffee machine, the latter having been one of the first essentials to be transferred from Torrejon to Aviano.

Shooter turned to note the arrival of this latest group of squadron pilots. He held a cigarette in one hand and his coffee in the other. The zipper on his flight suit was open to the TDY level, and his collar was turned up. He singled out Whiskey as the new arrival most deserving of his attention. "How was the 'Lump'?" Shooter used the colloquial term for the transportation of personnel via a cargo aircraft with more than a hint of contempt. After all, he had flown a fighter to Italy, these guys had only ridden the "Lump."

"Like one of your briefings, Shooter," Whiskey returned as he walked through the room. "Two and a half boring hours of solid bullshit."

"Wrong!" Shooter countered. He put his cigarette in his mouth, checked his collar and returned to his conversation with Carp.

Major Sherman pulled Alan to the side. "After the inbrief, get all your gear together, and I'll take you over to Victor Alert."

Alan jerked his head. "What for?"

"You and Nick Dawson are going on alert this evening to relieve Ron Butler and Sam Christopher." Major Sherman gave Alan a look that said, 'I hate to break it to you, kid, but that's the way it is.'

Alan was incredulous. "My first day in Aviano, and already I have to sit the Pad?"

"You're certified. It's your time in the barrel."

"But I need to fly!" Alan wanted to say more but realized the futility of his arguments. He was angry. That would not help either.

"It's no big deal. Three and a half days and you'll be done."

"Why me right now?"

"It's your turn in the barrel," Sherman repeated with a touch of heat.

Alan said nothing more. It was just as well that he did not. Sitting nuclear alert was not difficult and carried with it only a moderate amount of crew harassment. Some even volunteered for it just to get away. But the thought of being out of the loop and away from the guys who would actually be flying fighters, if only for three days, was almost maddening. Alan sighed. "When do I go?"

"Right after the inbrief. Pay attention, if you plan to take the money on the range." Sherman stroked him with the experience of a man who had been there himself.

Aviano's Weapons Liaison Officer, Dusty Rhoads, gave the inbrief, complete with the standard slides and sub-standard jokes.

"Because of the small confines of our little range here," he said, "you'll probably be pulling g's throughout most if not all of the conventional pattern to stay within the range boundaries ..."

"Shit hot!" Shooter yelled from the back of the room. And he meant it. Pulling g's all the time was what fighter pilots did. That was real men's stuff. That was "Shit hot."

"Shit hot!" Carp Fisch parroted.

After the inbrief, Alan and Nick Dawson loaded their A-3 bags and flying gear into the back of a blue Air Force "six-pack" pick-up truck. Major Sherman drove them down the perimeter road to the Victor Alert pad at the far end of the field.

As they approached, Alan became immediately aware of the difference between this secure area and any others on the base. Two tall steel fences surrounded the complex which consisted of four hardened shelters for the aircraft, a long, flat building that housed the rooms for the alert crews, a covered storage area as large as a Tab Vee, but open at both ends, a guard building at the entrance, and a cafeteria. The double fences were some twenty feet apart and topped with razor-sharp rolls of concertina wire nestled in branches of barbed wire.

Air Force security police patrolled as sentries between the two fences. Entry by foot into the complex required being cleared individually by an airman at the guard shack. Vehicles entered and left the area by way of two large gates that were closed and opened by electrical motors that moved the gates back and forth along rails in the asphalt.

Major Sherman parked the six-pack in the small parking lot marked "Victor Alert Vehicles Only." Alan and Nick carried their equipment to the entry gate.

"After the change-over," Sherman called to them, "you guys can drive Ron and Sam back to the Mike area in the Victor truck. Someone will be waiting there to take them to the other side of the base." He turned to go. "That person will probably be me, so hurry it up."

"You can't hurry a nuke," Nick joked. He looked at Alan who was not smiling. "Ah, come on, Puppy," he slapped him lightly on the back, like more of a touch. "We'll have a good time ... it'll be a barrel of laughs! After all," he stood back in regal stance. "You got your main most woozo with you here!"

They stepped through the smaller, man-sized gate that closed electronically behind them. "I'll go first," Nick suggested. "You wait here behind the red line."

Nick walked to the window and exchanged his regular badge for the special yellow Victor Alert badge. He stepped from the window and walked through an eight-foot revolving gate, which looked like a rototiller turned on its side. On the far side, he turned to wait for Alan.

They don't make it easy to get in this place, Alan thought, looking at Nick through the big prison-like gate. How much harder was it to get out?

After he had exchanged his badge, the guard yelled, "Turn-style for one!" and Alan heard the faint click as the turn-style was unlocked. He awkwardly maneuvered the bags through the narrow space, walking sideways as the gate turned. He stepped out the far side and heard a louder click as it locked into place behind him.

He was inside Victor. He looked toward the Tab Vees in the distance, aware that one of them shielded a Phantom he knew how to fly, loaded with a nuclear bomb he was trained to deliver.

He followed Nick around the cafeteria and into the crew lounge where they found Ron and Sam sitting, each absorbed in a paper back novel.

"Free at last! Free at last! Thank the Lord, you're free at last!" Nick said loudly, announcing their entrance. ""The A-team has arrived! You guys will soon be relieved to pursue a life of debauchery, along with the rest of the decadent free world," he said with a large grin.

Sam moved only his eyes to look at them. "Where the hell have you been? Do you have any idea what it's like when you think that at any moment you will be relieved from this fucking hell-hole and that moment just keeps slipping by unanswered?"

"I know, I know," Nick said a little softer, holding his hands toward Sam in a soothing gesture. He turned his head and looked glancingly between Sam and the floor as he spoke. "Don't get upset, Sammy boy. We had another one of them marathon inbriefs!" He lingered on the word 'marathon' to get the proper effect. "Filibuster style in complete and nauseating detail, full of dull speeches and duller jokes, and every swinging dick that wears an eagle on his shoulder at this base had to have his say."

Sam closed his book and stood up. Ron, near the end of a chapter, remained at his reading.

"But we survived it, and now we have arrived!" Nick started up again. "And we understand there's a nuclear bird around here somewhere, so if you guys will sign it over to us, you'll be free for a night of revelry at the Aviano NCO Club."

When Sam did not answer right away, Nick looked humorously at the book he was reading. "Must be a good one, Sammy," Nick said. "Is it a 'who-done-it'? Or more like a 'who's-doing-it-to-who'."

Sam placed a page-bent copy of *The Odyssey* on a nearby table. "Let's go."

Night was falling as the four of them, with Alan and Nick lugging their flight gear, walked out of the crew building. For the first time, Alan saw the nuke loaded F-4 in the lighted, open Tab Vee a hundred feet from them across the taxiway. In the twilight, the bright lights inside the shelter illuminated the fighter, glowing in marked contrast to the night, bearing witness to the fact that while the rest of the world slept, this aircraft was awake and alive and ready to perform the sole function that might well be its destiny. In the increasing darkness, their approach to this armed war machine gave Alan the ominous feeling that, right now, this fighter and its weapon constituted the only things in the world that were real.

Sam and Ron appeared tired and bored, but Nick walked lightly toward the Tab Vee as if to display both familiarity and lack of concern. He had never been called out to fly the mission in the past, and they would not be called upon this time, either. No one was ever called.

Two airmen crew chiefs silently joined them as they approached the Tab Vee.

Alan looked at the lights and the guards, and the reality of the Iranians and the hostages and the volatile Middle East crept into the back of his mind as the thought came to him: We could really go!

Just outside the "No Lone Zone," a security policeman dressed in camouflage fatigues and holding a loaded M-16 compared the badges Sam and Ron wore with his paperwork. Satisfied, the sky cop cleared them and their two crew chiefs to enter the area he himself had never been within. Sam and Ron stepped over the low chain suspended across the front of the Tab Vee entrance, doing so simultaneously to insure neither was in the area alone. Once inside, they cleared Alan and Nick in with them.

As they approached the jet, Ron said casually, "If we get scrambled before we sign the bomb over to you, Sam and I will respond, and you guys get clear of the area."

Nick furrowed his brow. "Okay, we'll do it."

Ron motioned to Alan. "Here's the paperwork on the bomb. You can check it over to make sure the number's right. You'll be signing for it after we look at the bomb. From that time on, it's yours." He handed the folder with the papers to Alan.

Alan followed Ron under the left wing of the aircraft to the belly where the weapon hung ready. He was surprised at the relatively small size of the 'device', as it was called when people did not care to refer to it as a nuclear bomb. It was shiny and sleek with a pointed nose, and the outward appearance of the weapon casing was indicative more of the care taken in maintaining the device than the awesome destructive force that waited patiently within.

"You can see the numbers match," Ron was saying. He opened a small panel on the side of the projectile. "You can check the numbers with me to insure they're right for the line. No one else will come out here and check up on you to make sure they are. They don't have to. That's your life, your safe escape from the explosion. I don't have to tell you if these numbers are incorrect, you could hurt yourself in a very permanent way. Fragmentation damage from a nuke blast is just a tiny bit different from that of a Mark-82 500 pounder. It could ruin your whole day." He laughed, and Alan laughed with him.

"You satisfied?" Ron asked.

"Look's good to me," Alan answered trying to appear both serious and casual.

Ron ripped Alan's name tag off the Velcro that held it to his flight suit and placed it on an empty Velcro patch on the bomb that served no obvious purpose.

"Then it's your nuke!" Ron said smiling. "Sign here."

Alan looked reflectively for a moment at his name attached to the nuclear bomb before signing for it. He removed his name tag from the weapon and replaced it on his flight suit. He had already removed his other patches, "sterilizing" his flight suit for nuclear alert. The name tag was his one remaining means of identification.

"You've just bought yourself a bomb," Ron said. "Want to take it for a spin?"

"Not today."

With the necessary work inside the shelter finished, all six men left the No Lone Zone, Ron and Sam doing so last and together. They finished the required paperwork, then Sam and Ron trudged back toward the crew quarters with their flying gear flung over their shoulders.

"We'll be right with you," Alan said.

Ron waved without looking back.

Alan briefed the bored-faced airman on the entry procedures and the distant recognition number they would use as a signal if they were scrambled and came to the jet on the run. The guard looked as if he had heard this speech too many times before, but it angered Alan that his disinterest was so blatant. He considered saying something in admonishment but changed his mind.

The dark of a moonless night blanketed Aviano as Alan and Nick walked wordlessly back to the crew quarters. Alan could see spots of light in the sky to the north that betrayed the hiding place of the mountains. The corn fields around the base bore a darkness in sharp contrast to the bright yellow lights surrounding the perimeter of the Victor Alert Area. The fences and areas several yards beyond them were illuminated by strong flood lights. The concrete apron between the crew lounge and the Tab Vees was relatively dark, but there were enough lights that anyone walking or running toward the Tab Vees would be seen soon enough for the guards to react.

Behind them, the fighter remained still and silent, poised and ready in its bright fortification. Alan's thoughts turned to those of war as he searched within himself to understand what he was feeling. It was almost spiritual, like being in a church dimly lit with candles, or on a mountain flooded with moonlight.

For the first time in his life, he was responsible, or at least partially so, for a nuclear weapon. If they ever took to the air with it, the bomb was his. His country trusted him to deliver it where and how he was told.

In a conventional war, shooting down MiGs and blowing up bridges would be fun. The inherent danger would make it exhilarating because of the equal possibilities of death and survival.

The idea of nuclear conflict did not thrill him. It was too final. No MiG killing. No glory. No one left to praise him as a hero. Just two sides systematically annihilating each other. Not a fun war.

As he lay back on the bed of his small room in the crew quarters, he thought about the situation. It was all so peculiar - the small room, the bright lights, the armed guards, the high fences, the waiting. The bomb. It was so real that it departed from what he had always considered to be reality and formed its own quiet corner of naked truth.

He was sitting upon a brain child of technology that, if called upon, he was trained to drop on a specified target with no questions asked. He was not in the decision loop. He could not say "Wait ... let's think about this ..."

"Come. Let us reason together," he said, laughing out loud.

If the balloon went up now, on this night, he really was not a part of his squadron. They would prepare for and fight in combat that would be, at least for a time, conventional. But he and Nick would be called upon to go, to respond to their aircraft, start the engines and wait for a message that could very well direct them in their sole contribution to the war, and perhaps the final act of their lives.

They would take off into the night and turn toward their starting point. They would then fly at very low-level in the dark – which they were not trained to do - into a foreign country they had never seen - alone, armed with a nuclear bomb and nothing else, while every available defense of that country sought to zero in on them and blast them from the sky before they could deliver their payload of devastation. And the defenders would be highly motivated, being certainly aware of the destructive power this lone F-4 carried on its belly.

He knew he would never return from a mission like that, though he had been trained not to think that way. His part of the war would last but an hour or so, but in that hour, he would fight a lifetime's worth. And that was the whole game, to go down doing something that mattered.

CHAPTER TWENTY-TWO

At mid-morning, Alan became aware that he was waking up in yet another strange bed. A beading, clammy sweat adhered to his forehead and cheeks like the remnants of some limbic glue that had unforgivingly held his face against the boiling surface of subconscious rage until, screaming in agony, those edges of his mind as yet untouched by the madness had mustered the strength to pull him back from the dream's horror and into the realm of conscious calm.

The sun, rising over a beautiful clear morning in northern Italy, pierced the one window of the small room, forming a faint array of pale colors above Alan's head. The foggy veil of disorientation clouded his mind like ghosts of denied memory as he stared at the shallow walls of the room. He remained very still, waiting for his waking mind to tell him where he was and what he was supposed to do. As a certain familiarity gradually returned, the brightness of the sun shining through the window told him this day was totally different from the one before.

He showered and shaved quickly in the community bathroom, slipped into his flight suit and combat boots and walked outside into the day.

The mountains, he thought, stepping outside. They put them back.

Silhouetted against the clear blue cloudless sky, they were beautiful, tan and green. The foothills closer in looked soft and inviting. In the distance, he could make out one or two of the jagged peaks more characteristic of the Alps. The absent roar of jet noise made the morning very quiet. In the distance, the lonely chimes of a Catholic church beckoned the faithful to mass.

There would be no thunderous sound of freedom over Aviano on this Sunday. But one day was like the next at Victor.

He walked the short distance to the cafeteria. Nick was already inside eating breakfast with the Victor Alert NCO. Several security police were eating or talking or both in booths that lined two walls of the dining room. Alan stopped at Nick's table.

"What's for eats this morning?" Alan asked.

"Mornin' Puppy! Good to see you among the living." Nick eyed him with amusement behind his stylish, nonregulation glasses.

"Well, I decided I might as well get up in case the world needs me."

"The world can always count on you, Puppy." Nick grinned. "Your mind may sleep, but your conscience is untiring."

"Is breakfast worth the effort?"

Nick looked at his plate as if to confirm what he had just consumed. "Usual stuff," he said. "Powdered eggs and bacon dripping with grease, pancakes you could skim across a pond like a dry cow patty." Nick picked up a bowl and frowned. "And whatever this watered-down stuff is ... if I knew what it was, I probably wouldn't be able to eat it."

"Grits," Alan said. He looked with mock disgust at the plates on the table. "But if that cook has ever been south of the Mason-Dixon line, I'll eat my shorts." He started for the food line. "If you're hungry enough, you'll eat anything."

"They cater to that," Nick answered.

After breakfast, they strolled to the loaded fighter for the daily status check. They felt no need to rush. There was an unmistakable air of seasoned casualness about The Pad. It seemed everyone involved from the cops to the VANCO knew exactly what they were expected to do and did so with no obvious urgency. Most worked with a sense of professionalism. Some did so out of boredom. They let things flow smoothly and easily now, knowing how totally different the area would be during an alert. If they were scrambled, or "smoked" as they called it, they would do everything, up to a point, as if it was the real thing. And they would know right away if it was the real thing since, with the exception of the daily noon check, the klaxon would never sound unless it was an actual wartime aircraft alert.

Alan radioed the aircraft on status at 1025 hours.

"What do we do for the rest of the day?" he asked Nick as they walked back to the lounge.

"Whatever you want. We're only imprisoned here, not in jail. You can catch up on your reading or love letters. They generally have a stash of 16-millimeter movies to watch, some good, some bad. We could go over to Intel and get an update on the world situation. Sam told me there's a good-lookin' new Intel officer over there now. How 'bout it?"

"Male or female?"

"Puppy, can it be you've already been out here too long?" Nick's eyes widened in mock dismay. "Female, I imagine."

"I'll bet you do," Alan returned. "Let's have a look."

They picked up a brick and keys to one of the Victor Alert trucks and exchanged badges at the gate. Walking to the truck, Nick keyed the walkie-talkie. "Victor Alpha and Bravo to Intel," he said.

"Roger, copy," a voice from the command post acknowledged.

Nick drove them around the perimeter road to the far side of the runway. Alan took in the scenic landscape with a growing sense of melancholy. Everything he saw was new to him and in stark contrast to the dry, barren landscape he had seen so much of in Spain and Turkey. Through the tall chain link fence that defined the boundaries of the base, he saw a green open countryside that reminded him of his home in Texas. The land was lush and alive, and the nearby green hills and more distant mountains added a touch of wonder that took him beyond his home. It was Texas and Colorado combined, he thought, and here he was in the very middle of it, yet unable to get to it because he was playing nursemaid to a nuclear bomb. For the first time since he had been in Europe, he felt a longing to go home.

Nick stopped the truck in a parking lot dotted with grass patches growing up through the cracks in the concrete.

"Another long, green, flat-roofed building," Alan noted.

"Yessir. And I'll bet you anything they used Victor's interior decorator."

"I'm surprised they're here on a Sunday," Alan said as he opened the front door.

Nick smiled. "Well, they have to be here, Puppy, to give us our intelligence inbrief."

Alan looked with surprise at the side of Nick's face as they walked down the long corridor. "I just figured we were doing this for a lack of anything better ... you even made me think it was my idea."

Nick gestured to downplay Alan's words. "I'll take care of you, Puppy. Just stick with your main most woozo!"

Nick rang the buzzer at a tall door that looked more like a fence gate. An Airman two-striper opened a thick door behind the gate and walked into the cubicle between the two. "Line badges, please sirs," he said.

He opened the gate, had them sign in, then led them through the thick door into the briefing and navigational planning room.

"Have a seat," the Airman said. "Lieutenant Marcum will be with you in a moment."

As they sat, Alan contemplated the large map of the Mediterranean Sea and the Balkan States on a sliding panel. It was identical to the map in the Nuclear Certification Room at Torrejon, and it showed the Aviano Line One route of flight from take-off at Aviano to the holding point, to the target, and back to Aviano. Alan thought again of the last half of that trip. It seemed superfluous.

"Good morning, gentlemen," a female voice from behind them said.

Turning in their seats, they saw a woman five feet five inches tall with short, straight brown hair. Her eyes were a misty blue and close together on her pale face that was not beautiful but nonetheless attractive in a plain sort of way. She wore very little make-up in her desire to look professional rather than pretty. An Air Force blue blouse covered her thin but not unshapely torso, and her blue skirt was hemmed at the knees to reveal average sized calves that showed a hint of muscular definition.

She wasted no time in beginning her briefing, although she did not appear to be in a hurry to complete it. Her motivation to excel found no inconvenience in working on a Sunday. Connie Marcum wanted to go somewhere with her Air Force career, and this was simply one of many steps in her chosen profession.

With a look of studious attention on his face, Nick folded his arms as he listened. To Connie, the two fighter pilots seemed serious about the job they were doing, but they might also be two men who were skeptical of the abilities and knowledge of a female Intelligence Officer.

Alan correctly guessed she was a recent graduate of Officer Training School. A "Ninety Day Wonder."

Beginning her presentation, Second Lieutenant Marcum referred to her notes only occasionally. She looked at Nick and Alan as she spoke, maintaining good eye contact with her small audience.

As Alan watched and listened, he considered what she was saying and what it meant - the problems with the hostages, the turmoil in Iran, the Soviet war in Afghanistan. He also could not help but wonder about Lt. Marcum as a woman, if she was as regulated on the inside as she appeared on the outside.

He crossed his arms and legs, reflecting a posture of serious and intensive concentration, an outward sign that he was every bit as professional as she. Lieutenant Marcum glanced downward at the partially exposed red-striped white socks that emerged from the tops of Alan's combat boots. Reaching a break in the first part of her presentation, she paused and cast a whimsical smile at Alan.

Meaning to sound detached from regulation while yet concerned for his bearing, she said, "Lieutenant Wayne, are you aware that the commanders of this base frown on the wearing of striped white socks with utility uniforms?"

Casually, and without changing his seating position, Alan turned his head to look at the lower part of his legs. He then returned her gaze and said, "You're right ... you've opened my eyes."

Connie detected the sarcasm in Alan's voice, but before she could decide whether to flash a caustic grin, his mouth formed an emotionless smile that made her flinch.

"My job is to cut Commies' heads off and shit in their necks," Alan said, "and I certainly can't do that to the Pinko bastards if I have stripes on my socks." With his eyes steadily on her the intent on his face was unreadable. He held her eyes with the same noncommittal stare he had often seen Ron Butler use.

She coughed nervously, glancing at Nick who unconvincingly acted preoccupied with something on the large map behind her. Alan's face remained unchanged. She shuffled her papers and cleared her throat.

Returning to her script, Connie mentioned a problem in the world that required her to reference the large map for clarification. As she stepped toward the map, she tripped on an electrical wire running from the overhead projector to the wall and nearly lost her footing. Regaining her balance if not her composure, her pale face flushed a mild pink as she pointed to the wrong part of the board. She glanced at Alan to see what reaction, if any, his countenance showed to the awkwardness she was feeling. His face portrayed neither subtle enjoyment nor open compassion.

She felt her face flush again as she struggled to regain her momentum, referring to her notes more frequently, taking regular glances at Alan in search of anything in his demeanor that would indicate he no longer took her seriously. She avoided eye contact with Nick altogether.

Alan sensed her regression was due to a conflict within her, fighting between cordiality and disdain. As she looked at him now, she seemed nervous. When their eyes met, she stopped talking.

An incredibly abrasive noise pierced the momentary silence.

The Klaxon!

Alan's head jerked toward Nick, his face flooded with disbelief. The short, fat horn high on the wall behind them spat forth the one obnoxious note for which it existed. Alan continued to turn his head until his gaze rested on the horn. The incessant, harsh blaring of the klaxon spewed invisibly from the instrument, piercing the emptiness of the room and splintering all other thoughts in the minds of Nick and Alan in search of the one it demanded: Respond! Respond!

Nick's mind was ablaze. He looked at Alan in wide-eyed amazement. In a very few seconds, the synapses fired in his brain, sending impulses to his body and creating a multitude of fleeting reactions that were immediately canceled as new orders from his brain raced to his extremities. The twelve o'clock daily check. That possibility soothed his mind for half a second. His watch ... he looked ... eleven o'clock! 1100 hours! Not a test? Impossible! He had not reset his watch from Spain ... yes, he had! Not a test! ... Real! ... Sit down. It can't be real!

Alan sat frozen as he watched Nick stand abruptly straight up, turn around to look at the clock, then turn completely around and look at Alan and almost sit down again before some thought caught him halfway there and brought him straight again. He turned to get his jacket from his chair back, realized it was not there and remembered he did not have it with him. He jumped slightly as he turned his body toward Alan again who by this time was standing with a look on his face that said he was ready to move.

Looking from one to the other, Connie dropped her briefing papers on the dusty floor. The brazen sound of the klaxon filled the air so completely as to make human conversation impossible. Nick grabbed the brick from the chair and followed Alan out of the room through the big door to the hallway, through the gate and out into the parking lot. Connie did not move but watched them leave, her jaw slack, her brain refusing to function. Nuclear war did not play into her Air Force career plans.

Nick threw the brick into Alan's lap and cranked the truck's engine. "Tell them we're responding!" he yelled and shifted into reverse.

Alan keyed the mike. "Victor..."

"Alpha and Bravo!"

"...Victor Alpha and Bravo responding!"

"Roger," was the curt response from the Command Post.

Nick flipped the switch that actuated the revolving yellow light on the top of the truck. They sped around the perimeter road, kicking up dust behind them from the shoulder when Nick took the corners a bit too tightly. Alan's elbow rested on the open window sill, his hand rubbing his lower lip. Neither spoke until the Victor Alert Area came into view.

"We'll drive the truck on through to the jet," Nick said. He could see the increasing activity inside the fences.

"Right!"

The first gate began to open.

"What do you suppose it is?" Alan could not help but ask. "Iran? The hostages? That doesn't seem right."

"No clue," Nick answered curtly as he drove the truck past the first gate. He obviously did not want to talk. He gave his line badge to Alan who threw it and his own to a guard as they drove past. The second gate opened before the first was closed. Nick floored the accelerator, speeding them directly toward the Tab Vee. The crew chief and his assistant were already there, standing outside the No Lone Zone with two guards.

One of the young guards, an airman named Short, held his rifle across his chest. As the truck approached, he lowered the M-16 in the direction of the advancing truck. He held up two fingers on his left hand. The distant recognition signal Alan had given him one hour ago was "eight." Now Nick was supposed to return the guard enough fingers so that the total would add up to eight, but he was driving, and the signal given by the cop should have allowed the crew member to respond with just one hand. Nick turned the truck to the right to park away from the taxi-line.

With growing apprehension, the guard watched the truck rapidly approach with no response to his signal. He pointed the rifle at the windshield.

"Stop, and I'll give him the signal," Alan said.

The windshield was shattered by a bullet that struck it just below the roof of the cab. Safety glass flew over the two fighter pilots as the bullet embedded in the padding between them.

"What the hell!" Alan heard himself say as he exited the now stationary truck. With two hands, he held up six fingers, five on his left, and the middle one on his right. "What the hell are you doing?" he shouted above the blare of the klaxon. "The number is eight! You know who we are! We were just here an hour ago!"

He ran around to the left side of the truck where Nick was using the door as a barrier between himself and the nervous cop.

"You all right?" Alan asked, keeping his eyes on Short.

"Yeah, no cuts, I think," Nick said, starting toward the chain barrier. "What's wrong with that asshole of assholes?"

"You recognize us, right!" Alan yelled at Short.

"Yeah, I ..."

Nick grabbed Alan's arm. "Come on, there's no time for this, now. We've got a bigger punch to throw."

Another security policeman removed the chain and took it to the side of the Tab Vee as Alan and the two crew chiefs followed Nick inside.

They donned their flight gear and climbed the ladder to their respective cockpits.

Alan turned on the aircraft battery, put on his gloves and gave the crew chief the signal to give him air on the number two engine. As the rpm of the engine began to rise, Alan heard Nick's voice on the intercom.

"Okay, Puppy, I'm up," Nick said, his breathing quick and labored.

"We're cranking," Alan said. He brought the engine throttle to idle and the engine rumbled as the fire within its belly ignited. At 55 percent rpm, he gave the signal for air off and the engine turned under its own power, stabilizing at 65 percent. He gave the signal for 'air on one' and watched the rpm rise as the radio crackled the message from the Command Post.

"Batman, this is Robin ... prepare to copy Hotel Mike ... Batman, this is Robin ... prepare to copy Hotel Mike ..."

Alan took the message formats from the glare shield and shuffled through them until he found the one with 'HM' in the upper left-hand corner. He took a pencil from his shoulder pocket and circled the letters. As the message continued, he circled more letters.

"Batman, this is Robin ... prepare to copy ... Hotel ... Mike ... Sierra ... Juliet ... seven ... three ... Romeo ..." the Command Post read the message to them with no interruptions then repeated it once more.

Alan stared at this all-important piece of paper with confused incredulity. The roar of the two engines was muffled to a whine by the padding in his helmet. He could hear his own blood pulsing through his ear. "I've got a valid message ..." he said to Nick.

Nick's breathing began to slow. "So do I," he said with a sudden easiness in his voice. "I've got an exercise message for a vertical dispersal."

Alan looked toward the broad gate between the Victor Alert taxiway and the taxiway leading to the runway. It was closed, and the large fire truck was blocking the gate from the inside, standard procedure for an exercise scramble. But he had heard the klaxon! They had all heard it.

"This is not right," he said to Nick. "There's something screwy here."

Nick breathed a deep sigh. "I'm ready to believe what we've got, sports fans. There must have been a heavy-duty mix-up with the powers that be in the command post profession."

"One way to find out," Alan answered and the intensity of his imaginings played a quick scenario of sabotage in his mind's eye. "I'll call for a repeat of part one."

"Roger." The relief in Nick's voice was ever more apparent.

The repeated message confirmed an exercise scramble.

"What the hell happened?" Alan said to Nick. "I was ready to go. I thought the balloon had really gone up. All I could think of was Iran and the hostages, but there was nothing we could do for them here. I had true motivation to live through this mission and come back to Aviano. If that stupid sonofabitch airman who tried to cancel our ticket managed to survive a nuclear counterstrike, I was going to take him out myself!"

The Command Post terminated the scramble over the radio.

"Let me get a flasher on the INS and I'll be ready to shut down," Nick said, his voice indicating business as usual. When the green "align" light on the inertial navigation system flashed, Nick turned the INS off and said, "Okay Puppy."

Alan gave the crew chief the cut-throat sign and shut down both engines. He opened the canopy, unstrapped and slid down the ladder to the concrete floor. His knees buckled slightly for a moment as his legs refused to carry his weight. The excitement of the scramble, the confusion of the outcome and the fear and anger he felt from nearly dying at the hands of an incompetent young Airman before he could do his duty swelled in his body, and the pressure from his still wildly beating heart made his head swim in a sea of irrational fire. Moments before, he believed he was going to war. He had believed he was going to drop a nuclear weapon on a country he had never seen and with which he had no personal argument. He had believed he was near death, and when he thought again how nearly he had come to the end from the bullet of an excitable sky cop because of a miscommunication from the Command Post, his temper flared. Still in his G-suit and harness, he walked toward the opening of the shelter.

"Puppy!" Nick called after him as he climbed out of the jet.

The chief security policeman on duty, Staff Sergeant Turner, was a big black man with large muscular arms and an easy, controlled manner. As Alan neared Airman Short, Sgt. Turner strode toward what he determined would be the center of the approaching storm.

Short held his rifle at port-arms, across his chest. His eyes glared defensively when Alan stopped in front of him.

"What the hell were you doing?" Alan yelled. His anger spewed forth like venom.

"Sir ..." Airman Short began rather weakly. "Sir, I am ... we are ... responsible for ..."

With a wide haymaker motion that made Short flinch instinctively, Alan grabbed the barrel of Short's rifle with his right hand and ripped the weapon from the startled man's grasp. In one motion, he switched the rifle to his left hand and poised his right arm as if planning to backhand

Short's wide-eyed young face. Alan felt the grip of a fleshy vise on his wrist that suspended the entire scene like a still-shot photograph. He turned. Sgt. Turner's strong hand held his own where Short's face no longer was. Short, recoiling from the anticipated blow, had fallen backward onto the hard concrete apron. His protective steel helmet flew off his head and bounced on the concrete with a dull thud.

"That bastard!" Alan said quickly, his rage held somewhat in check by Turner's grip. "How could he not know it was us?!" He turned to look at Turner who released him. "What kind of idiot can't figure out how to count to eight on two hands!"

Sgt. Turner did not point his weapon at Alan, but he held it at the ready in one hand and said flatly, "Give me the weapon, sir."

Alan looked at Short's rifle as if realizing for the first time that he had it. He handed it to Sgt. Turner, then turned to glare at Short. Fear was in the young Airman's eyes. He used the heels of his spit-polished boots to push himself to a sitting position and further from the angry officer. His steel helmet spun to a stop behind him.

"I want this man arrested," Alan said, looking again at Turner.

"Sir, it is a violation of regulations for you to relieve a security policeman on active duty of his weapon," Sgt. Turner said evenly, as if quoting from a book.

Alan stared wordlessly into the big man's eyes. His anger partially satisfied, he again felt the reality of the situation upon him, realizing the trouble it could mean. "If striking a superior officer is a punishable offense, then I'm damn sure shooting one is." Alan pointed at Short. "I have relieved a weapon from a man that I, in my best judgment and in regard for the circumstances, feel is a potential threat to the security of this area." He looked at Nick, then back to Turner. "I want him arrested."

Nick watched the scene develop like that from another world. Through careful planning and experience, Victor Alert operations were supposed to run smoothly and unobtrusively. Beyond the fighter pilot and the two enlisted men, the blue truck with the shattered windshield rested as a silent testament to the contrary. The scene was rapidly escalating at a time when he felt he could do without any further such stimuli for the rest of his career. He sensed Alan had, perhaps, dug himself a very deep hole.

"I'll have to report this on the blotter," Sgt. Turner was saying. "We may have to take the aircraft off status."

"If we have to," Alan said. "But I doubt that is your decision to make."

"Let's reason this thing out," Nick said. "What we have here is just a miscommunication ..."

With sudden surprise, Alan turned to face Nick. "Are you serious? If this incompetent bastard," he pointed at Short, "could shoot straight, one of us would be dead!"

"Now wait a minute, Puppy," Nick said, holding his hands out in his usual gesture of defense. "I'm not saying this isn't serious. It is." He turned to Turner. "As I see it, we've at least got a Dull Sword here, right?"

"Probably," Sergeant Turner said slowly. "This officer, after possibly giving the wrong distant recognition signal, did, on completion of a routine scramble, disarm and attempt to strike a security policeman who, in the line of duty, was attempting to maintain the security of a highly sensitive area for which he was responsible."

"You've got it all wrong, pal!" Alan's temper flared again. "This ignoramus did not properly initiate the code. Then, this fuckhead tried to kill an Air Force officer responding to what, at the time, was an actual nuclear alert."

Nick glided in front of him and lightly but firmly held his arms as the sergeant took a step back, still holding both rifles.

"Ease off, Puppy," Nick said, releasing his grip as he felt Alan's muscles relax. "Now, that's the situation, isn't it," he said, turning to Turner. "For all we know, this guy ..." he pointed to Short, "... was trying to deter the actual launch of a nuclear loaded aircraft."

"No, I wasn't!" Airman Short protested, pushing his hands against the concrete to stand. "Shit!" He raised a bloody hand to remove a piece of safety glass embedded in his palm.

Alan said, "I want this man detained. I want a report on his actions completed immediately." Not only had this incident become a point of honor for him, he sensed it was either him or the airman - one of them was in it deep. He looked steadily at Turner, awaiting his decision.

Sergeant Turner silently considered the possible reactions of the base commander and his staff for each of the actions he might take. He really wanted to burn this officer, but he knew doing so could blow up the situation to disastrous proportions. If his judgment was incorrect and he tried to arrest this officer, it could spell the beginning of the end for his own career. He was Short's supervisor. Precaution dominated his thoughts. In house. Try to keep it in house!

"Come on, Dave," he said to Short. "Let's go talk this out at Ops."

Short was distraught. "Are you serious, Earl?"

"Let's go," Turner said. He turned to the other Airman. "Call Billy from the front gate and tell him to take this post with you until I get another replacement in." He removed the clip from Short's weapon and unloaded the bullet from the chamber, then handed the empty rifle to Short. They walked away toward the gate.

"What do you think will happen?" Alan asked Nick as he watched them leave.

Nick shrugged his shoulders. "Depends on how they write it up."

"I'm going to follow up on this."

"That's an idea, but I would suggest you do so through our Ops, sort of indirectly." He gestured toward the retreating cops. "We won't raise a stink unless they do."

Alan managed an unconvincing smile. "That's the game, eh?"

'That's the game."

CHAPTER TWENTY-THREE

Victor Alert received an early morning phone call from the Command Post saying the replacement pilots would be arriving in the area within the hour. The VANCO woke Alan to tell him the news.

"What?" grumbled Alan sleepily. He shook his head to wake himself and to understand what the VANCO was saying. "What ...? For yesterday?"

"I don't know very much about what happened yesterday," the new VANCO lied. "All they said was that the replacements will be here after a briefing at the Command Post. You're to meet them there."

"I'm in deep," Alan muttered to himself as he rose to wash.

When Alan and Nick arrived at the Command Post there were no smiles being passed around ... only memos. A Captain in blues took their statements, then left them alone as Buck and Carp Fisch arrived looking very unhappy.

"Top o' the morning, fellow birdmen!" Nick greeted them.

Fisch glared at him with a comically sour look on his round face. "Yeah, right. You gentlemen ready to go?" He was not pleased with being called to sit Victor a day earlier than he had planned. He wanted them to feel his ire. He was supposed to have flown a range mission today.

"We'll be ready to go in a minute," Alan said flatly. He made no move to leave. "You can go ahead, get some breakfast at Victor if you want." He turned to Buck. "So, what did they tell you?" he asked. "Why'd they decide to relieve us a day early?"

Buck frowned and grabbed his throat. "There was a mix-up here," he said softly, "at Command Post. Heads will roll. They decided it was best, under the circumstances, to take you off."

Alan's face grimaced in a pained look. "The cop?"

"The word is out that you nearly floored him," Buck said. "But the way the Hefe's feel about cops right now, they're probably on your side. That's not why you're coming off."

"It isn't?"

Buck was silent for a moment, enjoying the suspense he had created. "No. Compared to all else that happened, that was rather minor. When they thought it was a real klaxon, the sky cops screwed up in ways you can't begin to imagine. They want your statements on what happened and how you almost got shot." He looked around the dark room, then added almost secretively, "These guys are in hot water. There's all kinds of shields out there keeping the heat off you. When this thing is over, you'll probably get a medal. I suggest you play it very low key."

"We just want to get on with this," Carp interjected. Obviously frustrated, he did not care whether Alan Wayne knew any of the details. He turned to leave. "We'll see you at Victor," he growled as Buck followed him out the Command Post door.

When Nick looked at him with a smile of dubious relief, Alan felt the tension noticeably recede from his body, even as he realized he could never be sure whose side Buck was on. Buck's allegiance tended to shift with the prevailing wind.

Lt. Colonel Groff, the command post senior officer, walked up to them. He put his hands on his hips. "So, you guys had a little excitement yesterday. Bet you thought you were really going!" He flashed a casual smile.

"Yes, sir, we did," Alan said coldly.

The Lt. Colonel folded his arms in front of himself. "Well, it was good practice, right? Now you know what it feels like. You are experienced in that feeling of thinking you are going to drop a nuke."

Alan said, "It's not exactly a prerequisite ... sort of like practice bleeding."

"How do you feel now?" Groff asked. With his arms still folded, he patted his left biceps with his right hand. He seemed to be searching for something other than an emotional response.

Alan met his eyes squarely and said, "Somebody cried wolf."

The forced smile disappeared from the face of the Officer of the Day as he decided this called for a knowing frown.

"Colonel Groff," someone called from behind him.

Alan recognized the voice. Looking around Groff, he saw intense curiosity in Lieutenant Connie Marcum's eyes as they blinked a silent greeting from across the dimly lit room.

"Thanks for coming in guys," Groff said. He pointed to an officer in blues. "Captain Spence will take your statements." He walked toward the Intelligence Officer.

That was all. It was going to be covered up, smoothed over. No one dared add more heat to this smoldering fire.

Nick smiled wryly. "Puppy, you must have a four-leaf clover stuffed up your butt."

As they drove silently to the squadron operations building in the Mike area, the green Italian scenery lulled Alan's thoughts back to Texas and home. He tried to imagine what his mother would say, how she would react if she was told her son had been killed by an American Security Policeman while he was responding to a cockpit alert on a nuclear loaded aircraft. She had always backed him in his military career, always been proud of him, even though, and perhaps especially when his father had cautioned against it. Back in his Academy days, she had been extremely disappointed when he had mentioned he might quit and go to a "regular" college. She had been very vocal with reasons why he should stay, which almost always came back to the theme of how lucky he was to be there. He had been equally as vocal with reasons why he should leave. But he knew she really did not understand, had never understood. She could not know the inside and still feel the way she did.

Alan's father had been to war. He had never encouraged Alan to do the same. Something had happened to him while he was in the army, something he had never talked about.

But it was the letter his father wrote suggesting he consider leaving the Academy that had fueled his determination to stay and graduate.

Now, when he read or heard of soldiers being killed in Europe, he thought of their mothers. He doubted they could ever understand completely. A soldier would die because a truck exploded, another would die because he got too close to the intake of a jet engine, and Alan would think of the mothers. Some of them would not have ever wanted their children to be a part of the world of combatants. Others would be quite proud of their sons and daughters, perhaps forgetting, or never realizing, the soldier's sacrifice of giving up his lifestyle so that he might someday lay down his life for them.

He wondered if mothers really considered that when they showed pictures of their uniformed sons and daughters to their neighbors.

And then there was Sloan. How would he tell her? Perhaps she already knew.

Nick stopped the truck at the squadron building. "Time to face the music," he said, bringing Alan out of his thoughts and back to the reality of their trivial troubles.

No further mention was made of the incident with Airman Short or the false klaxon, at least not in any context that could be construed as formal, so both Alan and Nick assumed the matter had been quietly dealt with and dismissed to avoid embarrassment on all sides. Alan never knew how far up the chain it had gone, but he was beginning to understand this facet of the Air Force. Had there been an obvious infraction with a necessary scapegoat, no doubt he would have received widespread attention. All sides understood this mutual conspiracy in no way protected one side from the other in the future. No one owed anybody anything.

CHAPTER TWENTY-FOUR

Sloan meandered at a measured pace around the room of the house in the finca, stopping from time to time to look more closely at a particular relic or a grouping of knickknacks, her mind traveling to imagined places where the McPhersons may have found them. The nutcracker certainly was from Germany, as were the Hummel figurines. The copper was probably Turkish. The onyx phone was from Italy and just like the one she remembered seeing her first day in Spain at the apartment where Jennifer and Ron lived. The phone was on Alan's list, along with several other possibilities.

The inside of the house seemed familiar, and she suddenly realized she had last been here for the squadron party that marked her first day in Spain.

Sloan's thoughts scattered when Demi McPherson emerged from the rear of the house, pulling a black cashmere sweater over her head as she padded down the hallway. Sloan was embarrassed to see she was not wearing a brassiere and turned her eyes away.

"Thanks for waiting," Demi said as her face reappeared through the neck of the sweater. "I had to get into something more comfortable."

"This ... the place we're going must be ... pretty casual," Sloan offered.

"The Rib House. I don't know the real name."

"Oh, I've been there," Sloan said, following Demi outside to her truck. "Good ribs. And sangria!" It would seem strange to be there without Alan. She always enjoyed watching him wolf down the "best ribs this side of Texas," as he described them.

Demi maneuvered her small truck down the bad road with the skill born of experience. Bouncing along roughly beside her, Sloan said, "I like all your things, the things from different places."

"Memories," Demi said as they hit the unavoidable bump.

"Places you and Robert have been?"

"Not all have been with Robert."

"Before you were married?"

"Some, but there are a several from since then." She turned onto a better road. "I love the man ..." a small pothole in the road jolted them. "... but I'm not chained to him."

"I'm not chained either," Sloan said, wondering if she meant it. "Just dependent."

Demi laughed at Sloan's use of the word the military used to describe them both.

"I'm envious of you, Demi ... well, envious is not the right word. I admire what you've done, where you've been."

"It's a way of thinking," Demi answered, looking briefly at her. "Of living."

"I'd like to see more."

"Then why don't you?"

"We will. I wish I could have gone to Aviano with the other wives. It just didn't work out."

"Did Alan want you to?"

"Yes," Sloan said hesitantly. "Alan and I enjoy going places, but sometimes we don't travel well together."

"Alan is not your everything," Demi said. "You need to broaden your horizons."

Sloan tried to appear indifferent to the idea, but she listened to the experienced older woman's words like a lesson from the Buddha.

"There's a great big life out there, Sloan. You have to be more than Mrs. Alan Wayne. I hate to see anyone settle into their life thinking that's all there is without being sure there isn't something more, something different."

Sloan felt uncomfortable. "Alan knows what I am ... what I want."

"Does he?"

"Yes. Why do you say it that way?"

"Don't be afraid to go with your gut."

"What do you mean?"

Demi was contemplative for a moment. "What do you think of Brandon Parsons?"

"He's a good racquetball player," Sloan offered.

"Yes. And ...?"

Sloan acted surprised. "I'm not sure where this is leading."

"Never mind, then."

Sloan blinked, then said, "He's nice. He's okay. Are you trying to set me up?"

"I've seen the way you look at him. You're obviously interested."

Sloan considered her words. "Not interested. Just ... curious."

Demi laughed out loud. She was driving faster now, avoiding fewer bumps. The ride was decidedly rougher. "He practically threw himself at you when I introduced you."

Sloan shrugged and glanced out the window. "He's just friendly."

"I think he's more."

"Why?"

Demi hesitated, then said, "The way he acts."

Sloan eyed Demi. "So?"

"So, go for it!"

Sloan returned her gaze out the window. "You like him, you go for it."

Demi turned into an open lane on the Autopista, and the ride became relatively smooth. "He doesn't go for me."

Sloan looked at her friend. "Or you would?"

"I don't know. Maybe."

Sloan gazed again out the window at the dry, barren scenery.

"You've got to be at least curious," Demi said.

"I do feel a little ... something," Sloan admitted. "But it hasn't changed the way I feel about Alan. I love Alan."

"He's a nice guy."

"Yes. He's good to me. He's good for me."

"He's also TDY."

"Yes."

"So ..."

Sloan laughed. "So, what?"

"Go for the throat!" Demi said with a growl.

Sloan laughed again, unable to think of anything to say. Why was Demi so interested? What was it about her that was both dangerous and exciting?

"It's not me," Sloan said finally.

"It's not your life?"

"It is my life ... I don't know. I don't want to think about it."

"Of course not."

They pulled into the unpaved parking lot at the Rib House, followed the attendant's dubious parking directions, then gave him 50 pesetas for his effort and went inside.

CHAPTER TWENTY-FIVE

Camron Ransom carried himself with quiet self-assurance and a casual confidence that, while lofting him above the "gang," smacked of neither arrogance nor indifference. He belonged without actually fitting in. He won his share of Top Gun bombing titles without the "of course I did" bravado that invariably accompanied Shooter's debriefs. He was an Instructor Pilot minus the smugness that at times characterized Ron. He held his own in the air-to-air arena, being neither peacetime ace nor assumed wartime fodder.

As far as Camron Ransom was concerned, what he did as a fighter pilot was an important part of his life, but it did not define him as a person. To many of his fellow fighter pilots, he was an enigma. They did not understand him and so left him alone.

Perhaps Cameron saw something in Alan that he decided needed cultivating. Perhaps he took a different tack in taking a young fighter pilot under his wing. Or maybe he just liked Alan and wanted companionship.

"What are you doing for dinner?" he asked Alan after their first Maniago range mission together.

"Pasta!" Alan answered. "Wherever I can find it."

"Let's go to deBep's."

"Never been there, but okay."

Alan was neither surprised nor intrigued by the fact that Ransom invited him along. Something about Camron made it nothing out of the ordinary.

An invitation from Shooter or Whiskey would have sounded something more like, 'We're going to deBep's. If you want to tag along, pup, that's up to you.'

Camron was different, being at once exclusive and inclusive.

For a while, they walked the narrow road that ran between Area 2 and Area 3 of Aviano Air Base in silence. Clouds formed quickly over this part of the Po Valley, darkening the late afternoon in the premature gloom of twilight. The rain began to sprinkle them as they followed the curve of the road past Leno's Gift Shop. Camron kept his hands in the side pockets of the yellow cloth jacket he always wore, but Alan involuntarily opened his palm to feel the rain drops.

"Looks like we'll barely make it," Boomer Bailey said, looking skyward as he hurried to catch up to them. He winced when a sudden gust of wind blew rain in his eye. Clarence had earned his new callsign, which even he liked better than his actual name, on his first flight to the Maniago bombing range. He threw up just as the flight approached the bombing pattern, but after calming his intestines, took the other three WSOs' money with multiple orange bomb bullseyes. That first flight had not been a fluke. He continued to take the money on every range mission he flew. And every mission began the same way - with Boomer puking.

The rain came down harder.

Hunching his shoulders forward, Camron said, "Shall we run?" and quickened his pace.

"I don't know," Alan answered. "Will we get wetter if we walk or if we run?" The cool wind subsided as the rain increased.

Shooter and Carp shuffled past them, collars up, hands in pockets, looking down to avoid the developing mud puddles.

"What are you guys? Ducks?" Shooter called over his shoulder.

Boomer broke into a trot, then turned to see if Camron and Alan would follow. "Duck doesn't have the same ring as Boomer," Clarence said.

The three fighter pilots trotted across the parking lot to the small restaurant. They could see the diners through the windows on the side street. Shooter and Carp were already inside, taking seats in a corner booth with Bull Boulder and Whiskey Wilson. Alan saw no sign above the entrance or toward the front as they hustled inside. How did anyone know the name of this place?

As they entered, the dining area they had seen from the street was to the left. To the right was another serving area with more booths. A mixologist was preparing drinks for a local couple at the room-length bar.

To the left of the bar, a hallway went straight back to restrooms and a pool room. Immediately to the left of the entrance were three video machines, two of which were being played by Italian teenagers.

A mixed aroma of smoke, vinegar and freshly baked bread invaded Alan's nostrils as he wiped the rain from his brow.

Seated at the corner booth, Bull rested his elbows on the table. His hands, folded one over the other, partially hid his face. He raised the fingers of his top hand in a subtle gesture of greeting to Alan, then turned his head as quickly to say something to Whiskey. Shooter was already taking deep draws from a cigarette, and Whiskey was lighting up again.

With the air of experience, Camron walked into the room to the left and led Alan and Boomer to a booth in the opposite corner from the four other Squids.

"So, what do you think?" Camron asked after they had seated themselves. He dabbed residual dampness from his nose and ears with a napkin.

Alan reached for the menu offered by the waitress. With soft brown eyes, she watched her own hands. Her long flowing hair wrapped loosely behind her back, and the smile she refused to give brought the words "sad beauty" to Alan's mind. She may have been a heart-breaker at one time, but she no longer seemed to care about such things. When she left them, Alan opened his mouth to speak, then closed it again. He knew better than to discuss women with Camron.

"It smells promising," Alan said finally.

Looking at the menu, Camron said, "I meant about our geometric question."

"Our what?" Boomer interjected.

"Would we get wetter if we ran or if we walked?"

Alan's mind wandered from women to water. "Well, let's see. If we walk, it gets mostly on our head and shoulders ... "

"Yes." Camron looked amused.

"But, assuming a no wind situation ..."

"Of course," Camron's eyes danced with the little joke.

"... no wind, most of our body stays dry, and just part of it takes all the rain ..."

"If we run," Camron continued for him, "we run into the rain. The drops that would fall to the ground are now hitting our chest."

"But the volume of water has not changed," Boomer interjected, thinking he might as well be a part of this conversation as another.

"Yes," Alan said, looking serious. "We have created a trapezoid of water with a constant volume."

"So, which makes us wetter?" Camron asked again.

Alan looked thoughtfully at his fork for a moment. "I guess the only true variable is time. Just like anything else, the amount of sh... stuff being dumped on you is constant. The difference is the amount of time you choose to stay under it." He grinned at Cameron. "Running is best."

"But it can also depend on where you choose to take it," Camron countered. "If you're okay with it hitting you in the chest, or don't like bearing it on your shoulders ... you've created another variable."

"And another topic for discussion," Alan added philosophically.

Boomer did not get it. "What difference does it make? A wet shirt's a wet shirt."

Cameron smiled. "I guess so."

Alan nodded at Camron and opened the menu, certain that Clarence Bailey was forever condemned to think two dimensionally. He would never be a fighter pilot. He would never be a hero.

"Have you tried spaghetti carbonara?" Camron asked Alan.

"No."

"It's great."

"What is it?"

"Kind of a breakfast spaghetti. Spaghetti mixed with eggs, bacon and scallions."

"Sounds different ..."

"Try it."

"Okay."

When the sad, pretty waitress returned, Alan ordered a salad, tortellini and spaghetti carbonara. "What kind of beer do you have?"

"Birra? Uh, Becks ...," she began.

"Okay."

"Okay?"

"Okay, I'll have a Becks."

"Okay."

Camron ordered a coke. Then Boomer ordered a coke.

As they waited, Alan recalled the rhetorical question Ron Butler had once thrown out to him. How could a devout Christian live the life of a fighter pilot? Now he sat on one side of the table. Boomer and Camron were on the other. Somewhere in between lay the misty trapezoid of life.

"What got you interested in flying fighters?" Alan asked when the drinks came.

Camron took a sip of coke, then looked knowingly at Alan as he folded his hands in front of him. "That's where a warrior belongs."

"You are a warrior ..."

"Yes." Camron's eyes were bright, he was almost smiling. This was not new.

Boomer sipped his coke as he watched Camron intently.

"For war?" Alan asked, "or for peace."

"For peace."

"But someday you may have to nuke an entire city back into the Stone Age."

"For my country," Camron Ransom said.

Alan rubbed his head. He wanted Camron to consider his next question as thoughtful rather than irreverent. "Should we worship our country?"

"No, we should worship God who has His hands in our country."

Alan leaned back and smiled a friendly smile. He tended to get terse when discussions got intense, and he did not mean for this one to go that way. "So, we are the chosen people," he said jokingly.

"There are other ways to look at that ..." Boomer began.

"Like what?" Alan interrupted him, though he had truly not meant to. He just could not imagine that Clarence Bailey really had anything important to say.

"God wants our country to be strong," Boomer continued rather uncomfortably. "He wants it strong because we are based ... our Constitution is based on the Judeo-Christian ethic."

"And kill those that are not?" Alan asked while trying not to sound offensive.

Boomer was silent as he searched his mind for the answer.

"No," Camron said. "The world is as it is. We fight to keep our country strong while the diplomats work for peace and change."

"Change as we see it?" Alan asked.

"Change from war."

"But, yea, verily, in the interim, we will kill."

"If called upon," Camron said. "Do you want to kill?"

"No," Alan answered, mostly in truth. "But I am a fighter pilot."

"So you are willing to kill."

"If called upon."

"Then, we are no different."

"Will you go to hell if you do?" Alan asked him.

"Will you?" Cameron countered.

"Probably."

"Then why do you take the chance?"

"You take it, too," Alan said.

Camron shook his head. "I don't think so."

"Then it's okay to kill as long as you believe."

"No, it is never okay to just kill."

"What?"

"You don't understand."

"You're right." Alan looked away. "I don't."

Boomer found himself unsure what to think of Alan. He felt vulnerable, naked. He longed to have Cameron's conviction, although he knew he never would. And he wanted to be a little like Alan. He wanted to be a crusty fighter pilot ... with convictions. He rubbed his hands on his wet cotton shirt. "Do you ... have faith in anything?" he asked Alan.

"I used to."

"What changed that?"

"Ernie."

"Ernie?"

"A friend. He died."

"I know," Camron said.

"The last thing he knew in life was fear, and knowing he was going to die," Alan said. "Did you ever think about that? The lucky ones die in their sleep. But for the rest of us, the last thing we will ever feel is the life ebbing from our veins. At the point where death comes ... that's the last thing we know."

"You don't believe in life after death?" Boomer asked him.

"Even if there is, your own death is your last memory. You get blown to bits and that is what you have forever."

Camron said, "Not if Heaven is next."

"But what if it isn't."

"It is."

"But what if it isn't!"

Camron and Boomer were quiet.

"So, what are you now?" Boomer asked finally.

"What?"

"If you think differently, what are you now?"

"I don't know," Alan said absently. "Hungry."

The melancholy waitress delivered their antipasto.

They ate in silence until Alan said, "I respect you, Camron."

Boomer twitched in his seat.

"Why?" asked Camron.

"You know what you believe, and, just as important, you know why." Alan wiped his mouth with a napkin. "Don't take me too seriously. I usually argue for arguments sake."

Camron smiled warmly. "There is something more than just being the Devil's advocate. You just have to argue yourself around to it. In the end, I think you'll come full circle."

"Does that matter?"

Keeping eye contact with Alan, Camron put his coke glass to his lips, swallowed and replaced the glass on the table. "Quite a bit," he said.

CHAPTER TWENTY-SIX

The carload of wives arrived in Aviano on the day of the "Elephant Walk" exercise.

The ladies had driven from Spain through France to Italy under the pretense of enduring the long, hard trip to cheer on the Torrejon women in the Mediterranean Conference Volleyball Championship. They fooled no one. They were there to sleep with their husbands and shop in Italy, and no one believed anything else.

Unable to talk his wife out of it making the trip, Major Sherman made her promise she would play it up as being a surprise, allowing him the opportunity to save face with his fellow fighter pilots, not to mention his job and any future promotion potential. Michelle Christopher was with Cathy Sherman, as were Denise Fisch and Camron Ransom's wife, Cindy. They had all promised the same lie. Even Cindy.

As the ladies settled into their hotel rooms, sixteen F-4Ds and their crews sat on simulated alert status along with the lone nuclear loaded bird on the Victor Alert Pad.

Impatiently waiting just outside the squadron building, Alan mounted the small horse on the rusted spring and began to rock back and forth. "Maybe this thing is for stress reduction," he said to Sam.

"Maybe it's a World War Two flight simulator ..." Sam was answering when the words "Scramble! Scramble! Scramble!" came over the squadron loud speaker. Despite the strategic seating Carp had taken next to the front door, Sam and Alan were well on their way to their jet when Carp emerged outside with Buck in trail. As they ran for the Tab

Vee, Sam said, “I get the impression that, exercise or no exercise, Carp intends to beat us to the runway!”

Alan glanced over his shoulder. In the corner of his eye he saw Carp Fisch running in the knock-kneed fashion of a man who either seldom did anything athletically, or who had done so much that his knees had finally given out.

“Not a chance,” Alan said. “Unless our jet breaks. And I have no intention of letting our jet be broken, if you know what I mean.”

“And if the security guards don’t shoot us ...” Sam added as they approached the Tab Vee.

“These aren’t real nukes ... they can’t be using real bullets.”

“For you, they’d make an exception.”

Alan pushed Sam ahead. “Then you go first.”

With obvious disappointment, the guard acknowledged the correct signal Sam gave him. “Did you see the look on that cop’s face?” Sam asked once they were inside the shelter putting on their G-suits.

Alan grunted. “Got the impression he would have blown the whole exercise just to nail us.”

“Nail you, Puppy.”

“Turncoat,” Alan joked.

“Hey, I’m a survivor.”

Alan had both engines running when the Command Post transmitted the exercise message.

“It’s a go!” Alan said.

“Roger,” Sam said. “Hit it!”

Alan gave the crew chief the signal to pull the chocks, advanced the throttles and guided the lumbering fighter out of the shelter and onto the circular taxiway past the Tab Vee where Carp’s jet was ready to move.

“Suck exhaust!” Alan said watching Carp give the “chocks out” signal to his crew chief.

“Gotcha!” Sam added.

They watched the fighter manned by Carp and Buck pull recklessly onto the taxiway behind them. What they did not see was that, in his failed attempt to beat them, Carp pushed the power of the twin J-79 engines up so much that when he turned the corner, the powerful exhaust blew an unoccupied step van over on its side.

Alan steered the Phantom onto the runway. Pushing the power up to 85 percent for a moment, he felt the exhilaration of a take-off unhampered by normal procedure. At 80 knots, Alan retarded the throttles to idle, slowed to taxi speed and cleared the runway. Taxiing back toward the approach end of the runway, he watched as the other jets followed the same simulated take-off run. He turned to angle the jet across the yellow taxi stripe and stopped. Clearing the runway, the other jets followed suit until all sixteen jets were angled line abreast on the taxiway.

After getting quick-checked, the tower cleared them for individual take-offs. "Now, let's go have some fun," Alan said shoving the throttles into afterburner.

Low clouds and fog made flying the low level difficult, and the marginal conditions made Sam nervous. He reminded Alan of the high terrain perhaps once too often. When Alan groaned, "Uh ... Sam ..." he realized he was acting more as a nagger than a navigator.

"My wife's here," Sam said apologetically. "I want to live long enough to get laid."

Seventeen minutes into their flight, Alan said, "There's the target."

"Tally ho."

"Bombs away," Alan said to simulate dropping their nuke.

To the south of the mountains, the clouds were broken just a bit. He found a hole and flew the jet to the blue sky above.

The cloud layer, though quite solid, was scarcely a thousand feet thick and uniformly level, spread like a white carpet at the base of the mountains. The jagged Alps pierced the undercast and silhouetted against the blue sky where, in their rugged youthfulness, the mountains expressed an eerily inviting silent majesty. The clouds blanketed the hidden valleys with a creeping fog. Below the thin cloud layer, the day was misty and dull. Here, it was bright, open and clear. In their jet, they soared amid the raw landscape between sheer peaks above the opaque bed of white moisture, unspeaking in their isolated admiration of this beautiful, fleeting portrait of Nature.

Alan banked the jet hard right, into a steep climb up and away from the mountains, pointing the nose of the Phantom in the direction of the air-to-air training area above the Piave River valley. Breaking the serene mood, he said, "Let's see if anyone is up in Zita."

Within moments, Sam said, "I've got two radar contacts about 12 miles, 20 right."

Alan felt the thrill of the chase rise in his stomach. "Don't lock. They're probably after each other."

"Ten miles, now, ten right."

"Tally one!" Alan's voice betrayed his excitement. "Tally two! They're wrapped up with each other. They won't be looking for us. We'll nail 'em both."

Sam took one last quick look at the scope, then turned his attention outside the cockpit.

"Check our six!" Alan reminded him. Overcome by that uncontrollable urge to roll in on some unsuspecting victim, he knew he was not alone in this feeling.

"Okay!"

The two fighters were close aboard, neither with an obvious advantage. They were fighting in a classic horizontal "scissors," pulling toward each other's six, but, as the fighter planes were evenly matched, neither was gaining the offensive.

"There's a fox 2!" Alan said to Sam.

"Don't transmit your shots!" Sam yelled. "Ops might be listening."

"Going for guns on the left-hand man."

"Roger," Sam said. "I've got the guy to the right!"

"Guns!" Alan squeezed the trigger as the gun sight settled on his target's canopy. Unable to resist, he keyed the radio mike and whispered, "Tracking."

The fighter in front of him broke away to the left.

"He sees us," Alan said. "He's breaking!"

The fighter rolled inverted and pulled for the area floor.

"Where's he going?" Alan said in surprise. "He's heading for the rocks!" He keyed the mike to speak, then released it as he watched the fighter level off above the cloud deck and disappear in a valley.

"The other guy's trying to get his nose around on us!" Sam said.

"Where is he?" Alan asked turning back to the right.

"Right three o'clock! You might get a snap shot on him, but that's all."

"We'll take the snap-shot and bug out." He lowered the jet's nose and lit the afterburners. Pulling his aircraft's nose in lead, Alan squeezed the trigger as the fighter appeared behind the pipper. "Snap shot," he said to Sam.

"Right, let's beat it!"

Alan turned away from his adversary. "Keep an eye on him, in case he reverses."

Sam looked over his shoulder. "He's reversing, but I don't think he has the energy ..."

"Roger." Alan looked for the bandit over his shoulder as he instinctively lowered the nose of the jet. "He's got to be at least two miles away now."

"Shit! Watch the Mach!" Sam shouted. He stared at the other instruments. "I don't know where we're going, but we're getting there like a scalded-ass ape!"

"Speed is life!" Alan answered.

"I'm not so sure this time ..."

Alan snapped his head forward into the cockpit. The altimeter jumped as it characteristically did at transonic speeds. The Mach meter registered 1.2.

"Damn! We're through the Mach!" Alan pulled the throttles back to idle. "Where are we?"

The Tacan distance read three miles, the bearing pointer was spinning. They were in the "cone of confusion," directly over Aviano. Alan pulled the aircraft nose up to decrease the airspeed faster as the realization hit them both.

Sam broke the ensuing silence, stating the obvious. "We just boomed Aviano."

Alan was silent for a moment. "There's sixteen jets up here somewhere above the fog. Who's to say we did it? Let's find another fight."

"How's our gas?"

Alan checked the gauge. "Oh hell, we're bingo. Better head home."

"Slowly," Sam said. "Let's don't bring this thing in too quick."

After they landed, Major Sherman contacted them on the squadron common radio frequency. "I want to talk to you," was all he said.

"We're screwed," Sam sighed.

"Just stick to the story," Alan answered.

"What story?"

"We don't know nuttin' 'bout no boomin'."

"Did you boom Aviano?" Sherman asked them when they returned to the squadron.

"Do what?" Alan said.

"Did you guys do a supersonic run over Aviano?" Sherman repeated.

"No, sir," Alan said defensively, and he felt truthful about that. It had not been a run. More of a quick getaway.

"Well, somebody did. The wife of the Aviano mayor, or whatever he is, was outside hanging laundry. She nearly had a heart attack. He's already called us! And some farmer claims his cow puked its calf prematurely, and he says his chicken stopped laying eggs." He looked squarely at them both. "You didn't do a supersonic low-level pass over the base?"

"No, sir," Alan said evenly. "We did not make a low-level supersonic pass over the base."

"Did you fight above us?"

"No, sir!" That was honest.

"Did you fight in Zita?"

Alan flinched. "We saw a fight going on up there."

"From what vantage point?"

"It was behind us," Sam put in.

Sherman eyed them both for a moment, then shrugged his shoulders. "It doesn't matter much, anyway," he said. "Fisch and Buck are the ones in real trouble. They blew over a step van. They'll be the heat shield for everybody else for a while."

"Shit!" Sam whispered.

"Yeah," Sherman answered and walked away.

Alan and Sam looked at each other, then began to laugh, Sam uncontrollably.

Maybe Nick Dawson is right, Alan thought. Maybe he did have a four-leaf clover shoved up there where the sun never shines.

CHAPTER TWENTY-SEVEN

The announcement of the first nine Torrejon selectees chosen for the coveted role of transitioning from the old F-4D to the F-16 caught most of the fighter pilots of the 401st Tactical Fighter Wing by surprise. Even the three squadron commanders had not expected it so soon, but that did nothing to subdue the buzz of excitement. The long-anticipated conversion was going to happen.

The F-16 Fighting Falcon. A fighter pilot's dream. Nine-g capable. Side stick. Single seat. Single engine. Advanced avionics. Internal cannon. Highly accurate weapons delivery system. A jet so maneuverable that the pilots who flew it jokingly boasted it could "turn up its own asshole."

Of the nine listed AC's, there were three from each squadron. Camron Ransom was on the list for the 613th, as was Major Sherman, who was presumed to be on his way to becoming Hargrove's replacement as Squadron Commander if he made Lieutenant Colonel.

Alan was the third Squid on the list. In a way, it had surprised him, but, then again, it had not. Good things like that happened to him.

Fisch seemed stunned that he had not made the cut. He was the only one who assumed he would.

Whiskey was also not on the list, but he had not expected to be. He was working an assignment in the States that he felt would be a quicker road to becoming a squadron commander, his career goal. Regardless, the omission bothered many of the squadron members who wanted always to believe merit to be the one true measure for reward. And

Camron Ransom, as a fighter pilot, was not and never would be in the same league with Whiskey Wilson.

Shooter was disappointed that he had not made the first list, but he and Carp tempered their mixed emotions to celebrate the lucky three with a trip to Orsini's restaurant. Camaraderie was important, sticking by your fellow fighter pilots was important. And there were three more lists yet to come. No need to panic.

Located in the small town of Grizzo, not too far from Aviano, Orsini's is remembered by many Air Force pilots, non-rated officers and enlisted Airmen even if the town's name has long since been forgotten.

Whiskey, Shooter, Carp and Denise, Alan, Sam and Michelle, Camron and Cindy, and Boomer were led to a long table adjacent to the salad bar where there was, among other delectables, a whole smoked salmon with garnish.

Too bad Sloan is not here, Alan silently lamented. He felt uncomfortable.

Whiskey sat across from him and winked knowingly as he lit a cigarette. "Will my smoke-straws bother anyone?" he asked in afterthought as he exhaled his first puff away from the table.

"No," Cindy Ransom lied.

Very little conversation developed, other than a few awkward short sentences, before Orsini approached. He put his order pad on a corner of the table and leaned over it, supporting himself with his left hand as he prepared to write with his right. He was of average height. With graying temples, he appeared to be in his early sixties, although his full head of brown hair was made childishly unruly by his continuous bustling between the dining room, the kitchen and the register at the front bar. He wore a gray herringbone suit and a brown tie loosened at the neck to reveal an unbuttoned top button. He looked like he should be sweating profusely, although he was not.

Orsini's pale blue eyes were underlined with the heavily wrinkled crescents that age and hard work had made of his skin. A large round nose guarded his large upper lip which rose to reveal a full set of yellowing teeth as, in a deep gruff voice and without introduction or interruption, he told them in English the evening's options for the main course.

"Tonight we have the smoked salmon," he began, "which is imported and delicately prepared or perhaps you would prefer the cannelloni this is a fine pasta prepared in a special cream sauce filled with meat very tasty very good or perhaps you would prefer the veal which tonight is prepared with a delicate Parmesan sauce or perhaps you would prefer ..." His rasping voice and nonstop delivery were only part of the reason Alan, seeing Orsini in action for the first time, had to ask him to repeat his oration.

On hearing it the second time, Alan ordered the cannelloni, the others made their choices and Orsini disappeared through the doors to the kitchen.

Orsini's middle-aged son presented, opened and poured the Chianti Classico ordered by Whiskey who lifted his glass, tipping it first to Camron, then to Alan before toasting, "To the single seat jet and the new breed of animals who hope to fly it."

The ladies smiled. Carp offered a half-hearted "Hear, hear," and they drank.

Sam said, "I suppose it doesn't need a back seater."

"Not even for lookout," Alan added quietly. "With the bubble canopy and no canopy bow blocking your view, they say the pilot can look back over his shoulder and see the tail, something even a WSO can't do in an F-4."

As if to retract some of what he had said in recognition of his present status, Sam said, "But it's not the airplane, it's the man inside that counts."

Carp snorted. "You'd fly one if they gave it to you."

Sam smiled, and his stomach burned in covert anticipation. "I suppose I would have no choice."

Michelle laughed lightly and touched his arm. Her diminutive dimpled smile enhanced the admiration on her radiant countenance.

"I wonder how strong it is," Alan said, feeling awkward. He looked around the table, feeling flushed. "The canopy."

"Interesting you should question our talented American engineers of foreign birth," Whiskey said. He paused for a drink of Chianti. "I worked on part of the test bed for the F-16 Have Glass canopy a while back." He lit another cigarette while the others watched him, anticipating the story.

Whiskey took a long draw, which had the result of luring Shooter to light up again. "They developed a cannon for shooting fodder at the canopy," he began, "to test its strength. The most obvious concern was how it would hold up against a bird strike."

"What'd they use?" Sam asked.

Whiskey smiled to himself. "Live yard perch."

"Yard perch?" Denise questioned.

"Chickens," Sam explained.

Michelle drew in her breath and did not smile. "Not live chickens!"

"Of course," Whiskey said with a wry smile.

"That sounds bad!" Denise again.

"It wasn't easy," Whiskey agreed, "trying to propel Henny Penny through a reinforced dome, which is essentially technology's answer to the egg. It messed up our results sometimes, but that's what the powers that be wanted."

"It messed up your results ..." Alan began.

"Well, you can imagine," Whiskey said. "First of all, not a single one of the chickens was a volunteer. After all, we were firing them out of that cannon at twice the speed of sound toward a stationary piece of industrial strength acrylic. We kept giving 'em pep talks, and they'd nod their little heads, but when we got down to business, they'd squawk and put their feet and wings out to keep us from shoving them down that black hole. They knew what was going on. You see what I'm sayin'."

The men laughed. Michelle tried to grimace, but her enjoyment of the story was making it difficult to look disgusted, something that was less of a problem for Cindy Ransom.

Whiskey continued. "We used mostly roosters because they were bigger. So we tried to convince them that as soon as this was over, they could go to the bar, lower the zippers on their little flight suits, and pick up chicks, maybe get some tail." He glanced at Shooter.

Denise was smiling broadly, now.

Whiskey went on. "That would sometimes get them in the cannon, but our results were still wrong. We couldn't figure it out, so we played back the recorded shots in slow motion. Sure enough, there were these rocket roosters, fired from the cannon at Mach Two approaching the canopy with their eyes bug-eyed wide!" Whiskey clinched his cigarette in his teeth and made a wide-sweeping wing-like flutter with his arms. "Flappin' their wings to slow their approach speed, squawking all the way."

Sam was laughing his staccato laugh which made Michelle laugh harder. Cindy looked at Camron who was smiling and so smiled with him.

"I suppose I'd do the same!" Michelle joked as she caught her breath.

"So," Alan said deadpan, "your measurements ran a-fowl."

"I don't know what I'd think if I saw a bird coming at me that fast," Sam said when he could speak again.

"You wonder what you'd think," Whiskey quipped. "How 'bout the poor chicken? The last thing that went through his mind was his asshole."

Orsini delivered the main courses to the loud, happy American GIs. He did not seem to mind. He liked them. They always came to his restaurant. And he heard things. He placed a plate of smoked salmon in front of Whiskey.

"Ah," Whiskey said. "A gourmet feast, gaffed, gutted and grilled to perfection." He put out his cigarette in the ashtray at his elbow. "Gracia!"

Orsini smiled to himself.

"I should have ordered the salmon instead of chicken," Denise said.

"Sam," Whiskey said. "I'm surprised you didn't get the sea spider."

"The what?"

"Calamari. Squid."

"I get enough in Spain."

Whiskey leaned toward him. "Seems to me, you've been getting it in Italy, too."

Sam felt his face redden. Whiskey looked from him to Michelle who giggled coyly. Cindy Ransom blushed a deep crimson, flinching when Camron lightly grabbed her knee under the cover of the table.

The wine had gotten to Michelle a little. "Well, you know," she began, "just because the hen's squawking doesn't mean the egg's getting laid."

Even Cindy laughed openly.

Alan looked playfully at Michelle. "It seems to me," he said, "the sad thing about an egg is that it only gets laid once."

Grasping at this opportunity, Carp chimed in, "You sound like the egg of experience, Puppy." His words were lost amid the ensuing laughter.

Alan did not acknowledge him but looked at Denise who returned his gaze warmly.

"Anyway, it's a good jet," Whiskey said when no one else spoke. "Not something for a young pup." He looked directly at Alan who flinched involuntarily. Carp's eyes widened in anticipation. "So, Puppy," Whiskey continued, "I guess you'll have to be 'Dog,' now."

"Right!" Boomer said too loudly.

When the third bottle of Chianti had been emptied into their glasses, Michelle suddenly said, "Okay, now, who boomed Aviano?"

The others looked at her in surprise. Carp said, "You heard that?"

"Who didn't?" Michelle answered.

"You heard of it," Sam tried to correct her.

Michelle grinned and tipped her head. "I heard it." She glanced at Alan, and he knew that she knew.

Alan straightened his back. "We don't know nuttin' 'bout no boomin'!"

Denise laughed as she fixed her gaze on Alan.

Carp whispered something in her ear that made her face form a frown which seemed to surprise Carp.

"The evidence is against you, Dog," Whiskey said, blowing a billowing cloud of smoke from his lungs. "It's time to fess up."

"Might as well," Sam said waving his hand. "The smoke has cleared."

Alan leaned back in his chair and half-smiled. "I suppose. But it was never that bad anyway, thanks to an alternate heat shield," he said. Carp's face reddened, but before he could offer a retort, Alan said, "Since we are laying it all in the open." He paused to look knowingly at Whiskey and then Shooter. "I've been curious who it was we were running from."

Shooter furrowed his brow in mock concern. "You can't mean to imply there was unauthorized air combat goin' on in Zita."

"We weren't running from chickens."

"No," Carp put in, "the chickens were running."

"Separating," Sam said quickly.

"From two fireballs," Alan added.

"I don't reckon so," Whiskey put in.

"Ah, ha!" Alan said. He scratched his chin when Whiskey gave no reply other than a puff of smoke. He leaned closer to Whiskey. "I don't think anyone else would use the ground for cover like that. It almost made me concerned."

"That's why it works," Whiskey said without emotion, but loud enough for them all to hear. "People are afraid of the ground. We can't train for it like we should because those with the biggest fears are the commanders. But no matter what developments they make in technology, if the bogie gets behind you, given enough time, he can gun you, unless you can scare him off or make him afraid to follow you. You respect The Rocks. You don't have to fear them."

No one offered an argument, but Alan noticed that Michelle's demeanor had changed. She shifted uncomfortably in her chair.

After dinner, Sam ordered a round of cold lemon vodka served in frosted, vial-like glasses which the men, excepting Camron, drank in one shot. The ladies sipped on theirs, and the men ordered another round.

Orsini was gracious and courteous as they filed out the door, insisting they return soon. They drove back to Aviano, to the bar, in search of the quality drunk.

CHAPTER TWENTY-EIGHT

It seemed a rather subdued night of drinking and watch-shooting at the Aviano Officer's Club when Whiskey's group walked in. Buck turned from the bar with a gin and tonic in hand. His glasses reflected the dim light, looking like circles of fog over his eyes. He went to Michelle and greeted her with a groping hug. "Hey, good lookin'!"

"How's it goin'?" Michelle said lightly.

Buck released her to hug Denise, doing so with less vigor. "How was Orsini's?"

"Good as always," Carp answered. "The ladies were impressed."

"We learned a lot about chickens," Denise said.

"And eggs!" Michelle added.

Buck took a drink. "How so?"

Carp laughed and, under Whiskey's bemused eye, recounted the story of the Mach Two Chicken, but his version was not funny, although he imagined it to be, and Buck's smile at the story's end was little more than a courtesy.

Opposite the bar, an Air Force enlisted man was working as a disk jockey, turning records. Buck asked Michelle to dance.

Whiskey pulled a dice cup from the end of the bar, shook the cup, then threw it open end down on the counter top and peered secretively inside.

"What's the game?" Alan asked.

"Liar's dice."

"For the round?"

Whiskey nodded and said, "Two fives." He passed the cup to Alan who looked carefully under it and then pulled out the two fives. He put his hand over the open end of the cup and shook it vigorously for a second before slamming it to the counter. He peaked inside, passed the cup carefully along the counter so as not to disturb the position of the dice and said to Boomer, "Three twos."

Boomer looked questioningly at him.

Alan said," Do you believe me or not?"

Boomer considered his question for a moment, then said, "There's two fives showing. There can't be three twos underneath," and pulled the cup, revealing a two, a three and another five. "Ha!"

"Ha back at you," Alan said. "I'll have a Beck's."

"But ..."

"Three twos beats two fives. All I had to do was better what Whiskey said and have at least what I called or more."

Boomer nodded in solemn understanding.

"You gotta trust your lead, Boomer," Alan said. "Beck's for me."

A smile crept across Boomer's face. The sting of losing some of his TDY money in an unfamiliar bar game was soothed by the fact that Dog Wayne was instructing him.

Whiskey watched with studied amusement as the young AC explained the game to the younger WSO. Alan Wayne had come a long way. It seemed it had not been that long ago when he had taken this young pup under his wing, and now, here he was with his own wingman, his own new meat to influence. It was time to move on.

Alan pushed the cup of dice toward Boomer and took the barstool next to Whiskey.

"Congrats again on the new air-'chine," Whiskey said. "Dog. You deserve it."

Alan took a long, thoughtful swig of beer as he watched Whiskey's eyes pour over the younger, less experienced men aggressively following the dice game. "We're gonna miss you around here," Alan said finally.

Whiskey Wilson grunted acknowledgment, put out the partially smoked cigarette and threw the half-empty pack on the counter top. "I should quit these things." He looked at Alan through the smoke and haze of the dimly lit Officer's Club Bar. "You'll be all right. You can fly on my wing any day. I reckon you might even be about ready to go autonomous ... just don't build yourself a corner you can't make."

Whiskey considered him a moment longer, then finished his whiskey. "Gotta drain it," he said and walked away toward the latrine.

Standing behind Alan, Sam said, "I'd give just about anything to hear Whiskey Wilson say those words to me."

Alan jerked around. "Where'd you come from?"

Sam laughed. "Somebodies got my wife. I might as well talk bar talk." He took a long drink. "I agree with Whiskey. In principle, anyway. You're the best young AC I've ever known, Dog Wayne, and I, too, would fly to war with you any time."

Alan looked at him and nodded. For a WSO to say he trusted his life to you was the greatest compliment a fighter pilot could get. Before he could answer, Michelle returned with Buck in trail. The words of praise hung in the air like a protective canopy.

"Are you about ready to go?" Michelle asked Sam as she took his arm.

He leaned closer to her and whispered, "I want to stay with my buds tonight."

She did not seem put out. "Walk me home." She gave him a playful tug.

Sam placed his empty glass on the counter. "Let's go."

"See you tomorrow, Sammy!" Alan called after them. He retrieved the dice cup, contemplating the start of another game and saw that Boomer was on the floor dancing with Connie Marcum.

Shooter eyed Alan who, seemingly engrossed in thought, was shaking the dice cup in one hand and drinking his beer with the other.

"Dog!"

Alan looked at him.

"Dog, are you ambidextrous?" he asked with a smile.

Alan laughed as he realized what he was doing. "Hell, Shooter, I'm Dambidextrous!"

Perched on a nearby barstool, Carp exhaled noisily and said, "Wayne, no one could have a higher opinion of you than you have of yourself." Smiling a self-satisfied half-smile, Fisch launched himself from the barstool and walked away, a slight but noticeable swagger in his hips.

Shooter took the cup from Alan. "We'll, if you aren't going to start another roll, I will. I got the hammer, anyway."

Alan surrendered the cup as he watched Bill Fisch walk toward the restroom. Denise noted the perplexed look on Alan's face with intense interest. She caught his eyes as he turned his attention from her husband and flashed a weak smile of apology.

"I don't know if we'll ever come around," Alan said to her.

"Maybe you weren't supposed to."

He returned her gaze without returning her smile.

"It's not a selfish desire," she said.

He looked at her eyes. They were pretty, but in the dim light of the bar, the unique circles of blue that highlighted them gave her the appearance of being haunted. "What's that?" he asked finally.

She stood closer. "It's not selfish to want to be liked. Don't take me wrong, I think it's one of your better qualities. But you do make it easier for some than you do for others."

He turned his head away from her slightly. "What else do you know of my qualities?"

The music was not very loud, yet she moved closer to him to whisper in his ear, "For one thing, I think Bill wishes he had more of them, but he would never admit it."

Buck sidled up between them and asked Denise to dance. With a last nod to Alan, she turned to follow her husband's Flight Commander to the dance floor.

Daryl Hargrove seated himself a few bar stools down from Alan and began to play with the pack of cigarettes Whiskey had thrown there. Alan sat next to him. "Buy you a beer, sir?"

Hargrove said, "Let me buy you one."

"It would be an insult to refuse."

"Fine. What's your pleasure?"

"Beck's."

Hargrove ordered the beer for Alan and a blended Scotch for himself. "How was Orsini's?" he asked.

"Good," Alan answered. "You should have gone with us."

Hargrove shook his head. "That was something for you young bucks. The commander being there might have put a damper on things."

"Buck didn't go," Alan answered, feeling flippant. He saw Buck pull Denise Fisch in tight for a slow dance. He was obviously getting drunk. "He should have. Whiskey's leaving".

"Yes, he is."

"He deserves an F-16."

"No doubt he'll get one someday."

Alan did not answer.

"When I first met you," Hargrove said in the wake of Alan's silence, "I was afraid you might be just another angry young man. Sometimes, I still wonder ... like when you floor sky cops guarding nuke jets."

Alan looked pensively at Hargrove who was smiling.

"There's something inside you," Hargrove continued. "The hurt from the loss of a friend, maybe. A fear of losing more."

Alan studied him. "May be."

"If you stay in this business long enough, you will lose some, you may lose a lot more. And it won't feel any better when you discover nothing you do will change that."

Alan looked away from Hargrove toward the Squids gathering around Shooter for another roll for the round. "I'll do my best."

"Did Captain Ransom go?"

"Go?" Alan looked at Hargrove.

His brown eyes seemed softer tonight. "To Orsini's."

"Yes, sir."

"Good. He'll do fine in the F-16."

Alan frowned at him. "You say that as if to convince yourself, sir."

Hargrove returned his gaze with a smile of understanding. "He's good, but not as good as you."

Alan was surprised. "Sir, I'm not sure ..."

Lt. Colonel Daryl Hargrove narrowed his eyes, removing all other expression from his thin, childlike face in a manner that stopped Alan in mid-sentence.

It was one of the few times Alan could remember when the Boy Colonel had shown an honest response that seemed to come from his heart rather than his head. It was at once pained and sympathetic.

"I know what you think, if you're in any way the fighter pilot I believe you to be. You think like the majority of this squadron." Hargrove nodded over his shoulder at the rowdy group of men deep into a game of 21 Aces a few feet from them.

Alan glanced for a moment at the graying temples of the Squadron Commander as he turned his gaze to a distant wall.

"This selection," Hargrove said, "was the first of several. I think you will find it interesting how they turn out. No doubt, of the three Squids on the list, the squadron members question Camron Ransom's name the most. They envy you, but I doubt they begrudge you. They probably think some general somewhere insisted on Camron."

Alan had to stop himself from asking if that was in fact the case. Hargrove may have seen it in his eyes.

Hargrove reached for Whiskey's cigarettes. "Camron Ransom is the finest young officer I have ever known. You may not realize it yet, but I think a lot of you guys will be looking to Camron Ransom for a job in the not too distant future."

Hargrove took three cigarettes from the pack and arranged them parallel on the wooden bar like the steps of a ladder. "You're a good fighter pilot." Hargrove turned to Alan and, smiling added, "Dog." He looked at the cigarettes. "This is the ideal officer and fighter pilot," he said pointing to the cigarette farthest from him. "You are not there."

Alan flinched, and Hargrove quickly added, "But neither is Camron." He pointed to the middle cigarette. "He is not as good of a fighter pilot as you have the potential to be. But he is not on the bottom. He's an IP ... a good one. And as an officer," he picked up the middle cigarette and placed it above the others, "I'd have to rate him above you. So, even though you are above him here," he moved Whiskey's cigarettes again, "he is above you here." Hargrove put Camron's cigarette on top. "That will always win in the Air Force." He touched the middle one thoughtfully. "If you think only flying is important, you will always be here. Just as in life, if you think only one thing matters. Flying is not the end. It is the means."

Hargrove picked up the top cigarette, put it between his lips, reached for a pack of matches, and lit up. His puff was weak, but he did not flinch.

"I didn't know you smoked," Alan said, watching the thin cloud rise toward the lights above them.

"I don't usually." Hargrove suppressed a cough. "I like this one." He looked at Alan and then beyond him. Alan turned to follow his gaze. Connie Marcum stood to his right with her hands in her pockets.

"Hi," Alan said simply.

"Hello, cop basher," she said.

"Acquitted." He glanced at Hargrove who was stubbing out the cigarette in a clean ash tray.

"You've been busy tonight," Alan said.

She looked puzzled. "How so?"

"You've been dancing with everyone. When's my turn?"

Her eyes were soft in the light. "Have you ever danced with an officer, Lieutenant?" She smiled at Hargrove and then looked back at Alan.

He held her eyes. "I don't think so, unless I was drunk at the time and don't remember."

Hargrove rose suddenly. "I'm going to bed."

"I'm sorry, sir ..." Connie began.

Hargrove raised his hand. "No, I need to go. I've got Stand Up in the morning." He eyed Alan steadily. "Congratulations. Dog." He shook his hand and was gone.

Alan and Connie watched him leave in awkward silence.

"Is that your usual state?" Connie asked.

"What?"

"Being drunk."

"I'm familiar with it. Can I buy you a drink?"

"No. I make it a point never to accept a drink from someone with stripes on their socks."

Alan pulled up his pant leg to reveal a hairy ankle and topsider shoes, but no socks.

She grinned despite herself. "Bourbon," she said.

"Really?"

"Yes."

Catching the bartender's eyes, Alan held up two fingers. "Bourbons," he said. He glanced at Connie.

"Neat," she said.

"Neat," Alan repeated.

"What about my dance?" he asked when the drinks came.

"I'm not much of a dancer." She looked at him with a degree of intensity Alan momentarily misunderstood.

"That's not the way it appeared from here."

Connie looked out onto the others on the floor. Alan followed her gaze. The fighter pilots and gators dancing in flight suits and combat boots looked rather awkward. He was secretly glad to be wearing civilian clothes, in case she changed her mind.

"Did you really think you were going?" she asked finally.

His surprise was evident. "What?"

She rested her eyes on his chin. "Did you think you were going to get a chance to shit in some Commie Pinko Bastards' necks?" She moved her gaze to his eyes.

He stared at her until she cleared her throat in discomfort.

He nodded. "I did. At first, I mean. But I thought it through, and now I find it ridiculous for anyone to think that way."

"You don't think you could do it?"

"There's no doubt in my military mind I could do it. But how was it possible? What could two men in a fighter with one nuclear bomb accomplish?"

"Has it changed how you feel about it?"

He seemed to contemplate the idea for the first time when, in reality, he had reflected on it quite a bit. The false nuclear response changed him, transfixed his previous understanding of his place and purpose. He could have gone. It could have happened. He could have destroyed the lives of vast numbers of faceless people because they did not believe as he did. And his actions would not have made any difference. He would have changed nothing. He would not have been used to start a war, but only to add to the world's insanity already in progress as the missiles filled the atmosphere, meeting each other 180 degrees out, passing en route to their respective targets.

"Are you still with me?" she asked, turning her head to get his attention.

"It changed nothing," he said.

Someone called out, "Sam!"

Alan looked up to see the smile on his friend's face and realized he envied his friend's popularity. He imagined Michelle alone in bed and knew he envied even more than he could admit to himself.

"Someday," Connie Marcum sighed, "I'd like to know what's inside your head, Alan Wayne."

"Not tonight?" He knew he sounded relieved.

"Another time. Not tonight." She turned to look at the fighter pilots lined along the bar. "Sometime, when you want to talk about flying, but not with them." She smiled warmly and walked away.

Boomer approached him.

"Hey, Dog! Where's intel's finest Lieutenant going?" Boomer asked. "It didn't take you long to chase her off. Don't tell me tonight is already booked?" Boomer smiled to hide his blush.

"Sammy!" Alan said, looking past Boomer. "Sammy Small! Back so soon."

"Yeah, even I'm not that quick!" Shooter put in.

"Not in the mood just yet," Sam said, turning to order a Scotch.

"Well, I'm in the mood," Shooter said. "What's her room number?"

"Eat me, Shooter!" Sam said.

"Not my first choice," Shooter countered.

"Is everything okay?" Alan asked quietly.

"Full moon, tonight," Sam whispered.

"Oh. Say no more."

"Yep," Sam nodded. "Time to get drunk and be somebody!" He loved his wife, but he was glad to be with the boys. This might become another quality drunk. "Where's Whiskey?"

"Drainin' it," someone said.

Buck snuck up behind Sam, grabbing his neck in a half nelson. "Let us now sing a hymn. Hymn. Hymn. Fuck him."

Someone began the song that rose in intensity, even as Sam joined in:

> Oh, my name is Sammy Small
> Fuck 'em all.
> Oh, my name is Sammy Small
> Fuck 'em all.
> "Oh, my name is Sammy Small
> And I've only got one ball
> But it's better than none at all
> So Fuck 'em all!

CHAPTER TWENTY-NINE

For the last ten minutes of the two-hour ride, the train crept slowly toward Venice. When they disembarked, Alan was surprised to see the Grand Canal as soon as they walked out of the far side of the station. Unschooled on the history and layout of the city, he had not known what to expect, or even that the city was an island.

Sam took Michelle's hand and led them across the Ponte degli Scalzi bridge and down a large walkway.

Michelle released his hand to look briefly at a vendor's table.

Alan watched her as she peered at the wares. "Where to?" he asked Sam.

Sam jutted out his chin and scratched under it. "We, uh, could try to find St Mark's square and go from there." As he spoke, his words and facial expression indicated a personal knowledge of the town, both the strength and weakness of which was that it was knowledge born from books. "Maybe find Harry's bar later," he added.

"Harry's bar?" Michelle said, looking away. She seemed distracted this Saturday morning.

Although her face maintained a cheery expression, she was disappointed. She liked Alan, but she had hoped for an intimate ride on a gondola with Sam, drifting gently along the canals of Venice, kissing beneath the Bridge of Sighs. They needed that. Instead, they were a threesome, and walking instead of riding. So much for romance.

Sam cleared his throat. "Hemmingway wrote about Harry's Bar."

Michelle smiled impishly. "The one in Venice, or Florence?"

"Venice ... I think."

"A bar ... that sounds good," Alan said. "Let's get moving." He nodded at Sam. "Lead the way."

"I'm not sure where the square is," Sam said. "I just know ... I think it's on the other side of the city."

Alan gestured with his hand in the fighter pilot's way of passing the lead. Sam turned and walked toward the inner city with Michelle and Alan in close trail. Alan was surprised to see so many walkways. In his ignorance born of Hollywood, he had imagined that the only way around the romantic city of Venice was on the canals. But they walked, and the canals along their way looked polluted and sour.

"Lots of junk," Alan said, peering into the water. "Makes it hard to remember that you're thirsty."

Michelle walked with her hands in her pockets. "At least if you fall in ..." she nudged Alan with her elbow, "... there's plenty of flotsam to grab on to."

Alan feigned being off balance to hide a momentary flush of panic. "If there's anything I'm going to grab on to, it's you!" He grabbed her shoulders in mock desperation and contorted his face in exaggerated fear. "If I go, you're going down with me." He looked again at the debris floating in the canal. "Would you call that flotsam or jetsam?"

Michelle said, "Hmm. Some jet ... but I think more flot." She flashed a smile that Alan enjoyed more than he thought he should.

Sam seemed unaware of this playfulness. When he walked, he did so with a purpose. He did not stroll. Looking to find the right path to where he was leading them, he checked each street and alleyway with his head cocked slightly forward as if that extra milli-second of early viewing would expedite the whole route-finding process and decrease their chances for wrong turns.

Michelle caught up to him, her hands still in the pockets of her loosely fitting trousers. Though she never offered alternatives, she glanced with a casual alertness at each turn in a manner that suggested she could feel if they were going the right way as well or better than Sam.

When he was sure he could do so discretely, Alan watched her. There was nothing especially arousing or sensual about her gait, and yet that made him enjoy it all the more. Her light angora sweater outlined her figure without accentuating it. Her long brown hair bounced joyously with each stride.

The enjoyment of life truly seemed second nature to her. Alan thought of this, then smiled to himself at his subconscious choice of words. He fell behind, looking up at a non-descript building that dipped down to meet the canal. He watched Michelle for a moment and decided, from that vantage point, Sloan looked the better.

They crossed the Ponte di Rialto.

"Is this the same canal we just passed five minutes ago?" Alan asked. "That collage of trash looks familiar."

"Could be," Sam joked. He knew where they were, now. "Let's see ... the sun was over there ... but now, it's behind the clouds ..."

"Oh no!" Michelle crinkled her eyes into a smile. "We're not even in Italy anymore!" She turned to Alan. "Do you know where we are?"

"No idea," Alan answered. "I'm Venetian blind."

Michelle started a groan that turned into a gentle laugh.

"This way." Sam turned down a larger alley that opened into a street. Passing an apparently popular restaurant, they were suddenly at a corner of St. Mark's Square. For the moment, none of them spoke as each in his or her own way took in the European splendor of yet another historical treasure too complex to be understood in one brief visit. The picturesque cathedral stood boldly to the left of them. The columns crowned by the Lion of St. Mark and the statue of St. Theodore were across the plaza, and beyond was the Grand Canal and Giudecca Island. Pigeons and people populated the square.

"I'm getting hungry," Michelle said.

"And thirsty," Alan added.

"Let's see the cathedral, then have lunch," Sam suggested.

"Sounds good," Alan said, looking at Michelle. "I wouldn't want the priest to catch me with beer on my breath."

They walked across the square through the bystanders and birds to St Mark's. Its facade was unlike any of those they had seen in Spain. They went inside, stopping near the entrance as always seemed required when looking at cathedrals. There was something in the tall ceilings of this house of God that kept them from simply strolling down the aisle. Reverence. Awe. The feeling of being small. Something held them back.

They gazed in silence at the glass windows and the ceiling for a time. Michelle began to walk slowly toward the front of the church, and the men followed.

As they walked, they each turned and looked, seeing the inside from different angles. The large basilica revealed itself with increasing majesty. Alan tried to imagine the peasants of another world walking reverently through this place in humble silence with backs lowered, tattered old hats in hand, willing to give the church their life's last lira in hopes of a better world in the next.

Alan turned to look at the large glass window over the entrance. He was lost in the splendid art work, the time and talent some man or men had invested in that window as an offering of their lives to God. Something made them do that. Nothing that looked like this church or that window could be created out of a desire for money alone. Or even fame. It went much deeper than that. Only something beyond this world - and it did not matter whether it was perceived or real - could drive a person to such works of devotion. Something inside a man that turned art and love into sacrifice. That was what this was ... a sacrifice of money, of talent, of time, of life.

"You must really like that window." It was Michelle.

"What?"

Her hands in her pockets, she nudged him out of his reverie with her elbow. "You must really be finding something in that glass window."

Alan looked around. Sam was at the far end of the basilica, near the pulpit.

"Found something?" He looked intently at her. "I was lost in it."

"It's beautiful," she said, looking up.

"It has to be."

"What do you mean?" She looked thoughtfully at the glass.

Alan gazed at the side of her face, then back up to the window. "Whoever did this didn't do so for his own glory."

Michelle did not answer.

"My father would have loved to be here," Alan said, looking back at the window, unsure why he had said that. "I could never even imagine something like this, much less create it."

"Well, you're a fighter pilot, not a glass cutter. You have other talents."

Alan shook his head. "No. I mean ... it isn't in me."

"The talent?"

"The beauty. The devotion. The motivation ... that's not it, exactly."

She glanced away and, seeing Sam was still preoccupied, turned again to Alan. “I’ve never heard you mention your father before. Is he ... still ... in the States?”

Alan looked knowingly at her. “He’s alive and well, I suppose, in Texas.” He looked away. “It’s been a while since we talked.”

“Oh.” She wanted to take his arm for the comfort he seemed to need. “Why would he like this?”

“He’s a preacher. This is his ... thing. He would see something more. He would feel something I don’t.”

Michelle did not answer, thinking silence better suited the moment. After a short while she said, “Sometimes, I don’t feel motivated ...”

“Passion!” Alan said slightly louder, then looked around to see if he had disturbed anyone. “That’s what I don’t have,” he said in more of a whisper. “I don’t feel the passion.”

Michelle removed her left hand from her pocket and touched Alan’s arm. “Sometimes I don’t feel the passion either.”

Alan felt at once exhilarated and uncomfortable. This could not be a pass of some kind. Not from Michelle Christopher. His heart beat faster. He did not look at her.

“You know what I do?” she asked.

The lump in his throat facilitated no answer.

She put her hand back in its protective pocket. “I read a book.”

Alan’s face flushed in embarrassment. He was glad the church was so dark. “You read a book.” It was a statement.

“Yeah. Steinbeck or Dostoevsky. Tolstoy, maybe. It reminds me of what is in the inner person. What can come out.”

I am not in love with this woman, Alan thought to himself without knowing why the thought had come to his mind. “You amaze me,” he said. “Most women I know read slightly more contemporary authors ... like the ones that write the Harlequin novels.”

She laughed. “That’s not the passion I mean!”

He felt embarrassed again. Was she playing with him?

“You guys hungry?” Sam asked from behind them. Michelle turned as if she had been listening for him.

“Let’s go!” she said lightly.

Alan glanced at her. She had switched from talk of passion to craving for food with no visible signs of being consumed by either.

As they left the cathedral for the sunlight of the afternoon, Sam again took Michelle's hand. "Let's go to that restaurant we saw," he suggested. He was already leading them that way.

"You sure look at a lot of cathedrals in Europe," Alan said, looking back at St Mark's. "Every town you go to, it seems like. Did you ever think of that?"

"What? How many there are?"

"Well, that," Alan began. "And the fact that so many of them are so grand."

"They are pretty," Michelle said, smiling knowingly at him.

A table by the window became available as they walked into the restaurant.

"Those are good seats there," Sam said, leading the way, not waiting for the waiter.

Alan pulled a chair for Michelle. "This is a good view," he said, looking from the outside back to her.

"Yeah. Good seats," Sam repeated.

When they were all seated, Michelle said, "There's Camron and Cindy with Clarence Bailey."

"Where?" Alan turned.

"Behind us ... behind you. Back there. And Bill and Denise."

Alan returned their silent acknowledgment.

"I guess they've been here a while," Michelle said, picking up her water glass.

"What do you think of them?" Alan asked the question looking at Sam, but his tone indicated an open discussion.

"Carp and Denise?"

"Camron. And his wife."

Michelle glanced over her shoulder. "Well, she's cute. She's obviously crazy about 'her Camron.' That's what she talked about all the way driving here. 'Her Camron.' She really admires him, I think."

The waiter came with a plate of bread, and they ordered,

Breaking off a piece of the fresh bread, Alan said to Michelle, "So, you read Steinbeck?"

"Yes!" she answered, becoming slightly animated. "Don't you think he's funny?"

"Funny? No."

"He can be."

Camron caught Alan's eye and gave him a nod of greeting. Alan returned the acknowledgment with a twist of his hand. They were preparing to leave. Camron paid the check and rose from his seat. Followed by the other four, he strolled to the table by the window.

Alan greeted them. "Enjoying the sights of Venice?"

"Yes! Again!" Cindy said enthusiastically. "Isn't the cathedral magnificent?!"

Carp stood behind them. He seemed all too ready to leave.

"Impressive," Alan answered. "Can ya'll pull up some chairs for a minute?" he asked to be polite.

Boomer turned to find a chair.

Denise moved toward them with a smile. "Sure!" she said, then, looking at Bill added, "... for a minute."

The five of them sat at a round table away from the window.

"The square is nice," Michelle said politely.

"They could shoot a few pigeons," Carp offered. "They probably have. I think I had one for lunch." He laughed to himself. "Don't order the chicken."

"Oh, dear!" Michelle feigned concern, then smiled her carefree, dimpled smile.

Carp gazed at her long enough to make Denise uncomfortable.

"Well Bill, you keep making them fly by walking at them," Denise said. "You probably chased a few into the restaurant." She laughed, although she knew this would make him uncomfortable.

"Did you catch one?" Michelle asked.

"I wasn't trying to catch one." Carp glared at Denise then looked away.

Alan said, "You just wanted to see if you could kick one through the cathedral doors, right? If you can't score the touch, go for the three."

Carp did not acknowledge him. Alan sat back in his chair and, looking at Sam, shrugged his shoulders.

"You know? You guys are always trying to cause trouble," Michelle observed lightly.

"Always looking for a reaction," Denise added. She glanced around the table. "They always want to see how people will respond to their antics." She looked at Cindy for confirmation, then back at Bill and, leaning away, said, "You are."

"Looking for attention?" Alan asked, sipping his water.

Denise smiled warmly at him. "Yes, but in a crude sort of way."

"The 'Desire to Disgust'!" Michelle said laughing.

"The what?" Cindy said.

"Desire to disgust," Sam answered for her.

"Yes," Denise said, eying Alan. "Your songs ... the way you act in the bar sometimes ... don't you think you are looking for a reaction?"

"Maybe so," Alan answered, furrowing his brow in amused contemplation. "But we seldom stop long enough to see if we got one." He turned to see Camron's reaction, but he was facing away toward the cathedral.

"But you want it," Denise said firmly. She was thoughtful for a moment, curling her lower lip as she moved her eyes. "Every winter, the sea gulls gather on the beach at Daytona ..."

"That's where you are from?" Alan interrupted.

"Yes ... Every winter, in February usually, there's thousands of them. The water is too cold, so they stand on the beach ..."

Carp exhaled heavily. "Where is this leading?" he asked impatiently. He was anxious to leave.

Denise frowned. "Well, it's just that, when people are walking along the beach, the guys almost always run after the large groups of gulls or walk into where a bunch of them are standing. To make them scatter ... to run or fly away. They're looking for a reaction, but it's one they know they're going to get. I mean, what else are those birds going to do? Why do guys feel compelled to do that?"

"It's in the genes," Alan answered, looking into her questioning eyes.

Carp said, "I know it is. At least, that's where I keep mine." He exhaled in exaggerated boredom.

Sam laughed.

Alan thought of something to add, but, glancing at Cindy, decided against it. Camron had become interested, but not in Carp's joke.

"It's beyond our control," Alan continued. "It's probably the same gene that gives you that uncontrollable urge to roll in on someone who doesn't see you."

"Over the Aviano TACAN," Sam added.

"Right!" Alan laughed.

Cindy sighed and tapped Camron's arm. "We have a train to catch."

"They're anxious to get back to the room," Carp said, rising from his chair.

Cindy flinched, and Camron suddenly flushed crimson. Carp had gotten another reaction. Apparently, their day together had been less than pleasant.

As the others rose to follow, Alan felt an intense disappointment that Carp was among them. Denise had been nice enough. Without Carp, she might even have been interesting. Camron had been so quiet. He would like to have talked more with him, too, perhaps about cathedrals. The waiter brought them their salads, and they were once again down to three.

CHAPTER THIRTY

"Whiskey Wilson is dead," Cathy Sherman repeated to Alan and Sam as she stopped midway down the walkway leading from the door of the BOQ building. The mist of the early morning fog that blanketed the Po Valley was bleak and dreary. "The rescue team just found the wreckage," Cathy said blankly. "There were no survivors."

Sam was stunned into silence.

Alan had not believed her, had not understood her. Something about her demeanor had made him think this must be a sick joke of some kind. How could Whiskey be ...

"He and an IP from the 614th crashed near Twin Buttes late yesterday afternoon," Cathy said with a look on her face that gave Alan the distinct impression she felt special to be the one telling them the news. She had known Whiskey. Now he was gone. She almost seemed to relish having known someone who was killed in a fighter. It was inappropriate.

Sam spoke the only words he could find. "What were they doing?"

She turned toward the car. "Doug think's they were trying to fly between the Buttes ... he says it can be done," she said, without explanation. "They must have been too low."

She said "too low" as if she had tried that many times herself and found it far too easy to die from.

"Whiskey found a corner he couldn't make," Sam whispered to himself.

"This has not been a good day," Cathy announced as she turned to continue down the walkway. In the car, unaware of the tragic news, Michelle, Denise and Cindy waited to begin the long drive back to Spain.

The mood around the squadron was one of restrained depression. Two fighter pilots were dead, but the world could not stop. There was unspoken hurt and sadness. There was also subtle movement, a quiet repositioning of status. Whiskey had hit The Rocks. The rest of them had not. He was dead. They were alive.

The best ones were survivors. But no one knew who the best ones were because no one knew who would survive.

Yet that was not completely true. Some of the least capable ones survived. It was not talent, it was luck. As Whiskey had once said, sooner or later, they would all face a situation. Most would live to talk about it, to warn the lesser mortals not to try it. A few would not be so lucky. You could not fly a fighter for 1000 hours or even 500 hours the way a fighter was supposed to be flown and not brush against the edge of catastrophe.

A turn would be made belly up to a rock. A moment of inattention. Nothing might happen. The rock would go unseen, or the pilot would see it late just as his plane missed it and would realize the potential but not have the luxury of time to think about it, except to think that he did not hit the rock because he was too good to hit the rock.

Or he might hit the rock.

His engine might quit.

He might follow someone else into the rocks.

Someone else might hit him.

He might get disoriented in the clouds or at night, the canals in his inner ear so confused that the instruments made no sense unless they were lying to him. And so he would pull for the lights in the rocks, believing he was pulling for the stars.

He might join up on lights he believed to be those of his leader but were actually a train.

He might pass out. Too many g's at the wrong time. His mind telling his hands to pull on the pole before it had told his body to prepare. The blood would drain from his errant mind, and it would fall asleep just long enough for a supersonic jet to point straight down. If this happened at 5,000 feet, he could be dead in less than ten seconds.

Alan was angered by Whiskey's death.

Cathy Sherman had said, "There were no survivors."

Alan had wanted to believe that meant nobody stayed in the jet and lived. "No survivors" sounded to him like more than two people, like no one on the ground was hit.

"What do you mean, 'no survivors'?" Alan had asked.

"They found the wreckage," Cathy had said simply. "There were no survivors."

"You mean, no survivors in the wreckage."

"There were no survivors."

Friday night came without fanfare. The Aviano Officer's Club bar was very quiet. Every fighter pilot who could be there was, but it was a very low roar this night. And when it appeared it might liven up a bit, someone would offer a glass held high in a toast. They would drink their whiskey and become subdued once again.

Saturday morning was bright and cool. A few leaves fell from the trees that surrounded the officers' quarters. There were few complaints of headaches. Even those that had gotten drunk had done so without conviction.

With the evening approaching like an unfortunate friend, Major Sherman suggested they go to the Halfway House. With notable restraint, the men agreed it might lift the fog that filled their minds. Bull Boulder grabbed the keys to one of the rented Fiats and piled Reggie Smith, Shooter and Carp in the small car with him. Sam found the keys to the step van. Alan, Boomer, and Buck rode with him.

At the last minute, Major Sherman decided not to go. It was just such good judgment that had thus far propelled him through a rather mundane yet practically flawless career.

Another car of four completed the convoy that headed up the winding road on the side of the mountain to the Halfway House.

They first drove through the northern half of the city of Aviano, then across an intersection where two cars were seldom seen at the same time and into the foothills that quickly became mountains. The asphalt road narrowed with the beginning of the winding climb.

The Halfway House derived its name from the fact that it was a restaurant and bar halfway up the mountain to the Pianca Valle ski resort.

There was also a "quarter-way" house that was sometimes called the Halfway House by those who could not wait to get to the Halfway House to begin drinking. In the winter, the road could be treacherous, but the snow seldom sneaked far enough down the mountain to eliminate the possibility of somehow getting there. At times in the spring and fall, hang gliders could be seen floating down from where the tight road traversed the steepest edges of the hill.

The road always appeared much steeper going downhill, especially if the Halfway House had been the reason for going up it in the first place. There were stretches that seemed to race straight down, piercing through the dark woods and then suddenly turning sharply along the edge, barely gripping the mountainside.

The drive took thirty minutes going up. No one ever timed it coming down.

The sun was just beginning to set when the three vehicles pulled into the parking lot. Inside, a few locals were drinking quietly at the bar. Until the fighter pilots arrived, the restaurant had been practically empty.

Soon after they ordered their meals, the whiskey, wine and beer began to flow freely. It was not long before Alan could feel the fuzziness he knew would distort his memory of this evening, the indisputable beginnings of a quality drunk.

When their dinners arrived, Bull ordered a bottle of bourbon. "Whiskey could down the booze like no man I have ever seen," he began, pushing his chair back to stand. "Tonight, we drink bourbon for him, in his memory." He paused. "In his honor."

The officers nodded.

"Frederick 'Whiskey' Wilson was a good fighter pilot, one of the best ... and a good friend. Gentlemen! Let us drink to remember him, that whenever we take a glass of bourbon to our mortal lips, we remember Whiskey." He looked at the small crowd of Whiskey Wilson's friends. "Tonight, we will drink it on the rocks ... Whiskey would have appreciated the gesture."

He poured, then passed the bottle.

When the ice in each fighter pilot's glass was covered with bourbon, Bull held high his glass and said loudly, "To Whiskey Wilson!"

"To Whiskey!"

Bull downed his in one large gulp. The others that could do so did likewise. There were a few subdued coughs, and the bottle went around the table again.

"To fighter pilots!" Fisch toasted. "There ain't many of us left!"

Alan sipped this second glass of bourbon slowly. Dammit, Whiskey! And Damn you! How could you let that happen? You tell me what counts, and then you just fly into The Rocks.

"I can't believe Whiskey did this to us," Carp said.

"What?" It was Sam.

Carp swallowed his bourbon. "I can't believe he did this to us. I can't believe he's dead."

Sam looked at Carp who was now staring philosophically into his empty glass. "He did it to himself," Sam said showing little emotion.

Carp looked at Sam and shook his head. "No, you don't understand. You can't understand. He proved it could happen to him. He did that to us. Whiskey was great. He knew the 'numbs'," Carp said, meaning "the numbers."

Sam was quiet, aware that it was not unlike Carp to turn a significant event into a personal experience with him at the center of its consequences.

After a brief silence Sam said, "Carp, it didn't happen to you ..."

"It did happen to me, dammit!" Carp flared his nostrils. His loud voice interrupted the conversations that surrounded them. Drunken eyes fell on him. He tipped his glass to empty this last drop down his throat. "Another bottle!" he roared. "On me!"

When the frightened waiter brought the second bottle, Carp opened it roughly and, clearly lacking Bull's natural grace, filled his own glass first before clumsily filling those near him.

"To fighter pilots!" He splashed bourbon on his shirt as he offered up the toast.

"To us," someone said.

A piece of bread hit Alan's ear. Shooter was grinning. Alan broke off a piece of the hard-crusted bread and threw it ably toward Shooter who ducked, letting the bread hit Boomer.

More bread began to fly.

Trying to avoid a direct hit, Buck leaned too far back in his chair. Before his alcohol swollen head recognized the deteriorating situation, he was well on his way to the floor. The wooden chair collapsed under the bulk of his weight, and his whiskey glass, thrown clear of the immediate area of impact, shattered against a far wall near an Italian couple who had just been seated.

"Monsieur ..." the waiter began.

"No parley frenchie," Carp mumbled.

"This is Italy, Carp," Sam said.

Bull raised his huge hand. "We'll settle down," he said to the waiter who looked at him in disbelief before scurrying off.

"Gentlemen," said Bull. "We are reminded of our station." He threw a piece of bread, catching Sam squarely in the forehead.

Sam returned fire with a piece of boiled potato, missing Bull and hitting Reggie.

Reggie lunged for Sam but fell short, hitting his groin on the table corner.

"Ahee!" he cried and fell sideways onto a table shared by two local couples, hitting his head on an occupied chair. He lay with his face in the middle of their salad, holding his groin with both hands, writhing and moaning. The Italians at the table, now covered with wine and water, leaned awkwardly away from the drunken American.

"Time to pay the check," Sam said, rising from his seat.

Bull went quickly to the table where Reggie Smith lay stunned and bruised. "Excuse me," he said in Italian. "I believe this is mine." He picked up Sweet Cheeks, tucked him under his thick, muscular arm and strolled toward the dining room door where he met the little waiter.

"Oh my!" the waiter gasped, realizing the noise he had come to inspect meant everything and more of the disastrous image he had painted in his mind.

Bull placed Reggie in a chair and held him upright with his knee. From his trousers he pulled a bright red check book, signed his name to a check and handed it to the waiter who looked at it questioningly.

"Do whatever is fair," Bull said, "and pay for those people's dinner." He pointed to the four now very angry Italians. "Be sure they know," he added.

He lifted Sweet Cheeks up on his shoulder and walked out of the dining room.

"You have an Italian account?" Sam asked in amazement as he followed him.

"The lira is at a great rate right now," Bull answered matter-of-factly. "Even if they empty that account, I won't be out too much." He looked back. "You guys ready?"

"Yeah," Shooter said.

Buck picked himself up off the floor. "Uh huh."

"Carp, you coming?"

Carp remained seated, staring straight ahead. "I'm going to the bar."

"Good idea," Bull said. "Let's go back to the base and get blitzed among friends."

"No," Carp said flatly. "I'm going to this bar."

"Come on," Bull cajoled. "We'll have a few back on the base. On me."

"I'm staying here."

"How will you get down the hill?"

Sam said, "There's a disco downstairs. Dog and I are going. We'll bring him home later."

Alan looked at Sam in surprise. "We are? We will?"

"Sure."

"I'll stay with them, too," Boomer said.

Bull looked the young officers over for signs of sobriety and saw none. "Okay, be careful." He walked out with the others, half-carrying, half-dragging Reggie who had fallen asleep like an infant on his shoulder.

Sam looked at Alan and said, "We can't leave him here," indicating Carp.

"No, I suppose we can't, even though it appears to be what he wants." Alan took one last look at Carp before turning away.

Sam, Alan, and Boomer left the restaurant and walked down the stairs, following the sound of loud music. Except for the flashing lights on the small disco floor, the room was dimly lit with only a short bar and a few tables.

"Maybe we'll get lucky," Sam said, raising his eyebrows.

"Yeah." Boomer looked around the room. "Lucky enough to stay out of trouble."

Most of the tables were occupied. Only a few people were on the dance floor. Alan noticed two females in their early twenties standing at the bar. He was sure he recognized one of them.

Sam and Boomer followed Alan. "Bourbon, I guess it is," he said back to them.

"And cigars," Sam answered.

Alan ordered the drinks, but the bartender had only Italian cigarettes.

"Might as well," Sam said and, lighting one, began to puff on it. "These are terrible!" he said, suppressing a cough. "Even Whiskey wouldn't smoke this shit!"

"They're all we've got," Boomer said puffing, but not inhaling.

The girl Alan recognized lit an American cigarette. Alan recalled seeing her during a workout at the base gym. Her weighty companion had a round, friendly face with wide eyes that surveyed the room as the two women talked.

More patrons were entering through the door. Stirring his drink with his finger, Sam said, "I suggest we find a table." Alan nodded assent.

When they were seated Sam said, "I think those two are interested in us." He indicated the young women at the far side of the room.

Boomer looked at them. "There's only two of them, and I'm not into anything kinky."

"I didn't know you were into anything at all," Alan scoffed. "Except Connie Marcum."

Boomer's light-hearted smile threw Alan off his attack.

"As if any of us would do anything about it anyway," Alan added by way of apology.

Sam followed Alan's gaze to the girl at the bar. He looked at Alan, grinning. "It's amazing what a little contrast can do."

"Oh, yes," Alan acknowledged. "And a little bit of the absence that makes the heart grow harder. I mean fonder."

Finishing his drink, Sam said, "I assume the absence of which you speak is from a particular person more than a particular thing."

"It's all the same, when you get right down to it," Alan said, knowing that would get a laugh from Sam.

"But it's after you've gotten down to it that the who comes into play."

"One of life's great truths, I suppose ... but she's certainly no coyote."

"Coyote?" Boomer questioned.

Sam and Alan laughed.

"It's not her, necessarily, is it?" Sam asked Alan.

"What do you mean?"

Sam said, "When I was at NAV Training, our instructor had a party. We went dancing afterwards. His wife was beautiful. The other two young studs and I took turns dancing with this lady who was only a few years older than us, yet old enough to have had all the experiences we could only hope were in our futures.

"We kept dancing with her because her husband never would. When one of the other guys was taking his turn, I grabbed a beer and sat down beside my instructor. Right out of the blue he said, 'Do you ever hanker for some strange poontang?' I thought he meant his wife, so I didn't say anything. I was really afraid he had read my mind. But he said, 'You'll understand after you've been married a while. You don't really want an attachment, you just want one night with some strange poontang you haven't had before.'

"I thought he was crazy. Here was this Venus, this goddess we all wanted to dance with and rub up against. He was married to her ... he could take her home right then and do all the things we could only imagine ... but here he was talking about strange poontang. I didn't understand."

"Do you now?" Alan asked.

"Yeah. But 'strange' is the word that keeps me away from it." He finished his bourbon. "Three more? My round."

"Absolutely."

Alan and Boomer watched the dancers. When Sam became overdue, Alan looked toward the bar and found he was talking to the round girl. Her easy laugh made her look pretty. Alan caught the eye of the taller girl then looked away.

After several minutes, Sam returned with the glasses.

"What's up?" Alan asked suspiciously.

"Nothing. Just casual conversation. She's the friendly type."

"She spoke first?"

Sam stirred the bourbon and ice with his finger. "Uh, huh."

They finished the round, then another. The booze was hanging heavily on them.

"Let's ask them to dance," Alan said, getting up from the table.

"But we're a woman short ..."

"We'll explain it to 'em," Alan answered, not wanting to break the momentum.

The suggestion was favorably received, and all five of them took the floor, passing their names between them.

Sam struck up a conversation with the girl named Betty who, though not seemingly athletic, was a sensuous dancer. Michaela was quiet and danced stiffly as she watched Alan, showing none of the grace he had imagined of the athlete he had seen at the gym.

"I'm going for more booze," Boomer said.

Sam said, "See you at the table."

"I knew he couldn't hang," Alan said to Sam loud enough for the girls to hear.

As the dance floor became crowded, Alan noticed Sam was dancing close to Betty and sometimes around her. Sam disappeared behind her, and she laughed then yelped loud enough that Michaela turned to see Betty grinning and shaking a finger at Sam who was acting the innocent. Alan had seen him bend over and gently bite her. In his overly-bourboned mind, it seemed a good idea. With Michaela's back still to him, Alan grabbed her legs and lightly bit her shaking butt. She turned quickly, almost throwing him off balance.

There was pain in her eyes. "Why did you do that?" she yelled.

"I'm sorry." Alan tried Sam's innocent look, but it did not fit him.

"Why did you do it?"

"Because I wanted to. You ..."

Michaela turned and stormed off the floor. Sam looked quizzically at Alan who shrugged his shoulders and followed her. She walked briskly across the room and outside into the cool air.

"Hey, I'm sorry," Alan called after her when they were outside. She stopped under a group of trees before turning to confront him.

"I am sorry," he said again.

"My mother didn't raise me that way!"

"What?"

"I don't know what kind of a girl you think I am, but I'm not that way. No, mais oui! I am a young girl, le femme petite, but I am not that way, no, no, monsieur."

"I'm sorry," Alan broke in. "I ... I thought you'd like it," he lied.

"Like it, mon ami? Why should I like it? Je no comprendo pas vous."

Amid the mixture of English and obscure, incorrect French, Alan came to the painful realization he had bitten the wrong butt. This was the payback.

"I am a good girl. Why would you do that to moi? Maybe you jocks think you can do that, but I am une bonne femme. You have hurt me!"

"I am truly sorry," Alan said honestly. He turned to leave.

"No, wait!" She grabbed his arm. "You cannot turn your back on me! You cannot walk away from me. No! No! No!" she said in her flawed French accent.

"I didn't have to follow you out here to apologize ..."

"But you did! And now you are here." She paused and eyed him intently. "And I do not accept your apology. I will walk away from you." She turned her back to him and took a step or two away.

Totally bewildered, Alan stood his ground. "I understand. And I am sorry. That's all I can say. I don't know why I ..."

She turned and stormed back to him. "Is that why you asked me to dance? To bite my ... to bite me?"

"No!" Alan recoiled. "I bit your ass because ... it's a pretty ass."

"Oh! So you like my ass! Pardon moi! You want me to shake it in front of you?" She turned around and shook her behind, then turned to face him again. "You like that?" She took his face in her hands. "You want to kiss me?" She surprised him with a kiss that smelled of cigarettes and wine. She pulled back.

His eyes wide with confusion, Alan did not move.

"You want to hold my ass while we kiss? You like that?" She grabbed his hands and tried to kiss him again as she maneuvered his hands to her behind.

"Yes ... well, no! Look, I'm sorry. Let's go back inside for a while."

"Without you I will go back inside!" She threw his hands away from her behind and walked quickly to the door. She grabbed the handle, then glanced over her shoulder at him with a look that was both sensual and mocking. Throwing her head back, she ran her fingers through her hair and disappeared through the doorway.

Alan stood in the darkness for several minutes, deeply breathing the mountain's cool air, letting its freshness steer him toward sobriety. He thought of Sloan and was ashamed.

When he went inside, Boomer was still at their table, Betty and Sam were slow dancing very closely, and Michaela was leaning against the bar with a drink. Alan went to Boomer.

"What was that all about?" Boomer asked. "I was just about to come outside to see if there was somebody I needed to bust up."

"That girl I bit on the ass is crazy," Alan answered as he quickly downed the drink Boomer had bought for him. The ice was melting in Sam's untouched bourbon.

Boomer shook his head. "You bit a strange girl on her butt, and you think *she's* crazy?"

Within five minutes, Michaela came to their table. Like an actor immersed in a role she said, "Let me buy you a drink."

"No, thanks," Alan said looking straight into her eyes.

She stood abruptly upright, glaring at the refusal on his face. Her mouth formed words she could not speak. She walked away.

"She's trouble," Alan said to Boomer. "Let's get Sam, find Carp and get the hell out of here."

"Could be tough ... I think Sam's fallen for some strange poontang."

Alan glanced at Boomer who was smiling congenially.

Alan went to the dance floor, keenly aware that Michaela's eyes were following him. As the dance brought Sam around, he touched him on the arm. "We're outta here. You staying or leaving?"

Sam looked at Betty whose smile was noncommittal. "Leaving, I guess. I don't know."

She looked disappointed but said nothing. Sam kissed her on the cheek. She took his face in her hands and kissed his lips.

Alan shook his head and walked back to Boomer. Turning around, he was surprised to find Sam right behind him. "Going with us then?"

Sam sighed. "Too much at stake." He looked back at Betty who had rejoined Michaela at the bar.

As they walked toward the step van, Alan said, "That Michaela was a strange bird."

"I hope it's not in the name," Boomer joked, elbowing Sam.

Sam eyed him evenly. "My wife's name is Michelle."

"Oh. Yeah," Boomer said apologetically.

"She's not someone I would want Sloan to find out about," Alan said remorsefully. "Especially since I ..." He paused.

Sam grinned at him. "Never confess!" he said. "I'll go get Carp."

Sam found Carp at the restaurant bar talking to an Italian man and two young women. "We're heading down the hill," Sam said eying Carp's new friends. "You ready to go?"

"No. I'm staying."

"Staying here?"

"I'm telling these guys about Whiskey." He was very drunk.

The two women turned to each other and giggled.

"How will you get home?"

"We will care for him," the man said with a heavy accent.

Sam looked at the people. "Carp ... I don't think that's a good idea." He put his hand on Carp's arm.

Carp whipped it away. "Don't worry about me."

Sam walked back to the van. "He's staying."

"How will he get back?" Boomer asked.

"He doesn't want to act like he cares. I guess he thinks this is the way you're supposed to be when another fighter pilot dies."

He wasn't like this when Ernie died, Alan recalled. But then the stakes were different.

They were quiet driving down the hill. A tight curve held their mutual attention midway down the hill and so kept them from noticing the totaled Fiat on the side of the road.

When Sam stopped the van at the BOQ, Alan and Boomer were nearly asleep. He quietly removed the keys, ran inside the building and returned carrying a fire extinguisher. Alan was just getting out of the van when Sam hit him squarely in the chest with a steady stream of water.

"Assassin!" Alan yelled.

Sam targeted his head.

"You scum-sucking sub-human Commie swine!" Alan laughed.

Boomer flung open the back door ready to run, but Sam cut him off and nailed him. Momentarily freed from the attack, Alan ran into his Q-room to get the fire extinguisher he kept there for just such an emergency. As he turned to leave, Boomer opened the door into him, sending him back onto his bed and the extinguisher to the floor. He lay there, eyes closed, head spinning and decided this was where he would stay.

Boomer grabbed the fire extinguisher, turned off the light, and headed back outside, locking the door behind him.

Sam went to his room where he found Reggie who looked as if he had just arrived there himself.

"Hey!" Reggie said excitedly, watching Sam dig for the extinguisher hidden in his closet. "Hey! I think we totaled the Fiat!"

"What?" Sam stood with his new weapon at port-arms.

"We totaled the Fiat!"

"Well, to hell with that! We've got a war, finally! Come on!"

Sneaking out of the building, they did not find Boomer quickly enough. He blindsided them from behind a small tree. Sam returned fire as Reggie ran for cover.

Sam yelled, "We need more fire power!"

"I'm going across the road!" Reggie said, hustling his pudgy body out of Boomer's range.

Boomer's aim had been sure. Sam was soaked. Seeking revenge, he ran toward Boomer in a blind assault, fire extinguisher ablaze, yelling, "Damn the CO2, full speed astern!"

The fight moved to the van, each man seeking cover while looking for an advantage.

Reggie ran across the parking area and into the first building he came to where he found a fresh extinguisher just inside the door. He pulled the pin and, thinking he was in another BOQ, fired a test shot into an open door.

A husky voice barked from the darkness, "Hey! What the hell's going on?!"

Reggie laughed and fired again. Turning away from the room, he was confronted by three large young men, none of whom he recognized. Sweet Cheeks Swartz had stumbled into a nest of angry sky cops, and they were swarming.

As Boomer and Sam dueled, a squad car with its lights out quietly turned the corner into the BOQ parking lot.

"Sky cops!" Sam whispered loudly and ran behind the building. Boomer was trapped, though they had not yet spotted him. He stayed in the shadows. As the door of the car opened, he threw his empty container into the bushes and crawled under the van.

The car was parked not twenty feet from him. He heard the two men walk toward him then stop. Together, they turned and walked into the BOQ.

The first room they tried to enter was Alan's. Finding it locked with the lights out and heavy snoring coming from inside, they moved quietly on, out of that building and into the next.

Sam decided on a new strategy. Hide in plain sight! Running into his room when he saw the sky cops go into the other building, he took off his clothes down to his undershorts, ran back into the day room, turned on the TV, picked up a copy of "The Stars and Stripes" and sat down in a recliner in a pose he hoped would indicate he had been there for quite some time.

Moments later, the sky cops walked in.

Sam's strategy might have worked had he not immediately lost his cool.

"You guys looking for fire extinguishers?" he heard himself say.

The cops looked quietly at each other.

"I mean, are you looking for those guys ... the other guys?"

"Sir," said the taller cop, "your hair is wet."

Like a child caught in the act, Sam reluctantly felt his hair. "Oh ... yeah ... well, I just got out of the shower."

"Sir, do you normally shower wearing your skivvies?"

Sam looked dumbfoundedly at his shorts. "Oh ... well ... those guys, don't know who they were ... those guys nailed me ... coming out of the shower ... I never saw them, though. Don't know who they were."

"Would you put your clothes on and come with us, sir?"

Sam and Reggie spent the night in the base detention area because Lt. Colonel Hargrove refused to bail them out. In the morning, he began the paperwork required for a totaled Air Force rental Fiat. Around nine o'clock, it began to rain heavily. Hargrove drove the SOF truck to the base jail.

Leading the pathetic duo of unfortunates out of Security Police Headquarters and into the driving rain, his only words were, "Get in the back."

He drove slowly in the downpour to the BOQ, leaving the young men to huddle against the chilling rain.

Dropping them at the "Q", he said, "Stay here."

In the day room, Alan watched a pre-taped football game while trying to recover from an incredible hangover that no amount of aspirin seemed able to corral. When Sam trudged in, Alan considered whether he should ask for specifics before simply saying, "Well, you look kind of down ... did your cellmates try to make you play 'Lucky Pierre'?"

Sam did not look happy. "Lucky ..."

"... Pierre," Alan added helpfully. "Middle man in a three-man butt-f ..."

"No, no," Sam cut him off. "But we're screwed just the same." He slumped into a chair. "It's Whiskey's fault."

"You'll be okay," Alan said, watching him with interest. "I think the Great Aviano Road Rally as performed by Shooter and company will prove to be your heat shield."

Sam wiped the rain from his forehead. "Yeah, Reggie mentioned something about that ... last night. He said they were run off the road by a red sports car that spooked Shooter as it passed them going down the hill."

"Oh, shit!" Alan laughed.

"Sounds believable," Sam said. "I'd believe it if I had to ... and I have to."

"Maybe," Alan grinned, "but Shooter and Bull told Hargrove it was a white Fiat going uphill that came at them head-on."

"Oh shit!"

"Oh, dear!"

Forgetting his predicament for the moment, Sam laughed his deep staccato laugh as he pictured the look that must have been on Hargrove's face as, even now, he knew Reggie was giving the Boy Colonel his version of the story.

"How'd you get incarcerated?" Alan asked.

Sam shook his head. "I tried to play possum."

"Possum, huh," Alan repeated.

Sam looked at him in solemn assent. A wicked smile was forming on Alan's face.

In sudden understanding, Sam said, "Now wait a minute!"

"I'll use it sparingly," Alan said. "Possum."

"I don't want to be ...!"

"Possum?"

Major Sherman walked in just as Carp drifted into the room from the outside storm, still in his garb from the night before. He was soaked completely through. Carp stopped to take his bearings, then sighed as if satisfied and said, "Made it!" before stumbling past Sherman and down the hallway to his room.

Watching after him, Sherman shook his head. "You guys are turning me into an old man before my time."

"There is no such thing as old age," Sam offered philosophically. "Life is simply a series of nights from which we never fully recover."

Glaring at Sam with the hint of amusement, Sherman said, "Keep a low profile for a while, okay Christopher?" He glanced at Alan, allowing a tight grin to form on his lips as he winked. "I mean Possum." He walked out of the building.

Sam looked at Alan and laughed again. As suddenly as he had begun, however, he stopped and looked sullenly at the television. "Now I'm screwed on two counts," he said. "Damn you, Whiskey!"

The four F-4s on the runway were ready for takeoff. Another four-ship flying overhead was coming up initial. A cloudy, overcast day. A mist. A fog.

Blue four of the airborne fighters was too close to number three. He turned into the formation, unable to control his jet any longer, the stress of staying in position being too much. The four ship on the ground began to roll, two ship formation takeoffs, ten seconds apart.

Blue four burst into flames as he collided with three who hit number two who was then thrown into the airborne lead. They were coming down in one huge ball of flames, now crashing on the first two ship of F-4s on the runway. The second two ship, so close behind could neither stop nor takeoff over the mangled mound of metal and flesh. There was fire, another explosion, then nothing.

Charred, black Phantoms, piled in a heap. And faces, in anguish, staring from the destruction. And Ernie. A skeletal grin creased his face.

The dream woke Alan in a cold sweat. He sat up quickly and surveyed the small dark room. He was disoriented and felt very much alone, as if he had suddenly discovered that he was dead.

The dream was so vivid. He had seen it all. He could save none of them.

Michaela shocked Alan, approaching him as he and Sam walked outside the squadron building on the way to their jet for the redeployment flight back to Torrejon. She was in fatigues, and, noting her rank, Alan realized that a few days earlier, he, an Air Force officer, had bitten the behind of an "airman two-stripper." She looked into Alan's eyes without speaking, barely noticing Sam was there.

"I'll see you at the jet," Sam said, leaving the man and woman together on the steps.

Alan returned the girl's gaze, wondering what she would say in the light of day. When she did not speak, he said, "I don't know what to say."

Michaela placed a finger to his lips. "Shh. No apologies." She looked out over the concrete at the waiting F-4s. "I wish I could go with you, to know more about you than comes in just one night together."

"What do you mean?" Alan asked defensively. "We didn't do anything ..."

"I know that," she said, cutting him off abruptly. She smiled. "I was drunk. Drunk enough to get angry, but too drunk to enjoy it." She moved a step closer.

Alan tightened the grasp on his gear. "I didn't mean to offend you," he said with conviction.

"Oh, I know that." She put her hand to a strap of his parachute harness. "You really didn't. But you were trying to get my attention." She laughed and looked into his eyes. "And you certainly did that." She flashed pale blue eyes that he decided sparkled more with danger than emotion.

He was afraid of what she might say next. Even in sobriety, this woman was unpredictable. "I have to fly home ..." he began.

"I know. Your fighter pilot thing." She drew herself even closer. "When will you be coming back?"

"I honestly don't know." He was glad to be able to answer her truthfully.

"I'd like to see you again, under better circumstances."

"I don't think that would be wise ... under the circumstances."

She touched the wedding ring on his finger. "What happens TDY, stays TDY. And you'll be TDY. Here. You can trust me."

He gently removed her hand. "I have to go." He turned to leave but continued to look at her face.

She laughed lightly again. "Oh, now don't be a bastard!" she said a bit louder. "Fly straight, Cowboy. I'll be here."

Alan said nothing more, but walked quickly to his waiting jet, looking back over his shoulder as he approached, concerned she might have the gall to follow him. She remained where he had left her, smiling and waving like a young lover who would grieve his departure until his return.

The redeployment flight to Torrejon was uneventful. But Alan's thoughts ran wild as he gazed at the Med from 35,000 feet. He thought of Michaela and shivered with guilt. Would Sloan be able to tell?

The air was clear but rough. Alan thought back to Undergraduate Pilot Training in Arizona, recalling the day Wheels Delong taught him the secret of chasing "clear air turbulence."

"Over there!" Wheels had said as they flew, together, side by side in the T-37 jet trainer. "There it is!"

Seeing only clear sky, Alan had turned the small jet to fly where Wheels pointed. There was nothing.

"You incompetent young puck!" Wheels said with great disappointment in his voice. "You missed it! Here! I've got the airplane. I'll show you how to find it." He put the "Tweety Bird" in a hard right turn that threw Alan's head against the canopy. "There it is! See?"

Alan, his head throbbing, had answered, "I think so."

Wheels had laughed, then said, "We're in it!" as the airplane began to shake.

Fascinated, even as they made a second pass, Alan never noticed Wheels was extending the speed brake to artificially induce the burble they felt.

Several months later, over a beer at the MacDill Officer's Club, Alan recounted the story to Ernie who laughed openly at his friend's admitted gullibility. Alan had forced himself to laugh as well, thinking that to be the end of the lesson.

"You see? You were just creating your own turbulence," Ernie said, waxing philosophical. "Nobody can see the real stuff coming. That's why they call it 'clear air turbulence.' Nothing warns you about it, and only experience gets you through it because you know it can't last forever."

When they landed and taxied in, Alan saw Lt. Colonel Hargrove standing near his parking place with a full bird Colonel and Sloan. He shut down the engines, unbuckled and slid down the ladder. Sloan came to him, ahead of Hargrove and the other officer.

"This is one of our future F-16 horses," Hargrove was saying to the man. "He's one of our most promising young bucks. He'll just talk to us, briefly meet you, before greeting his wife ..."

Alan ignored them both, grabbed Sloan tightly and kissed her deeply. Her lips were softer than he remembered, her body firmer. He could feel his mouth watering in anticipation of her.

"Well, er, he'll, uh, he'll be right with us ..." Hargrove was saying. "And this is one of our best young WSOs," he said, turning to Sam who shook the unknown man's hand.

Hargrove looked back at Alan. "Lieutenant Wayne! Do you have time to meet your new Wing Commander?"

"Oh," Alan held Sloan's waist with one hand as he reached with his other to shake that of the new Commander. "Alan Wayne, sir. Damn glad to meet you!" He felt exhilarated and peculiarly non-military.

"Al Wolgast. Good to meet you, Lieutenant." He was a big, hairy man with a prematurely wrinkled face, short salt and pepper hair, and wiry arms that emerged from his creased blue shirt. "I've heard a lot about you."

"From ... Colonel Hargrove?" Alan had to watch himself ... he had almost said 'the Boy Colonel.'

"Yes, and your lovely wife. We played some racquetball together." He glanced at Sloan and winked.

Alan looked at Sloan in surprise. She whispered, "See? I'm good for your career."

"People call him Wolf," Hargrove said as he watched Wolgast walk away toward Sherman's jet. Hargrove pivoted to catch up with the new commander.

Next to The Wolf, the skinny Boy Colonel looked every bit of his nickname. “For obvious reasons,” Alan said to Sloan.

WINTER: A NEW YEAR
CHAPTER THIRTY-ONE

Though the mountains beckoned him, and although his blood burned with a desire to be in the peaks, to look down upon the world and yet be a part of it, Alan was unhappy with the chain of events whose momentum had nurtured the inevitability of this ski trip. He knew without question he would enjoy the skiing. Indeed, since leaving Colorado and the academy, he had hungered for the sound of the edges of his skis cutting into the packed snow. But he wanted to be in Texas, or rather he felt he should be there, spending this holiday leave time with his disintegrating family.

In separate letters to his mother and his father, he wrote that he and Sloan would not be home for Christmas, knowing his mother would be disappointed, and his father would be truly hurt. He knew what his father would say, or rather what his father would want to say - that he needed to come home for his spirit.

There was too much Methodist preacher in that, and Alan knew he could not face that right now. Since Ernie's death, talking to his father had become difficult if not impossible. Perhaps it was the guilt.

After driving through the rugged dryness of northeastern Spain, the Pyrenees emerged, rising above the horizon in a refreshing green and brown mix that was increasingly accentuated in white. Not especially high mountains, the Pyrenees derive their majesty from their prominence - historically and geographically- and their youth.

In an average winter, the snow at the Baqueira Beret ski resort is not especially good when compared to Tignes, France, or Italy's Cortina.

Situated on the south side of the Pyrenees, where the sun is plentiful and warm, the lower slopes are often devoid of skiable powder.

This year was exceptional. Despite the drought of the central plains, the snow was very good. So good, in fact, that Alan was forced to stop to put the recently purchased chains on the tires of the Citroën while still several miles from Baqueira. Difficulty arose when he could not understand how the low sitting design of the car could facilitate the use of chains, and he cursed repeatedly while Sloan waited impatiently in the car. The black grill cover, designed to allow the air-cooled engine to remain warm enough to idle in these temperatures, was in place, but the car's heater struggled with little to show for it.

Laboring and now breathing too heavily to swear, Alan did not hear the man behind him until he spoke in schooled English, "Sir, I may be mistaken, but I do believe those are to go on the front wheels."

Looking up, Alan realized he was blocking the way for an increasing number of cars below him on the road, none of which were there when he made what he had assumed would be a brief stop.

"Are you sure?" he asked the man as he stood to stretch and examine his lack of progress. "How can you get any traction that way?" he asked, curious how the man knew to speak English to him.

"I may be completely wrong about this," the man said with intended courtesy and confidence, "but I believe this is a front drive car."

"Oh." Alan looked at the front wheels that obviously had plenty of area to work the chains. "I see."

"May I help?"

"Where do we go?" Alan asked irritably when they reached the village.

"I guess we'd better ask somebody," Sloan said, looking through the frosty window of the Citroën.

"Do you know the name of this place?"

"I have it written down. See?" She took the make-shift brochure out of her purse. "Show this to somebody."

Alan parked, grabbed the paper, and walked into a small currency exchange. In broken Spanish and some English, he asked the clerk inside, showing him the paper.

He returned to the car shortly but did not get in. Opening the hatch, he removed their luggage.

"Well?" Sloan asked.

"This is it. It's right above this tavern. How about a little help?"

"Okay." She gave him an angry grimace, then looked away at the building as if expecting to see something familiar.

They lugged their bags up two flights of stairs to the numbered apartment they were looking for.

"You said we could ski right up to our room."

Sloan puffed from the weight of her bag. "We can ... to the building. That's pretty close."

Alan knocked on the door.

Vernon Moreau answered. "Ah, you made it." He opened the door wide for them and stepped away.

Alan threw the bags into the middle of the front room. "We had a little trouble, but we got lucky."

"Yes, I can imagine. Being fluent in Spanish and French is a great advantage for me."

Sloan was about to close the door when she recognized the somewhat bulky form of Martin Rudd coming up the stairs with two pieces of luggage. Marty smiled. "So, did you guys just get here, too?"

"Uh, yes," Alan answered looking sideways at Vernon.

"So did we." Marty forced the bags through the doorway. "Had a little trouble with the directions."

Vernon flashed an angry look which Marty ignored.

"There's the front room sleeper sofa and the one bedroom with two twin beds," Marty said. "How shall we do this?"

"Why don't you guys take the bedroom," Sloan said quickly. "We'll take the sofa."

Alan thought to remind her that they were the married ones and she was the only female and might need privacy. The look she gave said she had already considered all of that.

They had a dinner of snacks and sat around talking about the good snow that was falling. Alan was reminded of his first meeting with these two men when Vernon invited them to dinner, having met Sloan through the ski club. Introduced by Sloan, Vernon had said, "Yes, I'm a knock out! An anesthetist. If you ever want to get gassed, I'm the guy to see."

Alan had retorted quickly, "I'm a fighter pilot. Gassed is okay, but if you ever want to get bombed, I mean completely blown away ..."

Being bettered had not set well with Vernon.

Later, with inflated pride, Vernon had shown them original hand sketches of Budapest he bought from a Hungarian artist while on a trip to Yugoslavia. "You'll notice there are two pictures ..." There were in fact. "People don't know that it's actually two cities. See. This is Buda ..." He pointed to the first. "... and that is Pesht." This pedantic arrogance had irked Alan. But as these were Sloan's friends, he did his best to be amiable.

"I think they're all a pesht!" Alan had said with a twist on Sam's joke.

The look that formed on Vernon's face then was no different from the one he wore now when Alan said he was tired and wanted to go to bed early to be fresh in the morning.

"Oh, yes, well," Vernon said. "Time for bed."

When they were alone with the lights out, Alan said quietly to Sloan, "I would prefer a little more privacy. This is a vacation. We should treat it as such."

She knew what he meant. "But I thought we should make the offer since otherwise they would have to share the double mattress."

Alan laughed softly. "You don't think they'll be sharing anyway?"

"No, they are just friends, but what difference does it make?"

"None, really. Frankly, I'm glad to see it. I was afraid you wanted to come on this trip just to be around other men." He kissed her.

She rolled over with her back to him and closed her eyes. "They're not gay."

CHAPTER THIRTY-TWO

When Alan awoke, the darkness was growing pale. He could see the night's shadows fading on the walls through the partially opened curtains. Unable to sleep any longer, he took a moment to savor the intimacy of sharing the first light of day with no one. It was already a little late. The sun would not warm the earth long in this arena of his life.

He looked at Sloan, beautiful in repose with the covers up to her neck. What a difference. In summer, almost nothing. In winter, she hibernated in flannel and socks. They were different in that way. He responded to the freshness of the air, she to the temperature.

He dressed quickly and quietly, enjoying the solitude. Using the coffee maker and small voltage transformer he had packed, he made coffee, knowing the aroma would wake someone. He hoped it would be Sloan. The noise he made putting the cups on the bar stirred her, but still she slept.

Vernon emerged from the dark back room. "Is Sloan up?"

"No."

"I'll take two cups." He looked back into the room. "He's still sleeping. Let us know when it's clear."

Alan went to Sloan with the coffee and gently nudged her. She sat up and looked at him. "Are you going to shower?" he asked.

"What?"

"Do you want to shower?"

"Yes. What time is it?" She took the coffee.

"Time to go. You're first."

When they were dressed, they gathered their skis and poles and went out. It was a beautiful morning. The sun was bright and warm. There were no clouds.

Marty was the first ready. "Where to?" he asked.

"To the top," Alan answered.

"Right away?" Sloan asked. "There's snow everywhere."

"The top's the best, the least skied."

"Because it's the coldest."

"That's why it's the best."

Marty stabbed his poles in the hard snow and pushed himself toward the first lift, raising his skis in the coordinated stepping motion of an experienced skier. "Let's go!" he called over his shoulder without looking back.

Vernon struggled to follow him, looking like an awkward child who believed the only way to move on snow was to bend forward and push himself along with his poles like a sled.

"Step and push, Vern." Alan's helpful advice was tainted with sarcasm.

Vernon did not look at him. He hated to be called "Vern." He pushed again but began his own version of stepping as he strained after Marty.

Sloan adjusted her gloves and hat and, pulling her goggles down over her eyes, adjusting them as well.

Some ski trip this is going to be, Alan thought. He alternately watched Sloan and the ponderous Vernon, thinking it would take half the day just to finish the first run. Beginning to lose his patience, he said, "Do you need your goggles just to get to the lift?"

Sloan did not answer. When she was ready, she moved past him toward the increasingly crowded lift line.

In and around the line, the skiers pushed and shoved. Kids broke in line when they could get away with it. No one spoke of it, but everyone vied to maintain or improve their position. Once on the lift, position was determined and that was it until the next lift line. Alan and Sloan sat together on the moving bench as it tucked them at their knees, and they were finally on their way up the hill.

The first tier was covered with skiable snow with little visible grass, although rocks appeared through the white ground cover like granite icebergs that could make the run treacherous to the unsuspecting novice.

They got off the first lift and skied the short distance to the second one where they caught up with Marty. Vernon's pants were already marked with the telltale white of his first fall in the snow.

Sloan was silent as they rode up the hill. As the mountain passed underneath them, she intently watched the other skiers.

Alan turned in the seat to look down the hill behind them, taking in the magic of the valley and snow-covered buildings below. The lift offered the best view. Going up, looking only forward, the rocks and trees and thick snow drifts under and around the large poles gave no hint of what was behind you if you simply turned and looked. That was where you would be going. On the way down, he would be too preoccupied to enjoy the view, going faster, avoiding trees, concentrating on negotiating the hill at a pace that was perhaps borderline on the uncontrollable. Taking it all in was easy now, relaxed on the lift chair, not having to work, being taken to the top.

He recalled the first pictures he could remember of snow and snow-covered mountains, before he had ever skied Colorado. The pictures had come first. The art before the reality.

"Why do you always have to look back?" Sloan asked somewhat irritated. "You're rocking the chair." She adjusted her thighs on the bench.

"It's pretty, looking back," he answered.

She wanted to look back, but the end of the ride was near, and she had to prepare herself. "You'd better get ready. We're almost there."

They rose together to get off the moving bench. Sloan reached to hold Alan's arm for balance until she was able to remain upright on her own. "Down now?" she asked when they were clear of the lift.

"One more," Alan answered.

The ride on the third lift to the top was colder, especially where trees blocked the sun. But the snow was beautiful. It rested in the trees, piled on the boughs. It lay smooth and even on the ground, in many places pure and untouched where it had fallen. It was Nature's muffler, warming the earth beneath it, subduing sound above, turning the wind that brushed the trees into a whisper of security.

Just like the pictures, Alan thought, unable to verbalize the image in his mind. Of all the paintings and pictures of scenery, those of snow always seemed the most accurate. So pure. So even. He knew the painter would have to see it himself, to know it, to paint it honestly.

At the top, Vernon's bindings released as he tried to get off the lift, and he threw out his hands as he began to fall. His pole straps were on his wrists, his skis attached to his ankles by the safety straps. His legs and arms diverged from his body, extending from him like flailing spokes from a human wheel. He landed face down in a snow drift. When they pulled him out, the silhouette sculpted in the snow was that of an out-of-control snow angel.

While Marty helped Vernon adjust his bindings, Alan opened the top of his leather bota bag and squirted Spanish red wine down his throat. Against the backdrop of the snow, the cheap wine tasted oaken and fine and settled warm in his stomach.

Sloan looked at him almost contemptuously. "Do you have to start on that stuff already?"

Alan looked where he imagined her eyes were through her goggles. What was back there? Why were they on each other's nerves? "It's warm. Just a little warmth in the sun for a day of skiing."

"Don't get drunk. You'll get hurt."

He took another squirt, then replaced the cap on the bota bag and draped the strap of the bag securely across his neck and shoulders. He glanced at Marty and Vernon. They were still working on the bindings. He skied the short distance to them. "How's it coming?"

Marty looked up at Alan. Vernon stared at his bindings. "Slow," Marty said. "You guys go ahead ... we'll catch up."

"Okay." Alan turned away. "Sloan, let's go."

"See you soon," she said to the two men as she followed her husband.

They skied the white packed powder of the third tier quickly, then returned to the line to ride up the hill again. The sun was warming them now as it angled higher in the southern sky. The mountain was beautiful, and with their first run behind them, they both felt more relaxed. Alan took a drink from the bota bag, then offered it to Sloan.

"Want a swig?" The look in his eyes was softer than it had been earlier.

She relented. “Okay. A small one.”

“Take as much or as little as you like.”

“I just want a swallow.”

When she finished, he took the bag, then put his hand on her leg. She pushed her free hand under his arm, and they rode up in silence.

Marty and Vernon were not at the top, though Alan half expected them to be. Sloan and he adjusted their gloves and began their second run. A few hundred yards down the hill, Alan saw a woman having trouble getting up from the deep snow there. As he approached to help, he recognized the figure.

Michelle’s eyes flashed with surprise and delight when she looked up from her troubles to see him coming toward her.

“How’s it goin’?” he said, imitating her usual greeting.

She struggled a little to turn, trying to get her skis pointed downhill. “Can you help a maiden in distress?”

“You’re distressed?”

“Well, you know?” She tried to raise her skis.

“And you need help?”

“Oh, all I can get!”

“Then I’m here to rescue you, my lady.” He took her outstretched hand, allowing her the balance she needed to push against the deeper snow.

Sloan came up behind them as Michelle regained solid ground. “Hey Sloan!” she said.

“Hi.”

“Imagine seeing you guys here!”

“Where’s Sam?” Alan asked looking down the hill.

Michelle brushed snow off her pants and arms. “He was headed down. When he realized I was stuck, he was too far down to come up. I think he went to the lift to come back up and get me.” She smiled at Alan. “I hope he did, anyway.”

Alan looked over his shoulder up the hill for a moment then back at Michelle. He was happy to know they were here.

“Hey!” Sam yelled, streaking toward them from above. He slid effortlessly across the smooth packed snow, turning his skis as he reached them, leaning and cutting the snow with the edges, pulling up suddenly beside them in a sliding stop born of experience. "What's going on here?!"

"I'm rescuing your abandoned wife," Alan returned. "How long have you been here?"

Sam poked his poles in the snow and helped Michelle brush the snow off her back. "Yesterday. We thought it would be a good place to spend the New Year."

"So did we," Alan said. He was feeling better. Sam and Michelle were here. It was going to be all right now. He pretended not to notice the glare on Sloan's face he knew was meant to remind him of his former lack of enthusiasm.

Sam opened a bota bag and drank. He held it toward Alan. "Take a swig."

Alan pulled his around from his back. "Got my own," he said and opened it to drink.

Sam offered the bag to Michelle who took it and squirted the liquid, holding it away from her mouth as Sam had. The red wine streamed from the bag as she squeezed, making a gurgling sound as it hit the back of her throat.

"Swallow while your shooting," Sam said.

She lowered the bag, closed her mouth and swallowed. "I can't do that."

"'Chelle, go for it!" Sam answered.

"Later." She drank again.

Alan held his bota toward Sloan, but she shook her head. He drank again, this time in the manner he had seen Sam and Michelle use, looking up the hill as he did so. Marty was coming down the slope alone. Alan lowered his head, swallowed, and yelled out to him.

Marty glanced around, then turned his skis and slowed as he approached them.

"Where's Vern?" Alan asked.

Marty took the bota Alan offered him and pointed. "Down there, I think. It's not just the bindings giving him trouble now. He's not used to this much powder." He pounded the hard-packed snow with a pole and laughed, then drank from the bota.

"Don't lip it," Alan said.

Marty returned the bag. "I'd better go find him." He sped away from them down the hill.

"Let's go, too," Alan said.

On the next run, Sam found a modest jump, and they decided to try it. With enough speed, they would be able to get high enough to make it exciting for fighter pilots. "Take our picture," Sam said to Michelle. She removed a pocket camera from her jacket and pointed it at the small mogul, waiting for the first jumper.

For the camera, Sam picked up more speed and flew high enough to make his landing hard and shaky, but he remained on his skis.

Alan walked the "crab walk" sideways on the edges of his skis, getting higher up the incline.

"Where are you going?" Sloan yelled at him.

"This has to be good!" he yelled back at her, thinking he would surpass the competition or go down trying.

By the time he reached the jump, the speed he was carrying was scary. At the last moment, he decided not to jump as much with his legs. He went airborne, stiff-legged, arms flung wide for balance. Even as Michelle snapped the picture, she imagined herself to be framing the portrait of a broken man.

He hit the snow hard, fought for balance, lost it in some heavier snow and rolled head over heels into a drift. The others skied to him, laughing guardedly when they saw him pull his head out of the white mound he had created. His bindings had released, his hat covered his eyes, and snow covered his purple ski jacket and pants.

When she realized that Alan was not hurt, Sloan became angry. "You could have broken your neck!"

"Such grace!" Sam called. "What do you call that? The dying prune?"

With effort, Alan rose to his feet. He ignored Sloan's stare and looked intently at Michelle. "Did you get the picture?"

"I think so."

"You think so? I nearly killed myself for you, for your picture, and you think so?"

"Yes."

He brushed away snow and turned to Sam. "If it's on film, that's what matters. Who cares what happened after?"

"Not so," Sam returned, grinning, "because every time you try to show someone that picture, I'm going to give them the actual story. Speaking of which, anything broken?"

"I wouldn't tell you if there was," Alan said, adding, "Possum."

They skied down the hill to the next lower run where they took a break.

Enjoying the scenery of the mountains, out of the corner of his eye, Alan saw Sloan wave as she said, "Hi!" Turning, he was mildly surprised to see Brandon Parsons skiing awkwardly toward them.

"Hello stranger," Brandon said. "Small world!"

"Major Parsons," Sam said in dubious respect. "What brings you to the Pyrenees?"

Brandon glanced at Sloan and smiled. "Well, this ski trip."

"Oh." Sam looked down at Brandon's snow covered Scotchgard-ed blue jeans. "How do you find the slopes so far?"

Brandon replied, "I just open my eyes every time I fall, and there they are."

Sloan laughed with him.

Sam was taken aback. At least the man could laugh at himself.

"Brandon!" a female voice with an accent called. Everyone except Brandon turned to see her approaching them. She addressed him in German which he answered somewhat curtly.

She looked toward Alan and something on the snow caught her eye. She spoke to Alan in German, and he shook his head.

"Sprechen Sie Deustch?" she asked.

"Nur ein bisschen."

She said something to him again, which he did not understand. She tried again. "Parlez vous francais?"

"No, I'm sorry," he answered, flattered that this new woman had singled him out.

"You are English?" she asked in an accent.

"Yes."

"Oh, okay, well ..." She pointed at his leg. "You are bleeding to death."

He looked at his legs. There was red snow at his feet. Liquid was dripping from his pant leg. He reached behind him and pulled the bota bag around. It was nearly empty from a burst seam. "What a catastrophe!" he said in his best imitation of W. C. Fields.

She turned to Brandon and, out of deference to what she assumed were his friends asked again in English, "Are you okay? You took quite a bounce yourself."

"I'm fine." Brandon seemed rather annoyed with this person who was nice enough to be concerned for his welfare. He seemed embarrassed and stole glances at Sloan who was watching him intently.

"Then let's ski more," Brandon's lady friend suggested with a slight frown of annoyance.

With a certain reticence, Brandon said, "We'll see you guys later."

"If we do, we do," Sam answered.

"Oh, we will, I'm sure." Brandon Parsons turned awkwardly on his skis and reluctantly followed his multi-lingual, obviously intelligent female friend toward the lift line.

Alan turned to Sloan. "Do you know him?"

"Yes. Sort of. We've met."

"How?"

"Playing racquetball."

"And you know who he is?"

Sloan furrowed her brow. "I think he's the new head of something."

"Wing Chief of Plans," Sam said.

Sloan smiled cutely at Alan. "That's it!"

"Did you know he'd be here?" Alan asked.

"No."

"You didn't seem surprised."

"Why would I be?"

"I don't know." He turned to Michelle and Sam. "You guys ready to hit it again?"

"Lead on." Sam said.

"To the top then."

Michelle smiled. "All the way to the top."

CHAPTER THIRTY-THREE

The day turned decidedly colder as the sun descended to the southwest. They decided to rest their skis and warm up in the tavern near the condo where Michelle and Sam were staying. Two bar stools were open where the counter angled, and Sam suggested the ladies sit. They ordered hot spiced red wine which they drank initially for warmth, sipping as the wine rekindled their spirits. Feeling more comfortable, Michelle removed her ski jacket, dropping it on the foot rail.

She smiled at Alan. Her cheeks and chin glowed pink from mild snow burn. Her eyes flickered brightly like living candles in the dim yellow lights. Her thick dark hair rested on her shoulders, overflowing down her back and across her chest. Alan could not take his eyes off her, and she seemed to realize it. Sloan noticed as well. Sam did not appear to.

Michelle talked about the skiing and was more animated than usual. The snow, the cold, the warmth, the Pyrenees, and the warm wine all seemed to enhance her radiance.

Sloan's ski boots did not fit comfortably. She went to their room to change into the fur-lined Pacs she had insisted on buying.

When she returned, her wine was cold, and Alan was saying, "Skiing the Pyrenees is not a bad way to bring in the New Year. What are you doing New Year's Eve?"

Sam shifted his feet on the floor. "Probably eat locally, then drink locally." He laughed. "Get drunk locally, and hopefully stagger back to the general locale of the condo."

"Why don't you have dinner with us? We'll ring in the New Year together."

Michelle's eyes flashed. "That sounds good. We brought a little something we could fix."

"We have plenty."

Sloan found it difficult to conceal her reaction. Alan had not consulted her, or Vernon. She realized then that she was not especially fond of Sam, or Michelle, for that matter, although she could not say exactly why. Perhaps it was because they seemed so fit for each other. She would not retract the invitation, but Alan would hear about it later.

Sam saw Sloan's face. "We shouldn't impose on such late notice."

"Bull feces!" Alan said, making Michelle laugh. "You can't greet the New Year with a quiet, boring evening. There should be revelry, merry-making, and debauchery with friends!"

"We'll help cook and bring the wine and champagne," Michelle offered.

"Sounds good."

Sam finished his second glass of cinnamon wine. "What do you think, Sloan? It's okay if your friends won't like it."

Sloan curled her lips into a welcoming smile that was convincing enough. "It'll be fun."

Someone tapped her on the shoulder. She turned in her seat to see Brandon Parsons.

"Hey, stranger. Mind if I join you?" He pulled an empty stool from around the corner of the bar, sat down heavily, and ordered a beer.

"Where's your friend?" Sam asked.

Brandon frowned. "In her room, I guess, or maybe out and about by now. We just met on the slopes. We're not here together.

"Sure seemed like you were," Sloan blurted, then looked away.

Brandon smiled in her direction. "Nope. She just sort of discovered me."

Several questions crossed Alan's mind that he decided not to ask, and one that he did. "Are you here alone, then?"

"Yeah. No roomie." He glanced again at Sloan.

"What are you doing tomorrow night?" she asked.

"Tomorrow?"

"New Year's Eve."

"Oh, I don't know. Dinner somewhere."

Sloan blurted, "Why don't you join us?"

Alan had felt this coming, and he was caught. There was nothing he could say now that would not lead to an argument.

"Well, I appreciate your invitation," Brandon said, "but I don't want to bust in on your dinner. I've sort of got plans." He paused and glanced at Sloan. "With the guys."

Sloan was disappointed and looked it. She wanted to ask who the guys were but changed her mind.

"Maybe I can drop by after dinner," he added.

Sloan was noncommittal. "Why don't you, then."

"I will."

The dinner was quiet for a while. Vernon felt abused and openly showed it. Alan did not care, being determined not to waste his life on people he did not like.

The little party livened a bit as the champagne flowed.

Dinner was barely over, and they were gathered around the sofa table in the living area playing a fast card game called "Slap" when there was a knock on the door. Vernon rose from his seat on the sofa next to Marty to answer the door. Brandon Parsons smiled into the room from the stairway. Seeing him, Sloan got up and went to the door beside Vernon. Brandon's grin moved his ears as she stepped aside for him to enter. Vernon exhaled audibly.

Sloan introduced him. "This is Brandon Parsons."

"Brandon." Vernon offered his hand limply. "Vernon."

Marty sat on the sofa, working on a Rubik's Cube Alan had bought at the BX and brought along to fill the void when there was nothing else to do. Michelle and Sam sat on the floor at each end of the sofa table. Alan sat at the corner, next to Michelle.

"Have a seat," Vernon offered without meaning it.

"Thanks," Brandon Parsons answered, looking around the small room. He plopped down on the sofa and immediately engrossed himself in what Marty was doing with the Rubik's Cube. Too late to make other arrangements, Vernon sighed audibly as he sank sulking into a chair away from the group.

Brandon quickly realized Marty did not know the secret of the Cube. "Have you solved it before?" he asked Marty.

Marty twisted the Cube in his hand, making another attempt to get the colors on one side the same. "No. The best I've done is get the colors right on the top layer." He twisted the Cube again. The pattern was worse. He let the Cube and his hands fall to his lap. "Have you?"

"I've played with it a long time," Brandon said. "I finally figured it out." He took the Cube from Marty's lap and began to twist it, explaining his moves to Marty as he went. The colors of the Cube slowly took organized form. He made mistakes here and there, then told Marty of his error and corrected it.

Alan listened to Brandon as the card game continued. Brandon's instruction did not make sense. Perhaps it was the champagne. Marty nodded methodically, but to Alan, the words sounded unreal. When Alan first bought the Cube, he also bought the book that explained how to solve the puzzle. He read through it once before deciding to try it alone.

In his slightly inebriated mind, it slowly occurred to Alan that Brandon was quoting that same book, solving the Cube from memory. Marty seemed fascinated. Brandon turned the Cube over, grinning as he explained his discoveries.

Michelle was on her fourth glass of white wine. As she reached for a card she needed, Alan kept her from it with his arm as he held his cards. She laughed, going with more force toward the card, over his arm. She did not look at him, but her chest pushed against his arm as she grabbed the card and put it into her hand. She threw out another card which Sam grabbed quickly, then realized he could not use it and threw it back on the table. Alan took it with Michelle tugging on his arm as he did so. He laughed a wicked laugh of success, playing the card with his others and discarding another.

Sloan lost interest in the game. Watching Brandon's hands work the Cube, she felt herself aroused. As he made order out of the chaos, her own feelings seemed to come together. The confusion she felt in her mind coalesced to a single shape that fit, to colors that worked. She began to covet the attention Brandon was giving Marty and the Cube, nodding in unrelated agreement as Brandon explained his moves.

The card game was getting lively, at least in the contest between Alan and Michelle. She moved to take a card. Alan grabbed her knee under the table which made her jump and utter a soft squeal and allowed him the advantage. He grinned in self-satisfaction.

Sam got up, staggering slightly as he retrieved another beer for himself and Alan. He was dimly aware of Sloan's attentiveness to Brandon's seeming preoccupation with the Cube, as well as Alan's attention to his own wife. But he decided to disregard it all. It was nothing. His best friend was flirting with his wife, but it was only the familiarity that came with being close.

When they first arrived in Spain, he and Michelle had noticed how overtly flirtatious some fighter pilots and their wives were. It was just part of being in a big family. It was above board and innocent, they had decided. A fighter pilot certainly could not have serious intentions for a fellow flying buddy's wife. Not if he understood this was the same guy who might someday save his life, in combat or out.

Alan, too, was unaware of the danger. It was acceptable to imagine things that he knew could not happen, as he had imagined them with Michelle. He felt perhaps Sloan was somewhat infatuated with this Brandon character, but he trusted that her upbringing and her love for him would restrain her from going over the edge.

Alan's continued playfulness with Michelle allowed Sloan an excuse to enjoy whatever attention might be directed her way by another man. She felt her blood tingle in her body.

Failure would come from misreading that tingle to mean something deeper, something stronger than it really was.

An hour before midnight, Sam suggested they find a bar to welcome in the New Year. Vernon whispered into Sloan's ear that he could think of few things more disgusting than being sober among a bunch of drunks before saying aloud that he had celebrated enough and was going to bed. He stomped childishly into the bedroom and closed the door loudly behind him.

There were no seats open in the tavern. They nudged their way into a corner close to the bar where they could watch the Europeans celebrate. Alan retrieved four plastic champagne flutes he had hidden in his ski jacket and handed them to Michelle. He turned to Marty and Brandon and said apologetically, "Sorry, I've only got these."

Marty ordered a liqueur from the bartender. Brandon ordered a beer.

Alan opened the new bota bag he had purchased that afternoon and poured champagne from it into the first flute and handed it to Sam. The second he gave to Sloan. He and Michelle took the others. Marty downed his Cointreau, then held his glass for Alan to pour.

Brandon sipped his beer and looked at Sloan when he was not casually watching the other women milling about in the room.

The patrons counted down the seconds from a clock on the wall behind the bar, letting out a wild continuous yell at midnight that threatened to grow to a frenzy well into the early morning hours. The Americans watched them as they toasted among themselves, turning their attentions to their little group.

Alan grabbed Sloan and kissed her passionately, working his hand up to her breast.

"You're drunk!" she laughed, pushing him away.

"On New Year's?" Alan laughed. "There's a surprise!"

Marty finished his champagne and clumsily kissed Sloan, dropping his glass to the floor.

Alan grabbed Sam, puckering his lips. Sam fought him off, spilling champagne as he did so. While Alan and Sam wiped the liquid away, Brandon gently put one arm around Sloan and pecked her quickly on her mouth.

Standing between Michelle and Sam, Alan noticed this embrace and looked away. He had considered kissing Michelle but realized now that he could not.

Sam turned to Alan and whispered, "Like Steinbeck said, 'Should old acquaintance be forgot and kiss your neighbor's wife'."

Michelle held her empty flute with both hands in front of her, smiling coyly and twisting slightly left and right. Her dark hair bounced off her cheeks as she looked up at Alan.

He reached out his hand to shake hers. "Happy New Year," he said.

She did not take it, suddenly hugging him tightly. "Happy New Year!"

Alan glowed as he looked at her. "It should be a good one."

The weeks that followed the ski trip were cold and wet in central Spain, and there was very little to indicate the beginnings of a good year. The nights were long, the days uncharacteristically foggy. There was little to ease the melancholy grasp of estrangement the Americans felt in being so far from home. With Christmas over and change in the air, there was a feeling of listlessness, an apathetic awaiting of the new order.

The Hostage Crisis was over, and there was no war. But there would be no shortage of TDYs.

It was good that change came in the wake of the lingering effects of Whiskey's death. The men and women of the 613th Tactical Fighter Squadron needed something to remove the dark cloud hanging over their lives in this place that was thousands of miles from their homes and the support of their families and friends waiting their return to The Land of the Big BX.

Alan was yet to learn the date when he would begin the F-16 Transition Training course at Luke Air Force Base in Phoenix. The 613th would be the last squadron to make the transition for the 401st Wing, but he was beginning to get the feeling that, while he was on the first list to know, he would be one of the last to go.

Sloan was proud of Alan and his selection for the F-16. It added to the recent events that were coupling to make her feel very good about herself. Inside, she was also happy that Brandon Parsons had made the cut. That meant he would be around longer.

Ron and Jennifer Butler returned to the states with a new assignment. They were going to Nevada. Ron would be transitioning to the F-15, which seemed a fitting consolation for his failing to make the Thunderbirds team.

Bull Boulder was going to the Pentagon. It was what he wanted. He would fly more later as one of the rare WSO Squadron Commanders. He desired and deserved a career as well rounded as himself.

And Lt. Colonel Hargrove became ever more the Boy Colonel as he was selected, once again below the zone, for a full bird colonel billet. He was too proud at the time to realize how that promotion threatened to be the beginning of the end of an illustrious career. Few generals could find a need for a full Colonel with so little actual Air Force experience. As the Squadron Commander of the 613th TFS Squids, he had grown in stature and knowledge. He had begun to learn how to be an effective and respected Squadron Commander, and they were promoting him out of what he now realized too late was the best job in the Air Force.

He came into the job of fighter squadron commander desiring to renovate the Squids and turn them into a fighting unit as he saw it. Ironically, his competence and adaptability had placed his career behind the power curve. He would never be a General.

PART FOUR

A CHANGE OF SEASON

CHAPTER THIRTY-FOUR

"I am not sure I'm going to enjoy this," Alan said, opening the passenger door of the Camaro for Sloan to get in. "They are much more your friends than mine."

Sloan's face glistened with angry determination. When Alan closed his door and put the key in the ignition, she said, "I put up with your friends all the time ... at the bar ... at parties. Your fighter pilot buddies don't exactly fit the normal definition of friends."

"Oh?" Alan cranked the engine and hurriedly backed out of the tight parking space. "I didn't realize you were putting up with them. I thought they were your friends, too."

Sloan shifted in her seat. "I just don't have that much in common with a lot of them. Sometimes they bore me." She stared out the window at the warehouses. "That's not always their fault," she added, somewhat apologetically.

"Demi's husband is a WSO, right?" Alan said after a time. "I don't see anything new or especially stimulating here."

"Robert is also a financial advisor, and Demi was a behaviorist, or something like that, in the states."

"Oh, it's Robert is it? Down at the Lucky Devils, he's known as 'Slick.' He gives tax advice no one asks for, and he's always trying to recruit investors into some get-rich-quick scheme."

"He's interesting," Sloan said defensively.

Alan gunned the engine, accelerating across the electronic train tracks. "Why do I suddenly feel like a fifth wheel with my own wife?"

"You're not a fifth wheel," she said, caressing his leg. "I love you. You interest me more than anyone I know." She leaned over and kissed his cheek. "You smell good."

Alan flinched. He felt uncomfortable, and so drove along the shaded boulevard to the autopista in silence.

Following Sloan's directions, Alan turned off the autopista and on to a side road that was vaguely familiar. A turn later and the ride on the very bad road jolted Alan's memory.

"This is the same crater-infested excuse for a road we took with Ron and Jennifer to that party when we first got to Spain," he said. "The finca."

"Yep." Sloan spoke as one with recent experience. "You have to change from one side to the other to avoid the rough spots. Lucky there's nobody coming at us."

That was true for now. The time-damaged, well-worn road required heads-up navigation for even the most experienced traveler. One side of the road was good for a while, but then it would be necessary to drive on the "wrong" side to avoid potholes that could be severely damaging to the vehicle and its occupants. If any opposing traffic appeared on the road ahead, you would be forced to either plow through the bad spots and risk the consequences or stop and wait until the traffic was no longer a factor before continuing. How quickly you wanted to get where you were going determined how much agony you were willing to accept along the way.

"So, they live in a house out here?"

"It's the same one we went to on our first night," she said, adding, "They like the seclusion."

Alan's memory of the place came with mixed emotions.

They turned right onto the dirt road that passed the old tennis courts, following it to the small group of houses.

A lime-green Toyota was parked in the driveway of a house with a pool in the back.

"That's Brandon Parsons' car!" Sloan said somewhat excitedly.

"Is it." Alan parked behind the Toyota. Sloan did not wait for him to open her door.

Hearing a door close at the next house over, Alan turned to see a tall, very slender woman with short blond hair walking toward them. With her bright blue, inquisitive eyes, large nose and dry-looking olive skin, she reminded Alan of someone who would spend five years in Africa studying gorillas or lions. She was, Alan guessed, in her early thirties.

"Over here!" Demi McPherson laughed. "That's Brandon's house."

Sloan's eyes twinkled. "He lives next door now?"

"Why else would we invite him?" Demi laughed again.

"I heard that!" Brandon Parsons said, emerging from the back of the house with Robert.

Alan could not shake the feeling that at least part of this meeting seemed staged.

The men shook hands, then followed the women into the house.

Demi gave Alan the customary grand tour with Sloan in close trail while Robert and Brandon sipped a Spanish red wine and continued their conversation briefly interrupted by the arrival of their guests.

"Nice place," Alan said to Robert when they returned to the big room that served as both den and dining area. "I wish we could get something like this. I'm sick up and fed with apartment life."

Demi giggled politely at his use of words, but her smile seemed condescending.

"All in good time," Sloan said, frowning at him.

Robert mentioned that both Alan and Brandon were on the first F-16 conversion list and asked if they would go to training together. The conversation turned for a while to flying. To his surprise, despite Robert's casual arrogance, Alan found that he enjoyed the attention. Parsons, on the other hand, though he contributed animated dialogue at times, seemed preoccupied, stealing periodic glances at Demi and Sloan in the kitchen.

"Would you care for some wine, Alan?" Robert asked.

"I'll have a beer, if you've got it."

"I think I can dig one up," Robert said, acting a bit snubbed. He started to rise.

"Hey, I'll get it," Brandon said. "I'll have one with ya."

"Fine," Robert said. "You know where they are."

Brandon went into the kitchen where he remained for a few minutes. Alan could hear him talking to Demi and Sloan.

Robert was quiet for a moment, making Alan feel uncomfortable.

"That's a tough road to get out here," Alan said finally to deaden the silence. "It must get frustrating, negotiating it twice a day."

"You get used to it," Robert said flatly. "Experience and determination make it easier to take."

Alan looked around the room at the collections of curios and marital mementos. "Is it worth it?"

Robert smiled and glanced toward the kitchen. "It has been so far."

Changing the subject, Robert said, "I hear you're kicking tail over at the 613th. Are you looking forward to the F-16?"

"I'll miss the extra set of eyes," Alan said, following Robert's gaze.

Nodding his agreement, Robert said, "Good answer." From the end table next to his chair, he retrieved a meerschaum pipe, yellowed with use, and began to pack it with tobacco from a colorful tin. "But we both know it's a hell of a good jet, one well worth flying."

"Yes," Alan answered. "It can turn. That'll be a new experience. And it's new. And, I admit, it's a pat on the back."

Robert placed his pipe between his teeth and spoke with it clenched there. "I find the fascination front-seaters have with turning very interesting." He struck a match. "Why do you suppose you are being rewarded?" He lit his pipe and looked at Alan through the thick smoke.

Alan considered Robert's question thoughtfully while disregarding his statement. "For being who I am, I suppose."

"First on the menu is the salad," Demi announced when they sat down to eat. She placed a steamed whole artichoke on each of the salad plates in front of her guests.

Curling her lip, but meaning to look cute rather than rude, Sloan stared humorously at the scaly green pod before her. "What's thith animal on my plate?"

Brandon laughed, pulling his chair closer and placing his right elbow on the table. "That ..." he said pointing, "... is an artichoke."

Sloan glanced at him then back at the object of discussion. "What should I do with it?"

"Eat it!" Demi said with fervor.

"It looks like the plant equivalent of an armadildo," Alan suggested.

"A what?" Demi giggled.

Sloan laughed. "Armadillo?"

"Whatever," Alan said indifferently.

Seemingly unaffected by the exchange, Brandon Parsons patiently waited, his facial expression unchanged. "I'll show you how," he said.

"How what?" Sloan asked.

"To eat it."

"Oh."

Demi stepped in. "Peel it."

Brandon looked momentarily disappointed.

Sloan repeated the instruction. "Peel it ..."

"And dip each piece into the melted butter," Demi said, peeling a leaf from her own artichoke. "There's a little bit of goody on each leaf."

"I'm not sure I ..."

Brandon Parsons saw his chance. "Like this," he interrupted. "Take the peel ..." He pulled off a petal, "... dip it in the butter ..." He did so. "... and kind of scrape the inside off with your tongue and teeth." He closed his large lips over the buttered leaf and pulled it back out of his mouth.

Shyly, Sloan imitated his actions. "There's not much there," she said, licking a drop of butter from her lower lip.

"There'll be more as you get down to the heart."

Brandon removed another leaf and ate. Then another. He made eye contact with Sloan when he could.

The others worked their artichokes slowly.

"What's the purpose of this?" Alan asked after a time.

"To get down to the heart," Brandon answered matter-of-factly. "The idea is to slowly eat away at the pieces until you get to the heart which is the best part. It's soft, and the work to get to it makes the enjoyment of it all the better. It's a lot better than just having it laid out ready for you. It almost makes me not want them when I get them that way."

He worked his artichoke quickly, much faster than the other four. When he got to the heart, he dipped it in the melted butter, popped it dripping and whole into his waiting mouth and chewed it with exaggerated relish. He finished, wiped his mouth, then leaned on both elbows, watching Sloan.

"Why are you watching me?" Sloan asked uncomfortably.

Gripping his hands like a platform, his rested his chin on his intertwined fingers and looked sleepily at her. "Because I know what you are coming to. I'm enjoying with you what I know you are about to enjoy."

Alan worked on his artichoke, silently curious if anyone else realized how ridiculous Brandon Parsons sounded. "Does your wife eat artichokes, too?"

The question caught Brandon by surprise. "I don't know ... That is, I'm not sure ... We're not ... we're separated. Which is why she isn't here."

"Oh." Glancing quickly around the table, Alan realized both Demi and Sloan were glaring at him, obviously distressed by his social faux paus. Robert did not look up.

After what seemed to be an extended period of quiet artichoke peeling, Sloan said, "Mine is soft, now."

"Dip it and eat it in one bite," Parsons suggested, sounding excited. The red flush subsided from his face, replaced by what could only be described as the glow of anticipation.

"How do you like the wine?" Robert's question to Alan seemed like a diversion.

"It's good," Alan answered, not wanting to admit his limited knowledge by offering anything further.

"It's a Marques de Cáceres," Robert said. "It's a pretty good, full bodied Spanish red, don't you think?"

"It's good," Alan said again.

"I like the German whites better, like a Spätlese or, especially, an Auslese dessert wine," Sloan interjected, glancing at Demi who beamed in recognition of her covert compliment. "But this is good," she added for politeness.

Alan looked at her in surprise. "Where did you learn so much about wines?"

"From Demi," she answered shyly.

"Let me show you this one," Robert said. He got up from the table and opened a cabinet at the far end of the room. He returned with a small bottle of German wine. "This is a Trockenbeerenauslese."

"Okay." Alan glanced at the label.

"A good, sweet, expensive German white, made from grapes left on the vine longer and then hand-picked. You can't even find this in America ... that is, I never have."

"Did you know to look before you came to Europe?" Alan asked.

Robert seemed embarrassed. "Well, I've looked during visits back to the states."

"I see."

"But this is a special wine," Robert continued, glancing at Demi who smiled knowingly at him. "We plan to drink this if we ever break up. To drink to the sweet times that were ... that are ... good."

Demi nodded.

Alan rubbed his chin. "Don't you have to keep it chilled? I've heard German whites are early wines."

"Not this one," Robert countered. Handling the bottle like a delicate china figurine, he carefully placed it in the middle of the table for them to admire as they ate.

Alan continued to peel his artichoke. His labor seemed fruitless. "Mine has no heart," he complained.

"That's unusual," Robert said.

They all leaned from their seats to look down into Alan's artichoke.

"Yes, it does," Demi said, poking it with her salad fork. "It's just very small. Sorry about that." She sat down again. "You can't always tell about the heart from the outside."

After they finished dinner, Robert relit his pipe, and he and Alan talked on the back porch, illuminated by the full moon, looking over a shallow valley to a far hill. Sloan helped Demi and Brandon clean up.

After a while, Alan said, "I hate to break up the party, but I have an o-dark thirty brief tomorrow."

"Do we have to leave so soon?" Sloan's voice was begging.

"I'm afraid so ..."

"We can bring her home," Demi offered too readily.

Alan looked at his wife. Her eyes were pleading. "That's a long, rough drive," he said finally.

"Oh, we don't mind," Demi said.

Alan sighed and briefly kissed Sloan's cheek. "Wake me when you get home."

"Okay!" Sloan sounded excited.

"I have to go, too," Brandon said. He got up.

"No, you don't," Demi cajoled.

"Yes, I do." He walked with Alan out the door.

Driving home, Alan felt tired and angry. He was willing to let Sloan have her own life, but, dammit! She was still his wife! He realized the TDYs could be depressing to her. She needed her support group, and she seemed to sincerely like Demi. And Robert, although a bit pompous, was okay. But what did Brandon Parsons want? The thought bothered him. He comforted himself by deciding that Sloan would never do anything to ruin their marriage, especially for such an obvious phony.

It was nearly midnight when Sloan quietly opened the apartment door. Alan was asleep on the sofa. She went into the bedroom, changed into a full-length nightgown, then returned to wake him.

"Alan," she said, shaking him gently. "It's time to get up and come to bed."

SECOND SUMMER

CHAPTER THIRTY-FIVE

More to pass the time than for any other reason, the Squids spent the late summer days readying the squadron for the dubious honor of being the first American F-4 squadron in many years to spend three weeks TDY at a small base in Greece called Andravida. In preparation, Hargrove had them repaint the inside of the squadron building before deploying. A "Happy Paint," Sweet Cheeks reminded them.

Even the jets were to be painted. Once they returned from Greece, it would not be long before they began preparations to deploy to Incirlik Turkey one last time in the aging McDonald-Douglas F-4D Phantom II. The "Phinal Phantom Phling," as Sam dubbed it. The initial F-16 transition was scheduled to begin soon after their return.

Two weeks before the Squids were to deploy to Andravida, Sloan decided they should go to church, and Alan's argument that he preferred a weekend of just the two of them could not deter her from an idea she had in her head.

"It's good for your career," she said. "Maybe the new Wing Commander will see us there. Where people see you is important."

"You don't go to church for career's sake," Alan answered.

Without hesitation, Sloan replied, "You go for a lot of reasons."

Having slept in, Alan was forced to dress quickly to accommodate his wife's unpredictable desire. They walked briskly out to the car to drive to the base chapel. Backing out of the parking space at Parque de Cataluña, he was the first to see the lime-green Toyota parked in front of the building next to theirs.

"Hey, isn't that ..." he began, slowing when he saw a figure in the car.

"Stop here," Sloan said.

"What?"

"Stop here!"

"Why?"

"I just want to see what he's doing."

Brandon Parsons sat in the car, reading something, or just sitting - they could not tell. The driver's side door was open as if he were either just getting out or just getting in.

Alan stopped behind a Red Spanish Seat, attempting to be inconspicuous, and the two of them waited.

Brandon remained in his seat.

"He doesn't live here now, does he?" Alan asked.

"No," Sloan answered curtly. She stared at the car. "I wonder what he's doing," she thought aloud.

Alan laughed. "Isn't it obvious? He spent the night."

"With who?" Sloan watched the figure in the car intently.

Alan released the brake. "What does it matter? Maybe one of the nurses who lives there."

"He doesn't look dressed for a date." Her face formed a frown.

"From what little I've heard about him, it was probably more of a pickup."

Sloan glared at Alan in a way that made him flinch. "What have you heard?"

Alan furrowed his brow, trying to understand what could make her suddenly so interested. "Only that having a wife back in the states doesn't seem to hamper his social life over here." He released the clutch.

"What are you doing?" she asked when the car began to move.

"Sloan, it's obvious he's not going to do anything. He knows we are here. You wanted to go to church. We're late enough as it is."

Sloan looked back over her shoulder as they drove away. Brandon Parsons never looked up, never acknowledged them, never moved.

Entering the base chapel, Alan felt uncomfortably. Looking for familiar faces, he found Boomer in a pew close to the front with Camron and Cindy but knew he would not feel right sitting with them.

Sloan spotted Sam closer to the back, and, after whispering to Alan to take off his sunglasses, slid in beside him. Michelle was singing in the choir, Sam told her when she asked.

The preacher, an Air Force Captain, bade the members of the congregation bow their heads in silent prayer, to pray to themselves for whatever they felt they needed to talk to God about. But he never gave them the chance.

"We pray for our loved ones," he said almost immediately. "We pray for our Commander in Chief ... we pray for strength in these trying times ... we pray for good training, we pray ..."

Alan leaned toward Sloan and whispered, "It's pretty hard to meditate when you're being told what to pray about all the time."

"Shhh!"

The preacher continued, "... knowing we are a little lower than the angels, we pray to Thee for guidance to bring us home ..."

Midway through the service, Michelle sang a solo. Alan found the lyrics uninspiring, but her voice was so beautiful that the words became unimportant.

She sang with an effortless grace that flowed like a clear mountain brook from the depths of her soul, cleansing all those lucky enough to be within the sound of her voice. She sang not necessarily from a deep belief in the words, but, more genuinely, from a simple, joyous desire to sing.

Alan caught her bright eyes and was almost sure she flashed him a smile.

When the service was over, they followed Sam to the Fellowship Hall for coffee and doughnuts. Michelle emerged from the adjacent choir room, her face glowing, her eyes lively and alert.

"Beautiful," Alan said in earnest. "Very nice."

"Very pretty, me guapa!" Sam said, hugging her slender waist.

"Well, it was fun," Michelle said. She smiled brightly at Alan and then at Sloan. "I didn't know you guys would be here."

Sam handed her a cup of coffee from the table.

"We've been needing to come," Sloan said simply.

Alan glanced at her, curious why she suddenly felt this need.

"Your song was very pretty," Sloan said. "I don't see how you do it. I can never sing in the morning."

Michelle's dimpled cheeks enriched her laugh. "Well, you know?" Her voice went up, as it always did when she said those words. "It helps to take a shot of Scotch in the morning to loosen the vocals chords."

"Scotch!" Sloan was unable to conceal her prudish surprise. "Before church?"

Michelle glanced at Alan. "It loosens me up."

Alan smiled at her. "That must be true." He turned to Sam. "Just like Friday night at the bar. A couple of Scotches and everybody starts singing."

Sloan coughed. "You mean your 'desire to disgust' songs?"

"That's the ones!" Michelle laughed. She sipped her coffee and nudged Alan. "I heard you sing those songs in Aviano. You have a good voice. Why don't you join the choir?"

He snorted, then quickly swallowed a bite of doughnut. "That would be a laugh." He looked sideways at Sloan then back at Michelle. "When is rehearsal? I'll bring a bottle of Scotch."

Sam laughed as Sloan smirked.

Michelle said, "Thursdays."

"What goodies are you bringing back from Andravida?" Sloan asked Sam.

"Well, you know," Michelle put in, "from what I hear, these guys won't have much time for shopping."

"Yeah, we'll fly everyday but Sunday," Sam said.

"That should keep you out of trouble," Sloan said to Alan. She had heard the rumors about the Aviano fire extinguisher wars. She hoped that was the only kind of trouble Alan was getting himself into.

The following Thursday, returning from a late afternoon flight, Alan found the note from Sloan telling him she was visiting Demi and would be home for dinner. When she had not returned by 7:00pm, Alan went down to the local bar and grill at the back of the building's bottom level. At 8:30, he met Sloan as he was coming up the outside stairs. She was looking for him.

His irritation was obvious, and, although she tried to apologize, Alan's anger was so focused that she grew defensive, like a little child who knows it has been bad but is unwilling to accept the consequences.

"I just wish you would show me a little more consideration," he said, looking into her eyes for signs of regret. "What can be so interesting about those people that makes negotiating that crumbling, pot-hole-infested road worth the effort?"

Sloan's eyes hardened. "I like Demi," she said defensively.

"Maybe you could invite me along again sometime."

"I didn't think you liked them."

"I don't mind Robert too much."

"Well," she sighed, "he's TDY to Turkey anyway. He left Friday."

Alan glared at her, but his rage was softening. "They probably won't want you around as much when he gets back."

"I don't know."

He touched her. "The squadron's leaving for Greece soon. I'd like to be with you as much as I can before then."

"You're leaving again already," she said, as if the realization that he would soon be gone had just occurred to her.

"Yes."

Sloan's eyes got misty. Something very heavy was welling up inside her. Holding back the tears, she said, "I wish you didn't have to go again, already. It makes it so hard. And after this, it's on to Turkey!"

"It's only three weeks." There on the steps, Alan embraced her, caressing her soft hair. "That's not too long. I'll bring you something Greek. Something special."

She pulled away slightly and managed a smile. "As long as it's not something communicable."

He laughed lightly and held her as tightly as he dared.

A song about leaving was weeping from the AFRTS radio station while Alan packed in the bedroom. Sloan trudged in sullenly, a pout on her pretty lips. Her eyes were red. "Would you do me a favor?" she asked him meekly.

He threw his favorite red cotton shirt that she had given him in the canvas A-3 bag and stood up straight to look at her. "I'll be careful."

Holding his shoulders, she turned him toward the bed. "Lie on top of me," she said without looking into his eyes.

"Sloan," he answered softly, "I love you, but we don't have time ..."

"No." She looked down and sniffed, unable to bear any rejection. "Just lie on top of me ... for a minute ... please."

He lowered himself gently onto her as she opened her legs and closed her eyes. Tears appeared from under her eyelids. Her grip was very tight.

When the song was played out, she let him go.

ANDRAVIDA

CHAPTER THIRTY-SIX

At the end of six days of flying, Alan and Sam sat in the back of the six-pack truck that Reggie drove with reckless abandon down the tight, winding road to Kyllini. Hanging on for dear life in the front seat, Jeff Cole and Boomer were unable to speak, the whole of their mental faculties concentrating on what each half-seriously considered might be Life's last moment.

On a small tip of land on the west side of the northern Peloponnesus, Reggie screeched to a stop. Thankful for their lives, the young men left the truck behind and boarded the Kyllini ferry moments before its last departure of the day to the Island of Zakynthos in the Ionian Sea.

The ferry shuddered, then released its grip on the old wooden dock as the sun crept toward the horizon, the seamless bridge between earth and heaven. The pier pilings on either side of the squarish boat appeared to march slowly toward the shore, and each whispered a quiet message as it passed: 'I am your last chance! Jump! Grab me!'

But to stay with the boat to its destination and whatever that might bring was better than cutting the ride short out of fear for the unknown.

The huge motors accelerated as the boat cleared the pilings, pushing its mass into a wide sweeping turn to the southwest. When the boat was halfway between the mainland and the island, the sun dipped below the horizon, turning the sky of layered clouds into a canvas of crimson and orange with detailed design having no particular form. The rage of the evening sky was vented passionately but quickly, and by the time they reached the namesake city of the island, stars were one by one replacing the evening colors with more subdued brilliance and tranquility.

As the fighter pilots walked away from the landing to Solomos Square, the city of Zakynthos spread before them in a thin crescent along the blue water bay like one of life's rare finds to be explored and savored.

"Let's find the beer!" Reggie called over his shoulder as he led the way. He walked with purpose, not waiting for an answer, assuming they were all of the same mind.

"And the food," Boomer added.

Sam said, "We're treading on a part of history, Sweet Cheeks, yet beer is the first thing that comes to your mind?"

"Not just first," Reggie answered. "Only."

In the plaza, stores, bars and restaurants encompassed crossroads of sidewalks passing small flower gardens. Balconies overhung the square, suspended from the upper floors of the white buildings that surrounded it. Tables and chairs placed casually, yet purposefully in front of the bars and restaurants invited the pedestrian to sit and eat and drink and pass the warmth of the evening in leisure.

Sam pointed to the marble statue that graced the plaza. "You know that music the Greeks play in the morning that you complain about, Sweet Cheeks? It's the national anthem, 'Hymn to Liberty.' That guy, Dionysios Solomos, wrote it. He was from here. Solomos Square is named in his honor."

Reggie nodded. "Looks like they might have Carlsbad over there." He pointed to an open-air restaurant.

"And food," Boomer repeated.

"Carls ... bad?" Jet said.

The fighter pilots took seats in front of the restaurant and placed their orders. The waiter quickly returned with five bottles of Carlsberg beer.

"Carlsbad!" Reggie exclaimed.

"Here's to it," Alan offered, and they drank.

Six straight days spent immersed in hard work and flying and each other quieted them for a time. They ordered another round, then another.

Sam gazed around at the white buildings, the shadowy arcades and the balconies. "This used to be called 'The Venice of the Ionian Sea'," he said distantly.

"People must really like Venice," Boomer said. "Just about everywhere you go there seems to be a Venice of Something."

Reggie looked at Sam with mock disdain. "Where do you get this shit, Possum?"

Sam did not return his gaze. "I know you'll find this fascinating, Sweet Cheeks, but there's this newfangled thing called books. Check it out when you learn to read."

"Oh. Hell, I figured it was just bullshit you made up as you went along."

"Why would he do that?" Alan put in.

"To annoy me."

"I'm not annoyed!" Boomer said enthusiastically. "Just hungry. I hope this Venice has lamb-burgers, or something like that."

Reggie and Boomer consulted the menu. Alan, Sam and Jeff decided they did not like the prices and got up to look elsewhere.

Walking among the white buildings and colorful balconies of the square, they found a small shop that was essentially nothing more than a place for an oven and the owner to operate behind a large open window. Several vertical rows of skewered chicken broilers turned slowly, cooking on rotisseries. The delicious aroma beckoned them closer. They ordered the chicken and more beer and ate standing near the shop.

The spices on the chicken, the method of cooking, and six days of eating military food in a hot canvas mess tent made the meal seem a delectable feast. They ordered another to split between them.

When they were finished, they roamed the plaza, eventually returning to the statue of Solomos. The night grew upon them, and the festive character of their arrival mellowed into a quieter, more contemplative mood.

Alan gazed at the balconies. "This place does remind me of Venice," he said to Sam as they walked toward the water past the 16th Century church of Nicholas-on-the-Mole.

"There's a lot of history here," Sam said without looking at his companions. His mind was on fire with what he knew of the place.

The night grew older and the quiet sidewalks of the plaza were gradually abandoned. There was no late-night revelry from tourists. Alan imagined they were observers in the midst of a typical Saturday night on Zakynthos, uninterrupted by the concerns of the outside world.

"These buildings don't look like typical European," Alan said finally. "I mean, they don't look ancient."

"The island is ancient," Sam said, "but so is Poseidon's wrath."

"How's that?"

"This place was practically laid to waste by an earthquake in 1953. The people rebuilt the city to keep its Venetian motif."

A moon in waning gibbous stage rose very low from the east over the mainland of the Peloponnese that they could not see. Reflected light shimmered on the water of the bay. They were quiet, each with an empty bottle of Carlsberg, but not wanting to leave this peace to go for more just yet.

Ages and history Alan did not understand filled his mind with possibilities. Civilization. The wars. Learning and relearning. That was history to him, a chronological documentation of man's unwillingness to learn what must be the most important lesson: how to get along.

After a while, Jeff broke the silence. "What will we do tomorrow?"

"Whatever the day brings," Alan answered. "Right now, we need a place to sleep."

"Cheap," Sam added.

They walked south from the square into the town and found a small hotel.

"Your friends are already here," the night-clerk said in concise English.

"Oh."

They took one room with one bed and fell asleep in their clothes almost as soon as their three heads hit the two pillows.

CHAPTER THIRTY-SEVEN

A pungent odor snapped Alan from a fitful sleep. The light of day and the noise of the morning filtered through the open window into the room and Alan's consciousness. He opened his eyes and, without moving his head, attempted to locate the origin of the foul smell. A white blur wiggled within the minimum focal length of his vision, and he instinctively moved his head far enough away to recognize the socks on Jeff Cole's feet. He rolled over and fell off the narrow bed. Jeff grunted as Alan pulled himself from the floor, sat on a nearby chair and looked around.

Sam was not in the room. Alan wiped the sleep from his heavy eyes and pulled on his shoes while looking out the window onto the sunny street below. He heard the tinny sound of a low horsepower motorcycle, then another. Under a tree in the open space near the hotel, Sam and Reggie Swartz parked a small Suzuki and a Vespa. The excitement of a new development woke Alan fully, and, slapping Jeff's feet, he said, "Jet! Let's go! We're mobile!"

Jeff grunted and sat up in time to see Alan leave the room.

Outside, Alan walked rapidly to Sam and Reggie. The morning town air was dry and dusty and calm. "What have you got?" he yelled through the sudden quiet that came as the two WSOs killed the little engines.

"Rental Vespas," Sam answered. "The island is ours! Let's go, Dog. Carpe diem!"

"Yeah, crappie diem. Where do I get one?"

"Hop on, I'll take you. Where's Jet?"

"Rousted, I think," Alan answered, throwing his leg over the narrow seat behind Sam.

"I'll wait for him," Reggie said.

"Good," Alan said. Sam started the engine, and as they whined away down the road, Alan yelled to Reggie over his shoulder, "Remind Jet to pay for the room!"

When they arrived at the rental shack, Boomer was in the middle of negotiations. "I've got the last one here," he said.

"Okay," Sam said, gunning the engine. "I saw another place." He took Alan there, and as Alan negotiated for two more Vespas, Reggie pulled up with Jeff on the back of his Suzuki, followed shortly by Boomer on a Moped. With all of them on two-wheel transports, Reggie took a "Hell's Angels" picture for posterity, and they were on their way west.

The edge of the city came quickly, and soon they were in a shallow forest of poplar, oak and eucalyptus trees. The sun flashed through the limbs and showered their bodies with the warmth and exhilaration of their new-found freedom.

A sharp curve caught them by surprise. Boomer's Moped could not make the corner, and it toppled, sending him skidding nose first, cutting a clear path through the fallen leaves as the friction between the ground and his face brought the rest of him to a stop just short of a large oak.

His fellow uneasy riders returned to assist him in his immediate return to the saddle. The delay was brief, and Boomer was none the worse for a little bloody wear.

In Laganas, they found a restaurant overlooking the water and stopped for a lunch of souvlaki, moussaka and fish. When the check came, Alan was disappointed to discover that on this island in the middle of the Mediterranean Sea, the fish was the most expensive item on the menu.

After lunch, they split up. Three of them went east.

Sam and Alan continued west. Riding past fields of currant vines and olive trees, they continued their quest, not knowing where they were going, knowing only they were following a road that led west to the Ionian Sea. The day was beautiful. The brush of the wind caressed their faces, pushing their short hair out of place. They sped along on the Vespas, determined to keep going until they found what they were looking for, something that would make stopping better than continuing on.

Following a dirt road west from the main road, they came to a sudden stop at a view that left them both momentarily speechless. This was it. This was the place. The place to stop.

The view from the side of the road was magnificent, overlooking the Ionian Sea from the sheer cliffs of the island's western shore. Below them, it was easy to imagine that the water from all the oceans of the world slammed against the steadfast wall of Zakynthos.

Alan parked his Vespa and walked away from the road. "Incredible!" he said. "I had no idea we would find something like this."

"I did," Sam answered. "Somewhere in Greece."

"But not here."

"No. Not here."

They walked together toward the edge. "Incredible," Alan repeated.

"It's a far cry from the trashed beach at Andravida," Sam offered.

"Yeah. That beach looks like all the junk of the Greek waters has been dumped on it. This looks virginal, uncorrupted by human touch."

Sam stood on a bald rock and took in the panoramic splendor of the view. "You would never know, standing here now, all the history this place has been through."

"Like what?"

Sam cleared his throat. He loved to talk of things like this, but he hated to appear pedantic. Alan never seemed to tire of his stories. And he did not think Alan was that way with everyone.

Sam spread his arms. "This place has been ransacked, and not just by earthquakes. In the fifth Century, the Vandals went on a tear through Gaul and Spain. Then they came here and killed over five thousand of the islanders before throwing them into the sea, maybe somewhere around here."

Alan was silently attentive, standing transfixed as Sam brought the island to life.

Sam continued. "About five hundred years ago, the Ottomans burned the place. It was so terribly devastated that nobody lived there for fifty years." Pausing, Sam glanced at Alan who seemed to be taking in everything he said. "The island appears in *The Odyssey*," Sam told him. He turned and pointed north. "Cephalonia is that way. Ithaca, the island of Ulysses, is just north of it. There was probably a land bridge between Zakynthos and Cephalonia during the Ice Age."

Alan laughed lightly. "The Ice Age again, Sam?"

Sam smiled, remembering their first flight together to Turkey.

"What happened to the bridge?" Alan asked.

"The end of the Ice Age." Sam glanced at Alan. "A lot of changes happen in the world just from melting the ice."

Until this moment, Zakynthos had just been a good place to drink beer and ride Vespas, a place for American GIs to rest and relax on foreign soil. Now it was more, and, for Alan, it always would be.

They were quiet for a time, enjoying the serenity and majesty of their new find. After a while, almost as if to himself Sam said, "The Ionians believe the saints are here on the islands." He stretched his back, gazing at the clear blue sky. "Not off in space somewhere. That seems more personal to me."

Alan remained quiet until the depth of his feelings made him blurt out, "I can't believe they pay us to do this!"

Sam laughed. "And fly jets! What a great life it would be if all we ever had to do was fly fighters and walk along the beach and find beautiful places like this."

"And explore them from the air."

"Yeah."

They sat and looked silently over the water, sometimes looking down to watch the waves breaking against the walls.

"We do put up with a lot of crap just so we can fly," Alan said after a time.

Sam shrugged his shoulders and sat down on the soft grass. "I always figured flying is the privilege and the bullshit is the payback."

"It has to even out somehow."

"Life is a zero-sum game," Sam said. "Like war."

Alan nodded although he was not sure he understood.

"Are you ever afraid?" Sam asked, not looking at him.

"Afraid of what?"

"Going to war."

"I don't think so. But how would I know?"

"You seem a lot closer to war when you're in the military," Sam said.

Alan looked to the water. "Only war can show if our training is any good." He paused and squinted his eyes. "But I sure don't care to put my ass on the line for some bullshit conflict."

Sam sighed and, mirroring his friend's image, looked out to sea. "Well, we didn't sign up to pick and choose when we'll fight."

"That's the part that bothers me."

"Why?"

Alan shrugged. "Should they own us so completely?"

"That's the contract. If we live through it, maybe someday we'll call the shots."

Alan exhaled heavily. "And maybe we'll have learned nothing, and we'll call them the same bullshit way. In the meantime, we'll fight other peoples' wars because they don't know how. Or don't want to." He tossed a rock. It went horizontally for a while, then curved down toward the sea. He never saw it hit.

"Then why do you ... why do we do it?"

Alan laughed again. "Because they let us fly jets! They let us fly supersonic, and they let us fly all over Europe and see great things like this." Alan looked intently at Sam. "The payback for the bullshit."

The breeze rustled their short hair and bowed the tall grass around them. They sat silently and stared out to sea, like gods contemplating the fate of humanity.

Alan squinted in the sunlight, watching a small cloud form out over the ocean and then quickly dissipate. "Did I ever tell you about my friend Ernie?"

"Just a little," Sam said.

"He was a great guy. You remind me of him." Alan looked at Sam briefly before turning his gaze to the western horizon. "Fisch knows him ... knew him."

"At RTU?"

Alan nodded, fighting the growing lump in his throat. "He died there."

Sam nodded respectfully. "What happened?"

Alan picked up another rock and threw it, watching until it disappeared somewhere beyond their line of sight. "Training. Air-to-air. 2v2. Our class against Fisch's more senior class. It was a kind of experiment, to see if the newer students could learn anything from the older students, and vice versa." Alan shook his head. "It sure seems stupid now."

"What happened?" Sam repeated.

Alan inhaled deeply. "We were out over the Gulf of Mexico. I guess Fisch was learning something because Ernie was kicking his butt. They were near the combat floor, and Fisch turned hard into Ernie. It was like a game of chicken. Fisch kept turning until he was nose-to-nose with Ernie's jet. I was above them, and I saw it all developing. I should have radioed 'Knock it off' or something, but I just watched. They came so close. Fisch expected the ROE to save him – 'Clear to the right, but don't cross flight paths to do so' ..."

Sam nodded in rapt silence.

"Ernie broke hard right to avoid the collision. He was already slow, and his airplane stalled and went out of control. The backseater got out ... Ernie didn't." Alan paused, inhaling deeply. "I think four fighter pilots would have died that morning instead of one if Ernie hadn't acted as quickly as he did."

Sam closed his eyes and lowered his head before looking up at Alan. "Was the valve rotated?"

"The Command Selector Valve?" Alan shook his head as if fighting off a demon. "No." He looked intensely at Sam. "It was set at Normal."

Sam clasped his hands together on his knees, resting his chin on them. "Didn't Ernie trust his wizzo?"

Again, Alan inhaled sharply, momentarily holding his breath. Had the WSO rotated the handle before takeoff, as most crews elected to do, when the backseater pulled his ejection handle, it would have initiated ejection for the Aircraft Commander as well.

"The wizzo was inexperienced," Alan said. "He testified that Ernie told him not to, that he would make his own ejection decision."

"That's always seemed odd to me," Sam said, looking away. "Since it doesn't work both ways. If the AC initiates ejection, the wizzo is going, whether he wants to or not." He looked back at Alan. "I've always rotated the handle when we flew together."

"I've always trusted you," Alan said.

Sam exhaled, and both were silent.

Finally, Alan asked, "Do you think one great act by one person can change another person's life?"

Turning his head, Sam caught Alan's concentrated gaze. He held it for a moment before looking away, out over the steep cliffs, into the invisible box above the Ionian Sea that was their air-to-air training area.

"Maybe," he answered finally. "Everyone wants to believe that what they do means something." He waited to see if Alan would say more. He could hear the ocean breaking against the island. Sea birds circled a ridge, squawking the noise of Life's daily struggle.

Sam looked at his friend. "I always wondered what was between you and Carp."

Alan rubbed his forehead. "That's part of it."

"What else?"

"Something about a girl."

As if suddenly called to attention, Sam sat up rigidly when the realization flooded over him. "Denise? Were you and she ...?"

Alan shook his head almost imperceptibly. "I'd never met her before that first night at the finca party."

"But Ernie knew her."

Alan nodded.

They sat quietly for a long time, neither certain where to begin again.

When Sam did not speak, Alan said, "After Ernie died, it was hard to get close to anyone." He looked away. "It still is. Even Sloan, sometimes."

"That comes with being a fighter pilot, I think."

"You get close, and they leave you." Alan closed his eyes and let the breeze gently caress his face. "But we all have to die."

"Yes, and we know we have to." It seemed funny to Sam that he had said that. They were so young, practically bullet- proof. "If you don't kill me, I won't die."

Alan looked at him in pain. "What do you mean?"

"I mean, I fly with you and you keep me alive, and maybe someday I can return the favor." Sam smiled and added, "The payback for putting up with my bullshit."

Alan started to laugh, but when he realized Sam was no longer smiling, he sighed.

Sam said, "There's a psalm I had to memorize when I was young that says, 'We are a little lower than the Angels'. I don't think so. We are the ones who have to put up with all the shit with only our faith promising a payback. The Angels are already in heaven and they never had to put up with the crap ... the suffering, the pain, murdering, betrayal, uncertainty ..."

"That's true," Alan agreed.

Sam continued, "They don't have doubts ... about God or themselves. If we make it, we pass a test they never had to take. I think that makes us higher than them."

Alan reflected on his friend's words. He thought again of Ernie. He considered him a hero. He had sacrificed. If Heaven was real, he was there.

Sam looked west across the water, thinking how the seas and oceans of the world spill their waters into each other, oblivious to and unaffected by Man's efforts to control them.

One mighty body of life-sustaining water covering so much of the earth, creeping into fjords and caves, moving in and out, but always as one. Men chose to divide it and label it saying, 'This ocean acts thusly' and 'That sea behaves so.' Sam viewed the ocean as one, not many. He thought of something the navies of the world always wanted to say: "We control the seas!"

Not likely, Mate.

Sam stood and glanced around from the cliffs to the sea. "I wonder if there's any way to get down there to take a swim before we go."

Alan rose and rubbed his hands together, brushing the grit and small rocks from his palms. He wiped them on his pants. "I can't swim," he said simply, looking at Sam.

Sam shook his head as if to dislodge an assumption made long ago. "But ... what about Sacedon? And Turkey? The pool TASMO thing."

Alan turned, eying the Vespa's in the distance. "No big deal. I can tread water with the best of them."

The day was fading as the two young men traversed a narrow dirt road toward the city, Alan riding in front, Sam in close trail.

Enlivened by the wind in his face, Alan was slow to notice the bee that had landed on his chest. When he felt the insect climbing up his neck, he instinctively brushed it away. The angry bee was thrown toward Sam and landed on his leg. Slowing as quickly as he could, without losing control, Sam could only watch the bee dig its stinger deep into his thigh. Alan did not see him stop, brush the doomed bee away, and pull the stinger out of his skin.

When Sam caught up with Alan again, his leg had begun to throb.

Boarding the evening ferry to the mainland, they found Boomer covered with scars and bruises and grinning like he was having the time of his life. He was with a beautiful Grecian girl who had found him trying to uproot more trees, hanging on for dear life to his out of control Moped. She was determined, despite his half-hearted objections, to "nurse him back to health" at her own house near the base.

Walking toward the front of the boat, Alan was surprised to see a familiar figure. Connie Marcum stood against the railing, looking to the mainland as the breeze created by the boat's movement caressed her face.

Walking up silently behind her, Alan asked, "How long have you been here?"

Connie smiled when she recognized the voice. She turned to see the silhouette of his head eclipsing the low-sitting sun. "I came over this morning."

"You got to Greece this morning, and you've already seen Zakynthos?"

She smiled. "No. I've been in Greece for three days. I went to the island this morning."

"Alone?" Alan looked around.

"Sure. Why not?"

"I wish I had known you were here," Alan said with a smile. "You could have gone with us today. We had a quality time riding Vespas."

"Riding what?"

"Vespas. Little motorcycles."

"Oh." Looking around him at the bruised and bloody face of Boomer, and then at Sam nursing his swollen leg, she said, "Vespa means wasp. Did you know that? Looks like some of you got stung." She smiled. "I think I did very well on my own, thank you."

Alan leaned against the rail beside her, watching the dock appear from the curve in the peninsula as the sun settled lower behind them in a cloudless sky.

Sloan sat on the sofa in Demi's den, sipping on a glass of German white wine, listening to Brandon accompany himself on his guitar. Demi sat across from her, stealing occasional glances between her friends. At the end of his song, Brandon immediately took a drink of wine from the silver Valero goblet he had placed on the coffee table in front of him, blushing humbly at their muffled applause.

"That's nice, Brandon," Demi told him.

Sloan added, "You know a lot of songs."

Delighted with the compliment, Brandon grinned, and his ears moved forward. "You've got to do something with your spare time." He stood and walked toward the hallway. "Excuse me a minute. Can I bring you anything while I'm up?"

Sloan giggled. "Not from there!"

He blushed but retained his grin. "I mean from the kitchen."

"No, thanks." She watched him walk quickly down the hallway and disappear into the bathroom.

"He's got a small bladder," Demi offered in a whisper. "Makes you wonder if room is at a premium in that area."

Sloan took a drink. "It doesn't make me wonder."

Demi leaned away from her, looking surprised. "You already know?"

Realizing the implication, Sloan laughed it off and said, "Demi! No. Of course not." She reddened. "I mean I don't think about it."

"You don't?"

"No," Sloan said emphatically.

"You wouldn't like to?"

Sloan flinched, which made Demi smile a peculiar, almost sinister smile. "Come on, girl, you can talk to me."

Sloan was not sure that she could, not completely. She decided to change the subject. "He doesn't sing very well, does he?" she said in a whisper that made Demi draw close to her again.

Demi laughed quietly so as not to be heard down the hall. "It's on a par with his playing."

"I don't care, though," Sloan said. "I like it."

Hearing the flush of the toilet, they pulled away from each other, not wanting him aware they were discussing him in his absence, though few things could have made Brandon Parsons happier. He would have assumed all they were saying was good.

He returned, still smiling, picked up his guitar and sat down. He glanced at Demi, and she nodded almost imperceptibly. He strummed a couple of cords, then deadened the strings with his hand and looked at

Sloan as if an idea had suddenly occurred to him. “Do you like to fly?” he asked her.

Sloan look questioningly at Demi then back to Brandon. “Yes,” she began. “I mean, I like to travel.”

He strummed the guitar again, rhythmically picking the same chord. “Do you like to fly in small airplanes?”

Sloan looked to Demi who only smiled with enlivened eyes. “I’ve been up in one once before, but I didn’t enjoy it. Alan took me. My stomach ...”

“Rough, was it?” he interrupted. “It can be nice in the morning on a pretty, smooth day.” The same chord continued from his guitar. “Would you like to see Spain from the air?” He looked at her. “I fly a Cessna at the Aero Club. We could go early, while the air is still, and I can share with you what I see every day.”

Sloan was startled by the idea, but she felt an exhilaration that bade her take the chance. She looked at Demi, who only smiled, then said, “How early?”

“When the sun comes up,” he suggested with a grin.

“I’d like that,” Sloan answered lightly.

He nodded and began to sing, looking deep into her eyes as he performed, his voice slightly off key, his guitar slightly out of tune.

CHAPTER THIRTY-EIGHT

"I want Wayne," Major Sherman told Buck. "I want Alan Wayne on my wing against that F-15 tomorrow."

"Who do you see in his pit?" Buck asked.

Sherman thought for a moment before saying, "Sam Christopher ... and put Boomer in mine."

Buck tried to make his disappointment appear as disapproval. "Is Alan ready for ..."

"He'd better be." Sherman smiled slightly. "You'll get your shot, Buck. You and Fisch can fly with Gunner in that 2v2 against the F-14s on Wednesday."

"Oh, I didn't ..."

"It's okay, Buck." Sherman waved his hand. "Be sure Alan knows about the flight. I want to brief an extra half-hour."

"Roger," Buck winked, implying his background and experience allowed him insight into the intricacies of such planning.

The "Eagle Jet" drivers welcomed the opportunity to come to Andravida to enjoy a brief respite from the perpetually overcast gloominess of Germany and have fun chasing F-4 drivers around the clear Ionian sky. The advanced technology of the F-15 Eagle made arranging fights of two F-4s against one F-15 a fairly even match.

Doug Sherman was just beginning to discuss the nuances of fighting against the superior abilities of the Eagle when their adversary, a Lieutenant Colonel, stuck his head into the room. He peered at Major

Sherman above half-lens reading glasses balanced precariously on the end of his nose.

"Squid Three One flight?' he asked cautiously.

"Yes, sir," Doug answered. "Come on in." He offered his hand to the Lieutenant Colonel. "Doug Sherman."

The Eagle driver stepped into the room. His scarf bulged un-uniformly out of the collar of his flight suit. Seeing Doug's outstretched hand, he clumsily tried to put his line-up card in the same hand that held a full cup of coffee and a pencil. When he shook Doug's hand, his glasses almost fell off their perch. "Pete Divine. Good to meet you," he said, quickly releasing his grip to catch his glasses. "Didn't you guys used to be Duddy?"

"A recent change, sir," Doug said. "Have a seat."

"Thank you," Pete Divine said. He shook hands with everyone at the table before sitting down. Pulling his chair to the table, he spilled coffee on his line-up card. "Sorry," he said and pulled a white handkerchief from a pocket to wipe the coffee from the Plexiglas.

Doug Sherman watched with amusement and a certain degree of skepticism.

Alan decided the odds were beginning to look even.

"Sir," Sherman said, "I thought we'd work this briefing by going over the standard stuff for getting to and from the area, brief the ROE, and then let you tell us a little about your jet."

"Well, that's fine," Pete said. As he lifted the mug to his lips, coffee dribbled down his chin and onto his flight suit. "Shit! That's hot!" he said looking embarrassed and quickly dabbed the coffee from his uniform and chin with the handkerchief that was now more brown than white. "I'm sorry, press on."

As Sherman briefed, Pete Divine scribbled notes on his card in indecipherable form. When it came his turn to speak, he took off his glasses, laid them on the table, put his hands behind his head and almost lost his balance as he leaned back in his chair. He was a dubious picture of confidence.

"The Eagle is a fine air machine," he began. "As you are probably aware, it has a faster turn rate and a tighter turn radius than anything the Soviets have to date. It will definitely out-turn your F-4D. I don't have to do a thing but pull on the pole. You may feel the urge to turn with me some today, but I don't suggest you count on that as part of your bag of tricks."

The Lt. Colonel took a sip of lukewarm coffee and managed to avoid spilling more on himself. He spoke almost apologetically, as if he was sorry his airplane was so much better than theirs, and he gave the impression that he was no great fighter pilot, that it was the airplane if anything that would allow him to come out on top today.

When he had finished, he placed the now empty coffee mug on the table and looked at Doug. "Anything else you want me to mention?"

"No, sir. That ought to just about handle us," Sherman answered with a sly grin. "We will use separate radio frequencies and let GCI pass our shot calls using the two-shot kill criteria."

The Lieutenant Colonel nodded his head.

"Any questions, sir, before we turn you loose?"

Pete Divine looked around the table, suddenly realizing he was being dismissed. "No, I guess not," he said and stood up awkwardly. "I know you guys don't have gun cameras, so I'll try to record what I can. See you over the Ionian Sea." He gathered his pencil, empty coffee mug and battered line-up card and strolled out of the room. Sherman closed the door behind him.

"This guy could be easy," Alan said as Sherman walked back to the head of the table.

"I don't know," Boomer put in. "He seems a little too easy."

"Are you kidding?" Sam said sternly. "By telling us how great his jet is he's already won the debrief."

"We've got to beat the man and the machine," Sherman added sternly. "He may be an average pilot, but he's flying a very lethal airplane. You don't have to be as good to win in the F-15." He began to draw arrows and lines on the chalk board. "Now here's how I want to do it ..."

Sloan squirmed to get comfortable in the little Cessna 150, adjusting herself on the small, threadbare seat as she tightened her leather waist belt. Sitting next to her, Brandon Parsons clutched the yoke with his left hand, his right casually resting on his leg. He looked at her with a knowing half-smile.

Sloan grinned sheepishly back at him. "My butt's asleep already."

"Maybe seeing Spain with me will wake it up," he said with a smile.

She turned her head as she felt her face flush crimson and glanced sideways at Brandon. He wore the same closed-mouth half-smile that made his ears appear to move forward. Sloan realized she liked to see him smile. It was boyishly charming. She felt herself beginning to relax.

"Let it sleep, then," she said loudly. "It could use the rest." She looked to the east. The sun was glowing beyond the plateau.

As the Cessna droned along at barely 90 miles an hour, Sloan giggled loudly in response to Brandon's joke about an enlisted man she had watched him play in a base-wide racquetball tournament earlier in the week. "I shouldn't laugh," she said loudly. "He couldn't help it, he just wasn't any good."

Brandon smiled his ear-filled, close-lipped smile. He was self-conscious about his teeth, thinking they were too large. He did not want her to think the same. "He did the best he could, but I don't think racquetball was his game."

"It's funnier now, the way you tell it."

Brandon beamed. "Well, I didn't look much better when I slipped and nearly fell on my how-you-doin'!" He patted his behind, then slowly banked the airplane toward the rising sun.

Sloan laughed again. "It was still a good kill shot." Somewhat self-conscious, she closed her mouth but continued to smile warmly. She felt fine. He was being very gentle, and she was enjoying the ride.

"Yeah." Brandon looked at her, then turned his head away.

She adjusted her seat belt. "Thanks for helping me relax."

He leaned forward slightly toward her, momentarily taking her left hand. "So. How do you like Spain so far?"

"It okay. Dirtier than I expected."

"It's what?" They were having to talk rather loudly over the drone of the engine.

"Dirtier!" She nearly yelled.

"Oh. It is, isn't it?"

"Uh huh." Sloan slowly pulled her hand from his and folded her arms. She looked out her window as he rolled the airplane level toward the mesa between Torrejon and Alcala. "It's sure pleasant from up here, though." She turned and flashed him a warm smile.

"So. You got this figured out, Dog?" Sam asked as Alan maneuvered the F-4 for a weapons-systems check behind Sherman's jet.

"Piece of cake, Possum," Alan said sarcastically. "I just maneuver my older, slower, smoking, big, ugly, flying brick to his dead six o'clock unobserved and shoot him in the ass with my old, been-on-the-shelf-for-twelve-years Aim-9 Papa."

"And don't try to turn with him," Sam said, adding the response he wanted.

"And don't turn with him," Alan repeated matter-of-factly.

"It sounds good when you say it."

After several attempts at contacting the Greek Air Traffic Controller, Major Sherman transmitted, "In the blind, Squid Three One flight is proceeding to the western training area. We will proceed with due regard. Contacting GCI now."

"What'd he say?" Alan asked. "We're proceeding with Beauregard? Who's Beauregard?"

"I don't know," Sam said, adjusting his scope. "God. Maybe."

Boomer threw up just as they went feet wet over the Ionian Sea. Clipping his oxygen mask firmly back in place on his helmet, he said to Sherman, "I'm clear!" as the GCI controller vectored them into the northern half of the area.

"Bogie dope," Sherman radio-ed.

"Roger," the GCI controller answered. "You've got one bogie, twenty-three miles, Angels 24."

"Deploy!" Sherman called. "I've got one contact 22 miles, on the nose."

"Slightly high," Boomer told Sherman inside the cockpit.

"Slightly high," Sherman radioed.

Alan pulled up and away from Sherman's jet to a position 2 miles away, 3000 feet high, slightly aft of his wing line. Sherman turned into him slightly.

"No contact," Sam said, keying the mike to inform both Alan and Sherman.

"Roger." Boomer's voice. "Single contact 10 left, 18 miles ... slightly high ... no, level now."

"Contact bandit," the GCI controller responded. "Still at Angels 24."

"24000 feet ... I'm looking, but no contact," Sam returned, beginning to breath heavily.

"Be calm, Sammy boy," Alan said flatly, his eyes searching the sky in the direction of Boomer's call. They were in minimum afterburner, brushing against the Mach.

"Go gate!" Sherman called.

Alan shoved the throttles fully forward. Their airspeed increased rapidly to 1.2 Mach before the drag from the wing tanks slowed their acceleration.

"Contact on the nose, 15 miles," Sam radioed.

"Good show, Sam!" Alan said. "Where ..."

"High. 5 degrees high."

"Above us?" Alan checked his repeater scope for the contact and saw the blip of the target.

"Yeah."

Inside his F-15, Pete Divine accelerated to 500 knots and made a hard turn to the west when he picked up both F-4s on his radar. His plan at the merge was simple: he would try to split the fighters and kill one quickly. Then if the other one stayed to fight, he would use his superior turning ability to try to make the remaining F-4 turn with him. If that happened, he would eventually win. How quickly he won depended on whether he fought the turning fight with the experienced leader or the inexperienced wingman.

"Contact, thirty left ... level," Sam said to Alan.

"Roger."

Sam keyed the radio, "Contact thirty left."

"Contact there," Boomer returned, indicating he had the same on his radar.

"Plan Alpha," Sherman radioed.

"Copy," Alan answered. He looked at his line-up card on his knee. Plan Alpha was a Hook/ID. Sherman would fly straight at the F-15. Alan would attempt to get turning room on the outside.

"Contact's still 30 left, now twelve miles," Sam said to Alan.

"Roger."

Divine had two radar contacts on his left side. One was a thousand feet below him and the other was four thousand feet below him, both with high aspects. "They're both pointed at me." He made a quick climb three thousand feet higher to get turning room in the vertical. At supersonic speeds, the targets marched down the radar scope toward him so fast that any erroneous information could result in incorrect analysis and a deadly error. For now, he would keep the fighters on one side to ease his radar work and, hopefully, gain turning room for an unobserved stern conversion.

"He's climbing," Sam told Alan. "Ten miles!" Sam called to the formation.

Pete analyzed his radar scope presentation. "One's still high aspect, coming right at me, and the other one's aspect is getting lower," he said aloud for his gun camera film. "Looks like the old Hook/ID. Might as well point at 'em." He turned left to put the lead aircraft on his nose at ten miles and got a radar lock. Looking through the Target Designator box in his Heads Up Display, he could not yet see the F-4. The numbers on his HUD told him he was in range for an AIM7F shot. He simulated arming his missile, counted to four and, at seven miles, squeezed the trigger. "Fox One on the western man," he called.

"We've got RHAW," Sherman called to Alan. "He's locked on us!"

"Roger!" Alan strained to find the F-15.

"Five miles!" Sam called, his voice sounding slightly anxious.

"Tally ho!" Alan said, keying the mike. "Two's tally ho!"

"You're locked," Sam said.

"Fox one!" Alan called immediately.

Pete manipulated the switches on his throttles that activated his Sidewinder heat-seeking missile. The green indicator diamond on his HUD centered in the TD box. He uncaged the missile's seeker head and the diamond enlarged. The characteristic chirping of the AIM-9L locked to a good heat source sounded in the earphones of his helmet. He simulated the missile launch. "Fox 2 Lima on the western man!"

"Damn!" Doug said. He pulled his engines out of afterburner to decrease the heat source and called "Chaff and flares!" to simulate countermeasures against the missile. None of the F-4D aircraft of the 401st TFW were equipped with the necessary dispensers.

Alan turned left toward the bogie. He saw the F-15 and Sherman's jet in the same field of view as they passed close aboard and 180 degrees out. Alan hardened his turn to five g's.

As the two jets passed, the F-15 went into a hard left turn. Alan sensed the Eagle saw only Major Sherman.

"Where's that other guy," Pete said to his camera. "He should be somewhere to the ... Tally ho!" He took his jet into a near vertical climb and continued the left turn.

"He's zooming for the moon!" Sam yelled. "They love to do that."

"Tally ho!" Alan said. "I've got the energy. I'm going up with him!" He keyed the radio, "2's engaged with the bandit in a vertical fight!"

"One's tally, visual," Sherman responded.

"He's coming up after me," Pete said for the camera, "but I don't think he can get up here." He continued his climb at a shallower angle and turned enough to deny Alan the AIM-9P shot at his tail.

"I can't get up there!" Alan discovered.

"Run!" Sam said. "Let's get out away from him and come back into the fight nose on."

Alan lowered the nose and accelerated downhill.

As Pete watched the F-4 below him begin to fall off, he pulled five g's back down toward it, all the while looking for the other F-4 he no longer saw.

Sherman turned away from the fight when he saw Alan take it up toward the bogie. He began a sweeping right bank to gain turning room as Alan fell off and the F-15 started down after him.

"He'll be pointing at us soon," Sam said to Alan.

"Roger, I'm coming hard left!"

"No! Keep running!" Sam grunted as he looked over his left shoulder. He grabbed the glare shield and twisted himself around further. "I'd say he's about two and a half miles. We can run from here."

"We'll turn and meet him head-on," Alan said as he pulled back on the stick. "If he turns with us, Sherman will have a chance to get into the fight."

"Not something I would bet my life on," Sam said heavily.

As Alan turned left, Pete Divine took his Eagle once again into the vertical. The result was an old F-4D turning horizontally with an Eagle circling above it, ready to swoop down when the chance came. That chance was not long in coming.

"He's still fighting us!" Alan said, groaning under the g's.

"No shit!" Sam screeched at him. "We can't go into the furball all balls, dick, and no forehead and expect to live. We'd better meet him close aboard and bug out."

The Eagle dove down on the Phantom. Alan pulled hard up into his adversary.

"Watch the g's!" Sam groaned.

When they passed, Alan reversed his turn.

"Don't turn with him!"

The Eagle and the Phantom were now across the circle from each other. Alan continued to turn as the F-15 quickly made angles on them. Alan pulled hard right. As he watched the F-15's silent approach, he realized this coffee-spilling, gray-haired, four-eyed Lieutenant Colonel was really a crafty old sonofabitch!

"You can't turn with him, Puppy!" Sam grunted in desperation. "You can't will this airplane into doing more than it's capable of!"

Out of the corner of his eye, Alan saw Doug Sherman's jet below them in a right turn that would put him at the bandit's deep six o'clock if the fight continued in its present direction. "I'm visual on Sherman ... he's below us."

"Separate!" Sam yelled.

Alan unloaded violently, throwing Sam unexpectedly against the top of his canopy.

"Nice unload," Sam grunted sarcastically as he pushed against the glass.

Sherman squinted as the sun glinted off the airplanes against the blue sky, momentarily blinding him. He searched the sky, unable to regain the tally. "I lost them," he said calmly to Boomer.

"Tally ho above us!" Boomer called.

Sherman squinted in the sun. "I don't see ..." He blinked a bead of perspiration from his eyes.

"Right three o'clock high, now ... going to four o'clock."

The hair began to stand on the back of Doug's neck. "No tally."

"Come hard right! He's going after our wingman."

Doug banked and turned the F-4 hard right on Boomer's call, still unable to find the bandit. The bright midday sun glinted on his canopy. "I still don't see him!"

"Keep coming!" Boomer directed. "He's three o'clock still, slightly high ... Okay, I'm visual on Dog and Possum. Tally, visual! Tally, visual!"

"Keep talking!"

Alan saw the Eagle pass to the right of his leader in a right-hand turn coming for him. Two lines of fine white mist formed off each wing tip as the F-15 turned. Instinctively, Alan brought both engines to idle to thwart the head-on heat-seeker shot. He turned hard into the F-15, and they passed within a thousand feet of each other, canopy to canopy.

"Passing us on the right!" Alan said.

"Tally," Sam said, straining less now.

"Roger, you've got the tally, I'm watching lead."

"Roger, the bandit hasn't turned."

Alan saw Sherman coming toward him in a tight right turn that was beginning to look like a collision course. He banked hard left, and Sherman's jet went by them to the right and toward the bandit. He unloaded the Phantom to zero g and began a downhill acceleration to get energy and turning room. "Lead is coming back toward you," he told Sam.

"Okay, tally, visual."

Pete Divine found the other F-4 coming up toward him from the rear and reacted to this new threat with a seven g turn. The F-4 was closing on him rapidly, and he expected to hear a 'Fox 2' call.

There was nothing. He's going to try to gun me, he thought. Looking rearward as he strained audibly to fight the g's, he saw the F-4 reverse its course momentarily, then turn back into him. He unloaded to get what airspeed he could then pulled on the pole again to keep this F-4 out of his vulnerable cone.

The F-4 overshot to his left. Pete lost him for a moment as he unloaded and reversed his turn. He found Sherman's F-4 abreast of him about three thousand feet away. They were in a vertical scissors. He pulled to the F-4s high six and watched the older jet, unable to match his turn rate, slide underneath him. Now he was in control of the fight. With Sherman's airplane on the defensive, Pete took a moment to sweep the horizon in search of the other F-4, cursing the fact that he could not find him.

"Shit! I'm in a phone booth with this guy!" he said to the camera. "I've got to finish him and leave." He closed in for the kill.

Alan was nearly supersonic when he turned back toward the fight. At first, he saw two planes close to each other and descending. He began to climb above the fight. He then saw that one of the aircraft had a definite advantage. As he continued to get closer, he realized Major Sherman was defensive. He stroked the burner and continued to climb as the fight turned toward him from below. He could see the F-15 closing to within gun parameters on Sherman. "Jink, lead!" he called.

There was no response verbally or visually.

"JINK!" he repeated.

Sherman began a series of violent, unpredictable maneuvers.

Pete looked behind him, trying unsuccessfully to find the mystery wingman.

Alan descended directly behind the Eagle going nearly 300 knots faster than the two fighters now in front of him. He brought the throttles from burner back to idle and opened the speed brakes to decrease his speed and control his massive overtake.

"You've got boresight and ten!" Sam said excitedly. "Get an auto-lock!"

Alan hit the throttle switch, and the radar locked on the bandit. The ranging bar showed Alan to be 2500 feet from the F-15 and closing rapidly. He watched the big sleek Eagle as it seemed to float effortlessly in the clear air, silhouetted against the low mountains of Greece in the distance. The large canopy made the single pilot look rather lonesome and aloof.

At fifteen hundred feet, Alan pulled on the stick until the pipper in the center of the gunsight was just in front of the F-15's vertical stabilizer. He squeezed the trigger. Three seconds passed before he realized how large the F-15 appeared in his windscreen. He pulled away from his target, keying the mike to call, "Tracking guns kill!"

Alan pulled hard to the right to avoid a collision with the F-15. The Phantom shook violently as it tumbled through the Eagle's jet wash.

Sam said, "Looked like a good shot ..."

The jet shuddered and rolled further right. The rudder pedal shaker vibrated to indicate a stall. Looking quickly at the airspeed indicator, Alan was astonished to see it showed them to be supersonic. He knew they could not be going that fast. He looked at the engine instruments as he pulled the throttles back on both. The right engine faltered then began to unspool, and the fighter shuddered violently.

"What the hell was that!" Sam yelled.

"I don't know! We weren't going super, but we've lost the right engine."

"You sure, Dog? Did it maybe just compressor-stall?"

Something caught Alan's eye over the nose of his aircraft. "Shit!" he exclaimed through his teeth.

"What?" Sam's voice was noticeably strained. "What is it?"

Alan began a climb. The airspeed showed them decelerating rapidly back to 300 knots, and the indicator seemed normal now. Three thick metal wires at the front of the jet flapped in the airstream. In the very back of his throat, he felt the dryness of Fear. "We've lost our radome ..." His lips smacked from lack of moisture.

"What ... "

"Our radome, Possum ... the nosecone is gone!"

"Gone?"

"Gone to the great radome Beauregard in the sky!" Alan quipped.

"How the hell?!"

Out of the corner of his eye, Alan saw the fire light. "I'm pulling the right throttle back ... I'm going to have to shut it down. There's a loud noise, but I'm not sure ..."

Sam stared at his instruments, trying to make sense of them.

"I think part of the radome may have gone into the engine," Alan said. His voice shook from the vibration. "If we look this one up in the book, I think it'll just say YOYO."

"You're on your own ..."

"Roger."

Sam's voice was raspy and broken. "I think I see something black on the right intake."

"Probably radome paint ... the right engine's shut down, the shaking should stop." Alan trimmed the ailerons to maintain level flight.

Sam swallowed. "Is the fire light out?"

Alan took a deep breath as the precious seconds passed. "No."

Since their arrival in Spain, Sloan had sensed that something of the experience Alan seemed to be enjoying was missing for her. She had tried to see it as a country of grace and beauty, as the books she read before crossing the Atlantic described it, but, until now, she had mostly known loneliness and an intense feeling of being out of place and out of touch.

Brandon Parsons' quiet demeanor was somehow bringing everything back into perspective for her. She looked at him and he was smiling at her, a sad, intense smile that made her excited and uneasy.

"Thank you, Brandon," she heard herself saying. "This is like a gift I cannot explain."

He put his right hand tenderly on her thigh. She patted it, then placed her own on top of his to keep it there.

"Andravida Tower, Squid Three Two is declaring an emergency," Sherman called over the radio. "They've lost their radome and their right engine. Squid Three One will go chase."

He signaled for Alan to turn northeast toward the airport. "Do a controllability check on the way in, away from the towns," he said over the radio. "We'll follow you, then land first."

Sam's voice trembled ever so slightly. "What kind of controllability check? What do you plan to do, Dog?"

Alan looked at the fuel remaining. They had plenty. "Try the gear first, then maybe the flaps. I don't know what else the radome hit. It may have hit us under the jet, too, I don't know."

Sherman pulled up to the right and a bit behind the crippled jet. "See anything?" he asked Boomer in the pit.

Clarence Bailey squinted to show he was looking intently at the bad jet, despite the fact that no one but God could see his face. "I see no nose cone and what's left of the radar is still moving back and forth."

Sherman flew below and behind, crossing to the left of the crippled jet, then back to the right. "The lower part of your right intake looks like something hit it," he said over the radio. "There's a crack, or something ..." He furrowed his brow in concentration. "How's your utility hydraulics?"

Alan checked the gauge again. "Gone."

Sherman said, "Yeah. Your radar just stopped sweeping."

"Turn off the radar, Sam," Alan said.

"The radar's off."

Alan keyed the mic. "We'll let the gear freefall down. If it's good, we'll land no flap."

"Roger," Sherman answered. "How long do you plan to head north?"

Alan realized in the heat of the moment, he had continued north past the airfield. "We'll head back in one minute."

"We're still kind of heavy," Sam reminded him.

"We can't stay up here all day burning gas, waiting for something else to go wrong. I'll dump fuel."

"With a fire?"

"Do you see one?"

Sam checked both sides of the airplane as far behind him as he could. "No. Maybe we should just jettison the tanks."

Alan looked below them as he turned over land toward the air field. Little towns with the white steeples seemed to be everywhere. He lowered the gear. "Three green," he announced. "We'll ditch the tanks if it gets worse."

"How much worse?" Sam asked brusquely.

"Squid Three Two," the tower called, "say your intentions."

Alan ignored the call from the tower. "How's our gear look?" he called over the radio.

"Three good gear," Sherman answered. "Put her down."

"Okay, tower, we're going to land in 2 minutes. We plan to take the cable."

"We do?" Sam asked. "Great! A single-engine no-flap approach to take the cable ... no problem. We do this kind of shit all the time."

"Squid Three One is coming in now," Sherman called. He saluted, then banked away.

The disabled Phantom jerked left, then right. "Damn it!" Alan exclaimed.

"Now what!" Sam's voice was urgent.

"I don't know what's causing that."

Sam was silent.

Alan said, "All I can think of is that the disrupted airflow still has the static ports confused. I'll turn the yaw aug off."

The blunted nose of the F-4 began ever increasing throws to the left and right. Alan turned the yaw augmentation switch on again. "That's no good. We'll just have to take the occasional jerks and hope they don't get worse."

"Do you still have control?" Sam asked, tightening the restraints of his ejection seat. He straightened his back.

"I've still got it." Alan turned southeast toward Andravida. He thought of Sloan, and, for a moment, allowed himself to fantasize what she might be doing right now, oblivious to what was happening to him. At this moment in time, they were in two different worlds. Time, Alan mused. He wished he had more of it.

"Shit!" Sam said under his shallow breath.

"Shoot!" Sloan said, rubbing her arms. "These little airplanes are always too hot or too cold." She rubbed her bare arms and looked at Brandon.

He smiled. "Do you want my coat?" Awkwardly, he took it off, making the airplane dip forward as he momentarily released the yoke. He handed the coat to her before she could object, brushing his hand against her breast as he did.

"Careful!" she warned, her hands reaching for the glare shield. "You don't want to see me lose my breakfast."

He regained control of the plane with his left hand. "Sorry. It's okay, though."

She took the coat. "Thanks. Let me know if you get cold. I'll give it back."

"I'll be okay." He watched her put it on with keen interest. "Have you ever been to Germany?" he asked suddenly.

"I've only seen a couple of places outside Spain. Not there, though. Why? Have you?"

"I was stationed there for three years ... at Ramstein."

"Flying F-4s?"

He shook his head. "OV-10s."

"What are they?"

"Two engine prop-jobbers. I was a Forward Air Controller. Not actually at Ramstein, but I went there a lot. I know a few restaurants. And some bars."

"You do?"

"In the city. I wish I could show it to you. I know more about it than I do of Spain."

"Oh." She paused. "You were there three years."

Brandon knew what that meant to her. It would be a touchy subject, but he needed to know how she felt about it. "Uh, yeah, on an accompanied tour."

She shifted in her seat.

"German food is good." He looked at her without the smile. "You'd like it, I think. Maybe more than Spanish food."

"Damn it!" Alan said.

Sam's voice was guttural. "Now what?"

"I wish I had more than eight thousand feet of runway to work with."

"We, Dog," Sam corrected him. "I'm not just along for the ride."

"Right. I'm going to come in fast and shallow and try to plant it on 'brick one.' If we're slow enough to take the cable by the time we get to it, I'll put the hook down on the roll out."

"Why fast and shallow?"

"To keep the angle of attack as low as possible without swapping ends in the flair. I want to have a few extra knots, in case the yaw aug decides to go bitmish or we have to go around on one engine."

Sam was silent. He looked out the cockpit as the island of Zakynthos passed beneath them. It was a beautiful day in southern Greece. There were no clouds and the haze was gone. Not a good day to die. After a while, he said simply, "We're in trouble, aren't we, Dog?"

Alan glanced outside the canopy, beyond the barren rocks of the ground below, to the concrete of the runway that seemed very short and a long way from them now. "This is no big deal."

The words were the reassurance Sam wanted to hear. Although he understood them to be just that and no more, for the moment, he allowed himself to savor the lie.

"We'll be all right," Alan said calmly, and he meant it. Things always turned out okay for him. This would be no different. He thought again of Sloan. He wanted to be with her.

He knew she had no idea what was happening to him now. For that, he was thankful.

Over the radio, Alan and Sam heard Major Sherman call clear of the runway.

Good, Alan thought. If they took the cable, the airfield would be closed until they could reset it. He allowed himself to fantasize again, for a moment, that Sloan was here. She would meet him at the airplane as she had when he returned from Aviano, and he would tell her what had happened, and she would hug him and kiss him and tell him how good he was, and everything would be fine.

That would have to wait. He still had to get this disfigured hunk of flying debris in the hangar.

"Are you ready, Sam?"

"No."

"Okay, let's go. Checklist."

Sam's reading of the checklist items lacked enthusiasm. "'Shoulder harness - locked' ... we'll need that if we take the cable."

"I still don't know if we're going to," Alan answered, locking his shoulder harness.

Sam unlocked his shoulder harness and continued the checklist.

"What did you like to eat in Germany?" Sloan asked loudly over the drone of the little engine.

"Veal. Mostly, different types of veal."

Sloan screwed up her face and looked out the window at the rolling hills of Spain. She looked back at him. "Baby cows ..."

Brandon flinched. "Well, yeah. They cook a lot of them ... it. I like it because it's tender and easy to eat."

Sloan batted her eyes. "I guess I like it, too. I just hate to think about it. It makes me feel guilty."

Brandon Parsons relaxed. "Guilt is over-rated." He smiled. "You don't think about it, you just enjoy it."

Alan flew the approach at 220 knots, 40 knots faster than the maximum recommended speed for cable engagement for an F-4. Approaching the overrun, he sensed that if anything was going to happen, it would be now. And it would be so sudden that he would be unable to control it, and it would be all over within a few heartbeats.

He did not want to die at the end of a runway, not quite making it all the way. If he made it past the overrun, he knew he could handle whatever happened after that.

Watching himself land in his mind, Alan saw the flames from the fireball of his dream. He saw himself scream Ernie's name.

"Are you still with me, Dog?" Sam's voice broke Alan's trance.

"Uh, yeah, Possum. I'm ready."

In a heartily fatalistic voice of defiance to the possibilities, Sam blurted, "Then let's park this pig on the patio and go to the bar!"

"Amen!"

"How long have you ... were you together?" Sloan asked after an extended silence.

"Seven years," he said without emotion.

"Seven years ..."

"It took that long to figure it out."

"That's a long time ... to figure it out."

"It was for me. It doesn't usually take that long for me to see something." He pointed to the right, his arm close to Sloan's chin. "That's Lake Sacedon."

"Oh!" Sloan exclaimed. "I've been there!"

"You have?"

"Yes." She looked at him. "Camping." She looked back. "It doesn't look like I expected."

"Few things do from up here," Brandon said.

The F-4 touched down less than 200 feet beyond the runway threshold, and Alan immediately applied the brakes. He poised his hand over the hook deployment handle as he watched the decreasing airspeed indicator and the rapidly approaching cable. He had it under control. "We're going to make it!" he announced to Sam and hit the handle. The hook caught the cable at 175 knots. The tension of the arresting gear rapidly decelerated the heavy fighter to a stop. Alan planted his feet on the brakes to keep the cable from pulling them backwards.

The emergency rescue team swarmed around the airplane. The leader, wearing an asbestos suit, gave Alan the signal to allow the jet to back up slowly to release the tension from the cable. When the chocks were in place, Alan raised the hook and cut the good engine.

"Made it." Alan's voice quivered with relief. He could almost feel his phantom four-leaf clover.

"We've got another problem," Sam said. His words were muffled, but Alan realized the edge in his voice was clearly gone.

Alan turned in his seat to look for Sam behind him, but he could see nothing. "What are you doing?"

"When you said we weren't going to take the cable, I left my shoulder harness unlocked," Sam answered. He sounded giddy. "That stop threw my oxygen mask into the radar scope. It's stuck on something, and I can't get up!"

Within a few minutes, Major Sherman arrived at the edge of the runway in the SOF truck driven by Shooter. Getting out, with a brick in hand, Sherman walked briskly toward the fighter. As he approached, Alan noticed his countenance was exceedingly drawn and tired. He looked worse than Alan felt and displayed no reassuring smile when he stopped in front of the jet and waited for the rescue team to put the ladders in place.

Alan climbed down, jumping the last couple of feet to the runway, then bent over and released his parachute harness.

In silence, Sherman watched Sam do the same. Sam patted Alan on the back. "Good job, Dog!" He laughed as if he did not mean it, but Alan was sure that he did.

He felt fine. He had "fought" over Spain, Turkey, Italy and now the Ionian Sea of Greece. He had never fired a shot in anger, and yet he felt hardened to the life of the fighter pilot. He had returned a crippled jet safely to earth, and, although he could not tell what had made the radome depart the Phantom, experience assured him it could not be his fault. His career had attained a new high. Not yet twenty-seven years old, he had reached an intermediate peak from which he imagined he could see the mountain top.

CHAPTER THIRTY-NINE

At the beginning of the party given by the Greeks to celebrate the end of the Squid TDY, the American fighter pilots kept to themselves, as did their Greek counterparts. To fulfill the requirements of protocol, their commanders stood together, making light conversation out of diplomatic necessity.

The wine began to flow, followed shortly thereafter by the whiskey, but it was the arrival of the food to the long serving table that narrowed the cultural gap to within a communicable range. As caution gave way to social custom, the Greek pilots began to intermingle with the Americans. Their conversation, guarded at first, became more open when it appeared the Americans were actually listening. They spoke of flying, and the commonality of their language nurtured the conception of fledgling friendships.

After a while, Alan realized the Greek fighter pilots were stealing glances behind him, glances that occasionally lingered into stares. Sipping his drink, he turned to look.

Lieutenant Connie Marcum stood talking with Major Sherman and Squadron Leader Demopoulos, the Greek Squadron Commander. Dressed in civilian clothes, Connie's persona was decidedly enticing. Being the only female in the room accentuated the goodness of her looks. Her black hair, sleek and shiny, betrayed her Greek lineage. The extra make-up she wore for this evening gave her face a character that was strikingly non-military. Her figure had subtly acquired a sensual tone.

The men continued to talk and listen, but now divided their attention between two loves: airplanes and women.

The music grew louder. Demopoulos encouraged everyone to dance. He took a few willing Greek pilots and, grabbing Sherman's hand, led them to the middle of the floor. They held hands and danced to the Bouzouki music. Individuals danced and then joined the circle, sometimes clapping. Alan, Boomer, and Sam joined them, dancing and holding hands. It was fun, it was a foreign country, and it seemed right.

Demopoulos placed a full glass of Robola de Cephalonie wine on the floor and danced around it. Then, picking up the glass, he downed its contents in one swallow before placing it on the floor again. Putting his fore finger on the rim of the upright glass, he suddenly slammed it down, giving the appearance that he had driven his finger right through it. Shattered glass dispersed over the floor as the revelers applauded, garnering a humble bow from the head Greek.

Leaning against the wall, Connie did not join them, believing herself to be of the wrong gender. Alan went to her, took her slender hand and led her to the celebrating men whose eyes widened with delight as they vied to join her in the dance.

The booze had played its vital role. The music and dancing gave way to more talking and drinking. In one corner of the room Sam and a newly made Greek friend passed a bottle of Ouzo between them, yelling "Koleós!" when it was the other's turn to drink.

In the white finca house on the outskirts of Madrid, Sloan sat with Brandon Parsons on his sofa, watching a movie on his new video tape recorder. Demi sat near them in a recliner.

"This is great!" Sloan said, her eyes bright. "I can't remember the last time I saw anything on TV, much less a movie."

Brandon Parsons was enthusiastic about this new freedom. "Yeah, and the movie you want to watch, too. Pick a movie and it's yours."

"How much was this one?" Demi asked.

"Well, my first one was sixty dollars, but for five dollars, I traded it for this one."

"Oh."

When the movie was over, Brandon rewound it on the VTR to run it a second time. Halfway through, Sloan began to blink sleepily.

"I'm tired," she said. "I can barely keep my eyes open."

Brandon put a sofa pillow on his lap. "Here," he said. "Put your head on my lap, if you want." He slapped the pillow gently.

Sloan looked at Demi, then relented. Ten minutes later, she was sleeping peacefully.

Demi got up. "I should leave."

"No," Brandon said very softly and even less convincingly. "Stay."

"It's okay," Demi said. "Her car's at my house. Don't let her drive until she's fully awake. And sober." She winked and walked out his front door, grinning in the dark.

When Sloan awoke, Brandon was leaning over her. She was disoriented for a moment, then remembered she was lying on a pillow in his lap. Something had awakened her. His face was very close to hers. Had he just kissed her? Looking into his eyes, she could not tell. She brought her left arm up past his face to look at her watch.

"Where's Demi?" she asked, looking around the room.

"She left," Brandon said.

"I should go, too."

"I wish you wouldn't." His eyes were pleading.

She looked up at him. She was comfortable. "Why?"

His throat was dry. He swallowed. "I don't know. I like you ... your company."

"Even when I'm asleep?"

"Yeah. I like being witcha".

"I like it, too." She felt her hips move on the sofa and wondered if he noticed. She had not meant to do that.

A feeling of exhilaration flowed through him in anticipation of what could happen next. Take it easy, he cautioned himself, don't spook her. He stroked her fine hair. "We have a lot in common," he said. "I'm glad we are friends."

Friends. She rolled the word around in her mind. This was too arousing to be friendship. This was sexy. Yes, that was the word.

He leaned over her, close to her lips, continuing to stroke her hair. It felt good to her. She did not need to see, she wanted only to feel. She closed her eyes. He kissed her soft lips.

She kept her lips and eyes closed. He put his hand on her stomach and kissed her again. She moved her mouth, then parted her lips. Her head swam deliciously. Was it the wine? Yes, she decided, it was the wine. His hand moved on her stomach as they kissed again. His tongue lightly touched her lips. My horizons, she thought, are broadening.

She touched her tongue to his, and he responded. They were both breathing deeply through their noses. As he rubbed her stomach, a little higher now, she put her hand on his arm. Somewhere in the back of her mind she felt this would put her in control.

He held her head in his right hand as they kissed, stroking her stomach with his left. He moved up to her arm, then around to her head, massaging her ear. Then down her pretty neck and onto her small breast.

She felt saliva flow in her mouth and wetness between her legs. Her mind was in chaos, confusion. As he rubbed around her nipple, she felt the uncomfortable paradox of the body that ached for pleasure muted by thoughts that created guilt.

She pulled his hand away from her breast. He continued to kiss her, stroking her stomach, then moving his hand down past her waist to the inside of her thigh. This time she pushed lightly with both hands and moved her mouth from his. They were both breathing noisily. He opened his eyes.

"No," she said. "Please. You know how I feel."

His breath was warm, his voice raspy. "I was beginning to see."

"No. I'm sorry. I can't do that."

"It's all right." He kissed her, and noticed the kiss was very moist. He stopped to look lovingly at her. Tears escaped through her closed eyelids.

"I'm sorry," she said again. "I have to go."

He continued to look at her and stroke her stomach and hair, unmoved by the obvious pain of her betrayal. When she sat up, he neither helped nor hindered, but only witnessed, letting his arms fall from her, brushing past her breasts again.

She ran her fingers through her hair, then looked at her watch. She stood unsteadily, gathering her coat from the floor. "Alan is coming home in a few days. I'm not ready for this now." She left the door open and walked carefully in the dark to the Camaro. He did not follow.

Despite the blackness of the night and the treacherous road, she did not feel afraid. She did not cry. The thoughts running through her mind were not totally unpleasant. In fact, they were exciting. She replayed them, not realizing that her stopping him was the reason she could enjoy it this way.

She knew she would feel the guilt later, when she saw Alan. And she knew she would have to have it under control tomorrow. For now, she let the fantasy play in her mind.

The stars flickered staccato in the clear Peloponnesian night as Alan and Connie walked out of the building. The trees and dry earth swallowed the sound of their footsteps in a quiet so intense that they felt their souls drawn close to the surface, seeking escape in the timelessness of the night. So different was it from being inside, oblivious to the darkness. Here, there was nothing for them but the earth and the sky and perhaps each other.

"I had to get out of there," she said. "I sensed the real reason for my popularity."

The words of Denise Fisch returned to him. "It's not selfish to want to be liked," Alan paraphrased. "I would think you would be flattered."

"Flattered? As the only female? With no choice to be made, where's the compliment in that?"

"Not flattered, then. But ... exalted ... as a woman. A very interesting woman."

She tilted her head back to gaze at him with close-set eyes that ever so slightly flickered the need for comfort.

He did not touch her. "But I was not the only man. It should be me that is flattered."

She looked at her feet as they walked in the darkness. "Sometimes I think my whole life has been spent in search of flattery ... of acceptance." She seemed preoccupied with an idea she needed to express. "Acceptance of my abilities, my intellect. My father never really accepted me because I wasn't his little boy. Now, tonight, I am reduced to being merely a woman." She paused. "That's what makes me interesting."

"I don't see it as merely, like something lesser," Alan said. "I see the character of a woman the same as a man, the difference being that you are a woman."

"Being a woman meant something different to my father ... something inferior."

"I'm sorry. He was wrong."

She stopped and gazed up at Alan. "What does it mean ... to you?"

"It means you have the same potential, the same capacity for intelligence as any man."

"Do you really mean that?"

"Yes. But you're also a woman."

She searched his eyes. "Do you think I could fly a fighter?"

Alan was taken off guard, realizing his casual advances on her senses had rebounded with a question that burned deeply in her soul. "Yeah, I believe you could." Was he lying? If so, to whom?

"You would fly on my wing." It was a statement. "In combat?"

"If you were as good ... good enough to lead a flight, why not?"

"You wouldn't be afraid I'd crack up or have PMS or something?"

"Not any more than I would Bill Fisch."

"Who?"

"Look. Nobody knows how they or anyone else will react to a situation until they get into it," he answered truthfully.

She looked away. "Like the ones you've been in?" she asked.

He shook his head. "I know nothing of real combat."

"You've faced some pretty harrowing experiences."

"Like being shot at."

She nodded. "And recovering a crippled airplane. It seems to me that training for combat can be as dangerous as the real thing."

"I've never fired a shot in anger," he countered. "I'd sound ridiculous trying to compare that to the real thing. It's more like practicing emergency procedures in the sim. The pucker factor is lower."

"Pucker factor?" Connie turned her gaze to Alan.

He smiled. "The consequences of busting a simulator check-ride are a bit less than those of busting your ... ass."

She did not return his smile. "You've had a real emergency. I'd say you overcame the pucker factor."

He shook his head again. "Imagine if that happened over enemy territory. Trying to limp home. A lot of fighter pilots have actually done that."

"So. It's still a mystery."

"A mystery?"

"How you'll react to a particular situation."

He rubbed his chin. Yeah." He paused. "Do you want to be a fighter pilot?"

She looked away into the darkness. "I don't know. I don't think so."

Alan touched her arm, camouflaging a sigh of relief as one of assent. "I consider that a feminine quality."

She focused her eyes narrowly on him. "You mean it's not feminine to want to be a fighter pilot?"

"No. It's just a feminine quality I prefer. It's got nothing to do with intelligence or ability. I have no desire to bear children. Does that make me any less of a man?"

"That's the woman's job, right?"

"Anatomically, yes. But that isn't what I mean. Would you think more of me if I wished I could bear children? It doesn't make me any more sensitive. For whatever reason, genes or testosterone, I desire to do man things."

"Like flying fighters."

"Yes."

She reached out and touched his arm with her hand, then returned it to her side. "I wish I could go with you," she said. "To fly. To know what you know. To understand you, to understand why you talk about the things you talk about. But because I can't, it adds to the mystery ... and the attraction."

"That makes you no less desirable."

"Being desirable is not all there is to life," Connie said softly. In another time and place, she would have argued against his chauvinism, however well-meaning. But not tonight. "I don't want to go through my life being insignificant."

As if by instinct, Alan wrapped his arm around her shoulders and hugged her loosely. The wind stilled as he looked skyward to the distant worlds.

She returned his hug. "A friend of mine at Aviano called you a rough diamond. It fits, I think." She did not release him.

Hoping her friend was not a certain Airman Two-striper, he looked down at her eyes and found a beckoning tear whose origin he could not know.

She seemed soft and purposefully vulnerable. He put his lips to hers. She tightened her grip on him and opened her mouth slightly. He touched her tongue with his, and together they felt a ripple of shaded desire flash between their bodies.

Too much! Alan thought, but he did not let up.

Her breathing became fast and shallow, making their lips part slightly from each other.

She was not kissing him now. Her mouth was open, her eyes closed with anticipation. The obvious willingness she felt thrilled him, because he had made her feel this way. His heart beat faster as he tried to remain in control.

"My god! What are you doing to me?" she moaned. "What are we doing?"

"We are being man and woman."

She pulled away slightly, her eyes still closed. "But you are married."

"Does that matter tonight?"

Fighting the fire raging through her body, she opened her eyes and forced a smile. "It matters every night. It has to if it is to mean anything."

Alan stared at her. He had wanted her. He had wanted her so much that he had been willing to break every vow. He felt ashamed. It should have been him putting on the brakes.

She touched his arm gently. "I want more than a fling."

"You deserve more," he said. He put his arms around her.

"And you can't give it to me."

He shook his head. "No."

She lowered her head onto his chest. "I think you are a good man," she said. "You are what I want." She sighed heavily. "I have no ties to anyone. I'm a free agent. But you are not mine to have. This would just be a fling. You could not give me your heart. If you were the kind that was willing to do that, at the expense of your wife, I wouldn't find you ... desirable. Isn't that crazy?"

"No," he said, stroking her hair. "It's the truest thing I have ever heard."

He took her hand and guided her toward the door, allowing her fingers to slip from his as they returned to the party.

CHAPTER FORTY

Wearing only cutoff Levi's, Alan sat on the white flokati rug he had brought Sloan from Greece, listening to CBS Mystery Theater on the radio. When the apartment bell rang, he stood and walked quickly to the door. Looking through the eyepiece, he was surprised to see the distorted figure of Michelle Christopher peering from the other side.

When he opened the door, he could not help but notice her eyes widen momentarily at the sight of his bare chest.

Alan said, "Please," and was immediately sorry he could think of nothing more casually inviting.

She smiled, but her face did not glow with its usual enthusiasm when she said, "How's it going?" and walked past him into the small foyer, glancing again at his chest.

"I'm sorry," he said. "Sloan isn't here. I think she should be home soon." He looked at his midriff, then to her. "I should put on a shirt."

She laughed. "You don't have to for me." She lightly touched his arm, then withdrew her soft hand. "Besides, I saw more than that of you at the lake."

Alan feigned sanctimonious shock. "You didn't peek! Did you? You said you wouldn't."

She laughed. "No. I didn't have to peek. I saw all I needed to see." She winked at him.

Perhaps she had been at the water's edge longer than he realized. Perhaps she had witnessed his naked hesitation. "Would you like something to drink? Coke? Wine? Scotch?"

"No thanks. No Scotch tonight."

He led her into the living room, to a recliner into which she eased herself without a word. He returned to his seat on the flokati.

"How was your last week in Greece?" she asked.

He looked at his bare outstretched legs. "It was okay," he said.

Michelle nodded and then shook her head. "Everything seemed so unreal here. I could tell from talking to people that most of them felt the need to re-evaluate their lives, but nobody talked about it. When somebody almost dies like that, it's not only you fighter pilots that are affected."

Her seemingly perpetual smile was gone. Alan had never seen her like this. It was a whole new side. He detected a deeper anger.

"We were never in trouble," he said, but he knew she did not believe him. "Beauregard was watching over us."

She eyed him quizzically. "Who?"

"Never mind." He decided to lighten the mood. "You're the one who could be in trouble."

"Why is that?" She eyed him with amused suspicion.

"I decided I was tired of waiting, and that I was going to make love on this rug with the next woman to come through that door." It seemed he should laugh now, but he barely smiled.

"I'd be an easy target." She giggled to clear the air.

On the radio, the Mystery Theater played the music that led to a commercial.

"So," she said. Her hands were folded in her lap. Her elbows rested on the thick arms of the chair. Her legs were crossed. "Tell me what happened."

"Are you sure you don't want anything to drink?"

"It's that bad?" She grimaced cutely. "Hm ... you mentioned Scotch."

Alan was surprised again. "Uh, sure. Straight up or on the rocks?" He rose and walked toward the wall unit that served as a bar.

"With ice."

"I'll make two." He left for the kitchen. When he returned with two high-ball glasses with ice, she was standing at the glass doors, looking out over the night as if in a trance. He poured the Glenlivet, remembering the look Sloan had given him when he brought the expensive Scotch home. It was an extravagance, for special occasions, anticipated or otherwise.

Going to her, Alan could see her face in the glass. She looked at his reflection, and somewhere in the darkness, their eyes meet. He gave her the Scotch.

"So, what happened?" she asked.

"The Scotch will help."

"That's why they call it Scotch."

"What?"

She took a sip. "Scotch. Like the tape. It mends, it heals, it even puts things together. But use too much of it and what it's supposed to mend looks and feels so different that it's distorted and no longer genuine."

"That's funny! Where did you hear that?"

"I didn't," she took a larger sip. "I just made it up. Are you going to tell me?"

"What?"

"The story."

"Oh, yes."

Mystery Theater was over. It was nine PM, time for soft evening music. A song by "Styx" began to play ... "Babe, I'm leaving ..."

She returned to the recliner, folding herself into it as if in preparation for an epic tale.

Alan sat stretched out on the flokati and began with his simulated kill of the F-15. She listened intently to his story, as if looking for some hidden meaning. He was truthful but glossed over parts of their in-flight emergency he thought it better that she did not hear. At least from him.

When he finished, she said simply, "I need him," as if the entire reason she had endured his tale to the end was to deliver that one line.

Alan turned to her. There was pain in her eyes. Her lips tightened, and the tears gushed so suddenly that Alan was shocked into inaction. For a moment, he could only stare at his big bare feet. "I know," he said finally. "They should have let him come home with me."

Michelle nodded her agreement.

His eyes widened in realization. She was hiding something deeper in her soul, but she wanted him to find it. "That's not why you're here," he said.

She sniffed and looked at him. "What?"

"It's more than just our IFE."

She nodded almost imperceptibly. She wanted to tell him. She was not just a fighter pilot's wife, and she resented her life being so defined, resented the borders around her soul that were formed by what some assumed should be her station in life. Not that she did not love her man. She was sure he understood, at least as much as the image of a fighter pilot would allow. She had allowed her life to be put on hold, at least temporarily, for his career. And she loved living in Spain, despite the fact that the best work she could secure there was selling cosmetics at the BX.

But she would not say this to her husband's best friend.

A fresh flood of tears came, and Alan was immediately sorry. "It's all right to talk about it," he said. He did not sound convincing. "It wasn't as big of a deal as it may seem. We were never in any real danger."

He got up and went to her. She stared across the room and out the glass doors. Looking down on her, he could not see her face. Her hair was beautiful and soft and smelled slightly of perfume. He stroked her long thick curls. His touch brought a fresh barrage of tears. Kneeling beside her, he stroked her hair until the sobs turned to sniffles.

Opening her wet, red eyes, she looked at him questioningly for what seemed a very long time.

"I understand what you are feeling." He tried to remain calm and in control, but he was enraptured by the feel of her. His senses were on edge.

She closed her eyes, like a cat being petted. He placed his hand on the back of her neck and kissed her forehead lightly.

She moved away and turned to gaze around the room through bleary eyes. "So, where is Sloan?"

Alan suppressed a touch of guilt. "I don't know. She isn't expecting me. I was supposed to fly home tomorrow."

Michelle nodded.

Then it hit him. "How did you know I was here?"

She smiled gently, blinking away the fog that blurred her vision. "I wasn't sure. I came to see Sloan."

"So you could agonize together?"

"Something like that."

He released her.

Michelle smiled sadly. "You understand me better than I thought you did ..." she paused. "But not as much as you think you do."

"You are my friend," he said sincerely. "I hate for you to hurt. I want to be your comfort."

She stood and brushed back her hair with her hands. "I had better go."

She walked to the door. He brushed past her to open it.

Michelle said, "You do realize how important your friendship is to Sam? He likes you very much." She walked out of the apartment onto the landing and pushed the button. The only sound was the click of the ascending elevator.

When it stopped, the dim light poured through the glass door and onto her face. She turned to look at him. His eyes told her he was devastated thinking he could have done wrong. Spontaneously, she threw herself into him, hugging him tightly. He placed his cheek on the top of her head. His heart beat rapidly. He felt like he wanted to cry.

"I want to be important to you," he said.

"You are." She pulled away and smiled warmly at him, the way he was used to seeing. She opened the door, stepped in and was gone.

Opening the door to the apartment, Sloan was unnerved to see a glow coming from somewhere inside. For a moment, she stood still, debating whether to go in. Deciding she must have left a light on, she closed the door gently and followed the glow to its source. Light from Alan's study bled into the hallway. She turned off the desk lamp. Walking quietly down the hallway, she looked into their bedroom and saw Alan's long body stretched out on the far side of the bed.

As she turned away, Alan said, "Hey, babe."

She turned back and saw his eyes were open and he was staring at her.

"You said you were coming home tomorrow."

"Aren't you happy that I'm home early?"

She went to him. "Of course, I am." She kissed him. "I heard about your ... thing ... with the nose thingy."

"No big deal." He smiled.

"You could have punched out if you needed to, right?"

He nodded. "But we didn't need to."

“I’m glad you’re home safe.” Her voice sounded less convincing than she meant it to be.

“Then come to bed. I need you.”

She kissed him again. “I need you, too. Just give me a minute.”

She went to the bathroom and closed the door, leaning against it for a moment. She felt flushed with guilt. After opening the faucet to get the hot water going, she stripped her clothes from herself. She tested the water before stepping into the bathtub and pulled the shower curtain closed. She briskly washed herself clean with more soap than usual, toweled and buffed herself dry, and picked up her clothes, hoping that whatever she had just washed off would not find its way back to her from them. She turned off the bathroom light, tossed the clothes into the closet room and walked naked to her side of the bed. She reached for Alan, but he was not there.

“Alan?” she called out. She heard the flush from the far bathroom and saw the light in the hallway as he opened the door before it went dark again.

Without speaking, he crawled into the bed with her and kissed her cheek. She turned to him and kissed him roughly. She tugged at him, guiding him on top of her. The intensity of her love-making seemed driven by desperation rather than passion, and her groans intensified frantically as she labored to bring herself to orgasm.

CHAPTER FORTY-ONE

In the days that followed the squadron's return from Greece, Sloan seemed ever more remote. Alan sensed a certain confusion in her manner that she herself chose to ignore through a lifestyle he sensed was becoming increasingly dangerous.

She was spending more time at Demi's place. Their inevitable disagreements upon her return were increasingly argumentative to the point Alan no longer thought them anything but destructive. And when he chose not to talk of it, she became defensive and probing, as if looking for a reaction she could attack.

In the mid-afternoon on Saturday, as Alan was reading in the living room, Sloan walked in fully dressed. "Do you mind if I go to Demi's for a while?"

He looked up. "It seems all you lack is my approval. When will you be back?"

"I won't be gone long," she said, gathering her purse and jacket.

Alan tried again. "What do you want for supper?"

"Grilled steak!" She licked her lips in exaggerated anticipation. "They're thawing in that sorry excuse for a fridge. See you then!"

He watched her leave. What was it about Demi that Sloan found so interesting? She did not do a thing for him. He had decided Demi was childish and rather weird, and he had found no commonality with her or her pretentiously eccentric husband. Yet, Sloan seemed to really like them. He refused to consider any other reason for her regular trips to Finca Avalon.

He opted not to think that she might also be seeing Brandon Parsons on these regular visits, even though, on Fridays, when they went to the bar, she looked for him, often inviting him to their table or leaving their circle of gathered friends to lean against the bar and drink and talk to him or listen to him talk to others. It embarrassed Alan to think she might be making a fool of him in front of their friends, but he was at a loss for what to do.

She seemed to be distancing herself from him, releasing him quickly when they kissed, almost stepping away, as if to kiss him was a betrayal. There were, he decided, many perspectives he could have in such a situation, and he decided finally that this was a passing infatuation which time and honor would soon dispel. He trusted her to do the right thing by him.

To Sloan, the possibility of an affair seemed more thrilling than the real thing. She was enjoying Brandon's company and his attention. She was sorry if she was hurting Alan, but something inside made her do that which her conscience told her was wrong.

But, she decided, if those feelings proved to be true love, they could not rightly be ignored. She was frightened even as with each new turn, she felt herself pulled in deeper and more irrevocably. She was guilty of her imagined feelings, yet she basked in the excitement of that guilt. The contented life she was living with Alan now seemed dull and pointless when compared to the excitement of infidelity.

And Brandon Parsons spoke quietly, but passionately of their potential. It was a good word.

When Sloan returned, the steaks were well done. She apologized for being late. They ate in awkward silence.

FINAL FALL
CHAPTER FORTY-TWO

Alan awoke on Sunday morning to discover Sloan was already out of bed. He tugged on his shorts and strolled down the hallway toward the kitchen, stopping when he spotted Sloan seated behind the desk in his study.

Several books were open and scattered in front of her. He recognized one as a book on love and marriage given to him by Sloan's parents on their wedding day. A book of collected poems he cherished was marked in several places with strips of white paper. The dictionary was opened to the letter "L." His Bible was beneath the pile.

He leaned heavily against the door frame and crossed his arms and legs in front of him. When she did acknowledge him, he said, "You're being very quiet."

She looked up from her work, her eyes wavering around his face but never meeting his. "I know."

His stomach began to hurt. He could feel it tightening. "What's wrong?"

"I am."

He tried to swallow. "Am I?" He felt the guilt swell within him, remembering the evening in Greece with Connie, and was convinced that if she only looked him in the eyes, she would see it.

"It's nothing you've done."

He felt no relief. "Looks like a lot of research ..."

"Alan, I'm not sure I'm in love with you anymore."

He felt the blood rush toward his heart and away from his head and legs. The room was very bright. His knees buckled ever so slightly. Her blurted, simple words stunned him, even as his mind went on the defensive.

His lips smacked dryly as he asked, "Do you want a divorce?" He swallowed again. The dizziness was passing.

"I don't know what I want," she said, looking around at the open books.

The ensuing silence was long and uncomfortable.

He could feel his pulse in his ears as he strained to hear any words of comfort and assurance from his young wife. He expected her to say something like 'No, I just need to get my head straight.' Anything close to that would be welcome now.

Finally, when no words came, he walked away from the door to the living room and stared out the big glass doors over the barren quadrangle below him and across to the apartments on the other side. When he accepted the fact she was not going to come to him, he went to the closet room to change, walked past the silent study, out the front door, hurried down the eight flights of stairs and out on to the street for a long run.

Run the evil out, he thought. But the evil was getting deeper and harder to exorcise.

It was after noon when he finally returned. She had prepared a light lunch without much effort.

"Do you want to eat?" she asked from the table.

"I'm not hungry."

"Alan, I don't know what to say ..."

He put his hand up toward her face. "Unless it's the words you know I want to hear, don't say anything."

She silently returned to her meal.

Standing over her, he watched her feed herself. "Is there someone else?" he asked.

She said, "It began before that."

He had to think of that as a lie. He knew it was Brandon Parsons, it was all Brandon Parsons, but he did not want to mention the name, as if ignoring him would keep him from being a part of this.

"Then we can work on it," he offered unbelievingly.

She did not answer. There was something in her that did not want to discuss it, that wanted only to endure it until the end came. Still, she could not admit that to herself, even as she knew the pile of books on his desk was nothing more than a front, a scene, convincing her own mind that she was searching, that she was trying. But that would only be until a proper time had passed, when their friends, her family and the Air Force accepted her choice.

The following weekend, the Squids had a going away party for Buck and Kathleen at the Officer's Club. Though not a squadron member, Brandon Parsons showed up and sat with the other wing officers, obligatory attendees of these periodic hail and farewell soirees. Sloan sat with Alan but glanced regularly in Brandon's direction.

When the dining was over, Alan sipped on a Coke and watched Parsons boogie awkwardly on the dance floor with Sloan. A growing circle of their friends approached Alan out of curiosity and concern. There were rumblings.

"Aren't you drinking, Dog?" Boomer asked. "Can I get you a beer?"

"No thanks, Boomer. You can't get drunk at every party, you know."

Reggie thumped him on the back. "Why not? Works for me."

"Because not everyone who is leaving should be going away."

At the far end of the room, Sam nudged Michelle, and they walked together to the group of fighter pilots and their wives.

"Gents, if you haven't heard by now, I'm buying the strongest concoction you can handle," Sam said light-heartedly. "So, what'll it be, Dog? Water? Straight up?" He smiled at his friend.

"No," Alan said. "Give it to Carp." He started toward the bar.

Sam stopped him with his free hand.

"Dog," Sam said. "Let me buy you a drink."

Sam gave Michelle a knowing glance, then, quickly excusing himself, went to the bar. He returned shortly with four glasses, giving one to Alan, one to Boomer, and one to Reggie who asked, "What is it?"

"A real man's drink, Sweet Cheeks," Sam said. "The Glenlivet on the rocks! The Scotch that is Scotch. Drink up!" He took a healthy swallow. Looking at Michelle over the glass, his eyes lit up in sudden realization. "My lady needs a drink. Anybody else?" he asked loudly as he gazed around the small group.

Cherry Swartz, Reggie's wife of two months, sheepishly handed him her empty wine glass.

As he took it, Alan's new Flight Commander, Randy "Casino" Garman approached the group with his wife, Beth, in trail. "Never look a gift horse in the mouth," Beth said as she handed her empty wine glass to Sam. "What's the occasion?"

"White wine," Sam said knowingly.

"Come on, what's the occasion?" Beth was playful but insistent. "A rich uncle die or something?"

Sam grabbed her glass. "In a minute." He gave his own glass to Michelle and left to get the wine.

When he returned, the group had grown to include Denise and Carp.

"I've always appreciated you turning me into a Glenlivet man," Alan said, retrieving his gaze from the dancers back to Sam. He reached for his wallet. "Here's the payback."

Sam declined Alan's offer. "Not tonight, Dog." He took his glass from Michelle and finished the drink that was now more Scotch and water, with little ice remaining. He looked at Carp and Denise. "...'Livets all around?"

Alan glanced at Carp. "You've never been much of a Scotch drinker, have you Carp? More of a bourbon and coke kind of guy."

Carp bristled and said, "Bring it on."

"I'll take a Scotch, too," Denise said. "But I can pay for it."

"Not tonight," Sam repeated smiling. He turned quickly and walked toward the bar.

"You'll need more hands," Reggie said following after him.

Beth turned to Michelle. "What?"

With a contrived air of indifference, Michelle laughed and said, "It's his show." She turned to Alan and followed his gaze to Sloan and Brandon who were now loosely embraced in a slow dance. She reached to touch his arm but pulled it back as Sam and Reggie returned.

As Reggie distributed the drinks, Sam eyed Michelle while stirring his Scotch with his finger. He was enjoying the suspense he was creating. "Skol!" he said finally and tipped his glass to drink. The others looked at him in anticipation, so he took another sip.

"Well?" Beth demanded.

"Speak, or die," Reggie threatened.

Sam smiled, hesitating for as long as he deemed safe, then said, "This time next year, I'll be flying a 'Tweety-Bird' at Sheppard."

His eyebrows raised in total surprise, Alan said, "Possum! You're going to pilot training!" He reached to shake his hand. "Congratulations!"

Carp grabbed Michelle around the waist and hugged her. "We're going to miss you, darlin'."

"Oh. We're not leaving until next spring," she said. Her countenance glowed absolute delight, but Alan found himself questioning her true feelings.

"Well played, Possum," Alan said as he downed the Scotch. His eyes went to Sloan and Brandon Parsons on the dance floor, which brought the eyes of the others in the group on him.

"How about another one, Dog?" Sam asked.

"In a minute," Alan said absently.

He put his empty glass on a nearby chair and went to Sloan. Turning his back to Brandon he said, "I need to talk to you."

Sloan flinched. "Alan, I don't think ..."

"Now," he said as a father to a child, "unless this is the moment you choose to let the shit to hit the fan."

A few feet away, Sam's celebratory group quieted as they drank and watched their friends leave the room.

Avoiding the gaze of the fighter pilots and their wives, Sloan glanced over her shoulder at Brandon as Alan led her by her elbow out of the room and down the hallway to the entrance foyer of the building.

"What is it Alan?" Sloan asked, pulling her arm from his grasp.

They were on the other side of the quadrangle from the party room now, but through the interior glass walls Alan saw Sam approach Brandon and begin talking to him, perhaps as a distraction.

Don't let the Scotch get to you, Alan warned himself. "You know damn well what it is," he said loudly, then lowered his voice. "Why are you putting on this display? You've already stepped all over my balls. Do you have to cut them off in front of our friends?"

"Alan, I ..."

"Are you just trying to make it acceptable? To subtly become a couple? You wouldn't do this if we were back home. Don't you realize what you are to him?"

"I think I do."

"No, you don't, or you wouldn't still be lapping up to him like a bitch dog in heat!"

"Alan! Lower your voice."

"No, damn it! If you care for me and our marriage, if you ever cared for me, stop doing this to us."

"Someone's coming," she whispered with some relief.

He turned to see Buck and Kathleen approaching them. It was clear they had heard more than a little.

Buck offered his hand. "We're heading out. Got to rescue the babysitter. I just wanted to come tell the best young AC I've ever flown with ... well ... just that."

Alan took his hand. "I guess we won't be seeing much of you after tomorrow."

"Not unless we miss the plane." Buck grabbed his throat.

Kathleen took Sloan's hand.

"We will miss you," Sloan said awkwardly.

"I won't miss Spain," Kathleen answered. "Living over here away from family and your real life isn't easy. I wish you the best."

"Thank you."

"Remember," Kathleen said, "You have to do what is in your heart. Don't let anyone else tell you what to do."

Alan's ears burned red. He was stunned to hear her saying this in front of him. What the hell did she know about it, anyway? Perhaps it was fitting. A summer ago, little Jason had crapped in his tent. Now, here was Kathleen, rubbing it in his face. He said nothing more to her or Buck. After a brief, uncomfortable silence, Buck nodded and walked away with Kathleen in close trail.

Sloan turned to leave.

"Sloan," Alan called to her. "It's time to go home." He tried to give her his best look of loving forgiveness.

"If you don't mind," she said coldly, "I think I'll stay a while longer. I'll get a ride home."

"I do mind."

"I'm staying." She turned and walked away from him.

He burst through the door and out into the cold, dry night air. He stood there for a moment, shivering, looking for direction. He hated the

Air Force. He hated the people in it. Sloan had never known anything about it before him. Now she was wrapped so tightly inside it that he imagined she was contemplating her own personal advancement.

Brandon Parsons was a senior major. Sloan could become a Squadron Commander's wife in three years or less. She had come a long way from being the bride of a lowly "butter bar." Was that what she was thinking? Or was Brandon Parsons just the better man.

He felt guilty for leaving Sam on his night of celebration, but he could not go back inside. He went to the Camaro, gunned the engine and drove quickly down the road to the squadron building. He parked in the squadron commander's space just outside the front door, opened the combination lock and went in. He walked down the narrow hallway to the squadron commander's office and threw himself down on the ugly brown sofa. He would wait her out and sleep if he could. Maybe he would not get home until after she did, and maybe that would get her thinking.

After a few fitful hours, he rose and walked back down the hall to check the coming Monday's flying schedule. He went outside, locking the building behind him. It was very late when he got to Parque de Cataluña, and he had to search for some time before he finally found a place to park at the far end of their building.

He took the elevator to the eighth floor and opened the apartment door loudly.

She was not there.

He poured himself a glass of Scotch from the bar, downed it, then another. He went to the closet room, undressed, and went to the extra bedroom and crawled under the covers of the small bed.

He had not been there long when he heard her walk through the door. She turned on the living room lights, then checked their bed. She sighed and said, "Shoot!" before walking down the hall toward the kitchen. Glancing into the other bedroom, she stopped when she saw his bulk on the bed. She flipped on the light.

"What are you doing in here?" she asked.

Alan shaded his eyes and glared at her. "More appropriately, what am I not doing in here?"

"Well, I don't know, but why don't you come to bed with me?"

"You can't be serious," he sneered. He detected the faint aroma of cologne, not his.

"Yes, I am."

"Sloan, you are not my woman anymore."

She swallowed hard and looked at him. "Alan, I want to work on the marriage. Brandon and I decided ..."

He cut her off. "I don't give one piece of dog crap what you and that little nut-ringer decide! You pulled my heart out of my chest tonight and danced on it for all to see! Do you want to keep up appearances at home? Is that what you two adulterers decided? Kind of going at it bass-ackwards aren't you?"

She frowned horribly at him. "We are ... I am not an adulterer ..."

"I'm sorry. Adulteress."

"No, I ... no we are not!"

"You're not sure what he is, are you?"

"He's a good man. I'm trying to be a good woman. To you."

"A good man does not try to steal another man's wife. He's a thief, a fucking self-centered homewrecker. And I know what he will make of you. Do you remember that Sunday when we saw him in his car in front of these apartments? He spent the night with someone. And the girl he picked up on the ski trip ... All he wants from you is to get laid! And all he wants from me is to get what is mine."

"That's not all he wants. He wants me here with you. Please don't drive me away ... "

"Sloan. Get a grip on reality! He's playing with our lives! Do you really believe he's worth flushing all that is good about us?"

She rubbed her head. "I can't talk about this anymore tonight. Now, come to bed."

"No. I refuse to share mine."

"Alan ... "

"Turn out the light, Sloan, and leave me alone."

"Alan ... "

"I can smell his stench on you." He rolled away from her.

She flipped the large European switch and walked away to their king-size bed.

He lay awake long after the lights were out, listening to her soft sobbing, his own tears draining down his cheeks.

CHAPTER FORTY-THREE

In the middle of the week, Bear Bevins, the new 613th squadron commander, called Alan into his office. Once again, Alan placed himself on the brown sofa to wait for what would come next as the Bear talked on the phone. Unlike Hargrove before him, Bevins did not make Alan wait long, but quickly finished his conversation, saying he would call back.

He hung up and looked quietly at Alan, his big arms resting on top of the desk Alan was more familiar with than he was. Alan held his gaze which was gentler than the often condescending look for which Hargrove had become infamous.

At last the Bear said, "Captain Wayne, I don't know you very well, but the fighter pilots of this squadron seem to think quite a lot of you. I started the same way. I was rowdy, rambunctious and bulletproof. But I could fly a jet. Over the years, you learn the more important aspects of this job."

He paused to shuffle some papers out of his immediate view. He was busy with another matter, but he did not want to be distracted from what was a very important and very difficult task.

"One of the obvious lessons is that we, as warriors, have to leave to fight the wars. We can only hope that when we return, like Ulysses, our Penelope will be faithfully waiting for us."

He paused, hoping Alan might lighten his burden with a knowing response that could somehow make this easier.

Alan remained silent, thinking this respected new Squadron Commander could not be aware of the problems of his personal life.

Then the Bear said, "Rumors are spreading that you are the unwitting member of a love triangle." This time, he did not wait for Alan's reaction. "I can't tell you why one fighter pilot tries to hustle his buddy's wife. I can't understand it."

"Sir ..." Alan began.

"Now that I've begun, let me finish," the Bear said. He paused for silent compliance. "This sort of bullshit can destroy a fighter squadron. I can't let that happen."

"What do you suggest I do, sir?" Alan asked when the Squadron Commander looked away.

"Go to Parsons and talk to him man to man. Tell him to leave her alone until after the transition. If you haven't worked things out by that time, then she's ... I mean he can have ... I tell you what!" Bear's voice rose in anger. "If it isn't straightened out, someone is leaving, someone is going back to the states!"

Alan could not tell if the Bear meant that someone would be Brandon Parsons or himself.

The Bear was thinking of the woman. As far as he was concerned, she was the spur in the saddle. He could not fathom fighter pilots willingly stealing each other's wives, so it had to be the woman's fault.

"The Squids are leaving for Turkey in next week. You're not going."

Alan's mouth dropped in surprise.

"I want you to stay here and take care of your life, Alan. Major Parsons is leaving for three months of training in Arizona. That's a long way from here. Make the most of it."

With midday approaching, Alan offered to buy Jeff Cole lunch at the Mexican restaurant at the far end of the runway.

"Dog, can I ask you something?" Jeff inquired rather shyly as they drove along the perimeter road.

"Sure, Jet."

"Actually, it's more to tell you something."

"Okay."

He fidgeted in his seat. "Well, rumors are spreading that your wife is seeing a lot of that asshole Brandon Parsons."

"I appreciate the sentiment, Jet, but they're just friends."

"You think so?"

"Yes."

"Well, I didn't know how to tell you this because you don't seem to be noticing. But, well, some people think they are having an affair."

Alan's throat went dry, and he felt his face flush. "They may be spending a lot of time together, but I can tell you they're not having an affair."

"Are you sure, Dog?"

"Yes."

Jeff was silent, but his mind was working. Perhaps it was better to let his friend believe what he wanted for now.

"Jet?"

"Yeah?"

"I need a place to stay."

Jeff looked at the side of Alan's face. There was no emotion. "Sure, Dog. Whatever you need for as long as you need."

"I don't know how long. Maybe a week, maybe a year. I'll pay my share of the rent."

Jet looked outside the car across Alan's chest at the haze that was obscuring the mesa beyond. "Don't you want to talk about it?"

"Not now."

Jeff nodded. "When do you want to move in?"

"Is tonight too early?"

Jeff flinched. "Uh, no. I, uh, I won't be there." He reached into his flight suit breast pocket. "Here's a key. I'll have another one made tomorrow."

"Thanks, Jet."

"My pleasure, Dog. I've got a big place out there, but it's kind of Spartan. You can have the whole downstairs. There's even a fireplace."

"Yes," Alan answered. "I remember the house. I just don't remember how to get out there."

"Nuevo Camarma."

"Yeah, but which house."

"First street in, turn right. It's the corner house on the left. Big, white, with a wrought iron fence around it. You can park in the garage if you want, but it can't be opened from the outside."

"Okay, Jet. And thanks."

They drove in silence for a minute or two. As they pulled into the parking lot of the small restaurant, two F-4s were making a formation approach to the runway less than half a mile away. As they passed, Jet asked, “So, are you going on this TDY to Turkey, Dog?”

Alan turned off the Citroën, dropped the keys on the floorboard and got out. “No. I have to stay home and keep my wife from having an affair.”

CHAPTER FORTY-FOUR

Brandon Parsons' office at the Wing Headquarters appeared to be deserted. That was odd. Those working for their careers at the Wing generally remained at their desks long after everyone else had gone home or to the bar. If they had nothing to do, they stayed anyway, accumulating "face time."

Alan felt the fool having an appointment with his wife's probable lover. The Bear was right, though. Something or someone had to give.

Alan followed the faint aroma of cologne and found Parsons in his office in the back.

"Are you the only one here?" Alan asked.

"Yeah. I gave my staff the afternoon off."

"How generous."

Brandon closed his desk drawer and locked it, putting the key in a pocket in his flight suit. "What did you want to see me about?"

Alan glared at him. "Let's not play dumb on this one," he said, adding, "Sir."

Brandon Parsons eyed him evenly for a moment. "Let's sit on the couch." He lowered himself comfortably at one end.

Alan followed him and sat at the other end, trying to understand what his wife saw in this man. "I want to talk ..."

"Would you like some coffee?" Brandon interrupted. As much as anything else, he hoped to infuse a certain degree of civility into the proceedings at hand. He thought their coming words might change everything. He hoped they would.

"No! Thank you," Alan answered with a deep frown.

Brandon paused. "You want to talk about Sloan."

"Yes."

Parsons sighed through his nose. "Just about her?"

"About you and her."

"Okay."

Alan fully expected this to become a shouting match when all the cards were on the table. He wanted that. He wanted to make Brandon Parsons angry enough to say the wrong things, echoes of the dishonorable intent Alan knew lay at the depth of this man's soul. If he could expose the rat enough to convince Sloan of it, they might still have a chance. He was a bit unsettled by the unpredictable cool of his adversary.

He decided to work into it. "Why are you so interested in my wife?"

"In Sloan?"

"My wife. Yes."

"In Sloan. Well, we are becoming friends, I guess because we have a lot in common ..."

"So do we, she and I. We got married because of it."

"But Sloan doesn't seem to think the marriage is going anywhere, that you have stagnated." Parsons sounded more like a therapist than a thief, as if this exchange was nothing more than one friend talking to another. "Have you considered working on that?"

"She never said that to me. Those must be your words."

"We are friends, as I said. She has shared some things with me." Brandon reflected thoughtfully for a moment. "We have a lot in common," he repeated. "We're both athletes. She's very talented, and I like that."

"So do I."

Parsons brushed off Alan's feelings to better express his own. "She keeps in good shape." He seemed to wander off for a moment on a tangent that transcended the present. "She's very svelte on the court, very lithe ..."

Alan found it difficult to suffer this arrogant fool. "Was she lithe when you lay with her?" he said in deep sarcasm.

Brandon looked at him as if from a cloud. He squinted his eyes. "I haven't slept with your wife ... with Sloan. You shouldn't accuse ..."

"Excuse me for interrupting, but I think you have a very distorted idea of what I should do. I don't think you know what is right."

Brandon Parsons withdrew somewhat. "Right is how it turns out," he said after a few moments. "Don't you think?"

Alan's face formed the sneer of contempt. "You believe that?"

"Yes. How could it be anything else?"

Alan nodded knowingly, a contemptuous grin curled his lips. "Then, I hope you remember that. If you take her from me, what does your future together hold? If you steal another man's wife, you can't expect the rest of life to turn out right. You will come to despise each other. Contempt will brew in the morning coffee."

"I doubt that," Brandon said defensively. "But that's not what we want."

Alan was silent for a moment. Varied scenarios of what he might do ran through his mind in chaotic incoherence. None of them were what he would consider pretty. At worst, it could destroy a part of him. "If that's not what you want, then get out of the way and give us a chance. Let us work out whatever it is that we need to ... correct. Show some decency, some honor. We are man and wife. Leave us alone."

Brandon seemed to consider the idea. "For how long?"

"As long as it takes."

"Do you think Sloan would agree to that?"

"Why wouldn't she?"

"I think you know."

Alan recalled the Bear's suggestion. Maybe that would be enough to get Parsons out of their life. Maybe he'd meet somebody else in Arizona. "Until the transition is over," Alan said. "If we can't work it out by then, well ..."

Brandon leaned back and frowned. "That's a long time."

Alan's jaw tightened. "You said the two of you were just friends. This is my wife you're toying with! My marriage! I can't even believe I'm talking to you." Alan tried to calm himself. "Take this however you want, but this is a survival situation for me, and, personally, I can think of much more effective ways to handle it."

"Is that a threat, Captain?"

Alan said, "It's not so much about what I would do ... but rather what you will become. What the rest of this wing will think of you."

Brandon became genuinely angry. He pursed his lips. "I believe we have said all we can say, Captain Wayne." He stood up. "I have work to do."

Alan quickly stood and stepped nearer to him. They were roughly the same height, though Brandon was a bit more muscular. He had the stance of an awkward athlete. Hard, but not refined, not fluid.

"What do you want with my wife? Are you just looking for a quick lay?!"

"No, Captain."

"What then?"

"It's up to her."

"No!" Alan said loudly. "She's a young girl. You influence her in a way I cannot. You need to man up. Don't make this terrible mistake."

"It's not a mistake!" Brandon said heatedly.

Alan could contain himself no longer. "You ass! You'd better control yourself! Stay away from her! Stay away from us!"

Brandon's face was hardened. He looked squarely at Alan. "Or what, Captain Wayne?" He could feel himself losing the will power to maintain his calm.

Alan wished he was drunk. Then he would not be intimidated by rank. He could indulge his fantasy and deck this lowlife with one well-placed blow. His fists tightened involuntarily.

Brandon Parsons flinched but maintained his stance of awkward defiance. "You're thinking about of taking a swing, aren't you Captain?"

"This is beyond decorum. It has to do with you ..."

"And with you, Captain. And your failing marriage."

"The only thing making it fail is you, Major. It's about you getting beyond your petty covetousness." Alan turned toward the door. "Leave us alone."

"Your arrogance is your weakness," Parsons spewed. "I imagine Sloan feels the same way!" he said loudly as the door slammed.

Alan drove to Parque de Cataluña hoping to find Sloan there to tell her of his confrontation with Brandon. Some of the things her "friend" had said might seem interesting in the context he planned to use in telling her.

He unlocked the door and went inside. She was not in the apartment. At least she has not changed the locks, he thought. He contemplated whether he should himself. It was his apartment, in his name. As far as the Air Force was concerned, he had every right. That might bring her to her senses. He toyed with the idea before tossing it aside. He could never be that cruel.

He felt a pain in his stomach that rose to his chest. She was probably at Brandon's place now, out in the finca, waiting for him to tell her how the meeting with her husband went.

Alan angrily tossed a suitcase on the bed and packed a few necessities. On the way out, he picked up some books from the study and his bottle of The Glenlivet. He would return later and get some of the furniture and maybe the guest bedroom suit which had once belonged to his parents.

He got on the autopista toward Guadalajara, driving away from Madrid. In Alcala de Henares, he turned left after stopping at the light by the park and then the forty-five-degree right turn past the tall trees. The road, sometimes winding, sometimes very straight, had little but open fields on both sides. He stomped the accelerator on the straightaway, pushing the air-cooled engine of the Citroën to its limits. Sloan had the Camaro, and he would not have cared if this little French car exploded.

He slowed as he passed the small town of Camarma off his right, following the curve in the road that took him to the entrance of Nueva Camarma, the Spanish housing development on the far side of the city. He turned right on the two-lane entrance road past the abandoned guard shack overgrown with weeds. He turned right on the first street, stopped, got out and opened the gate, then drove down the descending driveway to the garage.

Jeff was not home. It was Friday. He was probably at the bar for one more good night of drinking before the Squids left for Turkey.

Alan walked up the sidewalk to the front door and opened it with the strange thick key that had indentations rather than teeth. There was a very small foyer with another door that lead into the house. The living room was on the left. Jeff Cole's bedroom was the first room on the right with its connecting bathroom. Around a corner in the hallway were three more small bedrooms, another bath and the kitchen.

Curious how a Lieutenant could afford such a place, Alan had once asked Jeff that question, to which Jeff had answered, "The exchange rate. 160 pesetas to the dollar!" Then Jeff had winked. "And I've got a little extra laid away. Or, rather, my parents do."

Alan walked across the living room to the stairs that descended to the finished basement. Once downstairs, he sighed and glanced around the open, sparsely furnished space. This would be his home for the foreseeable future. Two more bathrooms connected to this main room, the first of which was full of Jet's unpacked boxes. Alan tossed his Dopp kit in the sink of the other one.

He threw his suitcase on the floor next to the pallet that would be his bed. He opened the bottle of Glenlivet and took a long swig, a toast to his new "home." He considered going back to the base to the Officer's Club for a last night with the Squids. He doubted Sloan and Brandon would show up there, although they were becoming so brazen he could not be sure what they would do. The idea that Brandon would soon be leaving was as painful as it was encouraging. How would those two spend these final days?

Brandon Parsons! His mind spit out the name. He recalled the first party out at the finca. What was that guy's name? Nutter! That was it. JG Nutter. The guy who was giving so much attention to the wife of the fellow who was leaving. What was it Ron had said? You can't run away from all the JG Nutters in the world.

They were everywhere. Men with greed so vile, honor so twisted that they would not hesitate to take whatever they wanted from whoever they wanted.

"To the JG Nutters," Alan offered his toast out loud, echoing in the large near-empty room. "Whose world is all they know!"

He drank from the bottle again and sat on the brown recliner, the one piece of furniture Jet had moved downstairs for him. He turned off the reading light and drank in the dark until the bottle was half empty, finally going to sleep in the ragged old chair.

PART FIVE

THE PHINAL PHANTOM PHLING

CHAPTER FORTY-FIVE

The squadron deployed to Incirlik led by Lt. Colonel Bevins with Sam in the ceremonial place of honor in his pit. Alan stood by the RSU at the end of the runway watching the Phantoms depart in two separate six-ships, thirty minutes apart. The wind whipped his hair and twisted the roar of the engines that propelled the fighters and his friends away. When the last was gone, the C-141 carrying squadron personnel and equipment took the runway and rumbled down the long concrete pathway, slowly gaining speed until finally attaining enough to become airborne.

With his own personal war to fight now, Alan drove back to the squadron building, a shell of the bustling busy life it had seen some three hours earlier.

Except for an airman manning the desk, he was alone. He and a few of the other Squids who were left behind would fly sorties from time to time, but it would be nothing like the flying the rest of the squadron would be doing at the Lik.

Brandon Parsons was somewhere over the Atlantic now on a commercial flight to the States. In the resulting vacuum, Alan hoped to find his life had returned. He inhaled deeply, as if at the beginning of a long race.

The next afternoon, Alan went to the apartment to get more clothes to take to the house in Nueva Camarma. Sloan was not there. Walking through the rooms, he realized she had not been spending much time here. Something about the way things were in the apartment told him it was not getting much use. Going through their dresser, he found the letter. He began to read, slumping on their bed as the words of love hit him like coldly calculated fists of hate.

> ... now that you've gone, everyone must think
> I'm going to run back to Alan! Let them think
> whatever they will. I miss you. I miss being "witcha."
> I'm thinking about flying to Phoenix to see
> my parents. Maybe I can see you, too, but not
> with my folks knowing. Not yet.
> I'm writing this in bed. I miss you there, too ...

Tears formed in his eyes, but he held back. What could he do now? She had not mailed the letter. Perhaps that meant something.

When Alan strolled into the bar on Thursday evening, he saw Sloan almost immediately. Seated alone at a table in the shadows beyond the dance floor, she was nursing a glass of white wine which she placed on the table in front of her. He was sure he saw her eyes widen when she spotted him. She beckoned him to join her. He bought a San Miguel and went to her.

This is the beginning, he thought.

"Hi," she said.

"Hello, wife." He sat without further invitation.

She cleared her throat and looked around. "I heard you didn't deploy with the squadron. Are you going later?"

"No. I'm staying here."

"Why?"

"Why do you think?"

She looked into his eyes, seeing the hope, refusing to acknowledge it. "If it's for me, Alan, I understand. But I won't be here much."

He put the bottle on the table. "Sloan, we can work this out, whatever it is. Don't forget what we had from the beginning. Don't forget what we said we could be. Think of your parents."

"I'm going to do more than that," she said, avoiding his eyes and trying not to remember how soothing his voice had seemed only a few months ago.

Hope flared in his mind. Out of sight, out of mind might finally work to his advantage.

She spoke softly. "I've decided to go back to Phoenix to see my parents for a while. I think it will help." She dug into her purse. "Here's the keys to the Camaro. I'll take the Citroën to the airport."

He was shocked, caught completely off guard by something that, when he thought of it, he should have expected. "That's about a thousand dollars to Arizona. If you're planning a round trip ... "

"It will help me, Alan," she repeated. "Maybe help us." She jiggled the keys. When he did not reach for them, she placed them beside his beer bottle.

Alan's shock was replaced with anger. He took the Citroën keys from his flight suit pocket and flung them on the table. "This wouldn't have anything to do with one Brandon Parsons, also in Arizona, would it?"

"I need to see my parents," she said simply, taking the keys. "It could help ..."

"Help?" he interrupted. "How could your following that asshole halfway around the world help us?!"

"I think it will help me, getting back to reality, to talk to my folks." She smiled a beguiling smile. She was actually flirting with him. "I'm not following Brandon anywhere."

Alan was unmoved. He pulled the un-mailed letter from the leg pocket of his flight suit and threw it on top of the keys. "What is this, then?" he said loudly.

Wordlessly, she retrieved the letter and read it, refreshing her memory of what she had written, realizing what Alan now knew. The ineffectual smile left her face. "I didn't mail it," she said finally, looking directly into his eyes.

He quoted from the letter, "...I miss you there, too." He stared at her.

"It doesn't mean anything ..." she began.

"Bullshit, Sloan!" He concentrated his wrath on her, looking directly into her blue eyes. "Don't piss on my back and tell me it's raining!

You've hurt me, wronged me deeply. Doesn't that mean anything to you?" He could see the moistness forming in her eyes even as she refused to look away. "You might learn to live with that, but no amount of love you give to someone in the future ... nothing you do will ever be enough to erase the truth."

"Lower your voice," she said pleadingly as she looked around the bar.

He paused and took in a deep breath. "Think about it, before you make a mistake that may ruin your life. Stay here. With me. And at least try to make things right."

"I'm going, Alan," she said with finality.

"If you go ... Sloan, if you go, you take any last chance we might have with you."

"Alan, I ..." she paused and waited. "I'm leaving tomorrow."

"I hope your folks sent you the money," he growled, "because I'm not letting you do this with what we've saved together."

"I've already taken the money out. It's money I made at the BX, some of it anyway."

"You ... I can't believe this!" His eyes were turning red.

"It could help," she pleaded, on the verge of tears.

He did not answer. She drank the last of her wine and stood up.

"This is why you came here tonight?" he asked, picking up the Camaro keys and putting them in his pocket.

She nodded, avoiding his eyes.

As she turned to walk away, she was sure she heard him say something under his breath. She stopped for a moment, but the tears came, and she could not let him see them. She walked out of the bar without looking back.

CHAPTER FORTY-SIX

As the evening turned to night, Alan sat alone in the bar getting very drunk when he saw Michelle come in with Denise Fisch and join a few of the squadron wives at a table. The boys were TDY, and the "TD wives" were forming up. He remembered what Sam had said, quoting Steinbeck about when the women go away, the men start to fightin'. What did the women do when the men went away? He stood and strolled to the table.

"Well, Alan!" Casino's wife, Beth, called to him as he approached. "Did you stay behind to entertain us?"

"Why sure, ladies. I'm here to serve." He did not look at Michelle but could feel her eyes on him.

"I'll take a raincheck on that," Beth said. "I'll let you know how I'm doing about two weeks into this thing." They all laughed with her.

No one asked why he had not gone on this TDY, although some were jealous that he was allowed to stay behind while their men had to leave. He pulled up a chair between Beth and Denise.

"Mind if I join you, then?"

"Not unless you can hear what we talk about without judging," Denise said.

He laughed. "If it's sex, I'm leaving."

"Then hit the road, stud!" Beth said.

"Then I'm staying."

After they ordered another round, Alan glanced at Michelle. She was watching him quietly and smiling. He returned her smile, thinking how much he would like to talk to her. But tonight was not a good night.

At nine o'clock, a band from Germany that made the rounds to most of the military bases began to play. After a few more drinks, Alan asked Michelle to dance a slow one.

As they danced, Alan whispered in her ear, "I like your height. We fit well together."

She laughed and pulled ever so slightly away for the rest of the dance.

He did not release her completely, but looked at her face, the face that made him feel good about himself. But he could not allow himself to become Brandon Parsons. "I would never try to take advantage of that, no matter what I felt," he said finally.

She put her head to his chest and hugged him tightly. She could hear his heart beating quickly and strongly. "I think we should stop for a while ... go sit down," she said looking up at him.

"No," he said.

"Alan."

"No. I mean, you can. I'm going home."

She frowned. "I am not rejecting your friendship."

"I'm glad of that." He sighed, releasing her completely.

"Do you want to go to dinner some time?" she asked with the same sweet smile.

The question took him by surprise.

"Sure," he said, trying to appear at once nonchalant and enthusiastic. "Where?"

"Ever been to San Javier's?"

"No. Where is it?"

"In Madrid. A short walk from the Plaza Mayor."

"Let's go."

"How about next Friday?" she asked.

Here was a chance for atonement, to leave Friday night at the bar behind. "Sure!" he said. "It's a date."

Her face in a perpetual smile, she said, "You want to meet at the bar?"

"Why don't I just pick you up? It's on the way for me." Why had he said that? "About 7:30?"

"7:30. Friday."

They were quiet for only a moment, but the pause in conversation made Alan feel awkward. "I look forward to it," he said finally. He turned and walked out to the Camaro.

Michelle Christopher watched him go, saddened by the night and Alan's obvious pain. And yet, she felt a shiver of excitement she knew she could not allow to continue. She shrugged her shoulders, clutched her arms around them and went back to the table for her car keys and purse.

Alan's muddled mind wandered in and out between thoughts of Sloan and of Michelle. He felt he needed Sloan desperately now. She could help him more than she realized and more than he wanted to openly admit, even to himself.

He hit the steering wheel with the palm of his hand. Damn you, Sloan! he thought. Look what you're doing to me! He did still love her. Maybe she only needed to hear those words to be able to return to him. To them.

He would tell her that he loved her. That was it! He would drive to the apartment and tell her. He would plead with her not to go to Phoenix, to stay with him, let him prove his love.

He parked the Camaro at the front of their apartment building and bounded up the outside stairs two at a time. Rushing down the hallway, he passed the portero who, up for some late-night work on the furnace, turned to watch in bewildered amusement as the tall American in the green flight suit passed him en route to the elevator with a wild greeting of "Hola y adios!" The elevator clicked past the lower floors. Alan's intoxicated mind reeled with the things he would say. Maybe they would even make love and make it all right again.

When the elevator door opened, he stumbled out of the small compartment and knocked on the apartment door. That would be better than just going in. She would invite him to stay, and they would make a new beginning.

She did not answer. He knocked harder.

When she still would not answer, he pulled his keys from the breast pocket of his flight suit and, with some difficulty, found the proper one, fitted it into the hole and opened the door as gently as his condition would allow.

The apartment was dark. He tried to focus on his watch but could not tell the time. He turned on the light in the same foyer where she had greeted him with her love so many times after long TDYs. He walked quietly toward the kitchen, then veered left down the hallway to their bedroom. It was dark and the persiana was down, making the room very black. Had she changed her sleeping habits? As his eyes adjusted to the darkness, he realized the bed was made and she was not in it.

He walked awkwardly through the apartment, turning on lights as he found them. She was not here. She was gone. Was she at the finca? He could not bear that idea. Where was his wife? He needed her! He felt the pain of many months boil to the surface.

He stared at the wall unit in the living room, at the several Lladrós he had surprised her with. He focused dully on the big one of Don Quixote they had bought together in Valencia, elated to find it at the Lladró factory. They had packed it carefully in the car, then driven to the beach and eaten paella.

His reddening eyes came to rest on a squarish little aluminum biplane painted to look like tarnished copper. She had given it to him the day after he asked her to marry him. He wound the propeller, and the tinny music box began to play "Fly Me to the Moon."

Overcome, he lay flat on his back on the flokati with his eyes closed, and the tears gushed forth as his hurt surfaced. No longer able to hold it inside, the anguish erupted in deep sobs and open wails that rocked his body as he gasped for breath with his heaving chest. And each breath fed the uncontrollable convulsions of sorrow like a seizure.

At last, his cries turned to softer sobs, which became chesty sniffs. He fell asleep as a child after a fitful bout.

When he awoke, the tears had dried in his eyes and on his cheeks. He was momentarily disoriented, but the salty taste in his mouth refreshed his memory. He felt somehow better, more resigned.

Methodically, he turned off all the lights. Standing in the foyer on the hand-woven Yahyali rug he had bought for her in Turkey, he gazed once more into the dark apartment, then closed the door and staggered down the eight flights of stairs and into the night.

CHAPTER FORTY-SEVEN

Having every conscious intention of driving to Camarma to sleep off this horrible night, Alan found himself instead returning to the bar. There were many things he felt he needed to sort out, but he would allow himself the small indulgence of forgetting about them for now. And this was the way of the fighter pilot, a late-hour reattack on the bar to reconcile the day.

The grandfather clock in the foyer of the Officer's Club chimed the eleventh hour as he opened the large wooden door, put his flight hat in the leg pocket of his flight suit and rounded the corner. In the distance, the ornate timepiece chimed its last as he reentered the dim soothing light.

He bought a San Miguel, then turned and leaned against the counter, surveying the room as he took a long swallow. His eyes blinked lazily as he searched the tables and the dance floor, curious to discern who were the hard-core survivors of the night.

The crowd had not significantly thinned, but he soon turned his drifting gaze to the table where Denise Fisch remained with Beth and two other wives. He noted that Michelle was no longer with them. He strolled casually in their direction, going to them when Denise caught his eye, turning her head from the conversation at the table.

"You're back?" she said as he pulled up a chair.

"Yes. I just needed a breather."

She tipped her head to the side. "From what?"

He smiled, looking into the targets that were her eyes. "From life."

Beth turned to him with a curious smile. "Did you have a late dinner?"

"No." He drank from the bottle of beer and looked at Denise. "I'm drinking pork chops tonight."

"Drinking ...?" Beth began.

He held up his beer. "There's a pork chop in every bottle."

Denise smiled, watching him with curious, bright blue eyes, raised eyebrows and a closed-lip smile. The question her face posed was not of where he had been, but rather, where he was going. The table conversation among the ladies had begun to sag an hour or so earlier, and Alan's late return offered a diversion that sparked a renewed round of harmless flirtation disguised as off-color jokes and sexual innuendo.

At times Alan glanced at Denise over his beer bottle, and each time she was watching him, her eyes widening slightly when their eyes met. As the evening wore on, the band tended to play more slow songs.

Alan leaned toward Denise and whispered in her ear. "Would you care to dance?"

"Yes, I'd care to," she said as she stood, ignoring the casually inquisitive glances of the others.

They danced the first without talking. Agreeing to a second, Alan said, "I didn't know if you even liked to dance. I don't remember seeing you dance before."

Denise smiled shyly. "Bill doesn't dance, so I don't much either." She paused. "Except for him at home." She looked at Alan and her eyes widened.

The image eluded him, preoccupied as he was with the times he had seen a different "TDY Bill Fisch" on the dance floor in another bar in a different country dancing with whatever women were available. Alan returned an answer that implied he had never seen Bill dance either. She smiled a knowing smile, silently thanking him for the lie, and they did not speak of Bill again.

She was very close with her head on his shoulder. Her short blond hair smelled faintly of inexpensive conditioner, clean and pleasant. Uncomplicated. He led her in a slow circle. She moved with him so that from time to time one of his legs moved between hers, and he knew she could not help being aware of his slight arousal.

Alan was afraid he would offend her, but he was equally afraid to move away for fear of the other wives noticing the obvious silhouette in his loosely hanging flight suit.

Denise smiled to herself. She sighed heavily as the rhythm brushed their legs gently together. Touching here, pulling slightly apart there, her knee-length dress partially obscuring the recurring embraces. He took her hand up to his chest, resting his chin on top of her head. After a turn or two, she moved their clutched hands slightly inward until the back of his hand touched her moderate breast.

Yes, he thought, she is arousing herself, and me. It was just a dance, a chance to indulge a fantasy with no consequences, and that was all right with him.

"You know just what you are doing, don't you?" he whispered close to her ear.

She laughed lightly and squeezed his hand.

The song ended, followed by a fast one.

They returned to the table and sat with Beth and the others. Denise was noncommittal, for which Alan found himself relieved. He bought them another round of drinks.

The band began another slow song. Alan looked at Denise, and she nodded. They rose and went to the far side of the dance floor, putting the other dancers between them and the ladies at the table.

"I'm glad you were still here," he said as Denise pressed her head against his chest.

She looked up at him. "I'm glad, too. We've had fun."

"We've also gotten drunk."

After a brief silence, she asked, "What's going on with you these days?"

He looked at her almost in anger. She was smiling receptively. "I'm not sure where my life's going, now," he said, "but please don't ask me about it."

"Okay. Where's your life going now?"

"Denise!"

She giggled, and momentarily tightened her grip around him. She looked up and took his hand, placing it as he had before just above her breast. "Seems like you could use a friend right now." She shivered slightly.

Her hand felt good and warm and soft in his. "It's fun being with you," Alan admitted. "I could use a friend," he said. "But not to hear of my woes."

"Whatever you need," she smiled. "Within reason," she added with a cute smirk.

They moved around a very small portion of the floor.

"I'll bet it's fun," she said, breaking their silence.

"What?"

"Being the only male stud among a bunch of lonely wives." She tilted her head back to gaze at him with eyes that ever so slightly flickered the need for comfort.

He looked around them. "But I am not the only man."

She released him to brush her long fingers through her short hair before placing it at the small of his back.

He moved their clutched hands until the back of his was in the middle of her chest. He massaged her breast with his fingers.

"Alan ..." She moved unconvincingly away from him. "You are a very attractive man. But I am married ..." She sighed deeply as he ran his hand down her back.

"We're just having fun," he said.

She smiled warmly. "You know exactly what you're doing." She pushed her thigh against him.

When the song was over, he walked directly behind her to the table, seating himself immediately.

As the ladies gossiped, Alan glanced at Denise who laughed with the ladies but swapped secretive glances with him, smiling when their eyes met. He sipped on the beer Beth bought for him, suspecting she had retrieved it from Pepe primarily as an excuse to get a closer look at Denise and himself dancing.

When he had finished the beer, he stood to announce he had to get some sleep.

"I'm going to have to leave soon, too," Denise said. "I've got a long drive to Eurovillas."

Alan answered, "I have a long drive to Camarma, but I'm not going to make it."

"What do you mean?" Beth asked him.

He held the empty beer bottle to his lips, then realized there was nothing left. "I'm going next door to the BOQ, tell them I've drunk too much, give them my four dollars and take a room for the night."

"You can do that?"

"Sure. No questions asked, and, except for perhaps a persecuting stare from the desk clerk, no accusations either. All thanks to the Wolf's desire to return his drunken fighter pilots to sobriety without incident, that they may live to fight the real war."

"That's a good idea," Denise said.

"Yes, it is." Alan pushed his chair into the table. "Well, goodnight."

"We'll miss you," Beth answered. She winked at him.

Alan walked the short distance to the front desk of the BOQ in the building adjacent to the Officer's Club. He paid his four dollars to the night clerk, winked in return to the expected subtle sneer, and went to his room on the second floor. The place was familiar. Perhaps it was the same room where he and Sloan had spent their first nights in Spain. He was but moments away from the past.

He stripped and was asleep so quickly and deeply that he dreamed immediately of the intermittent sound of a soft hammer, or was it construction? The dripping of water on wood? The sound grew loud enough to bring him out of his sleep. He rose and stumbled in the darkness to the door, found it, unlocked and opened it.

No one was there. Thinking he heard retreating footfalls around the far corner, he took a step through the doorway, squinting against the light. The hallway was empty. He trudged back into the darkness of the room and flung himself onto the bed.

CHAPTER FORTY-EIGHT

Speeding and weaving around the smaller European cars, Alan fought his subdued excitement, even as he allowed himself the indulgence of imagining what she might wear.

When Michelle opened her apartment door, he was disappointed but not surprised to see that she was dressed comfortably in a modest dress with no special attention given to her face or hair. They were just two friends having dinner together.

"Hello!" she said brightly. "I guess you made it back home."

"Sorry I'm late," he said. "I didn't count on the Spanish Friday evening 'who knows where the fast lane is?' traffic."

She laughed without inviting him in and said, "I'm ready." She grabbed a sweater from a chair in the foyer and securely locked the door.

Their conversation was light enough as they meandered through the evening autopista commuters. Michelle avoided mentioning Sam. She had heard Sloan might have gone home for a while and so asked Alan if that was true. He told her Sloan had gone to Arizona to be with Brandon. She said she was sorry to hear that, and neither of them brought it up again.

Once inside the city, Michelle asked, "Are you getting lonely at the squadron? It must be pretty quiet there with most of the guys gone."

He stopped for a red light. "It is. Quiet." It's quiet everywhere, he thought, except in my head.

She smiled, and her eyes sparkled. "Well, you know, after a night at the O'Club, you need the quiet to recover anyway. Right?"

"That's true," he said. "Sometimes, I could use more than a week between Friday nights." He pressed the gas pedal when several car horns announced the green light.

"Especially after a Friday night dedicated to the desire to disgust, right?" Michelle said.

"I guess I won't be a part of those for a while," he offered rather weakly.

"Oh, you never know! A quality drunk can come at the least expected time."

He looked at her with a serious frown. "Not for me," he said as if to convince her he was being good. "Not for a while." He felt stupid, cornered between his guilt and insecurity.

The Meson de San Javier was one of the best kept secrets of Madrid, at least from tourists, which is a shame. It is no longer there.

People visiting Madrid or talking of Madrid often ask about Botin's, which is good, but not the only good restaurant, and certainly not the best. The service at Botin's, however graceful, carries an air of superiority. Their reputation has been made. San Javier's was personal, and the food simply delectable.

Alan felt uncomfortable following Michelle's feminine frame down the narrow side streets, but her step was lively and open, showing no concern. He followed her up the stairs and through a door that revealed the small front room of the restaurant where several wooden tables and chairs were arranged to seat as many as possible as comfortably as possible. She had made the reservation and spoke in Spanish to the Maître d', who was also the owner and chef.

After they were seated, the Maître d' explained their choices of entrees, much as Orsini had. Alan ordered the Tournedos Argent, Michelle the roast suckling pig. They decided on a rioja which arrived with the entremeses. They conversed lightly as they ate, sharing the plate of hors d'oeuvres between them. He liked the asparagus and eggs, she preferred the meats, especially the chorizo. Eating from the same plate was a small, intimate act, and Alan savored anything that hinted of intimacy, anything that he thought she was enjoying with him.

"How do you like it?" she asked.

"Very nice. And cozy. I like the atmosphere. It's what I've always imagined as European."

They ordered a second bottle of wine with the main courses. She talked of what she liked about living in Europe as they ate. He agreed, saying he wished he could spend more time in Spain, to experience it as he was now. He had needed this, he said.

He did not think of Sam, except to find ways in his mind to separate them. Sam was his friend, his closest friend. But here was Michelle, with him, seemingly enlivened by his company.

He was drawn to her because she was what he thought he wanted. Though his heart was callused, he let her in because she did not appear to want in. She was good, and he was vulnerable. He was so taken by her that he was losing all feeling of reality and of a valuable friendship. Refusing to rationalize his feelings allowed him the only means of coping with them.

They drank espresso and brandy from demitasse cups as their desert was readied, a raspberry flambé concocted with controlled flamboyance by the owner using a raspberry liqueur and more brandy. In the quiet that accompanied the table-side preparation of the specialty dessert, Alan gazed over the flickering candle into the soft brown eyes of Michelle. She smiled, then took a drink of her carajillo. When she returned the cup to the table, he took her hand in his, gently caressing her knuckles. He was clumsy from the brandy and wine.

"I am happy tonight," he said. "I enjoy your company."

He did not physically want her. That is, his desire was not born of passion. Physical bonding would be but a culmination, sealing his claim on her, a claim he could not reconcile. He wanted her beautiful mind, her sweet face. In the growing darkness of his soul, she was a refreshing beam of focused energy. He was enveloped in joy and pain. He was with her, but he could not have her. He needed her laugh and her reflective silence. He needed something good, and she was good, and he could see nothing better.

She smiled, watching his hand on hers. "I like you, too," she said.

As they walked silently back to the Plaza Mayor, she let him take her hand again. Spaniards strolled or sat around in restaurant chairs, talking, enjoying the unseasonable warmth of the night, but the two Americans did not notice them. The night was very full, and very serene.

As they followed the autopista out of Madrid in the quiet comfort of the Camaro, the instrument lights glowing faintly on them both, Alan realized that he felt alive again after so many months of stifled emotion. Michelle was rekindling a fire that had all but died, torturously quenched by Sloan as she drained his confidence and maimed his manhood. But Michelle did not belong to him and was therefore unattainable. She was his ideal, his Dulcinea - fair maiden to be defended and protected, even from himself.

He glanced at her, the soft shadows cast by the luminescent lights accentuating the fine features of her face and body. Her lips were twisted neatly in her inimitable half-smile. The left side of her pretty face appeared to be absorbed in the darkness as she returned Alan's glance with a wink.

Why was he driven to consider doing exactly that which had taken his wife from him? Were all the good ones taken? Or did they become desirable by marriage? As a challenge? Or just an easier target. He was balancing his soul on that fine line.

He parked the Camaro, and they walked silently inside the building and to the elevator.

She no longer held his hand. With the nearness of danger, she withdrew as the contest between mind and body threatened to thrust her over the line to a conclusion she knew, was, as yet, undetermined. Innocent flirtation inflamed with alcohol had made the barriers crumble, but she must not give in.

She put the key into the lock of her apartment door and opened it. Holding the door ajar with her hip, she turned to him and said, "So, I'll see you Sunday?"

"Sunday?" he asked blankly.

"At church!"

He shook his head as if shaking off a demon. "Church. Sunday. Yeah, okay."

"I am glad we are friends," she said.

"So I am."

"You are a good man."

Oh, Michelle! he thought. If you knew my mind, would you still think so?

He leaned a bit toward her. He could see it all happening, but in his mind's eye she suddenly flung herself away from him, stammering about trust and friendship.

"I couldn't take that," he said aloud.

"What?" She eyed him with a questioning smile.

Alan faltered. "I, uh, I was thinking how much it would hurt for you to have a bad opinion of me."

She put her arms around his waist and hugged him. The door closed and locked again. For a brief moment, she held him with her head on his chest.

Alan put his arms around her and said awkwardly, "Your hair smells good."

She giggled through closed eyes. "I'm glad you like my hair. It's real, you know."

He laughed.

"It's getting late," she said, pulling away from him.

"It's a long drive." He felt childishly awkward.

"I know," she said. "I'm sorry." She paused. "Maybe we can go to the Rastro afterwards!"

"After ...?"

"Church."

His mind was flooded with relief. "Yes! The Rastro. I've been only once." After church. More respectability.

He held her chin and kissed her cheek with his eyes open. She did not move but closed her eyes. He pulled back and pushed the button for the elevator. She waited until he was on his way down before reopening the apartment door.

CHAPTER FORTY-NINE

Alan awoke late on Saturday. The fire he had made when he returned from Michelle's apartment still smoldered in the fireplace at his head. He got up slowly and deliberately, showered, and made toast and coffee for breakfast. The day was beautiful, crisp and clear, but he remained in his "fortress of solitude" for most of it, reading Tolstoy. Or rather trying to. He was frustrated and on edge.

He began to understand Sloan, though his anger and hurt would not allow him to contemplate complete forgiveness. He reasoned that for her to come back now would be an insult in itself, the implication being that it had taken someone else to transform her into a better person. Someone perhaps better than he.

His thoughts turned to Michelle. He imagined an evening of pleasure with her, only to cringe, shuddering at the remembrance of his embarrassing advances. How foolish it would feel if, in the end, he coveted another fighter pilot's wife enough to want to take her from him. Having felt it himself, he could never wish it on anyone, whether his greatest friend or worst nemesis. Not even Brandon Parsons.

Well, perhaps Brandon Parsons.

As evening cooled the day and his imaginings, he decided to drive into Alcala to eat dinner at Oliver's. Upon his arrival, he recognized several members of the 612th Squadron there with their wives. He was surprised to see Denise Fisch among them. Alan acknowledged the group of Americans as the Maître d' led him to a small table on the far side of the room.

He had a dinner of biftec and white asparagus, followed by an after-dinner cognac. The fighter pilots and their wives stayed a long time, thinning out finally as some left and others retired to Oliver's bar. Denise was among those that stayed. Enjoined in various conversations, she glanced regularly at Alan. The repeated meeting of their eyes elicited a thin smile that curled her lips.

He ordered a second cognac. When the waiter returned with his order, Denise picked up a fresh glass of white wine and walked to his table. He watched her come toward him, feeling the arousal sparked by her walk.

"May I join you?" she asked with a guarded smile.

"Certainly." He pulled her chair. "I've been wanting to talk to you." A half-truth.

"What could we talk about?" She spoke as if they shared an exciting, guilty secret. The thrill of a sensual embrace. Something more than what had briefly passed between them two nights earlier.

"How was your week?" she asked, taking the seat he offered.

"It's been kind of hard."

She grinned slyly. "What made it hard?"

"You did." He laughed.

The dark edges around the iris of her eyes seemed focused on something in the deep recesses of his mind. She twisted her head slightly but continued to watch his eyes as she adjusted herself in the wooden chair. "Do you think less of me?"

"Should I?"

"I hope not." She drank her wine and gazed back at her friends. Some looked like they were planning to leave.

"Do you need a ride?"

She looked at him and the pupils of her eyes seemed open, wide and deep. "No. I drove myself."

He nodded almost imperceptibly at the implication. "Would you like some more wine?"

She downed her wine and placed the empty glass on the table. "Yes, please."

"I have a cold German Auslese at my place."

Her look was one of slight surprise. "Aren't you afraid?"

"Of what?"

"Of the possibilities."

"For the possibilities, I am anything but afraid."

She stared coyly at him. The arousal on her face was obvious. "I've spent the past two days dealing with my guilt."

"I will take that as a compliment."

"How so?"

"Because I made you feel guilty."

Her eyes narrowed in concern. "I've never done anything like that. Not since I was married anyway."

"Honestly?"

"Absolutely! Alan, you don't think ..."

"No. I don't. I'm flattered." He touched her leg under the table, moving it slowly up her stockinged thigh. "And more."

She reached under the table and touched his hand, stopping it shy of the hem of her dress. "How much more?"

"Let's go to my place."

She looked at him and then turned to look back at the bar as if contemplating which road to take. "I'll meet you there. It's Jeff Cole's place, isn't it?"

"Yes. Have you been there?"

"No."

"You know where it is?"

"Yes."

"But you've never been there."

"No, Alan." She stood up.

"Are you really coming?"

She looked back at him so that the others could not see her face and winked.

Alan anticipated that Denise would undergo a last minute change of heart and not show up. Even so, he placed two bottles of Auslese in the freezer of the small German refrigerator. If she did not come to him, he would finish one of the bottles himself and find the same retreat into decadent indulgence, the same detachment from reality.

There was a knock on the door. He went to it quickly, remembering he had turned the outside light off for cover. He opened the door, and she stood before him.

He moved to let her in. "Please."

"This is nice," she said, walking ahead of him into the living room. "Much bigger than our place in Eurovillas."

"Is it?"

She blushed, realizing her opening words had suffused Bill into their rendezvous. "I like my place, though," she added without enthusiasm. She looked at Alan and smiled. "You mentioned something about wine."

"Would you like some?"

"I'd love it."

He retrieved the wine and glasses from the freezer. "Come on." He started down the stairs. "I'll show you the Wayne wing of the Cole castle."

She followed him down the stairway and along the wooded corridor to the large open room. The old brown recliner faced the fireplace with the reading light on beside it. *War and Peace* lay open on the floor. His sleeping pallet, as neatly made as possible, was stretched in front of a fire that was rapidly coming to life.

"That's a big fire," she said.

"It'll die down."

"Slowly, I hope." Denise looked enticingly at him as she lowered her purse to the floor.

"Have a seat."

She took off her shoes and sat on the mattress with her legs to her side. The top two buttons of her dress were undone. Alan had not noticed that at the restaurant. He gave her the glasses, then opened the first bottle, filled the glasses and placed the bottle on the carpeted floor near her.

She smiled, watching him move. "I'm nervous about this."

He looked at her. She had a nice face and healthy features. How did a person like Bill Fisch ever land such a woman?

"Maybe we can just enjoy being with each other for a while," Alan said.

She was noticeably relieved. "Just no pressure, okay?" She handed him one of the glasses.

"Denise," he said, taking the glass and kissing her hand. "None."

"Okay."

He raised his glass. "Here's to anything that happens or nothing that happens."

Denise felt better after the second glass. She seemed to especially enjoy talking of Spain and where she had been. She was careful to avoid mentioning Bill. Neither of them spoke of Sloan. An outsider eavesdropping on their conversation would have assumed each had gone everywhere and done everything alone.

With the third glass, she stretched out on the make-shift bed, resting her head in her hands, looking at the fire. Alan rose and turned off the reading light, then settled in beside her. Together they watched the fire in silence.

He turned to look at her profile. Aware of his gaze, she continued her vigil with the flames. She was attractive, Alan noted, not quite beautiful. Her short hair gave her neck and ears a clean simplicity that was somehow erotic. He looked away from the fire. Her dress was creeping up, exposing shapely thighs he had never really noticed before that first midnight embrace on the dance floor. Looking back at her face, the shadows of the fire flickered on her nose and cheeks.

He kissed her neck.

"Hmm." She closed her eyes.

He kissed her again, slightly lower and longer. She moved. He slid his body the short distance between them until he was against her, and she rolled onto her side facing him. He continued to kiss her neck, then moved toward her chest. He touched her breast briefly. She swiveled onto her back. Encouraged by her soft sighs, he released the remaining buttons on her dress and opened it completely. Her head was back now, the glowing shadows of the fire tickling her tightly closed eyelids and slightly parted lips.

His heart was pounding. Never had he felt this passion, this primal desire with Sloan. Letting himself go, he felt at once exhilarated and anxious.

Her movements became demanding as he stripped her of her sheer underclothing.

She looked up at him. "Why are you still dressed?!" she moaned hoarsely.

"That's your job."

She breathed heavily as she removed his clothes.

The fire was burning softer as they lay holding each other, watching the flames leap from the logs to lick the flue.

"More wine?" Alan asked.

"Is there more?"

"I think so." He released her to get the bottle, and she rolled onto her stomach. He filled her glass and half of his. She was further from him now and he could better see her form. Why had he married so quickly when there are all these beautiful women out there? He felt a tinge of shame. There was so much more to it than that.

She watched the fire as he watched her.

"This wine is good," she said, licking her lips. "I love fucking in front of a fire."

"I like looking at you in front of a fire."

She looked at him with an appreciative smile. "You do?"

"Yes."

She rolled seductively onto her side, putting her hand with the wine glass in it on her hip.

"That's very nice," he said.

She raised her top leg until her foot rested on her knee. "It is?"

He laughed. "You know it is."

She smiled.

"That's all we're doing, isn't it?" he said.

"What?"

"Fucking. That's all this is."

"Oh, yes!" She put her legs together again. "You're not thinking anything else, are you?"

"No. Are you?"

"No! It would kill Bill if he ever knew anything about this. I couldn't take that."

"Do you love him?"

"Yes, I do love him."

"May I ask the hard question?"

She nodded.

"How can you do this?"

She rolled onto her stomach and stared into the fire. "I am attracted to you, Alan. You are physically exciting. I frankly don't understand your wife."

"Probably because of the circumstances," Alan said.

"Maybe."

"Otherwise, you would consider leaving Bill for me."

"I would never think of leaving Bill."

"I wouldn't want you to."

"He is my husband. I love him. I have cared for him when he was sick. We have dreams together."

"When he was sick?"

She laughed lightly. "You know what I mean."

"Yet, here we are."

She sighed. "Yes, here we are."

"Why?"

"I guess it's because I am more of a wife to him than I am a woman. The things I did to get him interested enough to ask me to marry him are the same things he no longer likes. Because I am now his wife."

"But you told me you dance for him."

"You don't understand."

"No, I don't, not completely. But I do wonder how it is that you marry someone because they like the way you are, then, after you're married, they start trying to change you to suit them. Then, once they've changed you, they get disgusted and leave you, asking 'Whatever happened to the man I married?'!"

Denise laughed heartily. "That's true!"

They did not speak for several minutes. Alan realized his father made more sense to him now. He tried to brush the image from his mind.

"If anything, I would have liked Sloan to be more aggressive," Alan said, downing the last of his wine.

"Don't be so sure."

"Why?"

"Because passion is a dangerous thing."

"It can be," he agreed. "But you know you love something when you are passionate about it."

"I think passion is something you can come back to. But sometimes you have to be careful because your husband wonders where you got it or worries that it is for the passion of sex rather than for the love of him."

"I'd like to believe they can be one and the same," Alan said. "I hope you know it was you I wanted. Not just sex."

She smiled warmly and turned again on her side, watching his eyes. "You want to know why I am here with you? You enjoy me. I like making you feel that way. With a lover, the passion is obvious, or you would not be there. It is all there already. The openness of it all drowns out the guilt. Or at least subdues it."

"You sound like the voice of experience."

"I swear to you this is my only time. But I have thought about it. I've been thinking about you a lot."

"I've thought about you. To be honest, I've thought about a lot of women." He reveled in the freedom of telling the truth to her.

"That's natural."

"For some."

"For everyone with blood in their veins. Some just can't admit it."

"But you never considered doing anything about it?"

"No. Until you. You're different."

"How?"

"I think you really like me for who I am. As a person."

"I do."

"And as a lover?"

"Very much so. I've never crossed the line with others I have ... thought about. There have been opportunities, but something was missing. Part of that was the freedom to do something about it. But I really never felt what I feel with you."

"That's very nice." She sighed. "You know what I can tell about you, if you don't mind another honest observation?"

"I guess I can take it."

"We'll see."

"Say it."

"I think you had a lousy sex life."

He was quiet. He could defend his love life, or he could lash out at it to be vengeful. "You mean I did not please her?"

"As far as I'm concerned, you could please her very well."

"More flattery."

"I don't think she would let you. I think she was like Bill ... afraid to let go completely, to give herself fully."

Alan nodded. Perhaps Sloan was like more him than he had realized. Guarded. Loving with a kind of controlled passion. "It's too bad we are not in love," he said.

"No. It's probably a good thing."

They quietly watched the fire grow softer.

"I'll have to go soon," Denise said finally.

"Why not stay?" Alan asked. "Stay the night?"

She gave a knowing grin. "I don't think it would be good for anyone to see my car parked in your driveway in the morning."

He nodded. "That's a long drive back to Eurovillas."

"I'm a big girl," she said. "I think I can handle it."

Alan eyed her form, taking in her curves, admiring her face and features. "I will always remember you as something special. And I never would have, none of this would have happened, if you had not come on to me."

"I came on to you?" She acted surprised and insulted. "You came on to me!"

"No, I didn't."

"Yes, you did. And you'll really have to work for it now!"

"I will?"

"Yes!"

She tried to roll away from him, but he was upon her.

CHAPTER FIFTY

Michelle knew where to go and where to stop, so Alan obeyed her directions, then followed her as she strolled into the heart of The Rastro. They were there to shop rather than to buy, and for him, this was another opportunity to be with her among an interesting aspect of Spain about which he knew so little.

The Rastro is a fine flea market that begins and ends every Sunday, covering several streets, beginning at Calle de Toledo, south of the San Isidro Cathedral. The regular shops along these streets are open during the week selling antiques and other cheaper collectibles and non-collectibles that people will pay good money for anyway. On Sunday, the vendors come in and set up the shops in the streets, and the crowds can be so thick you can barely get around to see the whole thing by the end of the day.

Alan felt good. Theirs was a good friendship, he decided, even as he realized that, until recently, he had never known her. All he really knew he had imagined in his mind. She seemed to be enjoying their time together. Yet, he realized that he was merely a man offering benign male companionship while she awaited her warrior's return.

And he could never suspect Sam of having designs on another man's wife. Still, he recalled the "strange poontang" story. And dancing with the girls in Italy.

Alan followed Michelle through the crowds, watching her walk and thinking how fine she was and how easily she could control a man if it was in her nature. She stopped to look at some antique wares a vendor had on display. She picked out a tarnished, discolored key and held it to the light.

"Would you like that?" Alan asked.

"It's interesting," she said. "Look at the ornate design."

"It's a good size. Let me get it for you."

"No, that's okay."

"No. I want to." He turned to the vendor. "Cuanto?"

"Esto?" The vendor took the key from Michelle, which she was reluctant to give up. "Esto ... mil pesetas."

"Mil?" Alan asked in disbelief. The current exchange made the cost only a little over six American dollars.

"Si. Mil pesetas. Es bueno, muy antiquissimo."

"A thousand pesetas'," Alan said to Michelle. "I think he's throwing us a line."

The man offered the key to her.

"I don't want it," she said.

Alan took it. "I do." He gave the vendor 500 pesetas.

The man looked at the money. "No, mil pesetas!"

Alan spoke in his best belligerent Spanish, "Esto, o nada!" He again placed the key in Michelle's open waiting hand.

The vendor took the key from Michelle. Alan reached for the money. The man looked hard at him, then slapped the key into his hand.

"Gracias," Alan said.

"Humph!"

Michelle followed Alan away into the crowds. He handed her the key, pleased with the bargain he had made. "To my heart," he said.

She hugged him, and he felt ten stories high as he walked with her on his arm among the shorter Europeans.

The blue Air Force six-pack truck tore down the road, blowing up dust from the shoulders to mix with the chalky haze that enveloped the landscape.

The Turk is driving too fast! Sam thought, stealing a sideways glance at his fellow passenger for signs of discomfort or outright fear.

Airman Chip Worth gazed out of his window from the back seat, the doubt in his eyes concealed by the dark Air Force issue sunglasses. He was accustomed to this now, but experience did little to ease his concern. I'm just the weatherman! he thought to himself. If this guy is dangerous, the Captain will say something.

Sam rested his gaze on the nape of the swarthy driver's neck in front of him. He hated being away from the cockpit, but a week of down time at the Konya bombing range might help him sort out some things. Serving as the range officer might even be fun, or at least interesting.

The Turk steered into the opposite lane and gunned the engine to pass a large truck. Sam saw the other car coming at them and tried to relinquish the involuntary grip he held on the door handle to check the security of his seat belt.

The approaching car slowed as the six-pack whipped back into the right lane in front of the other truck, throwing Sam and Chip to the left.

"Take it easy!" Sam heard himself blurt out to the driver.

"So sorry!" the Turk said. "It looked more far."

"Okay. But we're in no hurry."

"Okay!" The Turk pushed the accelerator.

"No hurry!" Sam repeated.

"Okay." The Turk eased off a bit.

Feeling frustrated and resigned to the fact that he held no control over the situation or the outcome, Sam tried to return to his book of Turkish phrases, but he could not concentrate. This was not the way to die, in a US government truck on the road to Konya, Turkey. There was no honor in it.

Sam smiled wanly to himself, thinking that the way this guy was driving would make it impossible to identify the bodies, anyway.

At least this wild ride had managed to take Michelle from his mind for a while. She was acting strangely, or, rather, writing strangely. Her letters were as personal as always, punctuated with upbeat phrases. But something was different. She was practically screaming about something she would not openly profess. Each letter choked away a confession that she alone understood. But to what? A loss of Love? Another man? Had she totaled the Fiesta?

The Turk slowed to drive through the town of Eregli. Sam had flown this route to the Konya Bombing Range many times, and he knew it well. Their route in the truck was practically the same.

How many times had he sat in the back seat of an F-4 while some front seater guided the jet at 480 knots through these passes, turning hard left and right only a few hundred feet above The Rocks?

Never had he felt the anxiety he did now.

They arrived near sunset at the hotel in downtown Konya, a beautiful city centered, at least culturally, around the Sultan Selim Mosque and the Museum of Mevlana. Sam looked at the number on his room key, searching to remember the Turkish words. Room 104.

The word for hundred was "yuz," and "dort" was four. "Used dirt!" he said, showing it to Chip with a laugh. Certainly a good description of Turkey, he thought. A lot of history had walked through this place.

He would go to sleep thinking of that.

In the dark of the Turkish morning, Sam rose from the surprisingly comfortable bed, shivered under a cold shower because it was too early for the hot water to be turned on, and met Chip downstairs where they waited for their Turkish Range Liaison Administrator to arrive.

He appeared on time driving a government truck. He introduced himself as "Adil" and asked them if they were hungry even as he stopped by a bakery where Sam bought some fine, hot bread that served as breakfast en route to the range.

On the range proper, they passed shepherds who used part of the range for the grazing of their sheep. Three very large dogs with big thorny collars chased the truck a quarter mile down the road before returning to the herds and their masters. Adil told them the collars gave the dogs an advantage when fighting wolves.

Following another boring day at the squadron, Alan drove to the bar for a couple of beers before heading back to Nueva Camarma. He was surprised and pleased to see Denise there, nursing a glass of Chardonnay.

Over a week had passed since their night together, and in that time, they had seen nothing of each other. At the beginning of their time apart, Denise dealt with her guilt by trying to keep Alan out of her mind. As the time went on, he was all she could think about, and her lust seemed determined to supplant all other emotions.

Alan bought a beer and joined her. After several drinks and some light conversation that hit all around the elephant in the room without actually addressing it, he suggested they go to dinner in Madrid.

Denise declined.

"Not tonight," she said.

To his feigned pout, she added, "But I'm free tomorrow. Are you interested in taking a small excursion?"

"Where?" he asked with deep interest. "For how long?"

"Just a day trip," she said smiling. "To Segovia. And The Valley of the Fallen."

"I'd like that. There's nothing going on for me at the squadron, and I've never been to either one. But why now?"

"It just seems we might enjoy it. We can meet on base tomorrow morning."

He whispered in her ear, "Why don't we just leave from my place?"

Denise smiled and shook her head.

"Your place?"

She considered his suggestion. "That would be closer." She looked at him with a half-smile. "But only if you promise to be good," she said softly while looking away.

"I'll try to be very good," he whispered.

"No. I mean good. Really. I can't ... I couldn't ... in my home."

"Then go with me." He leaned against her and secretly gave her breast a light squeeze.

"No, Alan. I can't," she whispered even softer.

"But you will take me home tonight."

"You know the conditions."

"Okay."

"I mean it, Alan."

"I will honor them."

Alan left the Camaro in the Officer's Club parking lot, thinking anyone who recognized it would just think he was sleeping it off in the BOQ. Denise guided her Renault along the worn, winding roads to Eurovillas with seasoned agility and slightly excessive speed. A couple of turns made Alan tighten his grip on the armrest, but, going with the carefree image he had fostered of late, he said nothing.

The house was a small white structure with a drive-in carport. He walked behind her, turning up his collar against the chilling wind. Once inside, he discovered the house to be no warmer.

"Burr!" Alan joked.

She nodded. "I'll turn on some heaters. There're no radiators, but Bill loves it here anyway."

"Oh."

As the front room gradually warmed to the glow of electric heat, she opened the wooden stereo cabinet and put on a record. The music of a single classical guitar enveloped them.

"What is this?" Alan asked.

"Andres Segovia," she answered. She handed him the album sleeve with a picture of The Maestro.

"I've seen this face," Alan said. "On TVs in the Spanish cafes. But the sound is usually turned down."

"He is Spain," Denise said with admiration.

"You obviously like him."

"I'd love to see him in concert."

"Does he have anything to do with where we are going tomorrow?"

She shook her head. "Just coincidence." She walked toward the kitchen. "Are you thirsty?"

"Do you have a beer?"

"I've got several," she said smiling.

She returned with the beer, then went into her bedroom to change, closing the door behind her. She emerged several minutes later in a full-length night gown, robe, and thick house shoes and socks.

Alan sat on the floor, eying the stereo in deep concentration. He turned to her. "You look warmer," he said, looking at her with a frown.

"You like this?"

"Very much," he lied.

"I usually sleep this way in the winter."

"I like all of this," he said. "I have never heard anything like this music."

"Spain holds many secrets," she answered with a seductive smile.

"All part of the Spanish experience," he said. He placed the half-empty beer on a coaster on the coffee table and gathered his clothes and Dopp kit. "Where do you want me?"

She came to him and took his collar in her hands. "With me, if you promise to behave."

"I promise."

"I need to trust you, Alan."

"I promise."

He found it thrilling to lie down beside her, knowing they were just going to sleep. He placed his arm around her, and she snuggled her head comfortably onto his bare chest with her arm across his stomach. He felt protective. He kissed her forehead.

"Alan!" she said, raising her head to look at him. "You've got nothing on."

"How very clever of you to notice."

"Aren't you cold?"

"Not now."

"I meant what I said."

"Okay." He brushed a lock of her short blond hair from her pretty eyes. "Bad timing? Or are you not protected?"

She sighed. "I'm very protected. Nature made sure of that."

"No pill?" He felt a flush of anxiety.

"They give me migraines."

"How?"

"The estrogen, I guess."

"Then what do you mean? By nature?"

She put her head against his arm. "I can't conceive. We've tried. I can't."

"It could be ... Bill," he offered, hoping that it was not.

"He says he knows it isn't his fault."

"How can he know?"

"I don't care to ask. He's a fighter pilot. I guess he thinks it couldn't possibly be him."

"Oh."

"Besides, he says he knows."

"How?"

"You ask him." She sounded rather cross. Amid the darkness, he felt the wetness of a tear drop to his chest.

"I'm sorry," he said sincerely.

She laid her head back on his chest. He felt her reach to him and cradle him with her hand. It was not sensual, just warm. "Is that okay?" she asked.

"It's nice."

"We have to keep them warm."

"Yes."

There was no noise but the hum from the heater fan.

"Denise?"

"Yes, lover?"

"I like you."

She moved her hand to his chest. "I like you, Alan."

Together, they found the innocence of sleep amid the solace of a quiet, secure place, a mere speck in life's broad complicated spectrum.

When the first flight of F-4s arrived on his last morning as range officer, Sam recognized the lead's voice as that of Carp Fisch.

"Letter drop!" Carp radioed as he opened his speed brake doors and released the heavily wrapped package near the foot of the primary range tower. Chip retrieved the bruised package as the fighters set up for their first conventional pass.

While Denise showered, Alan searched for a pen and paper. A short poem had formed in his head, and he thought it would be cute to write it down and give to it Denise. Feeling a bit naughty, he rifled through the bottom drawer of her rolltop desk. This was her personal stuff, and he really had no right to it. But he was only looking for a pen. He recited the poem in his head, 'Roses are red, I was so blue, thank you for letting me ...'

The small unframed picture took him by surprise. He raised his head and listened quietly. Denise was still in the shower.

Alan lifted the picture by a corner, bringing it closer to his eyes. A very familiar face gazed up at him. The young man was dressed in full flight regalia and standing in front of an F-4 with MacDill Air Force Base tail markings. His flight helmet was tucked under his arm.

The shower water stopped, and Alan heard the rings slide along the rod as the curtain was opened. He stuffed the picture underneath the notepad and smoothly closed the drawer.

Adil took Sam and Chip into Konya for a lunch of Turkish pizza, which was oblong and very thin, a flattened football-shaped piece of unleavened dough with lamb meat sprinkled sparingly on each piece.

While they ate, Adil told them he considered himself to be a fighter pilot. His explanation was not unlike that of a songwriter living in the Keys who thinks of himself as a pirate, or a country singer who might call himself an outlaw. More of an attitude than an actuality.

In the quiet after lunch, Sam read the letter from Michelle as he sipped on hot çay - Turkish black tea - from an ornamental glass.

Her words made him anxious. He had always trusted Michelle, but something was in the air. He thought about Alan Wayne. Alan was having some problems, and Sam felt for him. Maybe that was what was bothering Michelle.

He did not want the same to happen to them. "Yep!" he said out loud as he folded the letter. It was time to leave Europe and the Spanish experience behind. It was time to go home, back to the Land of the Big BX.

He pulled Bill Fisch's note from his pocket and ripped open the envelope. I'll have to rib Carp about sending me a love letter, he thought, smiling to himself as he unfolded the paper.

Reading Fisch's briefly scribbled note, he almost dropped his çay. He shook his head as if in a trance. Four F-15s flying in the weather near Nellis Air force Base in Nevada had slammed into the side of a mountain. There were no survivors.

CHAPTER FIFTY-ONE

Denise drove the Renault along the back roads from Eurovillas to Madrid, then through the middle of town along the Gran Via to the northwest side of the capital where the road became "N-VI," the main artery leading west out of the city. As she pointed out the University of Madrid, Alan understood he was seeing a part of Spain he had hardly known existed. It no longer appeared dry and dusty. This side of Madrid was green and alive. He decided when spring arrived, he would come here to see it again when everything was new.

The terrain sloped up to the northwest, and although there was not as much greenery as there had been, tall trees continued to mark their pathway to the mountains.

In Guadarrama, Denise pointed to a sign that read Valle de los Caídos. "That's the way to the Valley of the Fallen."

Alan looked at her in dull realization as they passed the turn, continuing northwest. They had spoken little of their plans, thinking to take the day as it came. "Are we going there after Segovia, then?"

She looked from the road to him and smiled. "I thought we'd have lunch in Segovia, then go to the monument on the way back."

"You know exactly what you are doing."

Watching the road, she smiled as much to herself as to him. "I have an idea."

They turned north off N-VI and were in Segovia within thirty minutes. Following the main artery, they found parking almost at the foot of that portion of the Roman aqueduct that spans the main road some 90 feet above it. He marveled at the double-arched stone structure as they locked the car and walked toward it. "I had not expected it to be in such good shape."

She turned to him with a knowing smile. "It's beautiful, isn't it. Technology in a time that was useful and beautiful, doing the job without being destructive."

"The good old days."

"They still use it sometimes, I think."

"They do? What for?"

"To move water."

Under the aqueduct on the far side, they found steps leading to the top. An old Spanish man was standing on the steps singing loudly but very poorly, and his hat was on the ground in front of him with a few coins in it. Nodding briefly at the singer, Alan started up the steps.

Denise strode after him, saying, "Men! You're all alike. You've got to get up on top."

"Aren't you interested?"

"Yes."

"But it's my nature."

"You've got it."

Halfway up, he turned to look at the singer. "I should give him a few pesetas. If he gets enough, maybe he'll stop."

Denise grinned. "Maybe."

At the top, they looked down the open, squared-stone trench that was much smaller than Alan expected, being little more than a foot or so in depth and width. It was dry.

"All this elaborate structure just for that little trench," Alan said. "It doesn't move much water, does it?"

Denise looked down the length of the aqueduct to where it turned left to the southeast. "It's enough if it's continuous, I suppose." She took in the panoramic view of the city, imagining simpler times.

Retracing their steps down the walkway, Denise led Alan to the Alcazar.

"You know your way around," he noted. "I thought you hadn't been here."

She tilted her head at him slyly and said, "I never said that. I just said I wanted to go with you."

Walking beside her but not looking at her, Alan felt alive and free. She made him seem welcome, important to her life. They were friends and lovers, unencumbered by the complexities and demands that accompanied relationships based more on a feeling of ownership than of mutual assent. What they had was certainly not without emotion. But he cared for her welfare and happiness as one cares for family, and yet he had the luxury of knowing her daily needs of food and shelter were provided without his personal effort.

To provide totally for her was, in a way, to claim title to her. He did not desire title, only presence. He had his life, she had hers, but they could be together.

After the Alcazar and a few other less interesting stops, he suggested they find a place for lunch. Thinking she must have an idea for that as well, he asked her to lead the way.

"I've never eaten here," she said.

"Why not?"

"Well," she looked away. "Bill doesn't like to spend the time ... or the money. He's right about the money. We're saving for a house when we get back to the States."

"And the time?"

"It seems to me time is relative."

They walked back in the direction of the car and found the Meson de Candido, a first-class restaurant practically in the shadow of the aqueduct. They both had the specialty, cochinillo asado - roast suckling pig - enjoying their meal as the owner and master chef worked his way through the dining area signing menus for the patrons.

After a leisurely lunch, they drove out of the city toward Madrid and The Valley of the Fallen. Following the signs, Denise navigated a smaller winding road along a river into the mountains. There were pine trees all along the way. The sky grayed in the afternoon overcast. Alan spotted the cross looming out of the hills in the distance.

"Is that it?"

"Yes."

"You've been here, too?"

"When we first got to Spain. It was our first excursion outside of Madrid."

Valle de los Caídos, the Valley of the Fallen, is a monument to the dead of the Spanish Civil War. To some, it is spectacular, breath-taking, thought provoking. To others less given to deep consideration of what it means, it is just another huge cathedral sliced out of a mountain and a monumental bore. And to still others, it remains a raging controversy.

To Alan, it was a revelation.

Inside the basilica, hollowed into the base of the mountain, the high walls and polished floor margined the cavernous hallway from the granite that surrounded all but the entrance. The ceiling, supported by columns, held back the mountain, but the quiet air of the hollow expanse swallowed all utterances of reverence as if to absorb them into the rocks, to sacredly preserve them for the ages.

They walked slowly, almost ceremoniously toward the far end. The heels of their shoes tapped on the black marble beneath them, echoing solemnly against the walls.

The names of the fallen were buried as well. Death and sacrifice. Victims of battle and of mass murder lent their dubious celebrity to the sanctimony of remembrance. The Virgin was above each chapel they passed en route to the altar where the painted Christ was crucified against a tree trunk. Beneath Him were the funerary stones of Fransisco Franco, and the founder of the opposing Falangist party, José Antonio.

They were there, together, in name. Franco, in his political wisdom, had assured this union, a symbol of unity for a country whose bloody civil war was still fresh on its mind.

They buried their hatchets with their dead, Alan thought hopefully. He imagined that the world might yet take a lesson from this exaggerated stab at healing wounds. The world needed overstatement, he reasoned, to quell its more offensive extremes in the names of Right and Wrong.

The Fallen. From earthly life. And from Grace? He could not imagine these warriors and victims dead. Their passion sustained their spirit. They had fought and died in righteous belief in their side and in vigorous opposition to the other. The sides of the Spanish Civil War, he knew, had not been geographical, but philosophical. There was no Mason-Dixon Line, no 39th Parallel. The lines in the sand were drawn in the hearts and minds of the people.

He thought of his own lines. Training to fight against an enemy he really knew nothing about, other than what he had been told, against philosophies and even religions his leaders insisted were different from his own and therefore bad. The "great" men will always be so, it seemed, as long as they can convince the "lesser" men that there is evil to be fought. And that they are the best and only judges of what that evil really is.

For some reason, the image of his grandfather and the squirrels came to his mind. His grandfather killed the squirrels in the trees behind his house because they ate the seeds he put out to attract the birds. He wanted the birds, but the squirrels got in the feeder. The old man could not outsmart the squirrels, or he would not make the effort to try. So, he shot them.

As a little boy, Alan hated to see the fallen squirrels, maimed and bleeding, left to die on the ground as his grandfather searched the trees for more, cursing the illiterate animals vehemently, venting the rage of his ineptitude on their small bodies. Alan would cover his ears, and through sobbing tears brought by youth's inability to comprehend cruelty, beg to know why they could not raise the feeder higher, or build another one for the squirrels.

He thought of his lines drawn against Sloan, against her lover, against the man whose wife was with him today. What had Whiskey said about square corners you can't make? What were his? Pride? Arrogance?

And he thought of those fallen he had known. He had his own valley. Ernie was buried in it. As was Whiskey. And his marriage ... Through misty eyes, he turned to look at Denise who half-smiled at him with curious questioning.

"Where have you been?" she asked with a touch of reverence.

He took her hand. "I have been inside this mountain," he said, looking at the high ceiling of the nave. "And this mountain has been inside me."

She flushed with a comforting warmth that quickly gave way to cold reality. "Alan, I ..." She cut herself short. She squeezed his hand, then released it. "Very poetic," she said simply.

The truth is so, he thought, without even trying to be.

The drive back to the base was quiet. Inside himself, Alan was troubled and concerned. He wanted desperately to know this woman as a person, as something more, and yet, he knew time would pass, and his physical desire for her would inevitably drive him back to her bed. He did not truly know the person of Bill Fisch, and now he never could. He could not even attempt to get close to the husband of a part time lover, and that limited his relationship with her as well. When the "Phinal Phling" was over, so would they be.

The face in the picture hidden in the desk was in his mind's eye. Throughout this day, he had replayed different scenarios to explain why it was there. At one time, he had considered his fling with Denise as merely sexual, or perhaps a quiet joke. Now he realized neither was true.

She dropped him at his car. "Do you want to go with me?" he asked weakly.

She smiled warmly even as she shook her head. "I enjoyed our day. It seems right to end it here."

He nodded and turned to open his car door.

"Alan."

He looked at her. Tears had erupted from her eyes.

"Alan, you are a special person. Don't let anything convince you otherwise." She looked forward through the glass of the windshield.

He stared at her as the truth became clear. "You're telling me it's over, aren't you?"

She barely nodded her head.

"Is that what today was about?"

"I suppose it was," she answered almost inaudibly.

He looked at the pain in her profile. "This was about more than just being good."

"Yes."

"What was it?"

Through moist, reddened eyes, she searched his face for the answer. Finally, she said, "It was about honor. I don't understand it, why honor is more important than love and even life itself. We make a mistake, and honor says either admit it or stick with it. You mistakenly hurt someone you love, honor says admit it ... you make a mistake and commit to the wrong person, honor says live with it. I still love Bill, but I have changed. I will have to deal with that on my own."

He nodded his head, trying to understand. "Please don't say being with me was a mistake."

She gazed into his eyes. “No, lover. Being with you was anything but a mistake. Staying with you would be.”

He touched her arm.

She blinked and shook her head. “I have to go,” she said.

He looked outside the car, searching for any familiar faces that might have seen them together. The parking lot was empty except for the vehicles, among them a baby blue Ford Fiesta. He squinted but could see no one in the car. When he returned his gaze to Denise, she was not looking at him.

“So, this is adios,” he said.

She nodded. It had to be over. She was creating too many demons. She was falling in love with a man she could never have because of a situation they could never resolve.

He stepped from the car and closed the door. Looking straight ahead, she drove carefully across the parking lot and out onto the road that led off the base.

CHAPTER FIFTY-TWO

Alan rolled out of his make-shift bed early on Sunday morning. After a short run to and from the edge of Camarma, he showered and dressed in his best suit, opting to forgo the tie. He felt freer without one. He arrived at the base chapel just as the service was getting underway. Taking the program the usher handed him, he crept inside and took a seat on the outside aisle. Michelle stood with the choir as they rose to sing the first hymn. He knew as she returned his nod that she had seen him come in.

The preacher spoke of renewal. He did not speak of raising the dead, but rather of the rebirth of infants through baptism. Redemption. Alan found himself thinking he could use a little of that.

When the choir sang, Alan considered Michelle in a way he had not before. He had placed her on a pedestal. He wanted to keep her there. He noted with some interest that the preacher also seemed to be watching Michelle intently, sometimes smiling, sometimes nodding his head to the rhythm, seldom taking his eyes from her.

After the service Alan found her in the Fellowship Hall talking with the preacher. As he approached, the preacher widened the space between them.

"That was nice," Alan said. He turned to the preacher. "I liked what you had to say today."

The preacher looked at him with only the hint of a smile. "Thank you." He looked beyond Alan and nodded. "Excuse me." He crossed to the far side of the room.

Alan shrugged and turned to Michelle. "The music today was nice, too," he said. "Did you have your Scotch?"

She laughed. "Couldn't you tell?"

"Of course." He put his hands in his pants pockets. "Can I interest you in lunch at the Officer's Club?"

"Sure!" Michelle said lightly

Once there, they found a table near the entrance to the dining room.

After ensuring Michelle was comfortably seated, Alan removed his coat and placed it over the back of the chair across from Michelle who glowed at him with a warmth that made his heart jump to his throat.

"You said you were going to sing with us," she said as he sat down. "Why haven't you?"

He leaned across the table, and said, "Someone took my song from me."

Michelle winked. "That's a bit dramatic."

"It would be, if that was what I meant." He looked away for a moment, in search of the simple words. "I really used to enjoy singing aloud. But someone important to me didn't like hearing me sing all the time. When something that gives you joy in life begins to get on someone else's nerves ... well, that's when you know things have changed."

Her eyes met his in a look of true sympathy and deeper understanding, but she said nothing more about it.

They ordered lunch with iced tea. "What did you think of the sermon today?" Alan asked as they ate.

She chewed and reflected for a moment. "It was okay, I suppose." She grinned. "What was it about?"

"You didn't listen?"

"I was thinking of something else."

He was curious but did not ask. She would tell him if she wanted him to know. "I usually don't care too much for that fellow's ideas, but I agreed with his words this morning."

"About what?"

"Children. I believe in the Holy Infant. The infant is holy because it is new, it is fresh, untainted. 'Holy Infant so tender and mild' ... one of the things I really like about Christmas is the songs about a child. It reminds me of the importance of our children. Of our legacy."

"You want children someday?"

"I think so. Don't you?"

She looked away across the room. Alan thought he saw recognition in her pretty eyes. He was about to turn when she said, "Someday. When I'm more settled."

"Aren't you settled now?"

She smiled. "Well, yes. But I'd like to see more first, you know? Do more."

"So would I. It looks like I'm going to have that opportunity."

She frowned. "I really do hate what you're going through."

He cringed slightly. "I wouldn't wish it on anyone."

She nodded.

"I will miss you," he said. "Both of you." He paused. "Sam going to pilot training. That's something to think about."

Michelle seemed to flush, and she squirmed. Alan did not see the figure approaching their table, and he recoiled somewhat when the preacher pulled back a chair, sitting himself down without invitation.

"Michelle." The minister nodded at her, then looked at Alan. "Alan Wayne. I didn't know you were such close friends."

"We are ..." Alan began.

"We're in the same squadron," Michelle said pleasantly, but quickly. "I mean, Sam and Alan are."

The preacher cast a critical eye on Alan, watching his face disapprovingly. "Sam's still in Turkey?"

"Yes," Michelle said brightly, aware of his intention but showing no signs of guilt or admission. "He's buying me copper, rugs and whatever else he can find!" She nodded to Alan. "It's the last time." She turned and smiled at the minister charmingly, but something passed between them.

The minister's mouth formed an answering smile, but his eyes were wide and intense with concern. "And your wife, Alan ... I'm sorry to hear you split up."

Alan's face reddened in anger. "I was unaware this was so widely known."

"For me to know does not make it widely known."

"I'm certain of that."

"I beg your pardon?"

Alan did not speak.

The minister cleared his throat. "Perhaps you should watch your step." He rose to leave. Looking at Michelle he added, "And your impressions."

She did not return his glance, but Alan could not help but respond.

"It's my wife that's gone astray," he said sardonically. He nodded at Michelle. "You don't need to worry about her."

The minister glared at him, then turned and walked out of the dining room.

"What's with him?" Alan said, watching the preacher leave.

"I don't think he meant anything," Michelle said, forcing a smile. "But he sure lit a fire under you."

"He insulted you."

"I'm sure he didn't mean to."

"Maybe he meant to insult me and warn you."

"Of what?"

"Of the wayward fighter pilot."

"You can be a loose cannon sometimes."

"I just don't want him to think anything is going on between us," Alan said defensively.

"There isn't. Is there?" She drank from her tea glass.

He looked suddenly at her. Was she flirting with him? "I couldn't even think of such a thing." He wondered if she could see the lie in his eyes. "I think too highly of you."

She smiled and gently batted her soft brown eyes. "I'm not really sure what that is supposed to mean."

He could think of nothing to say. There had to be a place where the line was drawn, regardless of his desire.

Alan glanced around the room. "Maybe the preacher is right. We should be careful."

"Should we go somewhere else?"

He widened his eyes, then narrowed them again and sighed. "I think you should go to your place, and I should go to mine."

She pouted playfully. "I guess you're right," she said, adding, "No keys to my heart today."

He knew she was merely flirting. She must be. "I will see you tomorrow?"

"No. The BX is closed."

He felt he understood. No invitations. No dinner.

Feeling confusion and guilt, he rose to leave. "I'll go first. Maybe our minister friend is out there and will see me alone."

She stood with him. "Don't worry about it." She smiled up into his face. "If you live your life openly, who cares what other people think. We are friends, right?" Her voice rose slightly.

He gazed into her face while trying not to appear enamored. "Yes." His stomach hurt. He walked her to her car and watched her drive away, then stuffed himself into the Camaro and drove the long road to Nueva Camarma.

He spent the afternoon thinking of Michelle, obsessing over images of them together. He physically shivered in anger.

Darkness came, and it served to capture his mood at its most foul. He ate bits at a time, pacing up and down between the kitchen and his bedroom, unable to sit to read or even to think. Michelle's face was ever before him, pleading. But for what?

He poured himself a drink, downed it, and poured another. The drinks slowed his pacing but not his thoughts.

By nine PM his mind was boiling, his body was on fire. He fired up his car and recklessly drove the twenty minutes of roadway between himself and the answer.

He took the elevator to the fifth floor, knocked softly on the door and waited.

Hearing a knock, Michelle rose quickly from the sofa and placed the empty wine glass in the small kitchen. She adjusted the full-length robe she was wearing and padded softly on her bare feet to the door. Looking through the peephole, she saw that it was Alan. She lowered her head a moment in thought.

After what seemed an eternity Alan heard movement on the other side, then a latch, a bolt and the door opened.

Michelle was partially hidden behind the door. Warm, dry air bled from the apartment into the cooler elevator landing, engulfing him like a comfortable blanket. Her eyes squinted from the light above Alan's head.

"Alan?" Her voice was not deep from sleep. She wore pale pink lipstick. "What's wrong? Are you back in your apartment?"

"I can't go there," he said. "Too many memories."

She nodded. "So, you've heard."

He flinched. "Heard what?"

"About Ron Butler," Michelle said simply.

Alan felt the blood rush from his face. "What about Ron?"

"He ... Alan. Ron Butler is dead."

Alan did not understand. He felt he could not believe her.

"They all four hit the ground," Michelle said as if anguishing for her own husband. "A mountain."

"How?"

"It was a four-ship, flying in bad weather. Ron was number four."

Alan caught his breath. "How could they all ...?"

"Ron stayed in position," Michelle said. "They all stayed in position." She paused. "They think the flight lead was disoriented or didn't know where he was. He must have pulled up suddenly because Ron's jet hit first."

"Four smoking holes ..." Alan said absently, immediately sorry for his words. I'm sorry, Ron, he thought. I am so very sorry.

"Four smoking holes," Michelle parroted.

Alan felt a flush of anger. It was senseless, and yet it seemed to fit an eerie pattern of fighter pilots dying in training before they could do what they were being trained for. He could see Jennifer's face and was glad the image was only in his mind.

"Do you need to talk?" Michelle asked. She opened the door wider but stood between it and the landing. She tightened the belt on her robe. "Would you like some coffee?" she asked.

"Yes, I would."

He waited for her to move to let him in.

"There's a place downstairs that stays open real late," she said. "The coffee's pretty good, and strong. I think they're open on Sundays. Just let me throw on some clothes, and I'll be right out."

He looked at his watch. It was late. He did not want to talk about Ron, or anything else, among people he did not know. People who could have no idea of the levels of pain that seemed to be stacking up on him. "No, I appreciate it. I'll just drive back to Jet's place."

"Is that where you just came from?"

He nodded with the innocence of a child caught with his hand in the cookie jar.

She leaned against the door as if weighing a life-altering decision. Finally, she pushed it back and stepped aside. "Come on. I'll make us some tea."

He entered, and she closed and bolted the door behind him, giving it a quick check.

"It's very sad about Ron," she said as she disappeared into the small kitchen. "That's got to be terrible for Jennifer."

Alan caught his breath. He desperately wanted to follow her and grab her and kiss her and to hell with the tea and Ron and Jennifer and everything else.

She stuck her head through the entryway as if suddenly surprised. "Why are you here really? Did you go talk to Sloan?"

"She's still gone," he said simply.

"Permanently?"

He could not tell if the look on her face was one of surprise or pleasure. "I don't know when she's coming back." Sloan must have heard about Ron. What affect would that news have on her? "I don't know what she's doing anymore."

"Oh." Michelle disappeared again into the kitchen. "So why not stay there while she's away?" Her voice had returned to its usual lilting manner.

"I need to be somewhere else." He paused. "Especially now."

"Oh." She reappeared. "Alan, you can't stay here, you know that."

"Yes, I know that." He could hear the water in the kettle rumbling toward a boil.

She approached him and looked up into his face. Was she waiting for him to hold her? Or, aware of his need was she pleading for him to turn around and leave. Either would be painful enough now.

"Maybe I should go," he said. "Forget the tea. I appreciate it. I'll be okay. We all will."

"I don't mind," she said, adding, "the tea, I mean."

He thought to take her in a lingering hug. Perhaps then he would know once and for all if the recent days had been merely flirtation or if deeper feelings brewed beneath the surface. But he fought it. And he felt better. He was doing something noble, if in fact opting not to have an affair with your best friend's wife could be considered an act of nobility.

"Are you sure you'll be all right?" She went to the kitchen and turned off the burner.

"I'll try to be," he said when she returned to the front room. "Better than I am now, anyway." He looked into her brown eyes. "Thank you, Michelle. Thank you for being who you are."

She yawned and smiled. He took her hand and kissed it. She watched with sleepy amusement. He held her hand and pulled himself to her, giving her a quick and clumsy kiss on her forehead, then pulled away. She did not resist, but remained alert, her eyes open.

The sudden knock on the door seemed to make their bodies repel each other like the same poles of two magnets.

She listened. "Probably a Spaniard on the wrong floor," she said softly. "He'll go away."

The knock came again, louder and more insistent.

"I guess I'd better chase off whoever it is," Alan said as he turned toward the door.

"No," she whispered, pushing him aside. "I'll do it."

"You shouldn't have to ..."

"I think I'd better. It is my apartment."

"That's true."

The knocking continued, and Alan could feel the intense beating of his heart as the possibilities occurred to him. Before he could think further, Michelle took his arm and guided him toward the back of the apartment. "It's late, and I'm in my night clothes."

"Could Sam be home early?" Alan asked softly.

"No. He knows better than to surprise me." She ushered Alan into the unlighted bedroom at the end of the hall and smiled sweetly. "So you stay back here."

After a moment, Alan heard Michelle open the door against the chain. There was a muffled exchange of words in English. This is it, he thought, cringing. Sam is home, and I'm a dead man. He crept closer, remaining in the shadows. Two voices, Michelle's and that of a man, were coming from the front door. Alan tiptoed down the hallway until he could make out words.

"... and why not let me in?" the male voice was saying. "I heard about the accident. I came to check on you."

"Not tonight," Michelle whispered.

"Why not?" The voice. It was not Sam's. Alan felt a flood of relief.

"Go on now," Michelle said. "Let me sleep."

Alan resisted the temptation to move close enough to see the man's face.

"Is there someone in there?" the male voice asked louder.

Come on, Michelle, Alan grinned to himself, give it your best shot.

"No," Michelle denied.

"I'll bet there is!" The man sounded annoyed, perhaps drunk.

Alan backed away into the darkness when he recognized the voice as that of the preacher.

"I wish you'd let me come in and comfort you," the preacher said rather loudly. "I've come a long way."

Michelle said, "Dan, I'm okay. Don't worry about me."

Alan could see part of her now.

"A kiss goodnight, then?"

Michelle laughed light-heartedly. "You know? Now, you're just being silly!"

"Come on."

Alan ducked into the shadows as Michelle looked quickly behind herself. She closed the door enough to release the chain, then opened it and kissed the man lightly.

"Now, beat it," she said.

"See you tomorrow," the preacher said. "I'm really sorry about your friend."

Alan's knees weakened. His mouth was dry. Hearing the door close and the chain and bolt returned in place, he walked dizzily out of the bedroom.

Michelle turned to him. "Alan ..."

He looked away, unable to meet her eyes. The picture on the wall ... it was a copy of Guernica, Picasso's surrealistic mural composition depicting the Nazi bombing of the town. Taking it all in as if for the first time, Alan could feel the chaotic torment, the screams of pain and confusion on the surprised faces of the dead and dying as the Nazi's maliciously attacked from the air without warning, without provocation, fully with Franco's assent. "That's everything," he said aloud. He walked past her and the artistic nightmare to the front room.

Michelle followed quickly after him. "Alan, where are you going?"

Fed by the mosaic of his entangled emotions, a full fury flew to the surface. "Why was the preacher here?"

"The preacher?"

"Michelle!" His eyes reddened. "I heard it. I heard it all!"

Michelle touched Alan's arm. "He has an apartment ... nearby. Sometimes he stops by to check on me when Sam's not here. He was concerned I might be, you know, hurting."

"Do you usually let him in?"

"Sometimes."

"But not tonight."

"Of course not."

He stared at her, feeling a rising rage that he had no right to possess.

The smile left her face. "There's nothing going on between us, if that's what you're thinking."

"I don't know what I'm thinking."

"Well, don't think that. Because it isn't true."

"It's not?'

She exhaled noisily. "If I was going to have an affair, it certainly wouldn't be with a preacher."

"Who would it be with?"

She crinkled her eyes. "I think you know."

Alan gritted his teeth and lowered his head. "I saw you kiss him," he said evenly, his eyes turning up to look at her from below his furrowed brow.

She reached for his hand. "I had to do that to get him to leave."

"Bullshit! Michelle!"

She whirled away from him. "You can believe what you want. I'm not having an affair! That's not me. You should know that."

"I should?"

"Yes!" She began to sob.

He felt the sickness of guilt and remorse. He had never seen her so distraught. And she was right. He had wanted more. What was it Denise had said about the dangers of passion?

"I'm sorry, Michelle," he said more quietly, still unable to face those brown eyes that had lured him, intentionally or not, to his greatest loss of faith. "I have no right to accuse you. It's hard for me to explain. I needed you to ... be above all this. I want ..."

"You need for me to be perfect."

Her words were accusatory. But he realized they were also true. He looked at her intently. "I've put you on a pedestal ..."

"Yes!" she blurted. "And trust me, no one can stay balanced up there for long."

After an extended silence, he asked, "Do you love Sam?"

She looked down at her robe, flipping a fold with her hand. "I need him. I need him as much as I love him. That's all I can say." She gazed up at Alan and sniffled. "What about you?"

"Sam means more to me than anyone has for some time."

"Then say nothing about any of this." She sat heavily in a chair and looked out the window. He took a seat near her, silently doing the same.

When their eyes met in the windows dark reflection, he said, "We never really think we'll get caught. We hope no one will ever discover that we are all phonies, that we are never what we hope people will think we are. We balance our lives on an image we create, hoping it will stick until that time when it is too late for anyone to do anything about it. It's like we all have this little agreement with each other. We never think of what the real price of all that will be." He put his face in his hands.

Watching him, Michelle said softly, "He's the one who's perfect, you know?"

"What?"

"Sam," Michelle said. "He's perfect."

Alan bowed his head. "No, he's not perfect."

"He is to me."

Alan nodded. "He's a good man. I guess that's all that matters."

She touched his arm. "He's a fighter pilot." She waited for him to look up into her eyes. "He's what I wanted most in the world. And he could get himself killed doing the one thing he loves more than me."

"And that hurts you."

"How could anyone live with that?"

Alan stood slowly. He dropped the latch, slide back the bolt, opened the door and turned to her. “It’s amazing, isn’t it? The difference between what is real and what we wish were true.”

Fresh tears streamed down her cheeks. “Alan. Why couldn’t it have been you and me?”

Alan shook his head. “I don’t know.” He called for the elevator. “God knows we deserve each other.” He closed the door.

LAST SPRING

CHAPTER FIFTY-THREE

Springtime in Spain. With Easter came a time of renewal, and the fighting of the bulls.

Alan had no desire to watch another bullfight, but Sam chose to have his going away party at the Plaza Toros de Madrid followed by a night of tosca hopping. The only workable time was the afternoon of Easter Sunday, when the Plaza would be full of celebrating Spaniards. The entire 613th Tactical Fighter Squadron descended upon the Spanish bullfighting tradition like a bus full of tourists demanding to be entertained. When the seating was arranged just as the procession began, Alan found himself poetically placed between Denise and Michelle, with their husbands on either side beyond them.

Michelle laughed her dimpled laugh and joked with Alan as she always had, and nothing in her eyes betrayed a shared secret, even when she looked only at him. He looked across her at Sam who, for reasons Alan could only speculate, had been distant with him since the squadron's return from Turkey.

Maybe that was as it should be, he thought. Getting close to people always seemed to hurt.

He shook his head. The whole idea smelled of bull dung.

Denise was different. When he joked with her, he could see it. She was telling him something was there, but he did not understand what it was.

Alan looked out over the arena and thought of the fight. Killing bulls this way was gory and dangerous. But the gore was expected, as was the pain. It was part of the sport. It was the sport. Some of that was good. Other parts were less appealing - cowardice at times, a lack of style.

After the killing of the first bull, Carp stood and faced the fighter pilots.

"Gentlemen!" he said, raising a bota bag. "I would like to take this opportunity ..." He spanned his gaze across the fighter pilots, avoiding Alan's eyes. "... to confront you all. My wife is pregnant. Which one of you bastards is the father?!"

"Hey! Congratulations!" Michelle said, reaching across Alan to touch the arm of Denise who was beaming and blushing appropriately.

"Congrats, you impotent puck!" Shooter yelled, offering a toast of a beer from his seat. "I'm the father! Now sit down, so we can watch more bulls die, okay."

The Bear stood in the middle of his boys. His pious, tall and skinny wife, her long hair rolled in a Pentecostal updo, watched him in calculated fear of what he might say or do.

"My fellow fighter pilots, let us congratulate the lucky lady!" the Bear growled.

"Hear, hear!"

The Bear was in a decidedly jovial mood. Another F-16 list had been announced, and he, Shooter, and Carp were the latest Squids to make the cut. Standing out among the Spaniards, the fighter pilots were loud, and these three were the loudest.

The Bear took a drink of beer. "Being the only man among a bunch of boys, my place is with the mother of my child." He tried to climb over the heads of the Squids to get to Denise but met fierce resistance from other contenders.

Fisch rose again as the next fight began and said, "Gotta drain it. Anybody need a beer?" He left without looking at Alan.

The picador rammed his spear deep into the bull's neck as the beast charged the voiceless horse with every intent of killing it.

"Congratulations," Alan whispered to Denise, his mouth close to her ear, his eyes on the fight.

"Thanks," she said, turning and noting the features of his profile.

"I didn't think you could." He knew she must be smiling.

"Neither did I."

The picador left the ring as the matador approached the bull. The first pass was frighteningly close, and it appeared even the matador was taken by surprise.

Denise clapped and leaned toward him. "It must not have been me."

"What?"

"It must have been Bill."

Alan swallowed hard. "Well, it must not have been Bill, either."

She stopped clapping and faced him with a look that said she knew he knew where this was going. He gazed at her briefly, then turned his attention to the fight inside the ring. The bull was a dangerous bull, not because of its size and strength but because it was proving to be unpredictable.

"We need to talk, then?" he asked when the crowd cheered loudly.

"Some time."

"Would you like some wine?"

"Yes."

He reached to his left for his bota bag and saw that Michelle was watching him with a curious smile. Poetic, he thought. As the truth invariably is.

"What's that look for?" he asked as he opened the plug on the bag. "Are you with child, also?"

"No. Are you?"

"Yes. I'm just waiting my turn to make the announcement."

Her eyes glowed. "I see." She looked around him at Denise.

He watched her eyes until they returned to him. "I see that you do not see."

Alan turned to Denise and handed her the bota bag.

"Thank you."

"What's my part in this?" he whispered softly.

"I would prefer you did not have one." She shot the wine down her throat.

He looked at her in surprise. "Is that all we have to talk about?"

"That's the heart of it. How does that make you feel?" She seemed genuinely concerned about his feelings while determined for him play it her way.

He smiled. "I feel like that is all right. I'm happy for you two."

She returned the bag to him. He raised it to her as in a toast, then took a drink. The red wine felt cool and dry in his mouth. He took a second shot.

He was a man torn from his wife, like a baby ripped from the succulent bosom. He was between two women whom he had wanted, and he had taken one who now would bear his child in honorable silence.

Through the other he felt he had uncovered the truth of fantasy.

He offered the bag to Denise again, but she declined. He lowered the bag to his lap and said, "If I was anything of a man, I would make a strong play for you, to claim you as my own."

There was a sudden look of concern in her features. "No," she said. "A real man would do just the opposite."

He nodded as he considered her words.

The matador raised the estoque for the kill. At each attempted estocade, the matador jumped well clear of the bull's horns, refusing to subject himself to the danger necessary for a clean kill. After two difficult passes, the sword stuck halfway into the animal, but the bull refused to fall. The peons to its left and right alternately shook their pink capes in the bull's face, making it turn its head repeatedly left then right to facilitate the sword sawing through the aorta. At last, the bull fell to its knees, then slowly to its side. A third peon stuck his knife into the back of the bull's head and scrambled its spinal cord.

"Not a good kill," Michelle offered to Sam who only nodded. She glanced at Alan.

"No," Alan said. "But the result is the same."

CHAPTER FIFTY-FOUR

The sun was just above the horizon when the three-ship Alan was leading passed Santos outbound. His wingmen followed him in a shallow climb to 4000 feet, passing the second check point. He felt good, in spite of himself, enjoying the still smooth morning air, the serene peacefulness of the early calm. Passing over the still sleeping villages of the world below, he was reminded of how his father would awaken him on Saturdays to go fishing, sometimes as early as 3:00 in the morning, to hit the tides just right. It always felt like a day not wasted.

He recalled when he and Sloan were first married, when he had to get up before dawn for an early flight briefing, she would get up with him. Only half-awake and wishing to remain so, she would fix him a honey dew melon for his breakfast, telling him it meant "Honey, do good." He knew she would return to the bed as soon as he was gone. But she had always been awake and ready for him on his return.

He shook off the memory. Those days were over.

There was a touch of fog, barely a puff, over the lake and in the valleys where the river ran. The fog followed the river to the narrow end of the lake where it nestled against a mesa. The town of Sacedon was hidden somewhere in the mist.

A good day to be up here with Beauregard! Alan smiled to himself.

To the left, in the distance were the Twin Peaks. He imagined Whiskey's soul resting there, thinking it really was not a bad monument. He had meant to fly past it with Sam as a gesture of their remembrance, but the opportunity had never presented itself.

Before sunrise on this morning, Alan had briefed his flight members on the conduct of his favorite type of air-to-air training: 1v1v1.

"We will each begin at a corner of the area," he began. "At the 'fight's on' call, we will fly toward the center where the fight will begin."

He considered this an excellent training scenario because every fighter was alone and in constant peril. Nobody was safe or could think to be safe simply by gaining the offensive. That third fighter was always out there somewhere, ready to pounce on the two fighters who were jousting with each other. Like war, it was not a gentleman's game. To win required fighting smart, staying fast and using a fighter pilot's cunning. Staying alive was winning. To die, for whatever reason, was to lose.

"If you are killed," he told them, "you will do an aileron roll, and leave the fight for thirty seconds. You're dead, but you'll soon be resurrected."

Looking to his right, he saw that his number two man, Jeff Cole, was working to stay in position. He smiled to himself, thinking that it was good. He liked the way things were turning out. Despite the familiarity of living together in the Camarma house, Jet was beginning to revere him just a bit, and Alan was honing his new wingman like a fine quality knife.

As the flight of three fighters turned south toward the LED-33 air-to-air area and began a steeper climb, he allowed himself the indulgence of reliving his first flight as an air combat flight lead. Jet, having run out of options, had turned to point straight at Alan's airplane, crossing his nose at the last minute in a right turn in violation of the ROE. It had been extremely dangerous, but it had happened too quickly to frighten either one of them.

In the debrief, Alan had only asked Jet what he was doing during the first fight that had allowed Alan to make an easy kill. Jeff had been defensively acquiescent, saying, "I was working the egg." Alan had quipped, "Well, that explains why you were overly easy."

Later, at the bar, he mulled over the fact that he and Jet and their back-seaters had survived the same situation that cost Ernie his life. He decided to make a lesson of it. After finishing his third beer, he turned to Jeff and said, "Aggression means that when I brief ten seconds between elements, you strive for ten seconds. I don't mean nine. That doesn't show more aggression.

"And when I tell you to abide by the ROE, it means just that ..." He had then grabbed his housemate by the collar of his flight suit and flung him against the wall of the O'Club bar. Amid the flabbergasted surprise of the younger fighter pilot, Alan had said, "... it doesn't mean doing something stupid and trying to kill me before I can save your ass in combat or teach you how to save mine!"

Alan smiled. He had enjoyed that. It was the stuff of real fighter pilots. The women in the bar had been stunned. That made it even better.

Entering the training area, Alan looked to his left at Bill Fisch's jet. Sam was in Carp's pit on his End of Tour ride - his EOT.

His smile receded behind his oxygen mask when he remembered Michelle's words about her husband. 'He could die doing the one thing he loves more than me.'

Leading this flight made Alan feel responsible for his wingmen, for their lives, for their training, for their future. The image of Ron Butler surfaced in his mind, and he felt a brief flash of anger. You do not lead people into The Rocks! he thought, and then decided to let it go. Life was now. Go from here.

Alan keyed the radio saying, "Two and three, you're cleared to your points."

"Two," Carp acknowledged.

"Three," Jet radioed.

"Any last-minute questions on our plan?" Alan asked his WSO.

Boomer cleared his throat. "Nope. We'll just put 'em both on the right side. Come in low out of sun at the speed of smell, and jump 'em when they go for each other."

"Sounds good the way you say it."

"All right, Dog! Let's kick some ass!"

"You're ready, huh?"

Boomer had not yet puked. "Let's do it!"

"You don't need to ..."

"Nope. I'm ready for love," Boomer said, sounding at once ballsy and fatalistic. He was confident and self-assured, knowing he would be able to find the targets. But if he did not, he was not concerned. He was not afraid of the merge. He was with the Dog.

Alan arced the F-4D gracefully into a left bank, putting more back pressure on the stick to increase the rate of turn while maintaining 21,000 feet. The horizon fanned across the canopy like a kaleidoscope. Halfway through the turn, he called "Fight's on!"

"We'll head about 150," Alan said to Boomer. "That should put them both at least initially on our right."

"Roger," Boomer answered, looking over his shoulder. The low sun was blinding. "I think we're right for the sun," he added.

"Okay, Boomer. Find the bad guys."

"Roger, Dog."

Today, Alan liked this set up for another reason. Sam was his friend, but in this fight, he was the enemy, as was Fisch. He could vent his rage on something he could not control with something that he controlled fully.

In this vacuum, Sam and Fisch were, together, the dragon to be slayed for hand of fair maiden. The objects of his frustration and anger. Attack, without mercy. Vengeful, unforgiving, unrelenting. Beat them into submission. And then knock it off.

When it was all over, they would return to the squadron as comrades. No one, not even Boomer, would know the passion that drove him. They would fight in simulated combat, and no one would see the pain, the distortions on his face. He would fight it out against that other airplane - and with himself - and then be done with it. Put it forever to bed. Then Sam and Michelle would leave for pilot training, and he would learn to fly the F-16. And Fisch? Well, he didn't care what happened to Fisch.

Carp flew his F-4 just under the Mach at 9000 feet MSL. The cockpit was silent. Sam searched the higher altitudes while Carp peered eagerly above and below the canopy rail for his adversary.

"I'm gonna kill that sonofabitch Dog today!" he muttered, more to himself. "He's lucky more than he is good."

"Let's take him!" Sam replied. "Getting killed on my last flight in Spain would be embarrassing. We get behind Dog, and we stay behind him."

"Roger!" Carp said. "That worthless bastard is as good as dead."

Sam concentrated on the radar scope. We all have our demons, he thought.

Then Carp said, “I think he’s banging my wife.”

The statement caught Sam by surprise. He could think of no retort that would reflect the proper reaction. With less than a minute to the merge, Carp was obviously not trying to strike up a conversation.

Sam said, “Bullshit!” He felt a sudden surge of anger and relief. He was angry at himself, at his doubts over the past several weeks. They sounded so ridiculous, so petty when verbalized by Bill Fisch. Sam understood now. Carp’s one ridiculous statement had made it all clear.

Inexplicably, Sam felt elated. “Clean scope!” he said almost with satisfaction.

“Look high!” Fisch ordered. “They’ve got to be high!”

“Clean scope,” Boomer informed Alan.

“What? No contact? One of them must be inside ten miles by now.”

“Nothing.”

“Where are you looking? High?”

“Yes ...”

“Look low.”

“Roger!” Boomer worked the radar. “One contact, low! Eight miles!”

“I’m tally one, high!” Alan said. “Where’s the other one?”

“Very low! Lost him! Dammit!”

“Look for him visually,” Alan said. “I’ve got the other one coming down!”

“Roger!” Boomer flipped the radar to the auto-acquisition mode. “You’ve got boresight and ten.”

“Okay.”

“Tally one!” Sam called.

“Where?” Carp responded with a directionless pull on the pole.

“High. Screaming down on us!”

“No tally!”

“Come hard left!”

“Shit! Where is he?!”

“Deep in our shit at nine o’clock! He’s overshooting!”

Carp grunted. “Can we reverse on him?”

“No! Keep the turn coming and look for the other guy.”

Alan watched Jet go through his altitude. “He doesn’t see us! Tally two! The low guy’s turning into him. I’m engaging the low man!”

Boomer grunted, “Shouldn’t we take the high man?”

“They’re both low now.”

“Yeah.”

Sam strained against the g’s. “The other guy is high at our six and coming in fast!”

Carp groaned, “He’ll overshoot into the rocks.”

“Maybe,” Sam answered, looking inside to the instruments, “but we’re a lot higher than we were ... and a lot slower!” He looked back again. “Eight o’clock now! About two miles.”

“Shit!” Carp rolled left and pulled to six g’s. “Keep talkin’!”

Sam’s strong neck muscles allowed him to keep his head up and moving despite the high g-forces. “Going to seven!” he said, beginning to breathe hard. “A mile or so.”

“How’s he getting back there? I’m pulling as hard as I can!”

Sam looked in at the g-meter. It registered “5,” and they were at 420 knots. They could pull another g and not overstress the jet at this weight, though that much airspeed could give them three more. “More g!” Sam said.

Carp said, “Not today, Dog-poop, not today!” and yanked the pole into his lap. The F-4 dug into the turn.

Sam turned his attention outside again when he saw the g-meter go beyond “6.” He began to gray-out and knew they must be pulling close to eight g’s now.

“Pretty good turn!” Alan said to Boomer as he watched the F-4 maneuver low and to his left. “I’ll have to reposition. Where’s that other guy?”

“I don’t see him.” Boomer answered. “But he’ll be back soon!”

“Roger! We’d better make this a quick kill.” Alan smiled to himself. “We’re above them like a falcon about to pounce on a rat!” he said with excessive fervor.

"They're overshooting into the sun!" Sam yelled to Carp. "Do you see them?"

Carp reversed the jet. "Tally! In the sun!" he groaned as if in pain.

"I've lost them!" Sam said. "Above us!"

"Roger!"

"You've got 'em?"

"Roger!" Carp grunted.

Alan's jet seemed to hang above Carp's head, hovering there with the sun blindingly beyond it. Taunting him, his enemy grappled. Fixed in space, his nose off, the enemy was not yet an immediate threat, and still the jet toyed with him, like a cat with a mouse. It said 'I am here. Do you see? I have the advantage. I have you!'

Carp rolled further right and pulled.

"Tally again!" Sam said, and his voice shook nervously. "Do you see them?"

"Tally! I'll pull to his six!"

"They're right above us!" Sam groaned.

Poised above the "fur-ball" Jet sized up his entry. One of them would spit out soon, and the other would probably run to gain energy. Either way, from this vantage point, he could take his pick and go for the easiest kill.

Fisch strained verbally, a horrible, desperate cry from his gut. He jammed the stick into his stomach to slow the jet's forward movement, willing his jet behind that of his adversary. Alan and Boomer saw the F-4 below them roll until they could see the full top side of the Phantom. From this angle, it seemed very big. Neither man spoke. Alan lit the burners and rolled right and up, putting 5 g's on the Phantom.

Sam keyed the mike. "Heads ...!"

Carp's canopy struck the other F-4 near the tail, below the burner cans, driving his immediately lifeless body down through the ejection seat.

The nose hit slightly behind Boomer's seat. He looked inside and thought, That was a big one! He reached for the lower ejection handle and, as he did so, saw flames coming into the cockpit from below his feet. He pulled the handle.

It was too late for Sam to pull the handle, and he had known that. It was either the handle or the warning over the radio ... and he had not believed he would survive ejecting anyway. When his F-4 hit the one Alan and Boomer were in, he realized in an instant that he was behind the impact. Maybe he could ...

The momentum of the collision flung Sam clear of his fighter and into the hellish roaring flames of Alan's afterburners.

All thought ceased. All remembrances near and distant vanished. The turmoil of earth was over, the betrayals, the deceptions, the loves, the losses. Of the possibilities there was nothing left. Sam was now a part of history. His charred remains hurtled without a parachute to the waiting earth below.

Twenty-eight minutes after taking-off from Torrejon on a calm Friday morning, Sam Christopher was dead.

Michelle was getting ready to go to the BX. It would be her last working day.

He might show up there. And she needed to tell him that it could not be, that it never would be. That she wanted and needed only Sam.

Nothing happened when Boomer pulled the ejection handle. He strained against it, then realized he had pulled it as far as it would go. The airplane was slowly disintegrating around him. His rear canopy was gone, but he was still inside the jet. Everything was happening so slowly around him. In a split second, he decided to try the over-the-head ejection curtain, but his hands would not release the lower handle. I need to move! he thought. A fireball rushed into his lap.

The airplane began to pull away from him, and he felt his neck pushed into his shoulders. The wreckage grew suddenly smaller below him as he realized his seat had fired and was taking him safely away from what was now a huge fireball in the sky. He could see the top of Alan's head under the front cockpit canopy.

Dear God! Boomer's mind screamed. I know I turned that handle! He should be coming out with me!

Boomer was kicked clear of the ejection seat. The parachute blossomed overhead, and he could not see the airplanes any more.

The last thing Alan remembered was pulling back on the stick to avoid the collision. The image of the disemboweled dog at the side of the street flashed in his mind and was gone as he thought So, this is what happens next.

When he regained consciousness, he was hanging from a parachute, and his neck and legs were aching. He felt a dull pain in his left arm. The meteoric trail of the two destroyed fighters was etched in smoke across the clear morning sky like a black rainbow, but there was no pot of gold at the end of this smoldering arc. There was only what remained of his friend and one who should have been. He watched the pieces of the wreckage impact the ground in the distance.

Parachutes! Look for parachutes! He twisted his head to search and cringed as intense pain shot through his neck and upper back. He pulled his mask away, raised his visor and carefully turned his head to survey the horizon. He saw three other chutes below him and felt the glimmer of hope until he realized two of them were deployed drag chutes from what remained of the two fighters.

The ground was coming up rapidly now. He put his feet and knees together, stared at the distant horizon and waited for the coming impact.

CHAPTER FIFTY-FIVE

There would follow, as in all military accidents, the required investigation, complete with a board of officers led by a full colonel to find the cause and determine the ultimate responsibility. The deaths of two fighter pilots would be reduced to dollars and make no sense as, "in the big bell curve of life," as Whiskey had once put it, the bottom line would be the ultimate measure.

And Alan would be questioned, as would Clarence Bailey and Jeff Cole and his WSO. Probing questions that all but assumed guilt. Then the wreckage would be examined. And things would be found that it was too late to bury.

The board would find that a hesitation of two or three seconds would have cost Alan more than a broken arm and a sprained neck. First Lieutenant Clarence Bailey had saved the life of Captain Alan Wayne.

And Alan would be grudgingly determined unblameworthy.

But it was still there somewhere. It was tangible. It was in someone's pocket.

For now, there was only ceremony. The solemn funeral. The vexing words. The mournful song. The fly-by of the missing man formation.

The chapel was full of family, friends, and fighter pilots in blue and green. Wearing a neck brace and a cast on his broken left arm, Alan sat in the balcony. Even people who did not know him would realize he must have had something to do with the death of these two fighter pilots. He tried to ignore the eyes he felt upon him, watching, listening, and remembering as the preacher instructed. The preacher also insisted that these two fighter pilots were believers, and as such, belonged in the

Kingdom of Heaven. Alan wondered if God was really so petty, if there were not more pressing matters in the world than insisting that everyone who died must be believers before they got the ultimate reward.

"If we confess our sins ..." the preacher was saying. Alan almost smiled when he remembered the look on Sam's face the first time he heard him say "Never confess!" Why? To keep life simple? Unhurtful? For the first time Alan thought that if people were always compelled to tell the truth, they would not be so inclined to try to get away with the selfish indiscretions that fester and grow, inflaming the mind and scarring the soul.

He found it funny that this preacher was talking about the confession of sins.

What were the truly deadly sins? Apathy? Pride? Hate? Blind faith? Inaction?

He listened as the preacher read the names ... "William Allen Fisch. Samuel Jonathon Christopher ..." and realized he had never known Sam's middle name. Alan decided that he would not sound good dead. He had no middle name.

He felt his eyes moisten when, as a congregation, they stood to sing "Lord, Guard and Guide the Men Who Fly." A tear trailed down his cheek. He did not move to arrest its flight, allowing it to drop to the floor from his chin. He stared at the tiny puddle, his own body's creation that seemed to burn as it slowly streaked his face, resting quietly now on the wooden church floor, and he thought of Ernie and Whiskey and Ron and Sam. And William Allen Fisch.

When it was over, the widows boarded airplanes to escort their husbands home. Alan bade them both goodbye in silence. Denise was in control, though obviously in pain. Michelle was devastated. And there was nothing that he felt he could say. Evidently, there was nothing the preacher could say to sooth her, either. She turned away from him when he tried.

Alan realized now that he and Michelle were so very far apart. He would never have understood her mind. She had been, for him, a concoction, a creation, a figment of his misguided desire. In this, Alan and the preacher were alike. The difference was that one of them still pined for Michelle while the other could only pity her.

Alan wanted to console Denise but did not feel he had the right. He wanted to hold her, but he did not possess the strength. He wanted to ask her to stay. But doing so seemed so tasteless that he spewed it from his mind as he would a sour grape from his mouth.

The distance he was putting between himself and all else created frightening questions. Did he truly love? Or was he seeking someone to love him? Were they all merely a composite of his need for passion and compassion?

There were any number of reasons not to get too close, any number of ways to avoid getting hurt. And all of them were selfish ones.

The following week, Casino Garman approached Alan and said, "Colonel Bevins wants you in his office."

Alan seated himself as the Bear closed both office doors then stared long and hard at Alan before deciding to speak. "I want to know what happened."

"The investigation, sir," Alan began, "I'm not supposed to ..."

"I don't give one good goddamn what you're supposed to do! Talk to me! Two of my boys are dead. You pushed it, didn't you. You pushed it too far!"

Alan withdrew physically as the Bear crouched over him. "Sir, the tape will show ..."

"I'm not talking about a goddamn cassette tape!" The Bear walked behind his desk, then turned to face Alan again. "I'm talking about you!"

"Sir?" He felt violated.

"You, dammit! And the competition! On the ground. In the air. You finally took it to this!"

"No, sir!"

"You know you did. You felt it! You and Fisch have been at it as long as I can remember ... and as long as Doug Sherman could remember."

Alan could stand no more. He was possibly saying his goodbyes to the fighter world, but he rose to his feet, confronting the accusations. "What did you expect me to do? I am a trained fighter pilot. He came after me from day one, and I fought him. My best friend died because of him!"

The Bear glanced at the cast on Alan's arm, then at the wall, then to the door before sitting heavily in his chair. "I don't know what I expected." He folded his hands in front of him, his elbows resting on the wooden table. "I know I expect to get fried on a skewer for this."

Alan sat down again and looked at the big man whose eyes were red from lack of sleep. Perhaps the Bear would have asked deeper questions had he not assumed that the lost friend Alan was referring to was Sam, but, rather, a young fighter pilot named Ernie Goddard.

"Why you?" Alan asked.

"Because it's my squadron." He spun his chair so that his back was to Alan. "They were my boys. You can't lose two airplanes ... and ... and expect to stay in command."

"This was not your fault."

"How can you know?"

"Because the only person you can really blame is dead."

The Bear shook his big head. "It's on me. It's in my pocket."

"And mine," Alan said. "But only insofar as we can reach." The fact that the Bear was on edge made it easier for Alan to be in control. "You can only go so far, do so much. It's just a roll of the dice who will survive and who will not."

The Bear was quiet for a time, his mind on another matter.

Alan was beginning to feel uncomfortable when the Bear finally spoke again, saying, "I'm sending you to MacDill."

"Well, that's okay, sir. I'd really rather not train at Luke."

"No, Dog." He turned slightly. "I'm reassigning you to MacDill to be an instructor. Someone else will fill the bill here."

Alan had not expected this, but now that he heard it, he felt a certain flow of relief.

"Is that alright with you, Captain Wayne?"

Show a little fight, Alan thought. "Sir, in spite of it all, Spain has become my home. It's really the only home I know. Does that make any difference?"

"Not really."

Alan nodded slowly. "Then it has to be right."

He knew he had pushed it. The pain. The hurt. The loss of so much. He sought to take it out on the world, to hurl his rage at the only things he could see. The Good and the Bad. Unable to distinguish between the two, he had destroyed them both.

It was late at night when Alan heard the knocking on Jet's front door. He was in the kitchen, looking but not hungry. He turned the radio down a notch, went to the door and opened it.

"May I come in?" Denise asked.

Moving to one side, in his surprise he could only think to say, "Please."

He followed her into the living room.

"Is Jet around?" she asked.

"No. He's at Aviano sitting the pad. He volunteered." Alan paused. "Would you like a drink?"

"No." She looked at the plaster cast on his arm. "Are you healing okay?"

"Everything still hurts," he said. "I didn't expect you back. I was thinking I might not see you again ... at least until I got up the nerve to call on you. Are you going home to Daytona Beach? Or are you staying here ... in Spain?"

"No," She answered. "I'm not staying here. But I had to come back ... to straighten our ... my affairs."

Alan felt a sudden wave of dizziness and realized no matter what she did or said, he would not like it. It would have been easier if she had simply flown out of his life with her memories - and his - forever altered, yet basically intact. "I guess that includes me." His words were barely audible, muffled by the sound of the ringing in his ears.

She caught him checking her waste-line and laughed slightly. "It's still there," she said.

He started toward her. "Denise, I ..."

She raised her hands between them and turned her head. "Please, Alan. Don't." She moved away from him.

"I want to do what's right."

"Then listen to me. I'm ready to say what I need to say."

"Will I ever see ... my child?"

"No! Alan!" Denise said curtly. "You must not think that way."

He was shocked. "Denise, did you not imply ..."

"No, Alan! Don't do that. This is my child. You must never think of it any other way."

"You can't expect me ..."

She cut him off. "I'm giving you a gift, Alan. I am taking the innocence of an unborn child upon myself. And giving you ..."

"My freedom."

"No. Your reputation. And mine. Not because you got some girl pregnant. Or even because of the Air Force. It's a small world. I know that what goes around comes around."

"I don't care about any of that anymore."

"But you will again, someday. You steal some fighter buddy's wife. You get her pregnant. You ... he ..." She paused as the tears began to form. "Your name would not be worth the tag it's stenciled on for the rest of your career. Maybe the rest of your life. You know it's true. At least, you've wished as much on another."

He sat heavily in the only chair.

She stepped closer to him. "And I am giving my child a gift. Bill Fisch was his father. That is his gift. His father was a good fighter pilot, a good person and a loyal husband who died doing what he loved best. No one will take that away from his only child."

Alan did not speak.

"Did you know his father was a general?" she asked.

"What?"

"Were you aware Bill's father was a general officer?"

Alan saw the tears draining down her cheeks. Softly, he answered, "No one ever told me."

"He revered his father. But his father never praised him, never made him feel that he had done anything right. Bill always felt he had something to prove to that bitter old man. That general wanted Bill to go to the Academy, but Bill went to Florida instead ... and met me there."

"And Ernie."

She flinched and looked at him. "Yes, and Ernie."

"Have you ever thought how different it would have been if you had married Ernie?"

She blinked again. "How long have you known?"

"That last morning. At your place in Eurovillas. When you were in the shower, I went looking for a pen and paper in your desk. I was going to write you a cute note."

She nodded her understanding. "Bill never uses ... never used ... that drawer. But you would have had to dig around a bit."

Alan grimaced. "Not as much as you might think." He paused. "I'm so sorry I snooped."

She lowered her head. "Why didn't you say anything?"

"I don't know." He looked away. "Maybe I hoped you would think as much of me as you did him."

She came to him, took his good hand in both of hers and held it in front of herself. "I was not in love with Ernie Goddard." She gazed into Alan's eyes. "Ernie was just an infatuated kid with a good heart who saw the world as a child would. In a way, it's better he never had to lose that innocence." She gently caressed Alan's fingers. "The innocence that makes you believe you can actually make a difference in this world." She smiled in remembrance. "Bill was a realist. For all his faults, he was at least an adult." She allowed a quick laugh to escape. "Except when it came to Ernie. He was so jealous. But I couldn't just toss his picture away. Not after the accident."

"Especially since Bill was the one that ..."

"Don't blame Ernie's death on Bill!" she said, cutting him off. She did not release his hand but held it tighter. "Maybe your soul felt something your mind would not accept. Maybe you felt it without knowing it. But Bill never got over Ernie's death." She flinched in remembered pain. "He had sleepwalking nightmares. Once, in the middle of the night, he grabbed me by the throat and pushed me against the wall." She shook her head. "By morning, he had no memory of it."

Alan sighed heavily. "Do you blame me for Bill?"

She shook her head. "We've all died ..." Her voice caught in her throat, "...a little. I don't see what is to be gained from establishing blame."

"I'll try to get over that."

She squeezed his hand again and smiled. "I really hope you do. Otherwise, what's the point in going on?"

He released her hands and put his good hand on her stomach.

She placed hers on his sides.

"What about here?" he asked.

She looked down where his hand was gently massaging her rounding belly and smiled. "The future lies with her," she said, suddenly sounding very maternal. "Unblemished, innocent and, so far, perfect. More than anything else in the world, now, I want to protect her."

"Or him."

She nodded. "Or him."

"And that's a secret you can carry to your grave?"

She rested her head on his chest and closed her eyes. "A few years from now, who can say how long, when a young man or woman comes to you and asks if you knew a fighter pilot named Bill Fisch, I want you to know what to say."

"It'll probably take me that long to figure it out myself." He held her as tightly as he dared. She possessed more inner character than he had ever imagined for Sloan. But she was never his. She might never be.

Denise looked up at him. "Just remember Aviano."

Feeling his soul being pulled into the pretty rings of her eyes, he shook his head. "What does that mean?"

She smiled playfully. "You don't know nuttin' about no boomin'!"

He returned her smile. "If that is what you want."

"That is what I want."

"Will I ever see you again?"

Denise pulled away, looking at but not focusing on his chest. "I don't know. I'm going to need time alone. I know this is not as simple as I have tried to make it."

She touched the front of his shirt. A song played softly on the AFRTS radio station. Their eyes met as, together, they recognized it to be the first song they had danced to at the Officer's Club. They had held each other dangerously close. So much had come from that night.

Taking her hand to his chest, he pulled her close, with only his broken arm between them. She did not resist. Slowly, they began to move with the music and to the rhythm of each other. Light caresses enhanced their embrace, and they ignored the world for a brief moment.

Sloan turned the Citroën into Nueva Camarma. She tried to understand again what she had convinced herself she would do. Alan was in a lot of pain, no doubt blaming himself for everything that had happened. Well, maybe not everything. The memory of his words cut her like a knife. He could not have said them unless he truly felt that way about her now.

And why should he not? Had she not thrown everything away chasing something that was probably no better but merely different from what she had? It was a mystery. She felt honor bound. To admit a mistake now was to admit a grave sin.

But she had to believe Alan still needed her, still wanted her. In the past days and weeks, she had come to understand how much she still cared for him. She had grieved so for his pain. These feelings must mean something.

She decided to go to him to find out.

The gate was open. There was a car in the driveway. A gray Renault. Bill and Denise Fisch's car, she realized and then thought, No, just Denise's car, now. Why was it here?

Suddenly, there was nothing. Through quiet, rushing tears she understood that it was over. It was gone. Completely. Finally.

She turned off the headlights and backed slowly out into the street. She was in Alcala, the tears on her face salty and dry, before she remembered to switch on the lights again.

The plane ride from Madrid to New York was unpleasant. You were wrong, Sam, Alan thought. Going west is much harder than going east.

He imagined Sam could see him, though he disliked the idea of Heaven. Yet, as the jumbo jet continued west, he could not stop thinking of it. There was something he understood.

Heaven, however it was conceived, was for the living. We need it, he decided, for something to cling to. So that Sam could be there, and Ernie, and Whiskey, and Ron. And Bill Fisch. Now higher than the other angels, right up there with Beauregard.

And maybe we need it to deny to others of our choosing, like Brandon Parsons. Maybe Beauregard would disagree with him on that.

Looking out the window, Alan decided he needed Heaven, if only to learn to live, to overcome the guilt, to forgive and be forgiven.

Sam had been right, though, about being higher than the angels. And now he understood. The angels are already there, they have it made. We have to earn it.

Alan recalled the paintings he had seen at the Prado. So many of them depicted the seraphs, the little children not called angels. But, in his mind, they were the only true angels, gone before they could live, before they could know, before they could make their own decisions. Given little or no chance at life, they remained innocent. They had not lied - except perhaps to protect themselves - had stolen only hearts, coveted only life, killed only time, polluted no one with inane thoughts and ideas. They smiled impish smiles, coaxing our hearts temporarily out of the black vault of survival, momentarily realigning our priorities and exposing our souls.

He was his father's son. But he wondered if his father would understand who he was now. Were they closer? Or even farther apart.

Alan thought about Sloan. With him, she had been content. Now, perhaps she was finding love. Although it cut him deeply, she had needed to capture that which she thought was true. And if emotions are not true, if passion is not true, then only living death remains.

If you choose to measure your life only by those things you cannot take with you, then it is all wasted. For, what do you take with you? Not money. Not the number of different women you've had. Or men. Maybe not even memories, which could be painful. You die with whatever nobility you had and take with you whatever love you shared.

In stoic silence, Alan stared out the small window of the big airplane, imagining reflections in the billowing white clouds above the ocean and considering what great truth he was bringing back with him. A single, shameless tear of regret formed in the corner of his eye, blurring the passage of time back to the Land of the Big BX. The truth was that none of them had survived the Spanish experience unscarred.

CHAPTER FIFTY-SIX

A FRESH FALL RISING

Beer in hand, Alan leaned against the bar at the MacDill Officer's Club talking to other fighter pilots and getting drunk with them. It was Friday night, and he knew how to handle Friday nights. This bar created a dazzling spectacle, and the Desire to Disgust was threatening to run rampant.

He had finally received a letter from Denise with an address in Daytona Beach, a picture, and a name: William Alan Fisch. The kid's middle name was a cute twist, but there was little if anything in little William Alan's features that reminded him of himself, and very much that reminded him of his last glimpse into the round-faced countenance of Carp.

Denise seemed to realize that as well. The letter was more a courtesy than an invitation. Evidently, Carps father was becoming a loving, caring grandfather. The general and his wife were even making plans to move to Florida to be closer to their only grandson. There was a silver lining.

In the privacy of his apartment overlooking Tampa Bay, Alan had reread the letter several times, studying both it and the picture before stashing them both in the bottom drawer of his desk. That seemed a proper ceremonial resting place for reminders of the past that no longer belonged in the present.

Almost involuntarily, he felt for the envelope he kept in the leg pocket of his flight suit. This letter was wrinkled and worn from multiple readings. In it, Connie Marcum explained why she was at Columbus Air Force Base in Mississippi, about an hour west of her childhood home in

Alabama. She seemed very excited for having just soloed in the T-37. Evidently, her father had at last found a reason to be proud of her.

He finished his beer and bought another as he watched two fighter pilots from his squadron rolling pigs. "Another double leaning jowler!" one of them exclaimed, looking at the resting position assumed by the pair of one-inch plastic pigs the other had just thrown. "How do you do that? Are these pigs loaded?"

Alan hit him on the shoulder. "No. But you are."

"Am too!" he hiccupped.

A rather rotund female patron returned from the restroom to join her group.

"Land whale off the port bow!" the one named Adam Smith called.

"Secure the 'eskeemo' pies!" his partner Marshall said.

"A gold doubloon to the first who harpoons her!"

"I've got a pocket full of snickers and plankton!" Marshall said. "Mayhaps we can lure the great white into our vicinity."

The girl went to her friends at the counter, looking around for the origin of the commotion.

"Arr, she's beached on the bar," Smith said as he returned to his beer and the rolling of the pigs.

These two were the most immature adults Alan had ever known. And the crazy thing was, their commander considered them the heartbeat of the squadron. Alan seriously doubted this commander had his finger on the pulse.

Alan walked away from them to join a game of crud.

Crud is a perfect fighter pilot's game. It is a perfect example of the old proverb that you could give a fighter pilot a dog turd on a string, and he would find a way to make a game out of it. All that crud requires is a pool table, two billiard balls, two rolls of toilet paper and a fighter pilot who knows all the rules. The toilet paper rolls are stuffed in the side pockets which are not used, and all the shooting is done by hand with one ball thrown, slid or otherwise propelled at the "live" ball which must always be kept moving until it is knocked into a hole. And all shooting is done from one end of the table or the other. Doing otherwise is called "balls" and is a foul. While shooting, you must keep yours inside an imaginary forty-five-degree angle from the corners at the table's end.

When the game was finished, and Alan's team had lost and relinquished the table, he looked up to see Clarence "Boomer" Bailey grinning at him from the bar.

"Boomer! You ovarian accident of an unwed trick turner! What brings you here?"

"A new way of life, Dog."

"How's that?"

"I'm gonna fly F-16s."

"Oh, feces! It's over now! You actually went to UPT?"

"And Holloman."

"Congratulations, Boomer. But what about the stomach problem?"

"I don't do that anymore. Haven't since ... before our last flight together."

"That's good." Alan looked around the dimly lit room. He had never expected Boomer to become a real fighter pilot. He still had his doubts.

"How'd you do at UPT?"

Boomer shuffled his feet.

"Come on," Alan coaxed. "Fess up."

"Well," Boomer said. "I graduated number one."

Alan raised his eyebrows. "Congrats!"

"It's how you taught me, Dog."

Alan drank his beer, nodding.

"Are you going to Weapons School?" Boomer asked.

"I don't know."

Boomer took a swig of beer. "There's another arrival, I hear," he said.

Alan said, "I know" and wondered how much Boomer really knew about little William Alan Fisch.

"Is he in your squadron?"

"What?" Alan said, then realized who he meant. "Oh. Yes. I scheduled myself to give him an instructor upgrade flight on Monday. He's going to be an IP here, too, when he finishes the training."

"You're kidding! You can do that?"

"They don't seem to know, or care, and I haven't heard a peep from him myself. But you can ask him, he's right over there."

Boomer turned casually to see Brandon Parsons talking with the commander of Alan's squadron, the one without his finger on the pulse. "Where's Sloan?" he asked.

"I don't know. Home, I guess."

"Phoenix?"

"No. I mean home, here in Tampa, somewhere. They're married now. She's got a young'un."

"Oh." Boomer drank from his beer. "Dog?"

"Yeah?"

Boomer slapped him on the back. "How the hell are ya, Dog? I been missin' ya!"

Alan laughed. "I've missed you, too, Boomer."

"Well, how are you doin'? Should I be worried?"

"Worried? Why, Boomer, I didn't know you cared," Alan said to the man who had saved his life.

"I'm worried 'cause I've been here five minutes already and you haven't said 'fuck' or offered to buy me a drink or anything!"

"Boomer, is that you?"

Boomer smiled coyly and shrugged his shoulders. "I'm a fighter pilot."

"Then let me buy you a drink."

"Maybe in a minute. I got one, now."

"Fuck you, Boomer."

Clarence Bailey laughed. "There you go."

Alan glanced at Boomer when he felt he could get away with it. The young man had changed considerably.

"Boomer," Alan said eying his receding hairline, "You're thinning a little on top. Did the accident ..."

Rubbing the top of his head Boomer said, "Hell, no. But I had a good time at Holloman. I set my hair on fire so many times that it's nearly gone. But I looked good doing it!"

They leaned on the bar beside each other and drank. After a time, Boomer asked, "Are you really okay?"

"About that?" Alan thumbed at Brandon Parsons.

"Yeah."

"Hell, no." He drank. "I'll tell you something though, Boomer. I think I'm better at handling death than I am at handling life."

"I know what you mean, Dog. On the big bell curve of life, I've always felt a little below the mean." Boomer finished his drink and picked up the one Alan had ordered for him. He took several swallows, then looked at Alan squarely. "You know, Dog, young fighter pilots become crusty old fighter pilots at a very early age."

"That's true."

"We're desperadoes."

"What?"

"We're desperadoes, outlaws. Gunslingers! That's all we are, aren't we?" Boomer was becoming very drunk. He had never been able to hold his liquor. He had always said it was because he did not want to. "Hell, I ain't afraid of dyin' young and quick, splattered up against the side of some mountain at the speed of sound!"

"Not too much worry of that, here," Alan answered. "Florida's not known for mountains, and they won't let you go super over it, anyway."

"Whatever." Boomer gestured with his beer. "I ain't afraid of that."

"What are you afraid of, you fearless wonder?"

"I'm afraid of dying an old man, looking back on a long life filled with regrets."

"You have regrets, Boomer?"

"Sure. Don't you?"

"No."

"Come on! None?"

"There are things that I am sorry happened, but I don't regret them."

"What's the difference?"

"You can't see it?"

"No, Dog."

Alan smirked. "That's regrettable."

Boomer laughed, but his face remained serious. "We're just outlaws. We need a war." He finished another beer and ordered two more. "What do you think?"

"I think your job is to fly and forget, so don't you fight it."

Boomer grinned at the twist of words. "I mean really, Dog."

"I don't get paid enough to think."

Boomer put on his most serious face. "I'd like to know."

Alan put the beer bottle to his lips and drank half the liquid before lowering it to his side. He held it at his hip like he was resting his hand on a holstered pistol. He arched his back against the bar and furrowed his brow. "I've floated on a sinusoidal curve of emotion and dedication. At times, killing with my fighter strapped to my waist was a constant fantasy of which I was obsessed. Other times, the fighter mission repulsed me to the point that I wanted nothing so much as to be rid of the Air Force and return to the outside world where I would be free to criticize and condemn the military and everything about it."

Boomer raised his left wrist above his head.

Alan smiled knowingly. "Saving your watch."

Boomer nodded. "That shit's deep, Dog."

"You asked."

"How about now?"

"Now?"

"How do you feel now?"

"I feel like I may have to go to bed soon." He paused. "And take a piss."

"Be sure you get the order right."

"Yeah." Alan stretched his arms over his head.

"Aw, Dog. Don't leave. It's Friday night. You gotta get drunk with me!"

Alan looked at him squarely, letting the half-grin fall from his face. "Yeah, I guess I owe you."

Calm eyes bridged the reddened cheeks of Boomer's inebriated complexion. "You don't owe me nothing, Dog. Except maybe what you owe yourself."

Alan searched his savior's face. Was Boomer throwing something out because it sounded right? Or was he, despite the influence of much alcohol, capable of spewing forth gems that stirred in the depths of a flawed man's soul. Did he need to forgive Boomer for saving his life? Or did he need to forgive himself for surviving.

"I'm sorry I didn't trust you," Alan said.

"I'm sorry I rotated the valve without telling you," Boomer countered.

"I'm not."

They were silent for a moment in the reverence of a shared past.

"How do you like this new air 'chine?" Boomer said.

"It's a good jet, Boomer," Alan said, emerging from his thoughts. "Sometimes I miss ... I miss the ... having a wizzo."

Boomer looked at him with the deep blue eyes of awareness. "I know, Dog," he said. "I miss him, too."

After a short, reverent silence, Alan asked, "You want a Scotch?"

Clarence Bailey's face glowed. "Yeah, Dog. I'll drink a Scotch with you."

"The Glenlivet," Alan ordered from the bartender. "On the rocks."

"Two," Boomer acknowledged.

When the drinks came, Alan stirred the glass of iced-down Scotch with his finger. The gesture was not lost on Clarence who raised his glass and said, "To Sammy Small!"

"Fuck 'em all!" Alan stared into Boomer's eyes, clinked his glass against the one his friend offered and said, "To Sam." He drained the liquid and slammed the empty glass solidly on the table.

Boomer stared at the fighter pilots drinking, playing games, acting like they might be trying to hustle women. He was having a quality drunk. "Dog," he slurred. "We've got a quote by Hemingway in the squadron that says a man can only lose his virginity once to fighters."

Alan ordered two more Glenlivets. "I was unaware he was a fighter pilot."

Boomer took his drink and clinked Alan's glass. "Do you think it's true?"

Alan looked at him squarely, then looked away, across the room at Brandon Parsons. "Boomer, I wouldn't try to convince you one way or the other how many times you can lose your virginity." He downed his drink and put the empty glass on the bar. "I'm a dot."

"A what?"

"A dot on the horizon." Alan patted Boomer's back. "I'm outta here. See you Monday."

"If not sooner." Boomer turned to watch the Crud match.

Alan walked out of the bar. He stopped for a moment at a pay phone, feeling he might call Sloan. The number would be easy enough to get, and Parsons was in the bar impressing his new boss.

When she answered on the fourth ring, she sounded tired. "Hello."

"Sloan Parsons?" Alan asked hesitantly.

Her second 'Hello' sounded nervous.

"This is Alan," he said.

"Oh! I thought ... Alan. Thank God. How are you?"

"I'm okay. How's your life?"

"Fine. I have a little boy. Garner. He's a handful."

"Garner ... A strong name."

"I know. Thank you." She was quiet.

There were so many things he wanted to say, but none of them seemed appropriate. After an uncomfortable silence, he said, "Listen, I'm sorry ... I'd better go."

"Alan?" Her voice was course. "Alan, I can't just say I'm sorry ..."

"I know."

"It's just that ... the place ... away from what matters ..."

"Look," Alan said, cutting off her apology, "the Spanish experience took something away from all of us. We gained so much and lost even more. But we were young, and we were all so busy looking for the chance to test our mettle that we just couldn't see we were flunking the basic tests of life and love."

"We just stagnated ..." she offered.

"How could you say we stagnated?" He felt himself getting angry. He consciously softened his tone, but the words were harsh. "How can you say that? You've lived in Spain. You've been to Italy and France! How many people your age do you know that have done that? I gave you something you otherwise would never have had."

"Do I owe you for that?" she asked softly.

Looking through the open door to the bar, Alan could see Boomer leaning against the counter with another beer in his hand. On the other side of the bar, Brandon Parsons was animatedly telling a story to the Squadron Commander. "No, Sloan," he said sadly but honestly. "You don't owe me anything. We just found a corner we couldn't make."

Sloan was silent. He could just hear her sniffling.

Embarrassed by her silence, he said, "Do you want me to check ..."

"No, Alan. There's no need."

"Okay."

Again there was silence. On the jukebox in the bar, Willie Nelson was singing "Always on My Mind."

"I'd better go," Alan said finally.

"Okay."

"Take care."

"Alan?"

"Yes."

"I came by that night."

He was puzzled. "Which night?"

"The night ... after the ... the accident ... when Denise was there."

His faced flushed, and he felt hot. Had she listened at the door? What did she mean to tell him? "You came? To the door? My door?"

She cleared her throat. "Well, no. I drove up, but her car was there, so I left."

Almost whispering into the mouthpiece, he asked, "Why were you there?"

"I don't know, but, whatever the reason, it doesn't exist anymore."

"I wish you had come in," he breathed.

"I couldn't, with her there ..."

"I wish there had been no reason not to."

"Maybe it's best that there was." She paused, waiting to see what he would say. When the silence became too long, she said, "Did I tell you I have a son?"

"Yes." Alan fought back a fresh flush of anger. Ernie was right. Children were never meant to be measuring sticks for indulgent adults.

"Congratulations."

"In fact," Sloan said, "he's crying now."

"Sorry. I've kept you too long." Alan's ear throbbed from being pressed so tightly against the phone. He hesitated, holding on to this one last time. He wanted to tell her that he was not angry anymore, that he understood. That he had learned a lot and been through a lot more. He wanted her to know that it was okay. "Have a good life," was all he could think to say."

"I'm working on it."

He hung up and walked out of the bar and into the night thinking about his own.

CHAPTER FIFTY-SEVEN

Alan maneuvered his F-16 Falcon behind Brandon Parsons', "S-turning" for spacing until the radar ranging on his Heads-Up Display showed he was 5000 feet in trail. He flew slightly to the left as they repositioned toward the middle of the working area.

Flying twenty thousand feet over the Gulf of Mexico, the beauty of the day accentuated the freedom of the fighter. It was the kind of day the Tampa television weather man referred to as JAPDIP - Just Another Perfect Day In Paradise.

Brandon looked over his shoulder to check that his "student" was in position for the next scenario. The fact that it was Alan Wayne detracted only slightly from his concentration. He was wary. He had something to prove. "Ops check, lead's 5.5," he said over the discreet radio frequency.

"Two's 5.9," Alan answered. So you want to be an IP, he thought. You dirty, commie, wife stealer! Let's see how you handle a stud who knows what he's doing.

"Cameras on, fight's on!" Brandon radioed.

Acting on instinct and experience, Alan slammed the throttle to full afterburner and, using his designated call sign, transmitted, "Risky Two's got a bandit right one o'clock, one mile, I'm engaged!" He turned to point slightly aft of Brandon's hard left turn.

"Good comm, Two!" Brandon grunted, ever playing the good instructor pilot. He pulled 6 g's, expecting to see Alan moving forward on his canopy. Instead he groaned as he lost Alan directly behind him. "Your nose is in lag, two!" His voice sounded tired under the strain of the g-forces.

"Roger!" Alan acknowledged, thinking Brandon Parsons must have slept though Pete Bonhams Basic Fighter Maneuvers class.

As Alan flew behind Brandon Parsons, the angle-off between the two jets increased. Parsons noted to himself that he would keep Alan's nose trapped in lag position for two turns and then knock-off the engagement and debrief this student of that common error. His airspeed bled down to 270 knots. He could barely see Alan's airplane. He began to breathe heavily as he worked against the g's. At this slower airspeed, the g's were less, but the fatigue in his body reduced his resistance.

Carrying 400 knots, Alan slid the throttle out of burner momentarily and pulled hard to 7 and a half g's to reach his corner velocity, his best turn, of 350 knots. He selected burner to sustain the speed. The nose of his F-16 was now in lead of the "bandit's." At 2500 feet and closing, he called up the gun sight on the HUD.

Brandon eased off his turn, allowing his airspeed to increase to 300 knots. Straining excessively, he threw his head back but could not see his student's jet. He stopped the turn for a few seconds to gain some precious airspeed, then pulled five g's into the hard left turn.

Suddenly, he saw Alan's jet less than 2000 feet away and in lead for guns. "Damn! He's playing for real!" he said aloud. The gun camera recorded everything. He unloaded, rolled and pulled straight up. "You're not gonna gun me, you ..." Pulling four g's, his breathing became labored. Straining and sweating, he turned to keep track of Alan who was repositioning high above him.

He could do nothing less than fight it all out. Although he stopped short of putting his inner feelings on the video camera film, he felt them and thought them. Hatred was a fire burning rampant in his brain as he thought of Sloan and of Spain and of what he truly wanted. Then he blocked it out of his mind to gain control. Everything would be won or lost here! And he must win!

Alan countered the defensive move by backing off 1000 feet, waiting to react to the next turn, knowing Brandon Parsons was getting low on everything that counted. The fight was taking them closer to the 10,000 foot "hard" altitude, where the fight would have to be discontinued.

"Gun this!" Brandon said aloud as he rolled inverted. He started a "split S" maneuver that quickly increased his airspeed to 350 knots. "Now I've got some smash!"

Alan rolled right thinking 'He's got to pull out of that sometime, or he'll go through the floor and be a simulated ground kill.'

Brandon's breath was coming in short, shallow puffs now. With the nose of his jet nearly straight down, he looked across the tail and saw the F-16 before it disappeared in a gray spot. He pulled the stick back to the limiter.

Alan keyed the radio. "Knock it off! Knock it off! You're through the area floor!" He paused for a response. "Watch your altitude!"

The radio was silent. There was no visual response.

Under the g's, the blood pressure to Brandon Parsons' brain had become insufficient to sustain conscious thought. Like a hard punch to the chin, he had been put to sleep. His arm dropped away from the side stick. The Falcon mechanically obeyed its pilot's bidding and unloaded to 1 g at 30 degrees nose low. The afterburner quickly accelerated the craft through 350 knots, then 400 knots as the earth and "God's g" pulled the combination of metal, petroleum, and flesh to Her bosom in reclamation.

"Pull out!" Alan screamed over the radio, watching the silent jet dip quickly away from him. "Pull up! Parsons pull up!"

The seconds were immeasurable. "Brandon! Knock it off! Pull up!"

Brandon awoke feeling peaceful. Euphoric. In barely conscious comprehension, he thought, I feel good! Everything is wonderful. There was something ... something ... or someone, deep in the back, in his mind ... a ... voice ... mad? no ... urgent, speaking ...

"Bail out, Brandon! Bail out!" Alan's voice shook harshly.

Brandon moved his hand around. What was I ... what was ... doing? Flying? Fly. His hand made involuntary circles in search for a stick between his lap but found none.

"Bail out, Lead!"

Brandon stared at the instruments. "I'm ... God! Look at that altimeter!"

Suddenly, full awareness seized him in a panic that rushed hot blood to his head and made his hands tremble in realization.

He pulled the ejection handle.

Alan saw the canopy, then the fireball. A parachute! But that was insignificant, his mind told him. He had seen it before, when Ernie died, and Sam ...

Brandon Parsons cleared the aircraft moments before it impacted the water immediately below him. He felt the deceleration of his opening parachute, and then ...

Pain! It took his breath away! Dark droplets spewed against the inside of his visor painting it red. Incredible, agonizing pain!

The F-16 disintegrated against the waters of the Gulf of Mexico. Flying debris shattered Brandon's legs and fractured his right arm at the elbow. He could neither inflate his life preserver nor pull his mask away from his face. He did not feel his broken body hit the water. The salt water seeped under his chin and began to fill the mask.

"Mayday! Mayday! Mayday!" Alan yelled on the UHF Guard channel. "Risky's got a downed jet, one soul on board! Two four zero degrees, 80 miles from MacDill!" He changed back to the Miami Center Frequency and repeated his Mayday call.

"Roger, Risky!" Miami answered. "I've called the choppers!"

"Roger," Alan said. "Prepare to copy ... coordinates are ..."

He flew a tight circle that brought him back across the wreckage. He jerked the throttle to idle and extended the speed brake, slowing to 250 knots.

"Stand by!" he said.

Brandon Parsons' head was in the water, bobbing with the waves. There was no inflated life raft, and the fire was out.

"Dead." Alan whispered.

Movement? He turned as tightly as he could and looked back over his shoulder. Brandon's head was at water level, and he was trying to remove his mask with his left hand.

"He may still be alive!" Alan said to Miami control. He looked at the Inertial Navigation Control panel and read off the coordinates.

"Copy, Risky! The choppers acknowledge they will reach your position in ten minutes."

"Roger."

Ten minutes! The arm of the fallen pilot moved slower. He would be dead by then.

In gut-wrenching disbelief, Alan watched the death throes of his life's greatest personal enemy. My nemesis, he thought, is dying in front of my eyes, at my own hand.

He made another turn toward the place.

What was the cost of an F-16 these days? And the value of a pilot? How many millions had the accident board said Sam was worth? And Fisch? Ron? Whiskey? Ernie? What was their significance now?

He thought of Sloan. He saw a tear. He imagined the face of a child he had never seen, and the face smiled in youthful gratitude.

He searched his soul. One great act. Was that enough to make a difference?

He might not survive this, and even if he did, his career probably would not. That did not matter. What did matter was that, whether peacetime hero or comic villain, he could not live if he did nothing. He would shrivel up and be dead for maybe fifty years before his scarred, calloused heart ceased to pump the blood of life through his undeserving veins. An old man filled with regret.

The S struck him that he had never been to Alabama. Maybe it would be a good time to drive up there. See what that was like. Maybe find Connie ...

With the decision planted firmly in his mind, he felt strong. Strong enough to face the danger. Strong enough to face the truth. It was time to live. It was time to forgive. He would teach that to his children.

As he approached the floating pilot, he saw there was still valor and courage. The left arm continued the movements in its determined but useless struggle.

Nearly there. Careful of the canopy ... and the seat. I need to be very close. Throttle to idle. The jet pointed out to sea. Here, this is good. This has to be good.

"Okay Beauregard," Alan said. He pulled the handle.

The wind forced his head firmly against the seat back as the canopy jettisoned.

After what seemed an eternity, the rocket motor fired.

"Here's the payback!" Alan yelled as the ejection seat propelled him up the rail and on his way.

EPILOGUE

I must return to Mother Earth, to Her rocks and seas that bind me to the past and the future and my fellow man. To fly means to see, but it does not promise that I will understand.

Every failure is a lesson. Every lesson, a feather. Each lofty success borne by a layer of lessons secured in the sinew of wisdom. From this I form wings strong enough to sustain me.

And on these wings, I can fly. I can really fly! But the day is coming when I will remain aloft. High above the earth, or perhaps yet among it, to look upon it all and finally understand what I have come to be.

Or perhaps there will be only silence.

I cannot answer the question of life after Death. That is a riddle for the Ages. But I know there can be life after Life.

THE END

ABOUT THE AUTHOR

Charles Williams is a United States Air Force Academy graduate, a former F-4 and F-16 fighter pilot, and a retired Delta Air Lines captain. He was the coach of the Niceville High School Forensics Speech and Debate Team for eight years and was the Northwest Florida State College Collegiate High School Forensics Team coach for another three. He was also the director of the Niceville Drama Department for four years, during which time he wrote two comedic plays entitled *I, Xombi* and *13-13-13* which were performed on stage by members of the Niceville High School Drama Troupe.

He has been honored to receive several awards in the speech and debate community, including being named the Florida Forensics League Coach of the Year, a Diamond Coach recognized by the National Forensics League, and was inducted into the Gator Guard by the University of Florida Blue Key Speakers Bureau. He also coached the National Forensics League Prose Interpretation National Champion of 2013.

This is the second novel Charles has published, which will soon be followed by his third, *Nor Tolerate Among Us,* a novel about the Air Force Academy and the young men and women charged with upholding and enforcing the Academy's Honor Code.

His continues to work on new projects, including the sequel to his first published novel, *In Close Proximity,* which will be entitled *Classic Deception: The Search for Rebecca.*

What Readers say about *Higher Than The Angels:*

I was riveted. I loved it!

Sabrina Afflixio

Although this book is written as a novel, the people, events, and flying are the real deal. If you want to get your head inside what it was really like to fly in a front line F-4 fighter squadron this is the book for you! Once I started, I couldn't put it down!

Sid "Fuzzy" Thurston, 613TFS Weapon Systems Officer, Torrejon Air Base, Spain, 1977-80

A great read! I enjoyed it immensely. Charles Williams does an excellent job of appealing to a wide audience: something for everyone. Thank you for refreshing my rapidly fading memory of my Torrejon tour, some good (the flying) and some bad (bull fights). Again, congratulations on a great book!

Gary Kaskela, 613TFS Weapons Systems Officer, Torrejon Air Base 1981-84

The book is very well written and has excellent descriptions. Although this story did not deal with my preferred subject matter, it held my attention well. It does give a vivid picture of the life of a fighter pilot, and it makes me appreciate what they must have experienced. I never knew how dangerous it could be.

Sherry Gardiner Varner

I especially liked the parallels and double meanings and foreshadowing. It was more literary than I was expecting.

Name Withheld by Request

Made in the USA
Lexington, KY
21 June 2019